MW00808431

Runes of the Prime

The Rune Fire Cycle, Volume 2

Lance VanGundy

Published by Lance VanGundy, 2021.

This is a work of fiction. Similarities to real people, places, or events are entirely coincidental.

RUNES OF THE PRIME

First edition. November 16, 2021.

Copyright © 2021 Lance VanGundy.

ISBN: 978-1735427232

Written by Lance VanGundy.

Table of Contents

Dedication

Creative works of art are laborious adventures, and while I have enjoyed my chance to escape to Karsk on more than one occasion, my efforts would most certainly have withered if not for the support, critiques, and enthusiasm of my beta readers. I'm so grateful to Madisun VanGundy, Colette Lothe, Ricky Bennet, and Thomas Palmer, who offered constructive advice and encouragement. Madisun VanGundy has been my most ardent motivator and provided meaningful insights. Jason VanGundy gave me invaluable, honest appraisals of character continuity. I have endless thanks to my wife Kristin for her ear, her patience, and her boundless enthusiasm.

Tremendous thanks to the entire VanGundy clan for unconditional support!

Once again, I'm grateful to the amazing editorial work of Courtney Andersson of Elevation Editorial and the fantastic artwork (cover and character sketches) of Jamie Noble Frier from thenobleartist.com.

If you have gambled with your time to escape to the world of Karsk, then mostly dear reader, I'm grateful to you.

Preface: Synopsis of Awakened Runes, Book 1 of the Rune Fire Cycle.

In *Awakened Runes*, Kaellor and his nephews, Bryndor and Lluthean Scrivson, had lived in exile in the Southlands with their ability to channel zenith restricted. The deceased king and queen of Aarindorn (parents to the brothers) long ago sensed that despite the banishment of the Usurper, Tarkannen, his abrogator minions would be able to track Kaellor and the boys if they employed their gifts.

Life in the Southlands was just starting to look up. After twelve years of struggle plying their trade in cartography, the three are richly rewarded for defending the niece of a Southland king. They return home to Journey's Bend and discover that the strength of the boys' mantle is fraying. The construct, created by their parents, is supposed to shield them from channeling zenith and mask their identities.

The brothers encounter some danger and drama at home with two main outcomes: first, the brothers dispatch a feral wolvryn. By default, they inherit two wolvryn pups, Neska and Boru. Second, as their gift leaches out, Therek Lefledge, the regent of Aarindorn, suffers a vision regarding the whereabouts of the lost royal family. The regent dispatches Warden Reddevek the Outrider to find them.

Reddevek journeys to the Southlands to find the Scrivson home, but an assassin follows him. The killer, a zeniphile named Vardell, botches an interrogation of Aunt Rona, accidentally killing her. Vardell and Reddevek skirmish, and the assassin, a guster, gets the upper hand.

Kaellor arrives to find Rona dead and also nearly falls to Vardell's skill, but a young girl named Ranika saves them all. She is a street urchin from Callish and followed Reddevek. Kaellor ends Vardell after learning of the assassin's employer, the Lacuna.

Rona is buried, and the Baellentrells (Kaellor and the nephews' actual surname) struggle to live without her. They decide to return to Aarindorn, seeking answers and with revenge on their minds. On the way, they are tracked by Volencia and Mallic, two faithful abrogators who have released hounds from the Drift that pursue the Baellentrells. During a skirmish with the shadow chaser hounds, Lluthean is bitten and struck with a necrotic wound that threatens to take his life.

Laryn Lellendule is a woman on a mission to find her destiny. She lives among the Cloud Walkers, and after her heroic journey into the high places of the Korjinth Mountains, she is able to participate in a ritual that transports her outside the mountain region. She arrives just in time to incapacitate Volencia as she and Mallic prepare to kill Kaellor and the boys.

Released from Volencia's power, Kaellor wields his sword and kills Mallic. After a brief reunion with his long-lost wife, Laryn, Kaellor's ability to channel zenith unlocks, and his runes are awakened. He fends off abrogator attacks until the Cloud Walkers' ancestral spirit transports them to the safety of the Valley of the Cloud Walkers. However, they arrive without Lluthean, who was unconscious and suffering the ravages of the deadly wound.

In Aarindorn, the kingdom of origin for the Baellentrells in the Northlands, Karragin Lefledge and her brother Nolan are Outriders. She is promoted as prime in her quad. They survive an assassination attempt and discover the presence of grondle in the Borderlands and a horde of grotvonen within the Great Crown, the mountain range that surrounds their homeland.

Awakened Runes ends with several questions about Lluthean's plight, the significance of the Lacuna, Kaellor and Laryn's reunion and the rising tide of grotvonen in Aarindorn.

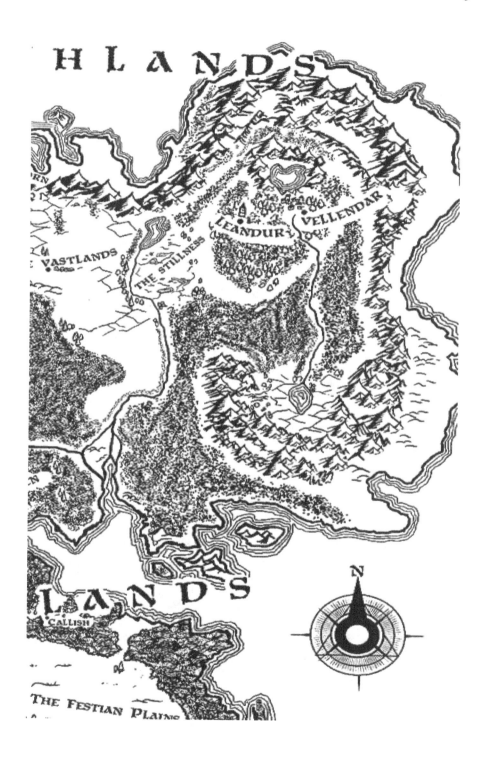

Chapter One: The Recruit

Wispy trails of glacier melt splashed down into a river canyon from the Great Crown. The water spewed out from a groove in a boulder high in the mountain, then dispersed into columns like sifted flour. A white cloud of moisture hovered over the headwaters and chased away the afternoon heat. Ksenia Balladuren sat on her Aarindin, gazing up at the streaming cascade. Goosebumps rippled across her sun-varnished forearms, cooled by the mists.

With little thought, she channeled zenith. The currents infused her core, and she funneled the power through delicate runes on her lower back and hips, linking her mind to the animal. The Aarindin perked its ears in understanding and released its grip. The zenith-powered magnetic attraction that held her fast to the mount's back lifted, and Ksenia stretched her legs.

She dropped to the ground and washed the trail dust from her arms, then considered her wavy reflection in a tide pool. Damp strands of honey-colored hair were gathered into a topknot, revealing smudges of dirt on her forehead. Her reflection wrinkled a slightly upturned nose blanketed with freckles. "That's a bit more dirt than Mother would allow at the supper table."

She plucked a handful of coarse, spongy lichen from a boulder and used it to clean her arms, face, and neck in the waters. A muscled cat the size of a wolfhound crept along the opposite bank. Ksenia's Aarindin, the only albino ever foaled to the Balladuren herd, nickered and shifted its weight with unease.

"Easy, Winter. That cat is no threat to us. That's a cave lark. You can tell by its underbite. They eat lichen and mushrooms. Be at peace and drink your fill."

Winter dipped her neck low for a drink but kept vigilant, pale blue eyes trained on the cat. The creature's mottled grey fur allowed it to blend in among the rocky shore. It wove around boulders, then circled into the shallows. A harsh rasping sound echoed across the river as the great cat attacked the vegetation draping the smooth rocks. After a few minutes, and with a large patch of rock picked clean, the cat padded back onto the shore. Cords of muscles undulated under its fur. The lark pounced once, and all the water fell in patters to the ground.

"Good trick," said Winter.

The cat swiveled its head back over its shoulder and licked its whiskers with casual arrogance. *"Don't walk on my food,"* the lark said before slyly closing its eyes once, then bounding up the rocky bank and disappearing into the misted haze.

Ksenia stifled a giggle as Winter turned to make eye contact. The Aarindin snorted. *"I dislike when you include others in our conversation. You never warn me."*

"I'm sorry. I wasn't sure if the lark could understand us. But now you have a story," replied Ksenia through her gift. *"None in the herd have ever spoken to a cave lark."*

Winter nibbled at shoots of grass on the bank and seemed to consider her words. She flared pink nostrils and turned to look back down the river valley. *"Another comes. The wind tastes like your brother."*

"You mean smells," corrected Ksenia.

Winter chewed a few moments in silence, then swallowed. *"No . . . maybe both. They are the same in my nose and mouth. All your brothers linger on the back of the tongue. Not you, just the brothers. It makes them easy to . . . taste."*

Ksenia humphed. In the last two years, her conversations with Winter had evolved from simple indications of emotion to complex sentences. As Winter matured, so did her ability to attend to more meaningful and abstract concepts. *"But at the end of the day, you are still an Aarindin."*

"What does that mean?" asked Winter with a tone of genuine curiosity.

"Sorry, Winter. I didn't mean to share that. Tell me, what does my brother smell, err . . . taste like?"

"The shiny green herb your mother puts in your food. It grows in bunches on the side of the barn that gets all the light." Winter trained her head back down the path.

"Oh. Mountain basil. That makes sense, I suppose, since we eat it nearly every day. What do I smell like?"

"You linger in the air like sweet apple blossoms in spring," said Winter.

"Why do I get the feeling you're just trying to finagle an extra scoop of molasses and oats from me when we get home?" Ksenia reached up and draped her arms around Winter's neck.

"What is finagle?"

The question made Ksenia giggle out loud. *"Another day. Here come's my brother."*

Riding an Aarindin reflective of the breed standard, her brother crested the rise to the headwaters. Kervin Balladuren, the fourth of four brothers and her elder by only a little more than a year, inhaled a deep breath with the appearance of relief. "By the moons, Kess. I've been looking for you for two hours. At this rate, we'll be lucky to get home before nightfall."

Ksenia tilted her head in confusion. "This is First Moon's day, isn't it? I'm supposed to have the day off."

"Why does the moon have a day?" Winter asked while nibbling at another cluster of grass.

Ksenia released her connection to zenith and pulled her fingers through the strands of hair tucked into her topknot, then pinched the back of her neck in frustration. "Did something happen? Why were you sent to find me?"

Kervin looked past her to the waterfall and headwaters. He seemed reluctant to make eye contact. "A messenger arrived late this morning just after you left. She waited a few hours past lunch to speak with you. When you didn't return, she left a sealed note with Mother."

Kervin forced his gaze to meet hers. "She came from the regent's offices in Stone's Grasp—fancy robes, embossed satchel, and even an Outrider escort."

"The regent's office?" she asked. A moment later, she realized why Kervin seemed both relieved and reluctant to find her all at once. "Mother sent in my application even after I told her and father I didn't want to go."

She felt heat blossom across the nape of her neck, and a tight feeling stole across her chest, preventing her from drawing relaxed, full breaths. "And of course, she sent you to find me, the one brother who might smooth it all over."

Kervin sagged his shoulders in mild defeat. "They sent all of us, Kess. I just knew where you were most likely to be."

She stared back at her brother. He was practically her twin in everything but her arca prime. They shared similar abilities in linguistics, and both of them could communicate with animals. A good seven years separated him from their next older brother. While her oldest three brothers favored their father with dark brown hair and thick beards, Kervin and Ksenia resembled their mother. The sun peppered their complexion with freckles, and they both had the same honey-colored hair.

"I got in. That has to be it." Ksenia paced a few steps back and forth at the water's edge and wrung a hand across the runes on her left wrist like she was twisting a bracelet. "I got in, or they would never have sent you. And I can't turn down a post with the regent himself. To the Drift with it all, when do you think I'll have to go?"

"I . . . you . . . we don't know. It could mean anything," said Kervin. She tilted her head and glared at him with incredulity. He collapsed forward onto the neck of his Aarindin. "But it probably means Mother sent in your application and that your post begins soon."

She blinked to prevent tears from welling and paced along the bank. With her hands interlocked on her head, she tried to slow her breathing, but her ribs constricted like the bars of a birdcage.

"It's just like Mother to plan everything without talking to me."

"It's not that bad. Only two days' hard ride to get home. To my understanding, you can return once a month, and you get out of chores on the ranch," said Kervin.

Ksenia dropped her hands, feeling some small part of herself accept the reality of the situation. "How long do you think I'll have to stay?"

"The post only lasts a year, and who knows what you might find in that time?" said Kervin. "I'll bet once you're there, we have to bribe you to come back."

"You can stop trying to sweeten Mother's bitter fruit, Kerv," she said.

She walked over to Winter and gestured. The Aarindin knelt on the ground, allowing Ksenia to swing a leg over. She clicked her tongue, and the Aarindin simultaneously rose and gripped her fast. Something about the warmth of Winter under her legs grounded her. They rode in companionable silence for a time, and the sway of the mount quieted the storm in her mind.

"Do you plan to take Winter with you?" asked Kervin.

"Father won't breed her, so I don't imagine he will mind. Why do you ask?"

"No reason. I just realized, though, you'll be the only person inside Stone's Grasp with their own personal Aarindin. All the others are deployed in service to the Outriders."

"Is that supposed to make my sentence any better?" she asked.

Kervin sighed. "Come on. It's not a punishment. There's nobody your age out here except me, and it's a fantastic opportunity. You can't spend all your days talking to Winter. You need to—"

"Don't you say it, Kerv," she interrupted. "If you say make friends with real people my age, I'll tell father how much you lost throwing dice last week."

Kervin flushed and stared out over the plains, then nodded. "I'm sorry. And I get it. Your last experience among the gifted at Stone's Grasp left a lot to be desired. But they aren't all awful. I'm still good friends with several people from my class."

"You're a prime in a quad of Outriders. It's not the same thing," said Ksenia. "I might wager Winter for the chance at that kind of opportunity."

"What is it that bothers you so much about the notion of going back to Stone's Grasp?" asked Kervin.

"Lots of things. They think about each other in terms of their gift and nothing else. If I can't push an object, send, or gust, then they find small value in my presence. When all I can do is communicate with animals, decipher strange languages, and magnify another gifted, I'm relegated to someone they can use when they have a need. Half the people in my class just called me sympath; they didn't even use my name. Then there are all the silly games they play, as if aligning with a specific house has anything to do with anything in Stone's Grasp."

"Anything else?" he asked.

"Yes, they all stink of meat," she said.

Kervin chuckled. "Oh, sister, you're hopeless."

"What?" Ksenia asked.

"Have you ever smelled yourself after a long ride? Just because you avoid meat doesn't mean your stink isn't just as bad. Some days you smell more of the Aarindin than the Aarindin," said Kervin.

She waited for him to look away, then dipped her nose down to the neckline of her blouse. A quick sniff caused her to lurch back in surprise.

That's not altogether pleasant.

Kervin interrupted her thoughts. "What if I told you there was a way for you to fulfill the post in the regent's office and avoid most of the house politics in Stone's Grasp?"

They rode on in silence as she considered her situation and her brother. Kervin rode with an odd, stiff posture like he was holding his breath.

"Kess? You there?" he asked.

"I was still deciding whether I should just take Winter and disappear into the mountains. But what did you have in mind?"

Kervin relaxed his shoulders. "I wanted to wait to tell you this, but Overwarden Kaldera summoned all Outriders to the forward base camp, and I leave tomorrow morning. If you take the post with the regent, we might not see each other for a turn of the seasons."

Ksenia squinted her eyes and turned to regard him, considering his words. "You're not worried about any of that. So, what is it?"

He wrinkled the freckles on his nose, then sighed once and continued, "I joined the Lacuna."

The words caused her to squeeze her thighs, and Winter stopped. Kervin casually circled back around to face her but struggled to make eye contact.

"Isn't that the group in opposition to the monarchy?" she asked.

"If you mean that we labor to see a free Aarindorn governed by the people and not a royal class, then yes," said Kervin.

"You know Mother and Father hold seats on the Assembly in Stone's Grasp. Blood moon Kerv, our oldest brother is in the city watch."

"Who do you think introduced me to the circle breakers?" asked Kervin.

Ksenia studied her brother, looking for some sign of a ruse. Sensing no telltale mischief in his eyes, she asked, "Who?"

"Rugen. But Mother and Father don't know, not yet. And you can't tell them. Rugen has a plan to let them know eventually, but it's still too soon."

Ksenia resisted her first instinct to berate Kervin for a fool; if Rugen had joined the Lacuna already, she felt like she should hear Kervin out. Rugen was nothing if not loyal to the welfare of Aarindorn. His sense of duty had lured him away from the ranch, where he'd stood to inherit a lucrative business.

Kervin directed his mount a few steps closer and leaned into her field of vision. "Say something, anything. What do you think?"

"I'm none too happy that Mother has set the path before me, but that doesn't mean I'm ready to join an organization that works against the Assembly, against Aarindorn."

"Come on. Do you think Rugen or I would have anything to do with a group that intended harm to the kingdom or our parents?" asked Kervin. "The Lacuna work to break us away from the never-ending cycle that sees Aarindorn ruled by a monarchy. That's all. There are no plans to dismantle everything good about the kingdom. I've attended the meetings for half a year now and not once has anyone mentioned breaking up the Assembly. In fact, I think a few of our members hold seats in the Assembly."

"I don't know. It sounds, just . . . why do you think the Lacuna would want anything to do with me?" she asked.

"We want all Aarindorians to see that Aarindorn can prosper under a new form of leadership. The noble families started and waged the Abrogator's War. It's taken the country over a decade to recover from that devastation. Grind it. There hasn't been a Baellentrell in the kingdom in all that time. Changes are coming. I think you could be a bigger part of it than you realize."

"I'll think on it. What would I have to do?" she asked.

"At first? Nothing," said Kervin. "You can help me move the herd to the south valley tonight, then come listen for yourself. The only thing I ask is that you keep my secret from Mother and Father for now."

It's not as if they have been completely honest with me.

Acting more out of anger with her mother than any agreement with Kervin, she nodded once, then nudged Winter ahead, passing her brother.

"Yes?" he asked. "Yes! All right, you won't regret it." He circled his Aarindin around to catch up to her, and they continued home.

"What did you mean when you said I could listen?" asked Ksenia. "We're two days away from the capital."

"You'll see," said Kervin. "I can show you tonight after we move the herd. But we need to pick up the pace. Fancy a race?"

Ksenia channeled zenith into her sympathy rune and opened herself back up to Winter. *"Can you outrun this other Aarindin in a race, Winter?"*

"Your brother wants me to run back but said he would give me sweet oats if I only follow," said Winter.

Ksenia responded, *"If we get home first, I will double that. What do you say?"*

Winter leaped into a comfortable gallop, racing ahead of Kervin's horse.

Kervin shouted from behind her, "Hey! That's not fair, Kess! I'm not gripped like you!"

Ksenia giggled and shouted back, "You tried to bribe Winter! Deal with it!" They raced down the river valley back to the Balladuren ranch.

Chapter Two: Straight Through the Heart

Karragin sat on a crude bench outside Warden Elbiona's command tent and hitched her leg up to inspect the bottom of her left boot. With her gift, she had reduced the worst part of the fatigue from the long march out of the Great Crown, but her boot soles had not fared so well. A bit of wool fuzz from her sock mushroomed out from a small hole over the ball of her foot. She ran a thumb along the arch to remove trail dust from the imprint, which read, *"EoB."*

Endule of Beclure . . . why am I not surprised that something crafted in a western duchy wears thin at the first testing?

The sounds of workers echoed off a large palisade erected to mark the division between the forward base camp and the Borderlands. Cutters felled trees, others carted lumber, and engineers raised timbers with pulleys. Zeniphiles worked side by side with the ungifted, using their talents to streamline the labor. Some trimmed branches while others directed draft animals or found creative ways to divert water and excavate soil. The telltale flashes of zenith rippled across the bare arms and chests of at least half the workers.

She inhaled the scent of fresh-cut pine that lingered sharp and strong in the air. The warden's tent sat behind the foundation of a sizable new building. Karragin had never invested much interest in timber craft or construction, but the progress made in just a week impressed her.

In stark contrast to the frenzied activity of the builders, Nolan straggled over to collapse next to her. Despite his apparent exhaustion, he'd managed to obtain a few biscuits of hardtack in their brief walk through the Outrider camp. He handed a portion to her, then slid to the ground using the bench as a backrest. Surrendering to fatigue, he ignored all sense of decorum and flopped his legs out before him.

We've been in camp for less than five minutes, and already you've found something to eat.

The biscuit proved predictably difficult to chew and yet was oddly satisfying after their long march. "We make it back here in one piece, and the first thing you fetch are molar breakers?"

Out of the corner of her eye, she sensed him shrug. He chewed in silence a bit longer, then swallowed with significant effort. "Water? Have you got any water?" His chin dipped low as he tried to swallow the ration, his words cut short and raspy.

She surrendered her waterskin, and Nolan drank several deep gulps before relaxing back against the bench. He handed the skin back to her. "Thanks." He bit off a smaller bite of the hard biscuit and chewed thoroughly.

"Where did Tovnik and Amniah wander off to?" she asked.

"Tovnik made straight away to the mess tent. Amniah muttered something about paying a month's wages for a hot bath," said Nolan.

"I thought you would have joined our medic at the first chance."

Nolan reached both arms back onto the bench to better recline. His legs remained sprawled before him, one foot pointing east and the other west. "It's a five-minute walk from here to the mess tent. I don't care what they are serving; nothing could make me take another step."

The warden's tent flapped open, and Kervin Balladuren stepped out. He nodded once. "It's been a long time, Karra, and well met, Nolan. I heard about your arca prime; respect, my friend. You both look like me after a hard day of mucking out the horse stalls. What happened?"

Karragin brushed a lock of matted slate-colored hair from her forehead and tongued the inside of the scar on her upper lip. She regarded the prime. In the half-year since she last saw him, the sun had painted his face with a patina of freckles.

"Hello, Kervin," she said. "We encountered a warren of grotvonen deep in the Great Crown just west of here. They gave chase, so we sent the Aarindin back to your family's ranch and had to walk back. Let's just say the journey was not a simple one on foot. We only just returned."

Kervin slid his hands into the back pockets of his pants and whistled in appreciation. "You ran across grotvonen? What was it like? Tell me about them."

"I think I should wait and discuss the details with the warden first. No offense," she said.

"Karra," he drew out her name, pleading to learn more. "You can't make an exception for a classmate? Moons, after everything I did to teach you how to use your sympath gift. You gotta give me something. Did you fight them?"

"All right, Kerv, settle down," said Karragin. "First, promise me you'll keep everything to yourself until the warden says otherwise."

"Done," he said.

She ran fingernails across the rune on her left forearm, scratching an annoying itch. "Nolan scouted a trail several ridges into the Great Crown. We were preparing to turn around when we ran across a warren of grot. They had taken up residence in a natural cave lying low in a valley.

"The little grinders had deforested at least a hundred acres in the valley. I fought a few. Foul-smelling things, but organized, and there were too many, so we retreated into the forest. I sent the Aarindin ahead, and we climbed high into the pine trees for the night. Amniah is a guster and used her skill to carry our scent with the horses. The trick worked, but I should not like to rely on that again. The creatures seem to have an unnatural ability to see in the dark, and their sense of hearing and smell exceed ours. That we made it back with only sore muscles to complain about is a blessing."

Kervin rocked his weight from one foot to the other. "By the Giver. Did they use weapons? How did they approach you? Were they in any special formation? I've heard from others that they wield spears and coordinate their attacks through some form of clicky speech."

Karragin recalled the strange way the grot communicated with a series of clicks, grunts, and occasional screeches. The memory caused a tingling shiver to ripple across her forearm, and she rubbed away the discomfort. "Yes. I approached them. No, and yes."

Kervin seemed to consider her words a long moment, perhaps replaying his questions in his mind. "Moons, you haven't changed a bit." He waited for her to fill the dead space in the conversation, but she just looked back at him. Eventually, he held his hands up in defeat. "All right, I give up. I'll wait to hear more later. How is your quad shaping up? You ride with Nolan and Amniah, right? Is your fourth a healer?"

"Yes, Tovnik," she said.

Kervin wrinkled his nose. "He's a good man in a scrap, but I wouldn't count on him for much more."

"Fortunately, we suffered more from the walk home than from anything the grot threw at us."

"Grotvonen, inside the boundaries of the Great Crown." Kervin spoke the words with disbelief. "I'm glad you all made it back in one piece."

Karragin sniffed. "All in all, not much of a heroic story there."

"Well, you managed to save the Aarindin and yourselves," he offered. "That's more than most, I'll wager."

"The horses made it back to your ranch?" she asked.

"Ksenia and I moved the herd to a canyon on the southern slopes about two nights back," said Kervin. "Two of them still wore their tracings. It didn't take us long to figure out someone sent them home. I should have figured it was you. There aren't many other sympaths in the Outriders."

"How is your sister?" asked Karragin.

"She's all right, I guess. She just earned a post with your father as one of his scribes. It's not the adventure she really craves, but I'm hoping it's something that can make her happy."

"You make it sound like she doesn't want to be there," said Karragin.

Kervin scratched the back of his head. "If she had her way, she would be here with us, but Mother couldn't stomach another one of us in the Outriders. Kess got to take Winter to Stone's Grasp, and that's about as much adventure as Mother would agree to."

Karragin arched an eyebrow. "Is Winter the albino she found foaled on the ice?"

Kervin nodded. "The very same. Not that my father would breed an albino, but if he even tried to separate those two, I'm pretty sure Ksenia would skin out in the dead of night with that horse, and we would never see either of them again."

The tent flap opened, and Warden Elbiona stepped through. She cocked her head to the side, making a quick inspection of the two primes, then Nolan, who lounged against the bench like a used rag. Nolan staggered to his feet to stand at attention. "At ease, tracker. Kervin, see to the new guard rotations. Lefledge—" she jerked her head, inviting Karragin to follow her into the tent.

Inside the tent, Karragin's eyes required a moment to adjust to the dim light. Twin posts cut from the local timber created two peaks more than ten feet high. The warden kept the interior utilitarian with little furniture beyond a few wooden chairs, a simple table, cot, and footlocker. An ebony bow and matching quiver rested against the cot.

Reminds me of my room in Stone's Grasp.

Elbiona knuckled the muscles in the small of her back and stretched before sitting in one of the chairs. "So, what happened?"

"Sir?" asked Karragin.

"You're going to make me ask why a simple scouting expedition into familiar territory left you returning days late and without mounts?"

Karragin nodded. "The Aarindin made it back in better condition than we did, but we made it back all the same, which is what matters, I suppose. Nolan was able to discern two separate trails from the blood left on Tovnik's knife. One led into the Borderlands, the other into the Great Crown just to the west. We followed this latter one and discovered a warren of grotvonen. The creatures had been there a while. They had cleared an entire valley of timber, and there were . . . hundreds of them."

Elbiona tapped her fingers in a rhythm on her knee, considering Karragin's words. "Why am I not surprised that a simple scouting expedition involving the Lefledge siblings ended up in near ruin? It seems the more I try to keep you out of the shit, the more you step into the sticky middle of it." The two considered each other in silence for a few moments. "Back up and tell me everything you learned up there."

Karragin offered a plain but specific narrative of their adventure into the mountains, the grotvonen horde, and their narrow escape.

The warden considered the report for several moments. Many people became uncomfortable standing before authority in awkward silence, but Karragin had weathered worse under the scrutiny of her father. If anything, she admired something in the intense power of the warden's stillness. Elbiona's disciplined bearing hinted at a cunning measure of all the factors rather than a moment of indecision.

The persistent burning sensation along Karragin's forearm caused her to check her rune of premonition. The veining remained dormant. *I must have rubbed against some itchweed on the way back here. I wonder if she's considering separating Nolan and me. I wouldn't blame her, I suppose, but what argument can I offer to keep him in my quad?*

Elbiona stood and walked to her footlocker. She removed a stack of folded papers and returned to the table, then unrolled a detailed map of Aarindorn. The warden tapped a calloused finger on the map. "Show me."

Karragin studied the region for a few moments. "Are we about here?" she asked, pointing to a spot between the Pillars of Eldrek.

"Yes," said Elbiona.

"Then I believe the warren is near this valley. It's perhaps four, no, five ranges in. If you ride west skirting the foothills, you will cross streams that exit the mountains. Turn south into the Great Crown at the third stream, and you should reach the area."

"You took your quad five ranges in?" asked the warden with an air of skepticism. "You mean up and down mountain valleys when you say ranges?"

Karragin shrugged. "You make it sound like more than it is, sir. Nolan was able to follow the trail such that we remained mounted all the way there."

A crease furrowed Elbiona's forehead as she considered the information. "We have to attend to the grotvonen sooner than later. Could you lead a larger company there if we decide to mount an assault?"

Karragin shrugged indifference. "Nolan would be the better person to ask about that. But from what I recall, he should have little trouble returning us there."

A clamor arose outside the warden's tent, interrupting further conversation. Cries of alarm and the unmistakable shouts of conflict erupted. Elbiona stood and retrieved her quiver and bow, leading Karragin out of the tent.

Workers dashed about in an unorganized frenzy. The harsh sound of rope tearing through canvas sheared into the air, and something bestial thundered past the warden's tent towing the remains of two or three tents behind it. The reek of decayed flesh lingered in its wake.

Karragin's attention detached from the beat of time as her rune of foresight flared a vision before her. Her gift rooted her in place before the image of a thick-muscled monster stampeding on cloven hooves. Where the neck should perch, instead a torso with burly arms sprouted, and on top of this rested the head of a bull with circular curved horns. In her vision, the grondle galloped blindly through the row of tents until it breached the larger mess tent. It trampled in a mad circle, throwing the bodies of unarmed Outriders like chaff tossed into the air by a massive winnowing fork.

"There's only one thing that size that leaves a stink like that." The warden's words brought Karragin back to the present, and her awareness returned to their surroundings.

"Grondle," said Karragin. "It's going to kill at least eight Outriders if we don't stop it."

"Why do you say that?" asked Elbiona.

Karragin pointed to the vestige of zenith as it flickered across the runes on her forearm. Elbiona nodded and tossed her bow back into the tent. "Grind it," cursed the warden.

"Sir?" asked Karragin.

"Arrows won't do any good against that thing at this point. We have to impede its progress, then spear it through the heart," said the warden. "See what you can do to slow it down while I fetch something stout enough for the job."

Karragin turned to her brother, who labored to string his bow. "Leave it. Elbiona said arrows won't do much. See if she needs any help and stay away from that thing."

Nolan nodded once and jogged after the warden. Karragin ran down the empty row left by the grondle. A mass of rope and canvas tangled about the beast's head, rendering it blind, and it ran a zigzag pattern interrupted by bucks, lunges, and kicks as it tried to free itself. It released a guttural sound between a growl and snort and continued its rampage through the line of tents.

Karragin caught up to the beast and gathered up a few of the ropes dragging along in its wake. She channeled a surge of strength through her arca prime and lunged ahead. Her effort allowed just enough time to loop the rope around the trunk of a felled tree three times before the beast pulled it tight. The grondle's torso wrenched back, and a loud crack erupted from under the canvas.

Its angry snort grew to a higher-pitched growl of anger or pain. The creature stomped in place a moment, then finally threw off the remnants of canvas. Dark ichor ran freely from the stump at the side of its head where one of its horns had broken off.

The twang of bowstrings preceded the hiss of a flight of arrows. Several arrow shafts sprouted from the humanoid torso of the beast. One even landed just under an eye along the hairy ridge of its snout. The grondle snorted once, a mocking sound, then roared a challenge. The beast followed the line of savaged canvas and ropes to Karragin, who stood beside the stump. Beady, dark eyes squinted at her. It pawed the ground, preparing to charge.

Karragin unsheathed the saber she carried on her hip and stepped in front of the tree stump anchoring the remnants of shredded canvas that had blinded the grondle. *Let's hope you're as dumb as Reddevek says you are.*

She slashed at the air a few times and shouted, "Come on then!"

Her taunt seemed all that the grondle needed. It lunged ahead, heedless of the arrows shot by other Outriders. More than eight shafts bristled from its torso, but it ran straight for her. Its curved hooves churned up the ground, lobbing clods of dirt into the air. The beast tilted forward as it charged.

Zenith saturated her arca prime as Karragin gathered her unnatural strength. At the last moment, she leaped and rolled to the side, slashing her saber along the grondle's flank. A deep gash opened up along the beast's side, sending an intense vibration through the weapon when the blade rattled against its ribs.

The grondle careened off the stump and rampaged in a wide circle through the camp. Several more arrows struck the muscled body. A few embedded; others seemed to hang for a moment, then drop to the ground. Still others careened off as if colliding with a target made of stone. Dark fluid flowed freely from the gash she'd opened along its flank, but the grondle raged on in a battle frenzy.

It picked up a splintered tent pole made of wood. The crude cudgel, perhaps six inches thick and five feet long, made a formidable weapon. The creature swung the wood shaft as it galloped through the camp, creating more mayhem. Karragin raced after as the beast upended two Outriders with bows, smacked a third one in the chest, causing him to fly back several feet, and crushed in the head of a young workman.

The grondle found its timing and ran in a winding path around a cluster of tents. On more than one occasion, a random swing caught someone trying to evade the fight. Eventually, it turned back in Karragin's direction.

She sheathed her sword and, using both hands, hoisted a medium-sized trunk over her shoulder. The bark bit into the skin on her neck, and sap stuck to her cheek. She walked to the edge of the woodpile and waited for the grondle. As the beast thundered past, she surged more zenith through her arca prime. Like a fulcrum adorned with cascading blue lightning, she pivoted and swung the log with all her strength. The grondle caught the blow along its lower chest between the legs. The crack of splintered wood rang out, and the beast stumbled back.

Karragin leaped forward and drew her blade. She sliced in a crisscross pattern, tearing deep gouges into the muscle and sinew of its humanoid torso. The cuts ran deep enough that she expected to see lung tissue bubble forth, but only fibers of muscle erupted from the ichor-slicked flesh.

With a grunt of surprise, she stabbed the blade deep into the grondle's chest. The beast ignored the wound and wrapped one beefy hand around her shoulder and the other around her neck. Coarse hide and hair scraped against her skin. Karragin reached up to pry herself free. Her efforts kept the grondle from crushing her windpipe, but clawed nails raked across her neck and shoulder.

Up close, the smell of the thing turned her stomach. Musky sweat mixed with the odor of rotting meat. Coarse whiskers from its chin hairs scratched her forehead, and she labored to extract herself from its powerful grip. The beast seemed to sense as much and casually turned its head, smearing the dark ichor from the broken stump of its horn across her forehead.

The viscous gore obscured her vision and matted her hair to her face. The grondle snorted with something that sounded derisive, and then it pulled her close and seemed to smell her. Only, the suction caused by its breathing didn't come from what she thought was the beast's snout. Instead, she felt the hot breath exhale from strange slits between its forelegs on its muscled chest. She set the awareness of that discovery to the side as the grondle began to squeeze.

Karragin flared her zenith again and tried to separate the grondle's arms, but her effort proved futile as the monster squeezed with inexorable force. A pressure swelled in her face, and scintillating lights streaked in the periphery of her vision.

She kicked wildly, but the grondle held her dangling in the air. Her inability to ground herself, to separate the beast's clawed hands, or even set her feet down threatened to overwhelm her composure. She tried to cry out, but only a raspy noise escaped.

Darkness pressed in at the edges of her vision just as something heavy throttled into the beast. The grondle grunted once, and she felt something solid wedge against her lower leg. Its grip loosened, and she was able to separate the creature's clawed hands enough to pull in a fresh breath of air.

The world tilted for a moment, and then her head cleared. Another vibration thrummed through the creature, and she dipped her chin enough to look down. A shaft of wood was skewered into one of the gill slits on the grondle's muscled chest.

"Again, Nolan!" shouted Elbiona. The warden crouched, shouldering the timber.

A thwack followed her command, and the grondle dropped Karragin to the ground. She looked back to see her brother swing the butt end of an axe against the other end of the makeshift harpoon. Another thwack, and something inside the beast cracked as the shaft of wood lurched half a foot into its torso. The grondle staggered back a few paces and collapsed.

Karragin propped herself on her elbows and watched in exhaustion. She inspected the two long gill slits edged with fleshy maroon edges, one over each side of the muscled chest of the grondle. The wood shaft pierced through one of the slits, around which the last death sigh of the beast escaped.

Nolan dropped to his knees beside her. "Karra, what can I do? Are you hurt?"

She tried to speak against the burning ache in her throat and managed to croak, "No, not bad, anyway."

"You can stop channeling now, or you'll pull in the draft for sure," said Nolan with a look of concern.

Karragin winced as she nodded and stopped channeling zenith. Her limbs felt suddenly thick and heavy, and she became aware of her heart thrumming against her ribs. A chill rippled across her shoulders as the breeze caught at her sweat-soaked uniform.

"So strong, I've never met anything so—"

"I told you the heart, Lefledge," Elbiona interrupted. The warden dropped to a knee and began inspecting Karragin for injuries.

Karragin lifted a shaking hand and pointed. "I buried my blade in its chest. Reddevek said the top parts are vulnerable."

Elbiona glanced over her shoulder, then sighed. "That top part, the part shaped a bit like a man, there's nothing vital there. It's all muscle and bone. You can limit their offensive capabilities if you cripple their arms or blind them. But all of the important stuff is buried deep inside the part that looks like a bull. We'll cover the finer points of grondle anatomy later. Can you stand?"

Karragin withdrew her attention to an inspection of her injuries. Aside from an intense burning in her neck and throat, she felt no pain. Nolan helped her to her feet, where she staggered a moment.

The warden looked out across the chaos of the camp, then turned back. "Nolan, get your sister to the medics. Seek out the docent, Venlith, directly, then find me after. They need to thoroughly clean and debride those abrasions. Tell them not to spare the embertang. Grondle are filthy. I don't want to find myself before your father explaining how Karragin survived the first grondle attack in a generation only to succumb to the soft touch of a tender-hearted medic."

"Yes, sir," said Nolan. He turned to lead Karragin away, but she remained rooted, staring at the corpse of the grondle.

"How, how did a grondle get into our camp?" she rasped.

"That's what I'm going to find out," growled the warden.

Chapter Three: The Taker's Price

The thick mists gathered by the ancestral spirit faded, and Laryn regained her orientation as the weightless, floating sensation subsided. She had experienced the ethereal phenomenon whenever she folded into the clouds but forgot how bewildering the transition could be.

Kaellor and another young man stumbled, then staggered to their feet near their empty litter. Two wolvryn pups sniffed eagerly at the mists. They all stood outside the gathering house ringed by the Cloud Walkers. The young and old of the Damadibo peered at the newcomers in silence.

Sensing apprehension, Laryn stepped forward, speaking in the tongue of the Cloud Walkers. "Everyone, there is no danger. These are my friends. And this," she said, looking at Kaellor as if for the first time, "this is my . . . husband."

The words reminded Laryn of kevash fruit. Though she had spoken them before, it now seemed so unfamiliar and new. She gazed again at Kaellor, taking a full inventory of him. His shoulders had thickened out in the last twelve years. *And is that a streak of grey I see in the beard that tries to hide his jawline?*

She found his eyes, azure blue with the zenith he now commanded, and her breath caught. Kaellor glanced at her, then seemed to survey their surroundings. He studied the collection of olive-skinned people as more emerged from the gathering house. Moving with purpose, he paced around their wagon and tossed aside the blanket that had covered the injured young man who was lying there.

A hardness stole across his face, appearing all the more stern by the ruddy color of recently burned skin. His penetrating gaze surprised her. "Laryn, where is Lluthean? He was on the litter when the fog collected around us. Tell me he wasn't left behind."

Laryn searched the group, equally surprised. "I'm not sure. The ancestral spirit should have brought you all safely here. But if that was Llutheandellen, then, is this Bryndorllean?" she asked, gesturing at Bryndor.

Bryndor stepped forward and bowed his head awkwardly. "Yes, ma'am, only it's Bryn if you don't mind." Bryndor looked from Laryn to Kaellor. "And where is Llu?"

Interrupting the moment, Ellisina stepped forward to pet Boru. The girl signed a question.

"Use the Kindred speech, the words I taught you spoken by those outside the valley, Ellisina," Laryn explained.

Ellisina nodded with a smile and cleared her throat, making her mouth form the unnatural shapes to produce the Kindred tongue. "Is he yours?" she asked.

Bryndor knelt down. "He chose me, but Boru belongs to himself."

"Many blessings, Bryndor, and honor to your house," she tilted her head. "Can I play with them?"

Bryndor pushed the wolvryn pups forward. Ellisina soon had them occupied chasing a piece of fur tied to a stick.

A firm grip around Laryn's upper arm interrupted the innocence of the moment. Kaellor stood at her side; an intensity darkened his expression and pressured his speech. "Laryn, is there some way you can find out what happened? Lluthean was injured, and the wound festers."

Her cheeks flushed with a mixture of surprise and anger. *Moons, I haven't felt anger in years.*

She resisted the urge to snap at him and pulled a shock of silver hair behind her ear, then placed her hand lightly over his. "Kaellor, you're hurting me. I know you're concerned. Let me go, and I'll see what I can do."

Her words struck him with more force than she intended. He paled, and she noticed for the first time the hollowed-out nature of his sunken cheeks, and the saucers of fatigue staining the skin under his eyes. He released her arm as if it were a hot kettle. "I'm so sorry. Laryn, I . . . it's all my fault. Please, anything you can do."

Elder Miljin interrupted their strained reunion. He scurried forth, outpacing the butterflies that usually hovered overhead. The elder signed with sharp gestures, *"Laryn child, be quick. The spirits have a task for you."* He turned, expecting her to follow.

She answered him in the Kindred tongue for Kaellor's benefit. Over the years, she had utilized the common speech on occasion, but more as a curious form of entertainment than significant communication. Several Cloud Walkers chose to learn the speech, Miljin chief among them. "Yes, Elder Miljin, but there was another in our group—a young man. He was wounded, and he's not here."

Upon hearing her response, Miljin paused and cocked his head, then nodded to himself. He turned with a slow grace. His brow creased with the effort of concentrating on the unfamiliar act of speaking aloud. "Yes, the ancestor dropped him into the spirit house. He is close to the spirits, I fear. Come now, they asked for you. He is well beyond my skill."

The olive-skinned old man ambled up the short trail to the spirit house. Something about the clipped manner in which he spoke instilled in her a foreboding sense of dread. She turned to Kaellor. "They have him in the spirit house. It's a holy place. They might admit you, but Bryndor should probably remain here. These are good people. He'll be safe."

Kaellor nodded and followed her up the path to the house. Miljin held open the doors and ushered them in. Laryn entered and found the young man lying on his back in the center of the room. From the corners of the room, familiar braziers burned, emitting multicolored currents of smoke. The wispy ribbons of color streamed around the periphery of the hut, outlining insubstantial figures. After the small group entered, a consort of diaphanous forms, the ancestral spirits, stepped forward from the smoke and mist with joined hands.

Laryn kneeled by the body of the young man. With one hand on his chest and the other on his forehead, she watched him draw shallow and infrequent breaths. A cold sweat beaded on his pale skin. Searching for a pulse, she grasped his wrist and, after lingering a few moments, found it at his neck, weak but steady.

She pressed her thumb deep into several places on his torso. His skin blanched under her firm probing and remained pale more than five seconds after releasing the pressure. The findings gave her pause, and she pulled back, folding her hands in her lap.

"He's . . . it's bad, Kaellor," she offered. "What happened?"

Kaellor pulled back the edge of a bloodstained dressing, revealing blackened skin over the young man's shoulder. "Abrogators found us. They sent some creature from the Drift, and one bit him here. I cleaned it with devil's tail, but the wound festered, and he took fever a few days back. I'm sorry for before. I wasn't myself. Please, whatever you can do for him. If there is a price, I'll pay it, anything."

"Devil's tail?" she asked.

Kaellor furrowed his brow a moment, then nodded understanding. "Embertang. It grows wild in the Southlands, but not as potent."

"Alright, let me concentrate," she said, then dropped her gaze to Lluthean's unconscious face. *By the moons, you have your mother's look about you. Where do I even begin? I haven't channeled in years, and you are so far away. Is your death to be the event that defines our reunion?*

She watched as Elder Miljin burned more butterfly wings, fueling the brazier and renewing the fragrant, colorful streams of smoke in the spirit house. He moved with uncommon alacrity, then stood beside her.

He dusted off his hands then signed, *"Laryn, the hour is upon you, my child. Only you can bring him back, or he will dance with the spirits forever. Let the spirits guide you."*

She looked back to Kaellor. "I'm going to try to bring him back, Kae, but you need to be prepared. I'll do my best, but—"

"That's all I can ask," said Kaellor.

Laryn adjusted to a more comfortable seated position. Through the clouded mist, she noticed a wispy silver thread drift from Lluthean's body. The thin filament caught in the currents of vapor swirling in the spirit house and thrashed like a single strand of spider silk caught in the wind. She reached forward to grasp at the errant tendril, but her hand passed through as if it had no more substance than the vapors in the hut.

Puzzled, she glanced beyond to the circle of elder spirits. The painted faces of men and women returned her gaze with intense expressions. Soothing waves of zenith flowed from the spirits, blanketing the young man, giving him a chance to remain in this world before passing to the next.

The only way to get anywhere is to take the first step. With one hand on Lluthean's forehead and another on his chest, she withdrew into herself. The lessons learned so long ago returned to her mind, and she summoned zenith.

Summon didn't really capture the feeling. Currents of zenith swirled all around her, waiting to suffuse her runes. She sensed it the moment she touched Kaellor and released their binding but had held the force at bay . . . until now. Laryn lifted her restraint and allowed the currents to cascade across her runes.

The symbols, once steeped with zenith, flared with azure light. The intensity of the blue and white radiance surprised her, and she sucked in a breath. The power shimmered from within, giving life to her gift that had remained dormant for so long.

With uncharacteristic reverence, Miljin's voice broke in, "By all the spirits, child, where have you been all these years?"

After a few moments, she gathered and funneled the swelling flow into her arca prime. A kaleidoscope of light burst from her neckline, then filtered into shafts of blue and white as she tightened her control.

The rune of the true healer flared as her arca prime suffused her with a sense of euphoria. She allowed herself to dwell in the moment, sensing the zenith infuse not just her runes but the flesh, muscle, and bone beneath them. The strength imbued by channeling allowed her to force the current to her will.

Her breathing slowed, and her heart beat in a synchronous rhythm with Lluthean's. She surrendered to her gift and allowed her power to permeate into him. As she did so, a soft humming murmur resonated into the spirit house.

Awareness of the world slid away as she focused on the supportive waves of zenith emanating from the spirits gathered in the hut. Somehow, they fed Lluthean's body while preventing his final departure. Tendrils of her inquisitive gift probed, searching for Lluthean's innate zenith stores. Though weak, his body answered with a faint vibration that gave her hope.

There you are . . . good. Thanks to the spirits, you're still here with us, even if faintly. That's one question answered. Now, let's see what ails you.

An inspection of his vital organs showed that the illness strained him, but his lungs drew air freely. His heart fluttered in a rapid rhythm and generated only a weak impulse, but not from any disease process in the muscle itself. *None that I can remember anyway. Too long; it's been too long since I've done any of this.*

Her assessment moved to his abdominal organs. His kidneys seemed withered or strained but still functional, based on the thin columns of urine she identified moving to the bladder. Blood flowed through his liver and spleen without congestion, so she didn't think the problem was there.

Fearing a more severe injury, Laryn directed her attention to his head. *What did Venlith always say? Lots of good folk could linger for a time, but no amount of healing could repair a cracked melon.*

At first, she couldn't sense any normal activity. His zenith stores seemed to flow with sluggish apathy. She increased the nature of her probing, sending and feeding zenith along his native zenith strands where she could.

The process felt both intrusive and infiltrative but necessary, so she pushed on. Within a few minutes, she assessed that there was no structural damage to his head. She sighed inwardly. *Great. Some of the most complex of maladies pertain to the blood and the arcane humors, and I haven't managed those in an age.*

She shrugged off her insecurity and directed her gift to survey his blood and lymph. A nauseating wave of putrescence stained the back of her tongue, and she began to salivate in anticipation of retching. She dialed back her zenith until the sensation became manageable and traced the corruption to its obvious source at the bite on his shoulder.

The wound festered, but underneath she determined that most of his vital tissues, muscles, bones, and even nerves were contaminated but not damaged. She pushed at the edges of the corrupted flesh and sensed the taint leaching itself deeper into his tissues. When she retreated from her probing, the corruption also receded to its original location.

She slashed an arc of zenith across the corrupted material, and it separated for a moment, then resealed. The contamination almost seemed sentient in its attempt to evade her ministrations.

Laryn withdrew, considering her options. *A simple incision and debridement won't do. It's too far along to overwhelm with purification. It's a risk, but maybe if I segregate his native zenith stores, then isolate and purge . . . There's so much risk.*

Her probing ceased, and she opened her eyes. As her awareness returned to the room, she tasted salt from the beaded sweat on her upper lip. Her hair was matted to her forehead, and she required a moment to allow her breathing to ease.

"It's not too late, and I think I can manage it, but the taint of that wound is like nothing I've ever seen before," she explained.

Kaellor took a knee then handed her a skin of water. "Please, do what you can for him, Laryn."

She turned the waterskin up and drank long, then searched his eyes and waited. He seemed composed, steady. "I'm going to isolate the contamination from everything, including his blood and his innate zenith."

She withdrew the sharp knife at her hip she used to cut herbs and handed it to him, hilt first. "When I do, you'll see his arm become bone white. When that happens, I need you to make a slice from the top of the wound all the way down to his wrist here." With her thumbnail, she traced a line from his shoulder, down the length of his arm, to the base of his thumb.

"How deep?" asked Kaellor with a grim expression.

"Plunge the blade all the way through the corrupted flesh until blood wells up, then keep it that deep all the way down to his palm. It will be deeper than you think, but don't worry about the damage. Once I purge the taint, I can repair the rest easily enough," she said.

She waited for him to process her request. He nodded once. "If this doesn't work, there's a chance he might lose the arm, but I can't think of any other way to get rid of the contamination."

"I understand. See him across the river, and we'll worry later about the Taker's price," said Kaellor.

Laryn remembered the old phrase. *But you don't believe in the Taker, as I recall.* She searched his face but found no humor there. He seemed ready for the task ahead. "Right then, when the arm turns pale. Ready?"

Kaellor reached over Lluthean's body and grasped the swollen, ruddy limb, positioning the wrist palm up, then grunted. "Like I said, do what you can."

Once again, she ignited her arca prime. The task ahead would sap her strength, so she committed to quick action and attached a delicate tendril of her gift to the thumb of Lluthean's affected arm. The connection served to sense his innate zenith and pulse.

Next, she created a sharp plane of zenith to act as a barrier, wedging it in place inside the inner edge of the corrupted flesh. The sensory tendril fell dormant as the barrier cut off the flow of zenith into his arm.

She channeled more zenith and shaped it into a constricting noose, then placed it along the barrier. A part of her awareness sensed something in the corruption lurch. Like a sentient parasite, the taint tried to seep deeper into Lluthean's torso. She fortified the zenith barrier and tightened the constricting noose as much as she could.

Lluthean's arm felt lifeless through her probing tendril. A moment later, she felt the faint vibrations as Kaellor cut across the wound and down the length of Lluthean's arm. Her head reeled, and a wave of nausea washed over her. With an effort, she ignored the sensation and double-checked that both the noose and her barrier were secure, then she began to pull.

The noose slid across the wound, milking the corruption down his arm. At first, the parasite flowed away from the touch of her gift. But somewhere near the elbow, the affliction gathered resistance, and her strength waned. She hovered in a deadlock as the festering ichor refused to drain into his forearm.

Self-doubt and recrimination entered her awareness. *If you lose control now, the corruption will surely retreat deeper and could kill him. Grind it, just push through.*

Her gift faltered under the strain, and a rivulet of the taint seeped under her noose and back toward Lluthean's shoulder. With frantic effort, she re-lashed the noose, trapping the parasite before it could spread farther, but the amorphous mass migrated back to its original position.

Kaellor's voice dashed away her fears. "Laryn, take what you need." She sensed his hand on her shoulder as zenith surged through him, fortifying her gift.

With confidence she had not felt until that moment, she grunted. "Back to the grinding Drift." She pulled with steady, unwavering resolve, milking the corruption down Lluthean's arm, where it swelled and gathered. All at once, the parasitic material spurted out of the deep cut along his wrist and palm. It fountained to the floor like a glob of blackened pig fat. Elder Miljin carefully collected the slimy material onto a thick kevash leaf, then discarded it into the brazier.

Struggling to keep both the noose and barrier in place a bit longer, she probed with the sensory tendril back through Lluthean's arm. Satisfied that none of the taint remained, she dispersed the plane of zenith acting as a barrier, then the noose.

In but a moment, Lluthean's arm pinked up, and arterial blood spurted from the incision Kaellor had made down the length of his arm. Laryn reached forward with both hands into Lluthean's armpit, occluding his pulse.

"Kaellor," she panted. "I need you to hold pressure here while I mend the cut. If you can do that, we'll be done."

Without words, Kaellor clamped thick fingers into Lluthean's armpit and stifled the bleeding. Laryn gathered the last of her strength and channeled zenith one last time. Severed tissues began mending and knitting together, responsive to her will. Excess tissue fluids were diverted and drained.

More than once, she found herself a bit surprised at how deep Kaellor had made the cut. She knew how much fortitude such an action required for someone untrained in the healing arts. Over the next hour, she completed the mending, and none too soon.

"That's it, that's all we can do," she said. She allowed herself to lay on her side on the floor. The room careened as she slipped into the draft. Her stomach emptied with a violent heave.

Elder Miljin approached and blew the smoke of a burning herb with a pungent clean aroma across her face. The scent refreshed her and dissipated her nausea. He wiped the sweat from her brow with a cool cloth and helped her to a sitting position.

Kaellor appeared equally drained and allowed his head to sag between his knees. Sweat matted his hair, and he panted heavily.

Inspection of her work revealed that Lluthean's arm had returned to its normal color and complexion and had a strong pulse. With tedious effort, she had mended his flesh together without any sign of Kaellor's incision. But over his shoulder, where the corruption had held sway for so long, a strange silvery scar blossomed like a crab extending onto his chest and back. Out of curiosity, she ran a finger over the strange phenomenon, but the pigmentation revealed no rise in the skin, no change in texture. It was as if some lingering part of the corruption had tattooed a remnant of itself.

"Let it be done," she mumbled to herself. She channeled the smallest trickle of power she could to probe one last filament into her patient. The tendril found nothing but vital, healthy tissue, rich with normal muscle and tendon mechanics, a good blood supply . . . but nothing else. Laryn held her breath, searching, probing.

"Laryn, what's wrong?" Kaellor's question broke into her concentration.

"Grind it all. I failed," she said. Hot tears streamed down her cheeks. "I don't sense the return of any currents of innate zenith into his arm."

"You removed all the decayed flesh and healed the damage I caused. He even has a good pulse," Kaellor offered as a rebuttal.

"I know, but it wasn't enough, or maybe it was too much, I don't know," she said.

"So, what is it then?" he asked.

A hollow emptiness settled into her stomach, leaving her defeated. "Without zenith, his arm will become withered and useless." She cut off her gift and stifled her channeling. "Right now, I can't sense even a flicker of zenith in his arm."

Chapter Four: Trek to the Torgrend

VOLENCIA STAGGERED across the mist-shrouded valley on the southern slopes of the Korjinth Mountains. Blood, warm and salty, streamed from the wreckage of her face where the branch had crushed into her nose and cheek. She ignored the pain, ignored the fact that she could only draw breath through her mouth, and gathered her seething anger into intention. Dense orbs of nadir coalesced in her fists, and she searched the area where the Baellentrells had stood only moments ago.

The clearing remained vacant save for the disheveled husk of Mallic's corpse. She examined his remains. Until now, she thought she understood the price demanded to wield nadir. After inspecting the strange obliteration of his corpse, however, she was not so sure. When Mallic collapsed in death, unbridled tentacles of pure nadir had erupted. *Erupted from where? From the ground?*

She maintained the compacted nadir in her fists but used the toe of her boot to disperse the scraps of Mallic's clothing. Fragments of bone and random hunks of flesh spilled from his tunic, but nothing recognizable. His breeches, on the other hand, were still filled with his bottom half. She was reminded of the two halves of Homnibus, the monk they had sheared in half to fill the blood pool.

She stared at the cauterized surface of his vivisected lower half. The softer bits of him left behind remained packed between the bony ridges of his pelvis.

It's like the Drift reached up to claim all the parts of him tattooed with nadir sigils but left the rest behind . . . left me behind, to finish it alone.

With a cry equal parts rage and equal parts rapture, she hurled the globes of nadir at the empty mountainside. The condensed orbs erupted, discharging random onyx fragments. A sharp clack echoed across the valley as black shards blasted against unyielding stone. Where they fell, anything living blackened. Swaths of trees and undergrowth withered, creating dark scars on the mountainside. A shawl of acrid and sulfuric smoke lingered in the air.

The snakelike black sigils on her forearms undulated with anticipation, beckoning her to delve deeper. Her thoughts drifted one last time to Mallic, of his routine undisciplined descent into the frenze and the way it clouded his judgment. There was something alluring in the shallow layers of that state. It conveyed a sense of heightened awareness, followed by euphoria.

But she understood all too well the false promise of those feelings, of how clouded her judgment became, and of the terrible recovery afterward. She was better than that. *Better than him, anyway.*

With a curse, she exhaled and stifled her channeling of nadir, then ran her palms across the sigils on her forearms. *Be still. There is nothing to be gained by shouting at the mountains.*

Her sigils became dormant and lay as sharply demarcated patterns on her skin. A drop of blood dripped from her chin onto one of the ebony marks, and she relived the brief battle in her mind. *Who was that cursed woman with the painted face, where did she come from, and where did they all vanish to?*

Volencia lifted fingers to inspect the injuries on her face and inhaled in surprise. Her left cheek swelled and puffed out unnaturally. Where her fingers probed across her nose, she sensed a significant deformity and the unmistakable crackling of bone fragments shifting under her touch.

But that was not the worst of it. A thick flap of her upper lip hung oddly on her chin, and she puzzled for a moment at what her fingers felt. Where soft lip should be, her fingers instead encountered smooth enamel. An image of her deformed face appeared in her mind, and she sucked in a breath.

With quivering fingers, she channeled a thin web of nadir and removed the blood staining her clothing and her face, but she had no further ability to heal her wounds. She'd given up any resemblance of that talent when she forfeited her ability to wield zenith to become an abrogator.

The removal of the blood only led to more bleeding from the wounds on her face and did not improve her ability to breathe through her nose. *Better to wait until it's all dried, then see what you can do. Gather what you can and regroup in Callish.*

A short walk through the timber led to where her Callishite strider stood picketed. From her pack, she removed a fresh robe and cut a strip of material from the hem. As gently as she could, she bandaged the hunk of her upper lip back into place then continued wrapping the dressing around her nose and face. When the bandage cinched tight, pain flared hot and searing from her lip and nose, pulsing through to the back of her skull. The sudden intensity of it all dropped her to her knees, panting.

The throbbing agony seeped into her, fueling her hatred and intent. No self-pity entered her thoughts. Instead, she made herself feel every pulse of her heartbeat through the damaged tissues until the pain subsided. She vowed to remember this moment and call upon the depths of this pain to fuel her rage and her power. An image of the woman with the painted face coalesced in her mind. *The Giver and the Taker together won't be able to shield you from my wrath if we ever meet again.*

Volencia tethered Mallic's pinto gelding to her strider and walked both back to the clearing. She lingered, wondering if Mallic deserved to have any of his remains buried. A moment of contemplative silence passed in which she waited expectantly to feel something . . . anything other than contempt for the man who had served as her partner for most of the last decade. A strange kind of peace came over her as she realized there was no part of her invested in him, no part of her that would miss him.

I feel . . . nothing. Is it worse that I don't feel anything for him now or that I put up with his incompetence all these years?

She raised her eyebrows once and ended the introspection, then bent to collect the glimmer stone lying on the ground near Mallic's lower half. The pendant she had looped around the shadow chaser's neck was her best chance to track the Baellentrells, but only if they had kept the artifact with them. The realization made her cheeks flush with anger and caused her face to ache.

Mallic . . . the Taker have you! Better yet, may Tarkannen find you in the Drift and cause you to linger in misery. I'll not spare another thought for your grinding arrogance and stupidity.

A short ride farther west into the mountain valley led to the corpse of one of the Baellentrell geldings. The animal appeared to have succumbed to the rotting effect of Mallic's nadir dart. A glistening, ulcerated wound spread from its flank across its rib cage, revealing blackened lung tissue.

She rummaged through the saddlebags hoping to learn something of value, but they contained only simple survival gear. Her journey home to Callish, empty-handed as she was, seemed to take a lot longer than the ride to the foothills of the Korjinth.

Upon returning to her estate, Volencia summoned several different healers, a black market alchemist, and an herbalist to treat her facial wounds. A talented mender stitched the desiccated remnant of her upper lip back in place. Collectively though, the best they could manage left her only slightly relieved of pain and free of infection but permanently deformed.

On the day the stitching and bandages were due to be removed, she sent the team away to consider the ruination of her face in private. A single glance in the mirror revealed all that she ever needed to see. Her nose still listed to the side like a foundering ship run afoul of the reef in the Bay of Callish, and the left side of her upper lip drew up in a permanently creased snarl over the jagged edges of her upper teeth.

She turned to consider the unmarred side of her face and ran her tongue across the wide stretch of her upper lip until it reached the imperfection. The rumpled, scarred tissue felt more like dried leather, but at least she could breathe through her nose . . . mostly. She inhaled once, considering her face one last time, then draped a swath of black silk across the bridge of her nose and lower face.

A final glance in the mirror gave her a measure of comfort. The ensemble left her still alluring to the imagination, if not a little bit mysterious. The combination of her nadir-stained eyes with the dark scarf also conveyed a menacing connotation she found appealing. She was imagining how strangers might receive her new look when a low gong reverberated through the estate.

Volencia descended through the vast empty halls to the library and approached the silver disc responsible for the resonant knell. The sounding still vibrated under her touch. Her fingers traced the image of an umbral etched into the surface. The outline showed the eyeless half-man craning its neck back in a cry of pain or ecstasy. The top part of its head was flattened into a disc with black sigils, which both empowered and enslaved the creature.

I wonder if Mallic will become one of you, trapped in between, unable to pass on and enslaved to forces in the Drift.

Her touch wandered across the cold surface to the depiction of a grondle. The image showed the half-man, half-bull holding a skewered body overhead and gorging on its blood. She always admired the simple brutality of the beasts: no morals, no thoughts, but base instinct. She wondered where Tarkannen had summoned them from. Their lack of any capacity to channel nadir made her think they didn't come from the Drift, but she was never sure.

The silver disc suddenly froze the moisture of her fingertips, and she snapped her hand back. Ice crystals spread over the surface, and the face of a dark apparition formed above the device. Volencia dropped to her knees and pressed her forehead to the floor, surprised by the ghostly image of her master, Tarkannen.

"Volencia, wounds and veils and dead man's tales, yet I see no Baellentrell kneeling before me," rumbled the abrogator.

"No, Master. They escaped. A third party intervened, a shaman, I think. She wielded power from the Drift and evacuated the Baellentrells before I could act." She remained poised on the floor.

A long silence stretched out before Tarkannen spoke. "I sensed as much, and what's left of Mallic filled in the rest. Your failure is a disappointment, but I have limited time. Rise, and let's have a look at you."

Volencia stood, dusting off her hands. "It is encouraging to see your face. Does this mean you are near to breaking the bindings?"

The visage of Tarkannen grimaced and stretched, testing the limits of his banishment in the Drift. Eventually, he resigned to his confinement and turned to regard her directly. "Perhaps . . . yes, the Baellentrell magic wanes. I have an important task for you. Travel to the Torgrend Range northwest of Dernegia in the Northlands."

Volencia rubbed a hand across her dormant forearm sigils, dispersing a feeling of confusion. "Master, I know the city of which you speak, but I don't recall any charts recording the Torgrend mountains."

"That is the name given by the grotvonen who dwell there. Their speech would not be recorded in the maps of men. Regardless, travel deep into the under spaces of that mountain range into the caverns and find the grotvonen known as the Brognaus Clan. Do not hesitate to employ force to bend them to your will. Find the clan leader there, Grasdok."

"Master," Volencia stammered, "the grot have not walked under an open sky since your banishment. If I can even find them, how can you be certain they will obey me?"

"After the turning of the moons, when I embraced abrogation, I left a consort of umbral behind. The Brognaus clan is different from other grotvonen. Among them are a select caste of shamans who possess some ability to channel nadir. I left the umbral behind with instructions to train the shamans in a very specific form of nadir weaving. Grasdok is the chieftain, but the shaman grot hold the real power, and they defer to the umbral."

"The umbral are . . . less than predictable," said Volencia. "I might have to impress upon them my strength as your agent to bring them to heel."

The shade of Tarkannen twitched his eyebrows in an expression of nonchalance. "It matters not to me how you obtain their obedience. I left twelve behind, and we will need only a fraction of their number once I return. Do what you must."

"It shall be done," said Volencia with calm resolve.

"Once you have Grasdok and his shamans under control, tell them to prepare for the Rite of Sundering," said the abrogator.

At the mention of the unfamiliar term, Volencia took a step closer. *All this time . . . if you had the means to return, why have you waited all this time?*

"It's not what you think, Volencia," smirked the shade. "Oh, I know you and Mallic tried for years to find a way to release me from my banishment. But the bindings keeping me here cannot be weakened from my side, from the Drift. We have to wait for the erosion of the banishment to occur from your side."

"Tell me what I can do. How can we hasten your release?" she asked.

Tarkannen's shade seemed to sigh. "The Baellentrells made certain I could not weaken the binding from this side, but they did not take into account the strength of their own nature. When they wove fibers of the mantle obscuring their children into my banishment, they created a weakness. All we have to do is allow the natural order of things to unfold, and the binding will weaken enough for us to shred it completely with the Rite of Sundering."

Stinging pain lanced across the fresh scars on Volencia's face, and she forced her mouth closed, thankful that her veil obscured her momentary outrage. She stood long moments considering his words.

A pained expression caused the apparition to shudder. "I will not be able to reach through to contact you directly again. Cease your pursuit of the Baellentrell heirs and find the Brognaus," Tarkannen commanded.

With a curt nod, she acknowledged his words just before the apparition faded. In the next moment, she stood alone in the vaulted library. The ice crystals of the sounding eventually receded from the edge of the silver disc, once again revealing the etching of the umbral.

"Much to do, much to do," she said to the empty chamber. After taking a mental inventory of her tasks, she summoned several couriers to acquire items for her journey. While she waited, her thoughts returned time and again to her master's words regarding the banishment.

What does he mean by the natural order of things? I don't know if I can check my anger if I run across the Baellentrells or their wild shaman. I don't know that I want to.

She relived the encounter with the Baellentrells and the woman with the painted face. With an effort, she dismissed the gathered foci of nadir collected in her fists. Some scores were best settled in the moment and others far in the future. For now, she dismissed her rancor.

I'll see that ledger even before I'm ground to ashes and fade to the Drift.

Chapter Five: The Seeds of Rebellion

The hallways of Stone's Grasp remained silent but for the soft footsteps of a man padding down a corridor on the north side of the castle. Though his hand lamp cast only a dim nimbus, he lifted his toe just enough to avoid tripping over the uneven edge of a crevice in the stone floor. He considered the imperfection for the first time in years and recalled the black hour so long ago when the foundations trembled from the assault during the Abrogator's War.

Images of the dead flickered in his memory. The mangled bodies of slain innocents had remained far too long in the places where the grotvonen hordes murdered them. This very hall was impassable for weeks before staff returned to remove the gore and blood, and the sweet putrescence of moldering corpses had lingered for months.

Chambermaids had burned incense and lamps oiled with the sharp, woody scents of the local mountain pine to cover the enduring taint of blood and corruption. Today they referred to the aromatic vapors as survivor's essence and still burned fragrant tapers in memory of the tragedy.

Those memories gave him pause, and he stopped, then turned back to the tiny fissure in the floor. With a grimace, he crouched to trace the seam of the fracture. Though the stone gaped wider than the width of his little finger, it was no larger than it was that first night. He traced the cleft to the wall, where dark grout appeared to fill in most of the crevice. Frowning, he scratched at the substance with a fingernail.

A sliver of dark putty released under his nail a moment before he realized that the material filling in the crevice was most likely the last lifeblood of some innocent victim. He stood against the protest of stiff knees, scraped the debris against the wall, then passed the hand lamp under his nose a few times. He inhaled slow, deep breaths, allowing the pine vapors to dissipate any lingering scent-memory from that night.

That I survived at all is no small blessing of the Giver. So let's not dwell on darker things, old man. Eyes to the horizon then, the hour of convening draws near.

A short walk led to the door to his private chamber. Once inside, he checked the lock, then made a fast inspection of the rooms. Keska, the chambermaid, had left a flowering sprig of crownberry in a vase on the small end table beside his bed, but nothing else appeared out of place. Secure in his isolation, he retrieved a hooded cloak from a small wardrobe.

The wool garment, dyed charcoal, appeared only as a smoky outline and masked his identity to any who received his communications in the Lacuna. If anyone learned of his actual station, so high in the Aarindorian aristocracy, he suspected that the group would either replace or simply abandon him. Yet, he had sown the seeds of independence over the years and labored to see a free Aarindorn emerge without the trappings of a royal caste controlling the fate of their nation.

If the Taker exists, he can have his way with me if I let it all fall apart now.

He walked into a small side room and pulled the hood of the cloak low so that his face remained shadowed. A simple embroidered pattern adorned the crown of the hood: a gold circle of thread, like a torque, interrupted by a small gap of black thread.

He checked his appearance in a wall mirror. All of his features, hair, nose and even chin remained shadowed as long as he kept a single candle behind him and tilted his head forward. Satisfied with his anonymity, he sat at the lone small table in the room.

Next to his chair, on the floor, rested a stout metal lockbox. A high-quality lock protected most of the contents inside—most, but not all. Instead of releasing the rather ordinary front lock, he channeled a thread of zenith along a seam on the back of the lockbox. A puff of air released the vacuum mechanism holding the secret compartment fast. The lockbox tipped oddly forward on silent internal hinges to reveal a small hidden compartment along the bottom of the box. Inside, he ran his fingers through a collection of nuts.

As a youth, his trainers had made him practice precise control of air currents with endless monotony. One of the drills involved directing opposing currents against a nut to crack it open without physically touching the shell.

Weeks had passed without success as the thick, woody husks resisted his earnest efforts. Though capable of gusting, the Giver bestowed this to him as only a minor rune. His two classmates, both of whom had inherited gusting as their arca prime, progressed rapidly beyond this drill.

In time, his peers left him to practice the exercises alone. One evening, after watching another nut bob and hover before him for hours, he tried something different. Instead of pinching a single nut with opposing foci of air, could he not direct two different nuts against one another?

He spent the next few hours attempting to modify the drill, but more often than not, one of the nuts careened out of control to dash against a wall. In a moment of anger, he'd channeled something different: emotion. Without understanding what happened, he drafted raw zenith into the shell.

Instead of rupturing, the nut and eight or nine others of its kind scattered across the room all began to glow. The phenomenon left him drained to the point of feeling ill.

His trainers had warned against allowing emotion to affect his channeling. All their gifts worked by shaping zenith through their unique collection of runes. If anyone channeled hard and long enough, the first stages of the draft set in as a sense of fatigue and nausea. Somehow, the shared connection of the zeniphiles in Aarindorn mitigated the effects of the draft.

However, if one allowed emotion to seep unfiltered zenith into the channeling, the result usually led to an accidental leaching of their innate zenith stores. A swift descent into a more advanced stage of the draft usually rewarded the clumsy channeler.

Keeping the strange discovery of the nuts to himself, the man worked for years to understand and perfect how the seeds connected. Over time, he became adept at shaping how much zenith he allowed into the channeling, and he discovered a few more crucial details. If all the nuts dropped from the same tree, they all illuminated at once. Yet, the phenomenon failed to spread to nuts from different trees.

With practice, he also learned how to reflect his image and voice along the currents of zenith. In this manner, he created a way to send communications to anyone else who held a nut from the same tree. As long as he controlled the source, he maintained a clandestine method to communicate with others.

A sense of accomplishment always blossomed in his thoughts whenever he sifted his fingers through the drawer full of nuts on the table. The clutch was procured from a trader just after the Abrogator's War. The rover woman explained that nobody cared to purchase nuts with such a thick shell and bitter fruit. He tolerated her rambling until she divulged that her caravan found the tree, a strange species from far to the east, and cut it down for lumber to make wagon repairs.

He purchased the entire bag and all these years later had shared them with members of the Lacuna as "zenith seeds." His secret methods of communicating through the seeds were shared only with select, trusted members.

He removed one of the thumb-sized nuts, then allowed the lockbox to close. Experience had taught him that if left uncovered, the images and sounds erupting from the clutch in the hidden compartment would create noisy feedback.

With his gift, he drafted a delicate column of air to suspend the nut over the table. Next, he allowed a thin filament of zenith to leach into the seed. Pale blue light emanated as a sphere. A version of his face coalesced within the ethereal blue nimbus, shrouded in the shadows of his hood.

Before speaking, he made sure to relax the muscles in his throat and altered the pitch and tone of his voice. "The time of convening is upon us. We are the Lacuna, those who seek a permanent break in the cycle. I am the Aspect who comes to you now through the zenith seeds. Who attends the meeting tonight?"

He refined his channeling and stifled his release of zenith to allow others to speak. A different face, masked with a hood and scarf, appeared from within the light of the zenith seed. A baritone voice spoke. "The Callinoran enclave is here, Aspect. I count over thirty in our number tonight."

The image dimmed, and another appeared, similarly shrouded with a shadowed face bobbing inside the pale blue light. "Dulesque gathers with over fifty, Aspect. We will need another seed to allow for an additional gathering place soon."

"That can be arranged," he replied. "Who else attends us this evening?"

In random turns, the seed before him pulsed with light and shifting images as enclaves large and small scattered across Aarindorn acknowledged their attendance. Some gathered in secret rooms and cellars, others in caravans along the countryside. The largest groups collected in the western duchies, but numerous cells gathered in small pockets secreted throughout Stone's Grasp and the rest of the kingdom. After ten minutes, the Aspect of the Lacuna continued.

"I am pleased to see our numbers swell. Be assured that where there are eyes and ears to hear our message, I will share more zenith seeds. You are drawn here by a single purpose this night, to see to the long-term welfare of our kingdom. Aarindorn has labored to crawl out from the rubble of the Abrogator's War—a war conceived and waged between the noble houses but costing them a fraction of what the rest of us paid.

"As I speak, the light shed by our zenith seeds spills on the faces of those who lost children, parents, brothers, sisters, and spouses. If you can see and hear me, then you share our belief that we cannot return to a state of dependency on this select caste."

The Aspect paused to allow his words to organize the thoughts of those who listened. He knew well that if he conveyed too much information in a short time, it was like overstuffing a crownberry pastry: all the glistening, tangy filling leaked out in a disorganized mess.

"Tell me, have we any members attending for their first time tonight?" he asked.

The voice of a younger man resonated from the seed, but his image remained poorly defined for several seconds. Eventually, the shifting, smoky image coalesced to reveal a cowled head. Bright blue eyes flared in the visage.

"Your technique needs refining, my friend. Stifle back your flow," said the Aspect. "Continue to release that much zenith, and you'll surely awake with the draft."

The blue eyes from the apparition diminished in intensity from azure to a softer icy blue. "Apologies, and thank you, Aspect. I bring another to our cause, my sister. She is gifted and has recently obtained employment in the offices of the regent."

"That is most beneficial," replied the Aspect. "Have her remain alert. I expect to be informed of changes in the regent's disposition regarding the succession. To our understanding, Lefledge sent an Outrider on a mission to the south in search of signs of the lost Baellentrell sons."

Chalk up another victim to the regent's folly.

The Aspect continued, "Hopefully, we can artfully persuade him of the need for free elections, governance that represents not just a fraction of the kingdom but all of it. And if Therek Lefledge, in all his wisdom, can't be persuaded, then and only then will we resort to stronger methods of persuasion. As such, your sister's employment is timely, indeed. Do we have any others joining us for the first time?"

The zenith seed pulsed, and a voice accompanied by the sounds of rushing water filled the room. A round face with a ruddy chin appeared, though the rest of the man's face was obscured by the shadow of a wide-brimmed hat. "My wife and son are here, Aspect, as are two of my hired hands—apologies for the noise. We are on caravan, camped beside a river. I'll be brief. Everyone here knows of your teachings. My boy Veln—"

The Aspect flared a strong pulse of zenith through the seed. The effect usually stopped anyone else from communicating. He knew well that the myriad of seeds scattered across the kingdom would throb with a burst of blue light and the sound of his voice. "That your son is here and committed is all I need to know at this time. Let me remind everyone of our strict need for secrecy. Divulge nothing of yourselves that might allow an outsider to learn of your identity. The day when we can step from the shadows draws near, but for now, we must maintain the veil of secrecy a bit longer."

The sphere of light from the zenith seed remained still for several moments. "Any other introductions?" he asked.

After a long pause, a feminine face covered with a dark purple scarf came into view. "There are four more merchants following your teachings in Stellance, Aspect," said the woman.

"Be welcome all who look into the light of the Lacuna for the first time," said the Aspect. The blue sphere of light emanating from the zenith seed flared in intensity as a chorus of voices welcomed the newcomers. As the clamor receded, he continued.

"As I foretold months ago, the gentle whispers of our desire to see a free Aarindorn have spread throughout the kingdom." He paused and inwardly berated himself for using the term in his address. The word "kingdom" only reinforced the old notions. He exhaled through his nose then continued.

"Authorities can confiscate your weapons, even your land. But how does one bottle an idea? It's like grabbing at a column of smoke. Once released, it permeates everything and persists until the fire dissipates. But ours is no simple brush fire on the plains. We kindle our fire from the embers inside of us. Its fuel is our collective desire to see a free and prosperous Aarindorn. And when the time is right, the winds of change will ignite a contagious inferno that spreads in the hearts of every citizen in our great nation!"

The Aspect watched as different cells responded by adding their approval. The blue sphere of the zenith seed flared, and different shadowed faces chimed in. "By the Giver!" and "By the moons!" were accompanied by the sounds of fists thumping chests.

"I have news that our ideas spill from the lips of countrymen in all reaches of Aarindorn and even bubble to the surface of conversations among our more affluent families. Our truths have reached even to the ears of the regent himself. And once the seed of our idea takes root, it might be the very instrument of change we need."

He inspected his likeness, bobbing in the sphere of light. Occasionally when passion entered his address, he lifted his chin, a move that threatened to reveal more of his face than he intended. Tonight, he managed to keep his head tilted just enough to obscure the significant details of his face.

"Now, a day might arrive when our members need our financial support. What news of our holdings? Do we have a representative from the merchants' guild in Stone's Grasp in attendance?"

"I can speak, Aspect," said the familiar voice of Valdesta. The subtle crease at her eyes and the way her cheeks lifted the scarf revealed a smile even through the veil covering her face. "Thanks to our friends among the merchants and vineyard owners in Stellance, the regent agreed to open up trade through the Pillars of Eldrek. Foreknowledge of these events allowed us to position ourselves to obtain lucrative contracts from both the offices of the regent as well as other affluent families. We estimate that we control at least a third of the contracts for the development of the road and construction of the forward base camp.

"Those supportive of our cause are involved in more than half of the planned caravans to the south. Finally, we control or serve as couriers for a quarter of the trade between Stone's Grasp and the outlying duchies. This includes the commerce from the scholars in Callinora. The holdings of the Lacuna remain fragmented among enough people that we are able to evade the notice of the bankers and the vice regent. If we amass much more, though, it will be more difficult."

"What do you plan to both maintain but obscure the size of our holdings?" asked the Aspect.

Valdesta cleared her throat and raised her delicate fingers to her lips, displaying a green gemstone. "First, members should see a modest increase in the return on any investments in these endeavors. If you work through a contract sponsored by the Lacuna, expect an additional eight percent in your pocket at the end of the day. We have several merchants working to purchase assets central to the caravans, particularly timber and materials used for wagons, tack, and gear. We control the market in textiles used for everything from tents to simple sheets and have begun negotiations to purchase a share in the Balladuren horse trade."

If we could control even a portion of the Aarindin, that would prove useful not only to our finances but our reputation. Something tells me that bending the ear of their patriarch, Elbend, will involve more time and money than she realizes. And actually bending Elbend . . . good luck.

The Aspect listened to the rest of the merchant's report and tolerated her mundane accounting of the rest of their holdings. "Thank you for that thorough review, my friend. The Giver knows we will all be grateful for your work in the months following our rise."

The Aspect fingered the embroidered stitching along the hood of his robe and considered the symbol of the Lacuna: a gold torque with a gap at the bottom. He rubbed involuntarily at the identical tattoo on the inside of his right arm, next to his armpit. Placed years ago, the mark blended as just another symbol among his pattern of runes but still left an irritating tingle from the scarring.

He redirected his attention to the zenith seed. "For any new members demonstrating serious intent, we will offer the next opportunity to earn the engraving of the Lacuna midsummer. For those who would sponsor any initiates, be certain of their commitment and true intent before bringing them to the ceremony. Are there any questions?"

He paused for a time, but the zenith seed remained dark. "Before we adjourn for the closed session, I would speak to our newest recruit, the one who earned a post among the regent's offices."

A silent shadow settled across the zenith seed. At last, a female voice rippled with a faint light across the blue sphere. "I am here, Aspect. What would you ask of me?" The woman sounded young but spoke with unwavering confidence.

Good. Perhaps she can be the sharp instrument required in the days ahead.

"Be at ease and welcome," said the Aspect in reassuring tones. "As you are new to our ranks, I would ask only that you listen. Get to know the regent and his associates, observe their demeanor and behaviors. A day will arrive when you might be among the first to learn of a piece of news relevant to our interests for Aarindorn."

"Alright," said the woman.

"Bear this one thing in mind as you work. We want the regent to be as successful as possible in his governance of Aarindorn. If we can learn of his stance on moving the country away from the monarchy, we can position ourselves to assist him. When he succeeds, the country succeeds for the betterment of all its citizens. Do you understand?"

"I think so, Aspect. Think on the regent, not as our adversary, but someone we can aid when the timing is right?" asked the woman.

"Exactly," he replied. "Keep your concern for his success and welfare foremost in mind, and we will usher in a prosperous future for Aarindorn."

"I will, Aspect," said the woman.

The Aspect bowed again to display the image of the broken circle embroidered on the crown of his hood. "Thank you all for coming. We will adjourn for a closed session of the officers. Until next time, eyes to the horizon."

The zenith seed pulsed as members across the kingdom repeated the greeting in overlapping echoes.

The zenith seed fell dark, and he placed it back into the secret compartment of the small chest. He reached into a pocket to retrieve a palm-sized snuff box. A sharp twist removed the lid of the ornate silver container and released aromatic vapors of resco, spice, and crownberry.

After inhaling the sweet fragrance, he stirred a calloused finger through the fine powder to reveal an unusual flat nut lying under the snuff and flush to the container. With a gentle touch, he lifted this new zenith seed, holding it up for inspection between thumb and forefinger. Veining ran across the wafer-thin surface. He brushed the residual powder off and channeled. The disk illuminated, and he placed it on the table.

"I call the closed session to order, are we all in attendance?" he asked.

One at a time, four different voices chimed in to indicate their presence. Inasia of Callinora and Valdesta, the brothel owner and merchant, spoke first. Burl, the gruff man from Midrock, and Kunzie, another merchant in Stone's Grasp, spoke in turn.

"What news do we have from the contract with the assassin, Vardell Becks?" he asked.

Valdesta responded, "Nothing to report, Aspect, which is, as you can well imagine, a concern. His last communication through the seeds indicated that he was close. He should have reported back weeks ago. We must entertain the notion that he might have failed or was discovered."

The Aspect nodded understanding. "If Becks was captured, was he in any position to betray our role in his employment?"

"It's hard to say, Aspect," said Valdesta. "He knew that the contract came from within our organization, but it was arranged through a third party in a brothel under our control. I do not think he would be able to reveal anything specific to our organization."

"Well, keep me informed of any new developments. How did the Spicer gang receive our proposal?"

"Very well, Aspect," said Kunzie. His veil obscured his high cheekbones, but nothing short of a trick of zenith could alter his nasal voice. "The information we provided allowed them to raid two smaller outfits, putting them in command of the black market in vivith. We haggled over the final percent of the cut coming to the Lacuna. Agreeable terms were reached just yesterday. The arrangement leaves them in a position to manage the brothels and gaming rackets through the Sprawl. Their leader, Salveen, was pleased and seemed in a mood to offer his services in the future."

The Aspect relaxed in his chair. *Another piece placed on the board.*

"Have we obtained a replacement for Gwillion?" asked the Aspect. "I understand he finally succumbed to his addiction to vivith. He was central in our ability to procure reagents for the manufacture of the drug."

Inasia, their agent in Callinora, chimed in. "We have identified a good candidate. A healer of the second order at Callinora; he ranks high enough to have access to materials but low enough for nobody to notice him."

"What's our angle?" asked the Aspect.

"Gambling debts have left him unable to maintain his residence in Callinora or provide for his wife, who suffers a wasting condition," she replied.

The Aspect inhaled through his nose and nodded in a knowing gesture. *And so we twist a man's vice like a knife.*

"He sounds like a good prospect. Apply a little pressure first, find out who holds his residence contract, and buy it if you can. Either way, once the man seems ready to break, offer him a way out through the Lacuna."

"Consider it done, Aspect," said Inasia.

"Does anyone have anything of significance to discuss?" asked the Aspect.

"I do," said Valdesta. "My girls at the Stag tell me Captain Oren might be another we can turn to our cause."

"The captain of the city watch? Here in Stone's Grasp?" asked the Aspect. "That Captain Oren?"

"The very same," replied the madam. "To begin with, he's sweet on one of my girls. Add a jigger of resco and his true nature practically tumbles out. He's been unhappy with the monarchy ever since the downfall of his extended family in the reparations after the war."

"Would he entertain a formal invitation, or do we need to entice him to feel compelled to enter our service?" asked the Aspect.

"Oh, I think he would come of his own free will, especially if Fendella suggested he escort her to a meeting. He's pretty taken with her," said Valdesta.

"Well, if we can enlist him as a true believer rather than someone compelled to the cause, he will certainly be much more useful. Make the arrangements then," said the Aspect.

The pieces on the board are getting a little crowded. We'll be prepared to make our moves soon if the regent doesn't come around to our way of thinking.

"Anything further then?" asked the Aspect.

"Just one more thing, Aspect," said Kunzie. "I received information that the runeless are organized."

The zenith seed remained dormant for a long moment as they all considered the news.

"Explain what you mean exactly when you say organized," said the Aspect.

"Just that," said Kunzie. "They have apparently been gathering in secret for several years now. They call their leader the Dedicant."

"Interesting choice," said the Aspect. "What do we know about them?"

"One of my sons is runeless; he attends their gatherings," said the merchant. "They started as a way to gather with others who could understand their struggles. But in the last year, the Dedicant has suggested a more vocal expression of their unrest."

"Do you think it's something that would benefit our cause?" asked Inasia.

"It's too early to say, but possibly," said Kunzie.

"We have enough irons in the fire," said the Aspect. "For the moment, keep close tabs on the group and any actions they might take."

"Consider it done," said the merchant.

The meeting adjourned, and the Aspect replaced the select zenith seed in his snuff box. He took a pinch, placed it in the crease at the base of his thumb and wrist, then snorted it back. Sweet aroma filled his senses, followed by a pleasurable flushing sensation across his chest and neck. He sighed and relaxed, thinking about the meeting.

If the runeless really are organizing, they could be an ally or possibly a scapegoat. We could make moves to clean the kingdom of two stains with but one pass of the cloth. Everything hinges on the regent. Cling to the old ways or embrace a new path? The old man better choose soon, or events will decide for him.

Chapter Six: Grondle Stained

Karragin awoke alone on a cot with the faint taste of anise lingering on the back of her tongue. She sat up and tried to turn her neck to orient herself to her new surroundings. Searing pain flared across her throat, made all the worse when she swallowed. The discomfort made her dip her chin to help make the muscles of her throat work. Reaching up to assess her injuries, her fingertips ran over the front of a thick gauze wrapping around her neck.

"Awake now, are we?" asked the voice of an old woman behind her. "Drink this. It will help ease the pain."

The woman hobbled into view and placed a cup of tea into Karragin's hands. She sniffed at the brew but didn't recognize the aroma. The thought of swallowing anything, even medicine, seemed against her better instinct. Without turning her head, Karragin set the cup on a bedside stand. The woman sighed once, picked up the cup, placed it back into Karragin's hands, then pulled a small rocking chair up next to Karragin's cot and sat down.

"First thing's first, then. I'm the docent here in this camp. My name is Venlith Lentrell. I'm a graduate of Callinora and a healer of the fourth order. I came here to help organize the medics at the forward base camp and only agreed to do so as a personal favor to a friend, one Therek Lefledge."

The docent paused and poured herself a cup of the same tea from the teapot on the bedside stand. She clinked the cup to Karragin's, took a sip, then continued, "Since I came all this way, and since you taxed most of my skill in removing the stain of grondle blood, the least you can do is complete my course of treatment. Don't you think?"

Karragin considered her surroundings more carefully. Two rows of cots lined the long tent supported by stout poles. Several patients lay resting, most with bloodstained bandages to show for their trouble. Seven cots down, a young man moaned in semiconscious pain as two healers straightened then splinted an obvious leg deformity.

She considered Venlith, dipped her chin in a subtle nod of agreement, then sipped at the tea. To her surprise, the liquid tasted faintly of honeysuckle and left her wanting more. They sat in silence, and after a few more sips, the pain in her throat eased. When she chanced a response, her voice felt and sounded like a wet stone over a dull, rusty blade.

"It's good. Thank you, Docent," she said.

"Finish that cup, and if you're hungry, you might be able to tolerate solid food in a little while," said Venlith.

"What did you mean when you said you had to remove the stain of grondle blood?" asked Karragin.

Venlith drained her teacup, then eased back into the chair. "People survived all kinds of injuries in the Abrogator's War, child. I channeled more zenith in those dark weeks than I did in the next decade. Some of the injuries were a challenge, those with internal bleeding or those that got knocked on the head. But none challenged us at Callinora so much as those stained by the creatures from the Drift."

"What makes those wounds any different?" asked Karragin.

Venlith rocked in her chair and stared out at the length of the empty medic tent. "That depends, I suppose," said Venlith, "on what caused the wound in the first place. Some of the creatures from the Drift leave a taint on any wound that will fester if not thoroughly cleansed. Grondle blood is like that. You have an hour, two at the most. If the foul humors of a grondle remain any longer, then the flesh is completely corrupted. That's not such an issue if it's on a hand or a foot. Lots of good folk over the years have managed well enough without a hand or a foot."

Karragin considered the crone's words and made a more thorough appraisal of Venlith. Nobby, arthritic hands wrapped around the arms of her rocker. The woman looked back at Karragin, apparently aware of her inspection, and smacked her lips, revealing yellowed teeth, before lifting the hem of her skirt. Two legs appeared: one weathered and veiny, the other an ebony wooden prosthetic. Both disappeared into common shoes.

"As I was saying, lots of good folk can manage without a foot. But that thing you wrestled with two days back smeared its corruption all over you."

"Two days? I've been here two days?" Karragin asked in a voice that sounded like rope sliding over rock.

Venlith smiled and kept rocking. "Do you know the hardest thing about being a healer of the fourth order? It's all the hurry up and wait."

"I don't understand," rasped Karragin. The pain in her throat subsided, but the muscles controlling her voice failed her still. She held out her teacup, and Venlith obliged, filling it back up.

"Seems at times I'm not much better at predicting outcomes than a backwoods midwife. A woman's water breaks, and they scurry around in preparation . . . then sit and wait. That's how it is with cleaning grondle-contaminated wounds. Lots of hurry, little bit of action, then lots of waiting. That's why I always travel with my rocker. Makes the waiting easier, even if it takes two days for a patient to declare."

Karragin considered her words. "Two days to . . . what, wake up or expire?"

Venlith nodded. "Wounds like yours, with all that taint, require lots of embertang. Embertang requires lots of bandle root and no small effort on my part to keep your mind removed from awareness of the pain. Your wounds were shallow and fresh, so I wasn't too worried. But with anything from the Drift, you can never be too sure."

"Well, thanks then, I think," Karragin croaked.

She sipped at the medicinal tea and listened to the creaking of the docent's rocker. Karragin thought about the old healer's words. "You said before that whether a person survives also depends on what caused their wounds."

Venlith nodded and placed a finger alongside her nose, then pointed at Karragin. "When I heard about how you fought that grondle, I imagined you must be all brute and no brain. But you pay attention, and I suspect you're better read than the average Outrider. That's good."

The docent rocked gently and continued to stare down the medic tent. "Grondle were just one of the strange beasts we fought in the Abrogator's War. Somehow, Tarkannen managed to pull a host of other nasty things from the Drift: creatures that resembled hounds with stingers for tails, others that seemed more reptilian, and all of them under the control of the umbral."

Venlith massaged the bone-swollen knuckles of one hand. "We had no trouble healing the physical injuries. But it just seemed that once a person's body was stained by the corruption of a bite or sting from some beastie from the Drift, we couldn't manage to ever get them back. They lingered, some for weeks, but ultimately it was like their soul abandoned any desire to return to a body so corrupted."

"I've read that, once drift-bitten, only death awaits," said Karragin.

Venlith raised bushy grey eyebrows and nodded in agreement. "Kissed by the Taker they were, every last one of them. That's why I'm not so sure the grondle are really of the Drift. You're the first person in a decade to survive a grondle attack, but there were plenty of others in the Abrogator's War who survived being stained by grondle blood, as long as we got to them fast."

Karragin puzzled at the strange twist in the conversation. "If they are not from the Drift, then where are they from, and where have they been for the last decade?"

"That's a question I'll wager your father is best suited to answer," said Venlith. "I can only tell you what I know. Drift-bitten does cause death for certain, but grondle stained is not the same thing."

A young man dressed in the burgundy garb of a novice healer approached. "Apologies, Docent Venlith. Warden Elbiona requests an updated report on your patient. If she is able to receive guests, her brother has returned, asking to see her again."

The docent pushed up from her rocker with a grunt. "I'll go see the warden. I could use the fresh air. If she gets hungry, she can trial soft foods first." Venlith grabbed the top of a cane and gestured it at Karragin. "Don't let me catch you eating anything more substantial than mashed fruit and porridge. Otherwise, whether you receive visitors is up to you."

The young healer raised his eyebrows in question to Karragin. "I'd like to see anyone from my quad, then maybe some porridge," she said.

The novice tilted his head then pushed through the entrance of the medic tent. A moment later, Nolan entered, wide-eyed. He happened to walk by just as one of the healers unwrapped the dressing of a new arrival. A spurt of blood splattered the tent ceiling. Nolan quickstepped to Karragin's bedside and sat in Venlith's rocker. He made a quick inspection of his Outrider uniform, dusting his hands across the front panels and sleeves.

"Did any get on you?" she asked.

"Hmm? I just had it cleaned, so it would only be my luck, I suppose." He grinned at her. "How are you feeling? The docent wouldn't tell us anything."

"My throat is still sore," she rasped, "but I'll be out tomorrow whether the docent approves or not. What have you been up to while I linger in this sickbed?"

"Well, the warden had me backtrack the grondle. Only an hour's ride south, I found the rest of Boljer's quad."

Karragin searched her memory. "He's the prime from Stellance, the one who jumps off the cliff and then asks how deep the river runs?"

Nolan leaned in. "Not so loud, I'm pretty sure that patient wrapped from head to toe in bandages just four cots down is him. Anyway, you got the right of it. It seems Boljer led a skirmish against a group of grot. The quad managed pretty well until that grondle showed up. It didn't take but a moment for it to mangle their mounts and kill two of them. Boljer and his medic climbed into the trees. They dosed a loaf of bread with all their bandle root. The grondle ate the loaf along with . . . other things."

"What do you mean when you say 'other things'?" she interrupted.

Nolan pushed back in the rocker and stared down the medic tent. "I only found parts of the other two Outriders, Karra. The grondle ate them."

They sat in silence a moment. Karragin tried to imagine how awful it would be to watch in fascinated helpless horror as a beast first killed her friend and then dismembered and consumed their corpse. She recalled the overwhelming strength the grondle possessed and rubbed absentmindedly at the bruising along her neck.

"Anyway, eventually, the bandle root must have sedated the grondle because it seemed to fall into a stupor. Boljer had the idea to cover its head with tent canvas and wanted to bring it back. I think he meant to hand it over to the warden for study, only—"

"Only the bandle root wore off right when they got to camp," Karragin surmised.

"You guessed it," said Nolan.

"Sometimes when you jump in, the river runs deep," she said.

"But Boljer's ran shallow," Nolan echoed the old phrase in agreement. "Still, Tovnik and I got a chance to study it, the one we killed."

Karragin scooted back on her cot to sit up taller. She tapped her empty cup on the side of the tea kettle. Nolan filled it to the brim. "Did you learn anything useful?"

"Lots of things," he said, "but nothing that you didn't already know. That entire part that looks like a man is all muscle. All the important stuff, the heart and lungs, and other organs—all that sits behind a thick rib cage."

"The warden said as much. Find any weaknesses?" asked Karragin.

"Maybe a few. Tovnik thinks the eyes are real enough, though by all the dead in the Drift, they give me the shivers. It's like the Taker shoved black marbles in and called it good. They breathe through those long gill slits, but you have to get close and personal to take advantage of that."

Karragin rested her head back and withdrew inside herself. She allowed the flows of zenith to infuse her runes and funneled the currents into her rune of premonition, waiting, hoping for some sign of the appropriate next steps. Only on a rare occasion had the gift bestowed anything useful to her, and usually, it was upon first waking when her sleepy mind hadn't had time to busy itself with the mundane details of the day.

The rune remained dormant and offered her no insights. "Only sometimes . . . sometimes the Giver gives," she muttered.

"You still trying to force your premonition to trigger? Give yourself a break, Karra. You know even Father can't manage that, and it's his arca prime," said Nolan.

Tossing back the sheet, Karragin realized for the first time that she only wore smallclothes. She pointed to her folded Outrider uniform sitting on a small trunk at the foot of the bed. Nolan retrieved her garments but held them on his hip, placing himself between her and the uniform.

"What are you doing, Karra?" he asked.

"We scouted an entire warren of grotvonen within our borders. Now another quad encountered more of them at the edge of the kingdom, and this time in the company of a grondle. Grind me if the warden thinks she can keep us in the stables."

Nolan smiled and handed over her uniform. She ignored the strain of stiff muscles in her neck and back as she shimmied into her breeches.

"The warden is not really somebody we can push around. I'm not even sure she'll agree to let you out of the medic tent," said Nolan.

Karragin sat back down and began to lace up her boots, but the pain in her chest and neck flared, forcing her to sit back on the cot. "Taker's breath. Nolan, just . . . help me get my boots sorted out. I can't stay in this place another minute."

Nolan bent down to attend to her laces. "What's the rush?"

"I need to pay a fast visit to one of the alchemists. Are any of them garrisoned here?" she asked.

Nolan shrugged. "I think I might be the closest thing to anyone from the guild."

"That's even better," said Karragin. "Grab Tovnik and Amniah, then meet me in the mess tent." She waved off the look of protest on his face. "I know, nothing more than porridge. I don't intend to ignore all the docent's advice. Just bring them. I think I know of a way we might be able to subdue a grondle. But unlike our friend over there"—she nodded toward the heavily bandaged Boljer—"I intend to get an idea how deep the river runs before we jump."

Chapter Seven: In Service to the Regent

Ksenia gazed out of the window overlooking Stone's Grasp. From her room on the second level, she could just make out the roof to the stables where she kept Winter. Beyond that, the morning sun streamed into the Crown's Timber, the royal gardens and forest of Stone's Grasp. The sprawling wood protected by the curtain wall remained unspoiled by poachers and was carefully managed by a huntsman. While she appreciated the chance to look across the wooded cliffs, she missed the freedom she'd once enjoyed whenever she disappeared with Winter into untamed parts of the Great Crown.

After channeling zenith through her sympathic rune, she cast her awareness into the stables. Without a direct line of sight, she couldn't be sure she would reach the Aarindin. *"Winter, can you hear me?"*

After a few moments and with no response, she tried again with a more earnest tone. *"Winter? Winter, are you there? Can you—"*

"I am here," replied the Aarindin. *"There is a boy. He gave me sweet oat and cracked corn, but the hay is flat and dry."*

Ksenia relaxed onto the windowsill. *"That's to be expected here, I suppose. Do you like the stables?"*

"They are small. Small and clean, but the boy took me on a long walk. I like the boy."

"That's good. I know the room is small. I promise we will ride later before dark. I will come to see you."

Ksenia ended the communication and turned to regard her reflection in the window. She hooked a thumb over the edge of a broad leather belt. Silver and blue stitching, marking her a member of the regent's staff, ringed the collar of her white blouse. She allowed herself to kick a leg forward, swishing the plain brown skirt. The brushed twill separated, revealing a division in the legs of the skirt that would accommodate her riding Winter.

I suppose I have you to thank for these, Mother. Small steps for big amends.

A knock on her door interrupted her thoughts, and she stood abruptly, the pantlegs disappearing and giving the illusion of more traditional garb. "It's open. Come in."

A young woman dressed in similar attire stepped into her room, her brown hair pulled into a neat bun set off a plain, round face. She pushed spectacles back on the bridge of a small upturned nose. "Hello, my name is Vinnedesta, but friends call me Vin."

Ksenia nodded. "Ksenia Balladuren, nice to meet you, Vin. I gather by your uniform you work for the office of the regent as well?"

Vinnedesta tipped her head and fidgeted with the edge of her collar, then seemed to regain a sense of poise and lowered her hands, smoothing the front panels of her skirt. "Yes, I only started last month. It's all a bit exciting, isn't it?"

"Can you tell me about your duties? How does the regent keep you busy?" asked Ksenia.

"Well, most mornings those of us who scribe for the old lynx—" Vinnedesta flushed at the slip of her tongue. "That's what we scribes call the regent on account of how his long eyebrows look like a lynx. Anyway, we keep rather busy penning and recording his missives. Sometimes we make entries into books of record and ledgers. Other times we draft memos for him to send on official business for the kingdom."

"That sounds . . ." Ksenia inhaled a deep breath to settle her frustration . . . frustration at the mundane nature of it all, at the way her mother had navigated her into the position, and at the feeling of being confined. "Simple enough, I suppose," she finished. "What else? What other responsibilities do we have?"

The expression on Vinnedesta's face brightened. "Well, I was told that you carry some skill with linguistics, as do I." She pulled back the forearm of her blouse to reveal two delicate gold bands that spiraled up beyond her elbow. In between the bands, small arcane symbols wove a pattern. Though it differed in specific shape, Ksenia recognized distinct similarities to her own lesser rune.

Ksenia cocked her head to the side, intrigued. "And that pertains to our work here how, exactly?"

"Why don't we make our way to the regent's offices and talk along the way? If we delay any longer, I fear we will be late, which is not a good way to begin on your first day, trust me. Be sure to bring your folio, the one with your identification papers. You'll need it your first few times past the guards on the upper levels."

Ksenia retrieved her folio, pocketed a few coins, and followed Vinnedesta into the hallway. They began the climb through Stone's Grasp to the restricted areas of the regent's offices. The young woman continued, "Aarindorn is currently without a steward of the archives. The old one, Weckles, passed this winter. May the Giver embrace him in the Drift. He was one of the only people in Stone's Grasp gifted in linguistics. Before he passed, Weckles had just begun to work on deciphering a text written in High Aarindorian, from the time of the Cataclysm."

"Alright, you have me interested," said Ksenia.

Vinnedesta hitched up her skirt as they began to ascend a long flight of stairs. "I'm glad to hear you say that because you and I are to begin work this afternoon to see if we can continue where Weckles left off."

"That could be fun," replied Ksenia, a bit out of breath. "Have you had the chance to start? How far did Weckles get before he passed?"

"Not far at all from what little I could tell," said Vinnedesta. "I've been at it a solid three or four hours and haven't learned a thing."

They turned onto a paved landing that wound in a lazy semicircle to the front of Stone's Grasp. Royal blue banners mounted on top of the distant parapet flapped in the winds gusting off the Great Crown. Ksenia pulled errant strands of hair behind her ear.

"Three to four hours every day for a month and not a thing? Not a noun or the understanding of gender or tense?" asked Ksenia.

Vinnedesta drew up short. "Oh, no, not every day, just one day. Three, maybe four hours is all the time I have had alone with the text. Come on. We just have to get past the guard, Bex. He can take a mood sometimes, but usually, I can sweet talk my way by."

Ksenia followed Vinnedesta through a set of double doors. Inside, a man stood with his butt cheeks resting on an oversized table. He wore a sleeveless leather jerkin with decorative metal accents designating him a member of the castle guard. The blue insignia of house Baellentrell decorated the sleeves of his white shirt and a short sword strapped to his waist. The man had his arms folded but waved a lazy finger at Vinnedesta. "Vin, you're cutting it close this morning."

"Good morning, Bex. This is Ksenia, newest scribe for the regent."

Ksenia stepped forward and handed her folio to the man. Bex opened the folio, inspected the papers a moment, then whistled an exaggerated tone before handing them back.

"You're a Balladuren, then?" asked the guard.

Ksenia nodded once and wrung her left hand around her right wrist. The guard resembled someone familiar, but she could not place his face. "Yes, that's correct. Nice to meet you, Bex."

"Never saw much need for them fancy horses your family breeds. But then, there's not much call for a mount inside the curtain wall," said the man as he reached to hand the folio back.

Puzzled by the hint of challenge in his statement, Ksenia reached hesitantly for the folio. "I imagine that's true."

Bex resisted, holding onto the folio. A half-smirk played across his face. "You don't see much need for a mount either?"

Ksenia suddenly remembered why she loathed being back inside Stone's Grasp. "Can I have my papers back, or do you need to keep them for further inspection?"

The guard lingered, refusing to release the documents, and spoke with feigned chagrin. "My apologies, high lady. I was just interested in why someone who sees the truth of my words would then bring her own mount to the royal stables."

Ksenia sighed and considered the man but held onto the folio. These word games always held more meaning than she appreciated at first blush. She knew they only mattered when you reacted to the baiting, but Bex had managed to provoke an itch, and she couldn't leave it alone.

She pulled lightly at the folio. "When I replied that's true, I was speaking to your inability to appreciate the value of a purebred Aarindin. Nothing more."

Bex grunted but refused to release the folio, dragging out the awkwardness of the moment.

Ksenia cocked her head. "Bex—your name is Bex, yes? You see, I want to remember to explain to the regent why Vin and I were delayed if we arrive late. I'm sure Therek Lefledge would welcome the news that one of his guards carried out such a vigilant inquisition of two young women. Women with proper papers and dressed in scribe uniforms without weapons. Surely such dedication should be brought up for review."

Bex snapped his hand away from the folio and walked around the table to take a seat. "No need for any of that. As you were, ladies." He offered a flat smile that failed to reach his eyes and gestured into the hall with a welcome hand.

Vin took Ksenia's hand and ushered them along. "Yes, thanks, Bex!"

Ksenia followed Vinnedesta down a wide corridor off to the right. The young scribe turned to her with wide eyes. "You gave better than you got, but I would step lightly around that one next time if I were you, Ksenia."

Ksenia found herself nodding agreement and wishing she had remained above the entire affair. "Believe me, I know. I suppose when anyone talks about Aarindin, I can get a bit touchy. But he's just a silly inner door guard. I bet he doesn't even know if the blade inside that scabbard is sharp or dull."

"Well, the kitchen maids whisper that he has more of a boot dagger than a sword if you catch my meaning," quipped the scribe. She giggled at her own joke, then leaned in with an earnest expression. "Regardless, that silly door guard is an Endule with a sister in the city watch, a brother in the Outriders, and another brother who represents the interests of three guilds in affairs to the regent."

They walked past a generous waiting room lined with padded benches and oversized chairs. Several well-dressed men and women, merchants most likely, were gathered, and a servant circulated the room with a pitcher of water.

Vinnedesta led them to a door that felt reserved for staff, and they entered a long, shallow room lined with writing desks. Above the desks, shelves housed sheets of paper and writing instruments. The scribe retrieved two of the writing tools and tucked them into the small pocket of Ksenia's blouse.

"I assume you've used a zeniscrawl before?" she asked.

Ksenia was more than familiar with the simple tool. "Yes, draft a bit of zenith through the tool to activate the dye, and it should last a few hours."

"Good," beamed Vin. "You can store your folio here and then grab any of the empty leather binders, fill them with blank papers, and we can take our place inside. I'll explain how the scribing is divided up as the regent receives the petitioners. Today though, you should just practice and write down everything I do. In no time at all, you'll get the format of the documentation, and we can split the responsibilities."

Ksenia retrieved the materials and prepared to follow Vin into the regent's chambers but stopped at the door. Realization washed over her like stepping out of a warm room and into a cold gale. "Vin, Bex Endule is Bextle Endule? Older brother to Craxton Endule? Is that the guild leader you're talking about?"

The round-faced young woman looked over her shoulder and shoved the door open. "The very same. You know him?"

"More than a little," said Ksenia. "We were in the same graduation class for skills and revealing and sort of . . . had a falling out."

Vinnedesta stopped in the doorway with a sympathetic expression. "Craxton is a linked sender born as a triplet. You pull the feathers on that bird and get the whole flock."

"And I just insulted his older brother. Here I thought this time might be different," said Ksenia.

"Look, Ksenia, you aren't the first one to be put off by that lot. Talking to one of the senders means you talk to all three . . . at the same time. What would it be like to kiss one of them? I mean, I might kiss Craxton; he's a looker for sure. But can you imagine if his brother and sister felt it too? That's just . . . I mean . . . ew."

Ksenia puffed out her cheeks and folded her arms, then shrugged her shoulders. "I can."

Vinnedesta arched her eyebrows. "Oh, just . . . oh. That does explain why Bex gave you the interrogation. Well, listen . . . squash all that for now. Let's get through the morning, and we can talk about it later."

Vinnedesta led them over to a table situated under a window with natural light. The young scribe was all business once they entered the room. Ksenia watched and mirrored Vinnedesta's preparation, setting out her zeniscrawl and several loose sheets of paper. The scribe drafted the date and time, then folded her hands and waited.

From a door at the backside of the chamber, Therek Lefledge, the regent of Aarindorn, swept into the room with strides that reminded Ksenia of a long-legged river heron. The tails of a silken blue tabard trailed behind the lanky man. He found purchase in a large chair raised onto a small wood platform.

The vice regent, Chancle Lellendule, followed him in but walked to stand before the table where the scribes were preparing to conduct their work. "Good morning, Vinnedesta. I see a Balladuren sits beside you today."

Giver, he's easy on the eyes, even if he is older than Rugen.

Ksenia rubbed at her wrist, the action allowing her to dismiss that small part of her awareness that surveyed the vice regent's manicured beard and the smart way his tailored shirt framed his shoulders. "Good morning, Vice Regent," she said.

"Welcome to Stone's Grasp, Ksenia. I'm so glad you accepted the position here. I know it's your first morning, but you couldn't ask for a better trainer than Vinnedesta. Consider everything you see and hear in these chambers a state secret. Sometimes conversations drag, and other times they break down into bickering and argument. Don't get lost in either, and record the simple details of the exchanges without any emotion, judgment, or bias. Any questions?"

Ksenia lifted her eyebrows. "No, Vice Regent."

Chancle offered them a kind smile of reassurance, then stepped back and addressed the regent. "If you are ready, Regent?"

The regent glanced over Chancle's shoulder and nodded to Ksenia and Vinnedesta but seemed preoccupied and offered no formal greeting. The sagely man drew his attention back to the vice regent. "The sooner we begin, the sooner we are done."

Chancle walked to the room's last door, which connected to the anteroom where the petitioners waited. Ksenia heard the zeniscrawl at work on Vinnedesta's paper and watched her write the date, followed by the words, "First petitioner to the regent."

Ksenia copied the entry on her own paper and waited for the vice regent to make introductions.

Chancle's voice carried across the room as she scribed. "Petitioning the regent pertaining to the allocation of timber for the wagoner's guild, speaker Craxton Endule."

Chapter Eight: Shadows in the Great Crown

Nolan Lefledge took a knee at the ridge of a slope deep in the Great Crown. He channeled zenith, filtering it through his arca prime, and assessed the surrounding valley. The remnants of numerous trails, some made by wild animals but more by grotvonen, appeared to him as wispy blue ribbons on the ground. He took care to search for any sign of the more formidable grondle, but his gift revealed no trace of the beasts.

The sun dipped below the mountain peaks, and craggy shadows crept across the ground. He pushed a wood toggle through a leather loop and cinched the high neck of his winter fatigues. The leathers made a poor ward against the early chill, but more than this, something in his search of the terrain caused him to shiver.

Intuitively, Nolan understood that the valley with the grotvonen lay a half-day's journey south by horseback. Under his scrutiny, numerous old trails appeared, but something strange had degraded the signal . . . something well beyond the typical passage of time. He studied the odd breaks in the tracks for long moments.

What am I not seeing?

His toes tingled with the nip of the cold, and he stomped his feet into the ground. Despite the cold, he continued to channel zenith and realized he had been doing so for a long while without the effects of the draft. Nolan thought fleetingly of the first time the malady leached away his stamina; the first time he discovered grondle tracks in the Borderlands. He dismissed the concern and allowed his gift to sweep one more time across the valley. No other answers came to him, so he stifled the flow of zenith and stood with a grunt of frustration.

"What do you see when you use your arca prime?" Amniah's voice, though soft and flat, caused him to jump to the side. He pulled an arrow from his quiver, holding it forward like a knife in a defensive posture.

"That's a strange way to shoot an arrow, Nolan," she said. He stood there, arm trembling, breath labored, and studied the strange guster. She stared back with a flat expression, and he waited to see if she would smile or wrinkle her lip in a sneer, something to betray what she was really thinking. After what felt like a long awkward moment, he realized she was just . . . making a simple observation.

He placed the arrow back in his quiver and retrieved his bow. "Amniah, what are you doing here?" *And how by the moons did you sneak up on me? Going to have to work on that.*

"Karragin sent me to find you. She believes we are close to the grot and ordered a retreat to make camp for the night," said the guster.

Nolan craned his head back to gather up all the unkempt, thick curls of cinnamon hair. He secured the tumbled mass into a tight tail with a strip of leather cord. The chill wind nipped at the freshly exposed skin under his ears and the nape of his neck. He turtled into his winter fatigues until he became accustomed to the cold.

"Why do you do that?" asked Amniah. She tilted her head to the side, and he was reminded of the way a bored house cat might regard the corpse of a dead mouse that no longer scampered about.

"Do what?" he asked.

"Why do you wear your hair loose? Does it have something to do with your ability to track?" she asked.

Nolan found himself again puzzled by the very matter-of-fact tone with which she always spoke. He wondered for a moment if she was poking fun but was slowly coming to the realization that these kinds of questions were just her nature.

"I don't know. Wearing my hair down is easy, and it's certainly warmer," said Nolan. "But Karra's been in a sour mood ever since we were tasked with this mission, and she doesn't tolerate a sloppy appearance."

Amniah stood still, gazing across the valley. "I hadn't noticed her mood. Why do you suppose she is frustrated?"

"She would rather be hunting grondle in the Borderlands. I think she has a score to settle," said Nolan.

"Mmm," said Amniah with a thoughtful expression. "Well, you're covered in trail dust and grass. Stand still then," said Amniah. She stood beside him and held her arms forward. "Have a care and close your eyes."

Before he could ask what she was doing, a straight line of wind dashed against the two of them. The gale roared in his ears for several seconds and caused him to step back for balance. The air stilled just as abruptly as it began. Amniah turned and made a brief inspection of his uniform, straightening the curled-in edge of the top of his collar.

"I don't know what your sister's standards are, but Mother would welcome you to dinner at our table in Stellance. We should go before it gets dark," she said.

"Thanks," said Nolan. He trailed behind her a few steps. Halfway down the backside of the mountain ridge, he triggered his arca prime for a moment, just long enough to learn Amniah's unique signature. Swirls and tiny currents of zenith revealed themselves to his awareness.

You might be as quiet as a cat, but I'll dance naked under the moons before I let you sneak up on me like that again.

After committing her pattern to memory, he walked to the tree line where they'd both picketed their Aarindin. They mounted and made a silent return back to camp.

Karragin was leading a full flank, ten quads, on their mission into the mountains. The assignment was Warden Elbiona's way of releasing her from Venlith's care while keeping her isolated from the threat of grondle.

The Outriders mostly remained grouped in their quads, with clusters of tents gathered in a circle. Nolan walked his mount through the lingering steam of their breaths, expecting to find a cookfire to warm by. His hopes withered when he realized that the only light to fall across the camp spilled from the slivered moon of Baellen, and even that was pale and anemic. Instead of inhaling the scent of a cookfire, the sharp and slightly sweet aroma of alpine cut through the night air.

He blew his breath under his collar and realized his chin felt numb from the cold. Amniah led him through the small camp. "Let me guess, ghost protocol?" he asked.

"Yes," she replied. "Tovnik and I set up your tent near ours over here." She directed them to a cluster of shelters that looked no different from any of the others.

Tovnik's head poked out of a tent flap as they approached. The healer worked his mouth, chewing something, then swallowed hard. "Welcome back. I saved a strip of jerky and two molar breakers for you. They're on your bedroll."

Nolan dipped his head. "Thanks, Tov."

With conscious effort, he overcame his reticence and slid off the Aarindin. The loss of the mount's warmth between his legs caused a shiver to run up his spine. After tending to the horse, he wandered to the center of the camp. Karragin stood in conversation with Kervin Balladuren and a few other primes.

She turned at his approach and held out a waterskin. Nolan waved it off. "I'm fine, thanks."

"It's hot tea, probably the last bit of anything warm to eat or drink for several days," said Karragin.

"Alright then," said Nolan. He unstoppered the neck and took a long pull. The subtle drink warmed his chest, but only as a tease. In moments, his core muscles shivered to resist the achy cold that penetrated his winter gear.

"I can tell we're in the right place. Did you find anything useful?" asked Karragin.

"I estimate the grot warren is two ridges in. If we break camp at dawn, we could make good time and survey the valley by midmorning," said Nolan.

"Anything else?" she pressed.

"I didn't find any signs of grondle, but I never made it to the warren. There were a lot of grot tracks and something else," said Nolan.

Karragin waited for him to explain, staring at him with a placid expression. Kervin interrupted the momentary silence as Nolan thought about how to explain what he didn't discover.

"Tracker, I can't feel my nose or my toes. Tell us what you found so we can catch a few hours of sleep," said Kervin.

"Right, well," he struggled to explain. "It's like nothing I've ever encountered before. The signs of grot are thick the closer we get to the valley. But there's something else. Something left skip marks in the grot trails."

Karragin squinted and tongued the small grooved scar of her upper lip. Nolan continued his explanation, "The tracks are only days old, but it's like something crossed through them at random places, erasing any sign of their passage. It's not bad enough that any one trail can't be followed, but I can't explain it."

Kervin shook his head. "You've had full use of your arca prime less than a season and, no offense, but you've only recently shed your tender uniform. It sounds to me like this is just something you haven't seen before. At least we are close, and you didn't see any sign of grondle."

Kervin turned to Karragin. "I'm turning in, Karra. I suggest we all do the same. See you at first light."

The group dispersed, leaving Nolan to wander back to their tents with his sister. She stopped in front of his tent and handed him the rest of the waterskin. "You'll need the rest of this more than me if you plan to eat the dry rations. Don't let Kervin distract you. He might be right. Maybe you're still learning the subtle parts of your craft. Is there any chance the breaks in the trails were natural?"

Nolan sighed and shrugged. "I don't know, maybe, but I really don't think so."

"Do you think the grot have learned to conceal their trail?" she asked.

"I considered that, but the skips were random, and the trails were still easy to follow. If hiding their passage was their intent, they wasted a lot of time and energy to little effect."

"Well, perhaps you'll learn more tomorrow," said Karragin. "I'm pulling you off night watch. I want you to break camp and scout ahead in a few hours." She looked past him into the night sky. "Baellen is just a sliver tonight. There won't be much light to go by, so you'll need to leave well ahead of the flank. Take Amniah with you."

"Yes, sir?" Nolan acknowledged his understanding of the order, but his words hung in the air with the question. *Why are you sending me with the odd duck?*

Karragin seemed to understand his confusion. "First, I don't want you without backup. Second, I like her instincts. She . . . sees the world differently; she notices the things others miss."

Nolan humphed in agreement. "I suppose she does. Anything else, sir?" A smile crossed his face as he deferred to her authority. Something in that formal address to her, to his sister, to his prime . . . something in all of it made him feel proud.

Karragin must have sensed as much because she allowed one side of her cheek to soften with a slight smile. "That's it for now. We'll regroup with you at the ridge above the grot valley by midday."

Nolan retired to his tent and made quick work of the rations Tovnik had left for him. He shrugged off his boots and pulled the bedroll over his head, allowing his breath to warm him. It seemed to take longer than usual, but sleep came just as his toes regained their feeling. He awoke several hours later and poked his head out into the cold. A survey of the night sky revealed the position of the slivered moon. *Just enough time to pack up and head out.*

He turned to Amniah's tent, fully intending to awaken the guster, but she was already sitting on her packed tent and bedroll, observing the sky. Nolan made quick work of his belongings, and then they stored the gear in a pile to be packed on a horse later.

With a silence that Nolan found either professional or strange, he couldn't be certain, Amniah led two Aarindin over. Once mounted, they headed away from the flank of tents and deeper into the mountains.

Several hours later, as the sun melted the shadows, they approached the last ridge before the valley where he expected to find the grotvonen warren. Amniah allowed her Aarindin to wander ahead a few steps.

"Amniah, give me a moment. I think the grot warren is past this valley and into the next one, but I want to check something," he explained. Without a word, she brought her Aarindin to a stop and tucked her chin into the collar of her winter gear. The cloud of steam billowing up around her face was the only sign that she remained awake.

Nolan retreated inside himself and allowed zenith to suffuse his senses, filtering the current through his arca prime. Ethereal, wispy tracks of grotvonen crisscrossed the valley, merging as dense trails on the far side. The strange skip marks still marred the trails at random places. He stared several minutes at the far side of the valley. From this distance, and laid across the heavy passage of grotvonen, the skip marks made sense.

"Grind me, that's not a break in the trail, that *is* a trail," Nolan mumbled to himself.

Amniah nickered, and her Aarindin retreated a few steps. She popped her chin out from the collar of her leathers and swiveled her head to regard him. Without blinking, she stared, then turned to gaze ahead. "When you forage for crownberries, it's best to find the clusters from far away. Up close, the leaves all look the same, but from a distance, the bushes with the sweetest berries carry darker leaves. One could waste hours picking through bushes with bitter fruit, but from a distance, you can easily find the good patches, you know?"

Nolan tried to react, but the cold numbed his forehead and chin, making any facial gesture impossible to discern. "I never thought of it that way, but you're right." He swept a gloved hand in a line across the valley's far side from left to right. "The grot trails run thick up there. But something else moved in a straight line over the break in the ridge on the far side, right where we entered last time . . . right where we're going."

"What do you mean something else?" she asked.

"Something . . . passed over the grot trails. I can see what's not there. I mean—" Nolan cocked his head to the side, considering how to best explain what his gift revealed. "Up here, the grot tracks appear to have skips and breaks. But up there, where the grot sign is thick, I can see a single path where the grot trail was erased."

Long moments of silence passed, and Nolan continued to study the phenomenon. Amniah interrupted his thoughts. "When your gift shows you a trail, are you seeing a pattern of zenith left behind?"

"I think that's right," said Nolan. "The first time I tracked the grotvonen to the warren, I was able to find the pattern left behind by grot blood on Tovnik's knife."

"Then something either hides its zenith or has none," stated the guster. "Do you know of anything that does that?"

"No, and I've never seen it before," said Nolan.

"Should we wait for the others?" she asked with a curious tone that seemed to lack any sense of fear.

"Maybe, but we have our orders. Let's make our way to that break in the ridge. We can picket the Aarindin there and walk into the valley the same way we did last time," said Nolan.

Over the next few hours, they crossed the valley, passing through clusters of evergreen. The only sound they made came from the steps of the Aarindin crunching over the carpet of fallen pine cones. They climbed the slope on the opposite side and picketed the mounts where the tree line thinned.

On foot, they crested the ridge, then dropped into the valley along a worn path through a cleft in the ridgeline. Nolan pitched his voice in a whisper. "This is the place." He crouched low among the thick dried grasses. Where the previous valleys remained covered with pine and spruce, this canyon stood deforested. Dried brush and grasses had already browned in the late fall weather. In the distance, a small black hole marked the bottom of the valley and the entrance to the grotvonen warren.

They hunkered down in silent observation for half of the next hour. Nolan periodically channeled zenith to check for any new tracks, any sign of movement. The air around them grew oddly still.

"Is that you?" he asked Amniah. She bent her head to the side to reveal the delicate play of zenith flashing across the top of her arca prime. "What are you—why are you wasting zenith?"

"I've always thought that was a strange phrase," answered Amniah.

"What?" asked Nolan.

"Wasting zenith. It implies a finite amount of zenith, or that I was charged a tax," said Amniah.

Nolan resisted an urge to bark a laugh, then studied Amniah. She continued to channel, stilling the air around them. The work of it did not seem to burden her, and she gazed back at him without expression. At last, he smiled. "Amniah, what I meant to ask is, why are you keeping the air around us still?"

"The wind carries our scent. From what we have learned, the grot have exceptional hearing and smell. The wind swirls around this canyon. Even if I directed our scent back to the ridgeline, it would eventually cycle around. Until we decide to move in or retreat, I'll do my best to keep our scent confined here."

"Oh," said Nolan. He studied the thick grass fields across the valley. The gusts through the canyon caused the amber stalks to undulate like waves on a lake. "That's . . . really clever."

They remained at their post, Nolan checking for new activity, Amniah stilling the air to hide their presence. Eventually, he suppressed the flow of zenith. "I don't see any sign of recent activity. All the trails are cold."

"Can you still see the not-zenith path?" she asked.

Her strange naming of the aberration gave him pause, and he considered her, not for the first time that morning. "Yes, it leads toward the bottom of the valley," he answered, then strung his bow and notched an arrow to the string. "The sun is out, you've got our scent covered, and I haven't seen any active sign of the grot. Let's make our way to the entrance to the warren, and then we can return to wait for the rest of the flank to arrive."

Amniah grabbed a fistful of loose pebbles, nodded once in agreement, then stood, stretching muscles in her low back. Nolan watched her with surprise as she stood from their place of concealment. *Right, onward then, I guess.*

A well-worn trail through the grasses led them directly to the bottom of the valley. They stopped about fifty paces from the gaping rent in the ground. He rekindled his gift and surveyed the area. The trails all converged at the entrance, though none emitted the bright residue of zenith he expected to find if the grot had passed by recently. The strange dark path of not-zenith led straight into the cavern.

He held his bow at the ready and stepped lightly toward the entrance. No grasses lived near the opening, and the ground was compacted from use. A faint smell akin to rancid meat wafted up from the darkness like a festering wound in the valley. As they approached, a strange noise carried from the entrance. It was a rhythmic sound, like the blade of a shovel stabbing into fresh manure.

The trunk of a massive tree lay on its side next to the breach, its roots draped down into the dark crevice. They crept around, inspecting the far side of the hole. It spanned a good thirty feet or more. Nolan couldn't see whatever was making the rhythmic noise. He stopped two steps away and motioned for Amniah to wait. With his bow drawn, he sighted along the arrow and advanced the last two steps.

Peering down into the depths, he spied something humanoid clinging to the side of the crevice, not ten feet below him. The creature used arms and legs like a human, but the similarities ended there. Instead of a rounded head, the thing was topped by a flat bony plate covered in thick grey skin and etched with strange, black symbols. From his vantage point, he couldn't identify any facial features, no eyes or nose. He could just make out the strange shadows that swirled under the surface of its leathered skin.

The creature gathered a small globe of oily shadow in its fist, then plunged the dark orb into the side of the shaft, leaving a small hole in the rock and clay. Nolan relaxed his draw on the bow and watched as the thing continued the same action over the next few minutes. It seemed utterly unaware of his presence.

Every time the creature plunged the black orb into the shaft, a strange noise echoed down into the darkness, like meat thrown on a hot skillet, like something being seared away. Indeed, Nolan could see a small channel in the side of the shaft where the creature labored.

There's nothing dropping below. Where is the loose stone and rock going?

Like a gangly spider, the flat-head climbed down into the darkness. An irregular ladder of stout wood shafts protruded from random places in the side of the cavern, serving as a lattice over which the creature climbed. It returned a moment later with another plank of wood and rammed it into the newly formed cavity. Then it climbed onto the new rung in its crude ladder and resumed its excavation work.

Nolan stood there, bow at the ready, transfixed by the sheer aberration of the creature. He shifted his weight without thinking, and a few pebbles of loose rock scattered over the lip of the cavern. They bounced off the plate of the creature's head.

In mid-strike with another fistful of dark shadow, the creature paused and cocked its head to the side. A mouth with lipless teeth opened once, then clacked down, emitting a single, sharp thwack like two stones struck together. The sound echoed down into the darkness. In moments, chittering, clicking noises answered the summons. From the depths, the grotvonen horde awoke.

Nolan drew and loosed his arrow. The shaft vibrated as it embedded into the plate of the creature's head. The flat-head screeched but continued to work on its excavation. Nolan fired another arrow and another. All three found their mark on the creature's plated head. Dark ichor oozed around the arrow shafts. Each time an arrow struck, the thing screeched and clacked its teeth, but it also kept digging.

"Umm, Amniah, you might want to come see this," said Nolan, the pitch and tenor of his voice betraying his alarm.

It took the guster only a moment to surmise the situation. "Only two more planks and it—they—will be able to climb out," she said.

He turned to her, surprised not just by her comment but her calm demeanor. "I know that, don't you think I know that? It's not stopping. I shot it . . . in the head . . . three times, and it's still coming up!"

The creature clambered back down the ladder of wood planks. A chorus of clattering and clicking noises erupted from deep below. They watched as the beast climbed back up and wedged the new plank into place. It screeched and clattered its teeth with what Nolan could only believe was malice and anger.

He looked around for something, anything they could use to toss down the hole. All he could find were small rocks. He threw a few of these, and they bounced off, causing no harm.

"Hmm, I don't imagine that these will do any good," said Amniah. She tossed the handful of pebbles into the air. At the apex of their trajectory, the rocks accelerated, propelled by a dense shaft of wind. The missiles struck the creature's flat plate, causing it to growl, but had no other effect.

"That trick still needs work," she muttered. Without warning, she lunged forward and stomped her foot onto one of the creature's clawed hands. It had jumped from the last wood plank and nearly managed to climb out. They watched as the flat-head tumbled back down the shaft. In moments, it returned up the lattice of wood planks, clacking its teeth in chattered anger, the broken shafts of three arrows sprouting from the plate of its head.

"Stand back, Nolan. Let me try something."

He frowned as she moved into a seated position just a few feet away from the edge of the hole. "Grind it, Niah! Whatever you're doing, make it fast. I'm pretty sure we made that thing mad, and we need to skin out of here."

"Step back, Nolan. I need to concentrate," she said.

The air around them grew quiet; even the undulating waves of grass in the valley stilled. Nolan felt painful pressure in his ears, followed by a sucking sound and then a loud *woosh*. He stumbled back from the force as a dense column of air speared into the cavern. Loose rock and debris scattered around the opening to the grotvonen warren. Nolan watched as the creature tumbled down into the darkness, splintering several of the wood planks in its descent.

Chapter Nine: Testing Lutney's Luck

A warm autumn breeze carried the fragrance of exotic flowers and fruiting trees to Kaellor's hut. He struggled to force his eyes open in the afternoon light. The offensive sunshine made his head throb. Muscles ached in protest as he rolled to his side and struggled to sit on the edge of the cot prepared for him by the Cloud Walkers. He curled his toes in the strands of a fur rug and oriented himself to his new surroundings.

The faint song of a strange bird echoed between gusts of wind, and the fragrance of exotic flowers wafted through the reed door. Someone had stacked most of their salvaged belongings from the wagon into a corner with his boots. The pommel of the Logrend sword protruded above the collection. A small stone hearth sat dormant, and a wood pitcher of what he hoped was plain water rested on a shelf just out of reach.

Attempting to stand made the room swirl. He staggered forward and gripped the sturdy timber frame of the door for balance. With pursed lips, he forced out a long breath of air. Unbidden, a memory bubbled to his awareness. The way he felt now resonated with a night years ago when he and his brother had found the bottom of a bottle of resco. Unfortunately, resco had nothing to do with his current condition, and he wondered how long the malady would last.

So this is the draft. Still, it's better than yesterday.

He sensed the footsteps of a child bound past his hut and pulled his long hair back into a topknot to better view his surroundings. One of the small, olive-skinned children scampered by towing leather cord attached to a tuft of fur. Boru yipped playfully and chased the girl around the backside of his hut. Something about the size of the clumsy pup felt off.

Either the draft affected my eyes, or Boru grew a paw length in the last few days.

He poured and downed two cups of water, relieved to sense the dissipation of the dizziness, then wandered next door to the hut Bryndor shared with Lluthean. Sun over warmed the tender ruddy skin of his face and forehead, which was still recovering from the burns he suffered in the cave only nights ago. *By the Giver's hand, that was only nights ago, and we've traveled to an entirely different world.*

He rapped a knuckle on the doorframe of Bryndor's hut. His nephew sat on his cot, sketching a rudimentary map, and looked up with surprise. "Kae. You're up. Can I get you anything?"

Kaellor shook his head and leaned in, letting his eyes adjust. "Not at the moment, thanks. How is your brother?"

"No change. He's . . . still sleeping." Bryndor sighed and walked across the hut to the cot where Lluthean slept. Neska lay beside him with her muzzle resting on her front paws. Bryndor took a cloth, saturated it with water from a basin, and wrung a trickle into Lluthean's mouth. Most of the liquid ran down his cheek, where Neska licked it away. Eventually, he coughed and swallowed a portion.

Kaellor took a knee beside Lluthean's cot and cupped Neska's jaw while scrubbing the top of her neck. "What have you been feeding the wolvryn? I thought it was just my tired eyes, but now that I've got my hands around her, I'm sure they're growing faster than weeds."

"Nothing new except what the Damadibo children give them," said Bryndor. Kaellor cocked his head to the side, his expression asking the unspoken question. "That's what the Cloud Walkers call themselves. Oh, and they have wolvryn here, Kae. A whole pack roams the southwestern part of the valley."

Neska pulled away from Kaellor's grasp and assumed a perch at the foot of Lluthean's cot. "She's a vigilant one, isn't she?" asked Kaellor.

"Boru comes in to check on us almost every hour, but the village children lure him away," said Bryndor. "She won't have any of it, though. She just sits here, keeping watch."

Kaellor threw back the corner of Lluthean's blanket. He lay naked except for his smallclothes.

The strange silver scar on his left shoulder remained as the only sign of his previous injuries. The rest of his arm appeared whole with a good pulse. The skin across his ribs, though, the way it sagged unnaturally between the bones as he drew shallow breaths, gave Kaellor pause.

Moons . . . you were lean before we started this journey, but I've seen more meat on a sparrow's kneecap.

Kaellor felt his forehead for a fever, but Lluthean seemed cold. "When was the last time he moved?" he asked.

Bryndor chewed on his lower lip a moment, then shrugged. "He hasn't, Kae. Where you see him is where we placed him two days ago. The elder has a few villagers help me change his soiled clothes four times a day. He doesn't even move when we do that."

Kaellor had surmised as much and nodded agreement. "Has . . . Laryn been around to check on him?" Speaking her name felt like stumbling around in the darkness to walk to the kitchen. The way should, by all rights, be familiar, but it felt so strange.

"Not that I know of, but you both looked pretty rough, and she looked worse than you. What really happened, Kae?"

Kaellor covered Lluthean back up then took a seat at the foot of the cot. He scratched errantly at a scraggly tuft of beard at his chin. "Laryn is the woman I was married to when we lived in Stone's Grasp, in Aarindorn. We were supposed to raise you and your brother together, but on the night of the attack, when your mother and father died, I watched as an entire wall of rubble fell on her. How she survived is . . . well . . . there are some mysteries only the Giver can explain, I suppose."

They sat watching Lluthean's shallow breathing in silence for a time.

"As near as I can tell, this valley is somewhere inside the Korjinth Mountains," said Bryndor. "How did she bring us here?"

"I've been asking myself the same thing. I believe she had some help," said Kaellor.

Bryndor pointed his writing quill at the weave of gold symbols on Kaellor's forearm. "She restored your ability, your runes. Do you think she'll do the same for Lluthean and me?" he asked. Something in his tone sounded suspicious rather than hopeful.

"No," said Kaellor with a hand raised in apology. "You see, Bryn . . . Laryn . . . she gave up everything to be with me, to be with us. She was the one who convinced me to bind my ability to channel so we could hide you from the abrogators. Giver's tears, we were even married in a secret ceremony. Afterward, we created the binding for one another, and by her touch alone, the binding was released."

Bryndor's eyebrows disappeared under his bangs. Eventually, a sly smile relaxed his expression. "Did Aunt Ro know you were married before?"

"She did," answered Kaellor softly. "But all this time, I thought Laryn was dead, so it didn't matter much."

"Hmm, that makes sense. Anyway, what you are saying is that she can release your binding, but not ours?" Bryndor asked.

"Your mantle and the binding it created are something very different, I'm afraid," said Kaellor. "Your parents wove zenith into a fabric the likes of which I've never seen, and I can't say I understand it at all. But the barrier that separates you from your gift is somehow tied to the banishment of Tarkannen. They wove all that sacrifice, your gifts, and their own lives into the Usurper's banishment."

Something drew Neska's attention to the entrance of the hut. She hopped down with tail wagging, showing the first signs of playfulness since they arrived in the Valley of the Cloud Walkers. A moment later, Laryn craned her neck through the doorframe. The sight of her with the pattern of tiny, exotic pigments painted on her cheeks set him off balance. A thick white shock of hair divided and pulled behind each ear framed her face. They shared a long look, and he became lost in the moment until Laryn bent to scratch Neska under the chin.

So different, but still the same. How could I ever forget those eyes? One blue and the other red, both with the ability to disarm. Can she ever forgive me?

Laryn stepped inside, and Kaellor shot to his feet, then swooned a moment from the lingering taint of the draft. "I came to check on my patient if that's alright?" she asked.

Kaellor nodded understanding and quietly stepped to the side.

Bryndor joined him and stood with a stiff posture. "Good afternoon, ma'am. He's been sleeping since we brought him here."

Laryn grimaced as if she tasted something bitter. "Ma'am? Did you have to teach them all the chivalrous nonsense, Kae?"

Uncle and nephew shared a look of mild confusion. "Never mind," said Laryn. She directed her attention to Lluthean. "Asleep all this time? I had hoped for more but didn't expect it. Give me a moment then."

They watched as Laryn sat on Lluthean's cot. She placed a hand on his forehead and another on his chest, then seemed to withdraw into herself. Flickers of blue light flared across the runes visible on her arms and neckline. A droning hum resonated through the hut. After a minute, the sound faded, and Laryn lifted her eyes.

Bryndor sat back on his cot. "Well, what . . . how is he? Can you tell?"

Laryn inspected Lluthean's arm and traced a finger over the feathery edges of the silver scar on his chest and shoulder. "It's so strange," she mumbled.

"When will he wake up? What else can we do for him?" asked Bryndor. Kaellor placed a hand of reassurance on Bryndor's shoulder and waited for Laryn to finish her assessment.

Eventually, she swiveled on the cot to face them but struggled to put her thoughts into words. "I have to be honest. I'm not entirely sure if he is separated because he was drift-bitten . . . or if it's just that I'm out of practice after all these years."

What do you mean, separated?" asked Kaellor.

"After I restored the damage to his arm, I couldn't sense the resonance of zenith running down the limb. But now, I can't sense zenith anywhere, except here," she said and lifted a lock of blond hair off his forehead. "It's like all the zenith retreated into his mind or is all bottled up in one place. I can tell you've kept him hydrated, but—"

"If he doesn't awaken soon, he'll remain . . . separated, and then what?" Kaellor asked.

"Over time, he'll fade away," she answered softly.

Kaellor sighed and placed a hand on Bryndor's shoulder. "How long? How long do you think he has?"

Laryn offered an expression of condolence. "I can't be sure. I'm really out of practice, Kae."

Hearing her pronounce his name with familiarity gave him more pause, and he swallowed the warmth gathered in his throat, struggling to keep his attention centered on the problem before them. "I understand, but so far, you're his best hope. Is there anything else you can do, or is it just a waiting game for now?"

Laryn looked back at Lluthean, then to Bryndor, and finally to Kaellor. She seemed to be weighing the options and eventually sighed. "I wish I could speak with authority. If we do nothing, he will likely fade to the Drift. If I attempt to draw him out from whatever has him disassociated, I might cause more harm than good. I really can't be certain."

She placed one hand on her hip and stretched her low back while they considered her prognosis. Kaellor recalled a time when a younger version of the woman before him stood with a hand on her hip, haggling with a spice merchant for a reasonable price at market. He pushed the memory away and looked at Bryndor. His nephew finger-combed strands of dark hair back, then locked his fingers behind his head, cheeks puffed out in obvious concern.

Kaellor calculated the facts before them and weighed the risks of both scenarios. *Better to die swinging the sword than watching it rust in the scabbard.*

"Laryn, after the Abrogator's War, there must have been others that were drift-bitten, others who survived?" he asked.

"After the war, I was a patient for almost a year at Callinora," Laryn explained. Kaellor felt his shoulders sag at the revelation. Laryn must have sensed something in his defeated body language and raised a hand to forestall any conclusions. "That's a story for another day. What I mean to say is, I was not able to participate in the direct care of anyone right after the war. When I eventually returned to my work among the healers, I remained separated from my gift, so most of my knowledge is secondhand. When I left Callinora, there were several patients with injuries preserved in a dozenth, a . . . cocoon of zenith. I think some of them were drift-bitten, but I can't be sure. Beyond these few, there were no survivors."

"The dozenth, is it something we can try?" asked Kaellor.

Laryn leaned forward, elbows on knees, and hung her head a moment, then sat back. "It's beyond me, Kae. I don't know how Venlith and the healers managed it."

Kaellor placed a hand on Bryndor's shoulder. "I don't like those odds, Bryn. That said, I can live with the knowledge that he lives or dies because we tried everything we could, but not because we did nothing. What do you say?"

Bryndor pulled Neska onto his lap and softly knuckled the front of her ears. "Better to dangle a bare hook in the river than wait for a fish to jump into the basket."

Kaellor grunted with humor. "That sounds like something a Tellend would say."

"It is, and after Aunt Rona, Emile was the wisest person back home," said Bryndor.

"Alright then, would you try, Laryn? Whatever you think you can do to restore him, it's better than nothing," said Kaellor.

Laryn considered them both a moment. "Did you ever catch a fish with a bare hook?"

Bryndor pulled his head back, appearing somewhat surprised by the question. He smiled with a wistful reply. "No, that kind of luck is something Lutney would give to Llu."

A strange combination of puzzled interest and confusion creased Laryn's forehead. "Who is Lutney?"

"That's also a long story, Southlander expression," said Kaellor.

Laryn raised her eyebrows and nodded. "Well, I, for one, would love to hear all about it from all three of you. So why don't we see if we can draw him out?"

"Thanks, Laryn," said Kaellor. "What do you need from us?"

Laryn waved for Bryndor to step close. "Come here if you would, Bryndor."

He stepped forward. Laryn took his hand, pushing up one shirt sleeve and then the other. She stood up, continuing her inspection in much the same way Rona used to whenever they returned from a long journey, turning his chin first one way and then the other. Then she sat and waved him back.

"After all these years, their binding still holds . . . neither of them can channel yet?" she asked.

"No, ma'am, not yet," said Bryndor.

"It might be for the best, I suppose," she muttered. "Kae, I'll need you to surrender everything you have for this. It will very likely throw us back into the draft, but mind yourself. If we push too far, just break away. You'll be able to sense everything I do once we are linked. If this works, I expect Lluthean will moan or cry out. Bryndor, I'll need you to stand on the opposite side of his cot. If he thrashes, keep him on the bed. Beyond that, I'll need you both to remain quiet, so I can concentrate. Any questions?"

"How will I know if we push too far? Will something happen to Llu?" asked Kaellor.

"It's not Lluthean I worry about. Once I begin, the task will require all my attention. I don't think I can safely monitor how much zenith I pull from you. You will have to break away if you think we are descending too far into the draft."

"Maybe I should sit on the floor next to you then," said Kaellor.

Laryn remained seated on the cot beside her patient. Bryndor stood opposite the two of them. He appeared ready to pounce on his brother.

"Eyes to the horizon then?" he asked. Laryn turned her gaze from Lluthean's emaciated face to meet his. He lingered there a moment, lost in the way blue pigments crystallized in her one red eye. He thought he saw the faint beginnings of a smile crease the edges of her eyes for a moment. Then it was gone.

"I'm ready when you are," she said.

"The Giver guide you." Kaellor withdrew into himself and allowed zenith to flood across his runes. The rush of power dissipated the achy fatigue in his muscles. He ushered the flow through the runes along his arms and torso, gathering his strength. But instead of shaping the force to his gift, he reached up and placed his hands on Laryn's thigh, channeling his zenith into her. She inhaled in surprise, whether from the surge of power or the intimacy of the touch, he wasn't sure. But he watched in wonder as she set to work.

Connected as they were, he witnessed, for the first time, her gift in action as if through her eyes. Probing filaments of zenith erupted from Laryn's hands, searching first for any remaining corruption. She lingered long over the silver scar on his chest and shoulder. Eventually satisfied with her prior work, she migrated the delicate azure fibers in a head-to-toe assessment. Her touch emitted a resonant, humming vibration when her gift connected with Lluthean's innate zenith stores. As she left his head and directed the examination into his neck and chest, the humming dissipated.

Through Laryn's gift, Kaellor sensed a dense collection of swirling zenith bottled up in Lluthean's head. But her search found no other trace of the force in the rest of his body. He watched as she redirected all of the probing fibers to Lluthean's mind.

Kaellor felt the room shift and became vaguely aware of a tickle as sweat dripped off his chin. Long breaths forced in through his nose and out through pursed lips dissipated the symptoms of the draft.

Laryn spent a long time probing, trying to breach the barrier that kept Lluthean's zenith encased and restricted in his mind. She grunted in frustration, then shaped all her probes into a curved pick. She struck at the dense swirl of coalesced zenith in Lluthean's mind, and vaguely, Kaellor heard Lluthean moan out in pain. Laryn repeated the strikes, forcing numerous small holes into the barrier.

Kaellor felt himself panting and salivating as if he might retch but swallowed back the sensation. He had never delved so far into the draft and struggled to keep his head upright, but as long as Laryn needed him, he would feed her every ounce of zenith he could muster.

Despite the haze of overwhelming exhaustion, he watched in amazement. Through each of the tiny holes she created, Lluthean's innate zenith leaked out as pale blue filaments no thicker than spider silk. Whenever this happened, Laryn sent her own azure filament to act as a tether. In this fashion, she gently drew out his innate zenith stores. With meticulous care, she anchored fiber after fiber throughout Lluthean's body.

She worked like an industrial spider, weaving and fixing strands of zenith in intricate patterns throughout Lluthean's body. She spent an unusually long time reconnecting the threads to the arm damaged by the corruption from the Drift, but eventually, the filaments of zenith appeared to take.

Without warning, she pulsed a surge of zenith through the connections. Kaellor felt the strain as she siphoned power from him but dismissed the concern as Lluthean moaned and began to move on the bed.

Bryndor lurched forward and restrained Lluthean, keeping him on the cot. Kaellor met Bryndor's gaze for the first time since Laryn began. They shared a look of grave concern, but something in Bryndor's bearing resembled horrified shock. Kaellor couldn't work his mind around what the expression meant. The river of zenith that he had channeled saturated all his senses, and he nearly choked on it at this point. He blinked and directed his attention to Laryn's efforts one final time.

She appeared to gather the last of their combined reserves and again forced a surge of zenith throughout the network she'd created. Then she withdrew and watched. The connections seemed to hold for a moment but gradually began to fade.

Laryn opened her eyes and turned to Kaellor. She appeared utterly spent. Hollow circles like the half-moon of Baellen ringed her sunken eyes, and sweat matted the hair to her brow. Through shallow breaths, she whispered, "I'm sorry. You . . . we should stop now before it's too late."

Kaellor was so steeped in the draft that he couldn't register the finality of her words. She began to disconnect the tethers she had crafted when Bryndor broke through the silence. "Don't give up! You've got to be close. He moved. Please, don't give up!" Bryndor placed a hand on Laryn's shoulder, and a deluge of power rippled through them all.

The flood of zenith rushed through each of the connections. Kaellor watched as the meshwork of Laryn's design flared from a light blue to a rich azure to a burning intense white. A concussive wave threw Laryn off the cot, and Kaellor became vaguely aware of her weight on top of him.

As he lay there on the floor of the hut, a small part of his awareness registered the warmth of her body on his. She seemed lighter than he imagined, and up close, her hair smelled like the exotic flowers that grew in the bushes outside his hut. He had just enough sense to lift a hand and place it on her back, surprised at the slight nature of her delicate frame. "Giver's last breath, Laryn, that was something," were the last words he whispered before the draft claimed him.

Chapter Ten: Befuddling the Warden

Reddevek leaned over his plate at a table at the Bashing Ram. He used the last bit of bread to soak up the remains of egg yolk, then sat back in his chair. The pain deep in the small of his back and pelvis had dulled in the last month to a mild ache that bothered him when he slept too long and sometimes when he slept not long enough. A firm knuckle pressed hard and long into the right spot eased the sharp twinge as he stretched in his chair.

Della walked across the taproom of the inn and refilled his mug of water. "Thanks, Della," said Reddevek.

"Sure thing, Red," said Della. The stout innkeeper turned and placed two clean plates with table service at an adjacent table. "We got a new patron this morning. I know how you like things peaceful like; thought I would warn you. He's a pleasant enough fellow. Calls himself a representative of the Immaculine. Can't say I know anything about that other than he is to meet the rector over breakfast. Anyway, he likes to hear himself talk."

"That sounds like my cue to take Nika into the Moorlok for the day," said the warden.

"I thought you might feel that way," said Della. "She's already seen to Zippy's needs and is likely waiting for you in the stable. Ingram is smoking that boar you brought back from your last hunt. I should have a nice loaf of baked rye and something hot for you both when you get back."

Reddevek stood from his chair. "Don't trouble yourself on my account, Della. Nika and I can fend for ourselves."

"It's the least I can do. You still haven't spent half of the coin master Scrivson left us, and if you keep supplying Ingram with the spoils of your hunt, I don't think you ever will." She tugged at an ear lobe then pointed at him. "You know full well we folk of the Bend don't accept charity."

He allowed the beginning of a rare smile to soften the edges of his eyes. From what he knew of the proud woman, there would be no room in the conversation for any rebuttal. Besides, the more he considered her words, he did want to be away before the chatty stranger appeared. He held up a hand to surrender to her point, bowed his head in respect, and turned to find the stairs when a middle-aged man dressed in unusual white garb descended to the taproom.

His clothing, cut in the tailored shape of a uniform, fit his pudgy frame more like a box than anything functional. Reddevek was reminded of a decorative case used to hold herbal teas sold at some of the finer apothecaries in Stone's Grasp.

The man even wore white gloves, which he stroked along a thin, neatly manicured beard along his rounded face. He stepped forward with a presumptive air and reached out to grasp Reddevek's forearm. As his wrist extended from beyond a white cloak, an ostentatious gold bracer appeared.

On instinct, Reddevek shifted his weight and batted the man's hand away, leaving the stranger to grasp empty air.

"Master Strictor, this is Red, a friend from the Northlands. He doesn't like to be touched," said Della. She pulled back the chair for the stranger to sit down.

"Ah, yes, I see. My name's Gavid, Gavid Strictor of the Immaculine," said the odd man as he took his seat.

Reddevek allowed his lazy eye to drift to the side just ever slightly and glared at the man's outstretched hand. Strictor shifted his gaze from one side of Reddevek's face to the other, then flushed and made a pretense of organizing his table service.

After a moment, the warden broke the awkward tension. "Enjoy the breakfast. Miss Della's the best cook this side of the Korjinth."

Without waiting for a response, Reddevek marched up to his room. He gathered his day pack, axes, and leather overcoat, then stepped out of the window in his room. A sloped roof under the window allowed easy egress.

Three steps led to the edge of the roof. A moment of indecision passed in which he eyed the short drop to a strategically placed cart of hay. With no more grace than a three-legged cow, he plopped down onto the straw, expecting to feel a surge of pain in his low back. To his surprise, the old injury remained dormant.

He rounded the inn and approached the stables, where Ranika was feeding Zippy the end of a carrot.

"It's about time, Red. Mr. Zip and I were about to leave without you," said the girl. She stood in ordinary brown trousers and a jacket, stroking the Aarindin's muzzle and jaw. A man's felt hat with a round, wide brim shadowed her face. When he approached, she looked up, and the morning sun showed her freckles and random bits of straw-colored hair.

"It's bad enough I have to call him Zippy. Now it's Mr. Zip?" asked Reddevek.

Ranika allowed the brim of her hat to shadow her eyes and spoke to the horse in a voice intended for him to hear. "Don't mind old Red, Mr. Zip. He's just mad because he can't find me in the woods."

Reddevek watched the girl. Something about the way she'd managed to follow him from Callish to Journey's Bend in total secrecy still left him unsettled. Three times in the last two weeks, they'd played a game in which he tried to find the waif after she obscured her trail. Each time, he'd given up and called out for her only to be astonished when she appeared from behind a tangle of underbrush or from her perch in a tree.

"Don't get cocky. Just because I haven't figured out your trick yet, doesn't mean I won't. Besides, there's fresh snow on the ground today. We'll see how well you hide your tracks."

"Hmm." Ranika looked back at him with a matter-of-fact expression. "I will. And then you have to honor our deal."

Reddevek smiled ruefully. When he was recovering from his injuries after the conflict with Vardel the guster, Ranika had been a constant presence in his room. She hovered about him singing, humming, playing, and asking random questions about Aarindorn or why horses wear shoes. He took to calling her "Gnat" but couldn't shoo her away. She finally agreed to let him recover in peace as long as he would take her with him when he returned home.

He had scoffed at the idea and wagered that if she threw dice and won four times in four throws, then the Giver must be sending him a signal, and he would take her on. After a brief conversation in which she peppered him with questions about the Giver, she countered, stating that if she could elude his tracking skill four times in a row, he had to take her with him . . . and so their game began.

They rode Zippy north into the Moorlok along game trails to a small glen where the morning sun melted a late autumn snow off the tall grasses. With a click of Red's tongue, Zippy knelt. They dismounted, and the warden paced a slow circle while the Aarindin grazed. After affording Ranika a thirty-minute head start, Reddevek channeled zenith into his arca prime.

The power suffused him with a feeling of liberation, allowing his senses to perceive not just the dull world around him but the totality of the pattern of zenith. Gentle currents flowed under the snow, indicating the tangle of roots from the trees and underbrush. Vibrant ribbons of blue streamed on the ground where a rabbit and then a fox skirted the glen. A wave of zenith shimmered and rippled where a herd of blackstripe deer had crossed not more than an hour ago.

He allowed his attention to dwell in that moment, lost in the beauty of the natural world around him. Eventually, he sighed and got to work. With his gift, he sifted through the different patterns with surgical utility, separating and diminishing all the signs of life that were not Ranika. In moments, he focused in on her resonance. Her peculiar trail led over deadfall and headed under a patch of brambles, then up a steep rise in the Moorlok.

He turned to Zippy and issued a hand command for the Aarindin to remain in the glen. As he stepped over the log, the familiar ache in his back flared a bit, and he regretted chancing the drop onto the hay. Her trail disappeared under the bramble patch. *Damn, girl's not gonna make it easy on me.*

Reddevek walked around the bramble, expecting to find her pattern on the opposite side. The thorny patch of shrubs covered only about ten feet. When he reached the logical spot where she should have emerged, he cursed and laughed in disbelief.

By the Taker's short and curlies, how does she do that?

He fell back on the familiar basics of tracking and scrutinized the area until he found signs of her passing. First, a scuff mark where old dropped leaves lay overturned, then confirmation from a place where she'd brushed off fresh snow from a tree trunk indicated her trail. A quick scan with his gift proved that no other animals might have caused the marks. The process frustrated him and took far longer than it should have.

How does she mask her resonance of zenith? It makes no sense.

A further survey of the wooded hillside failed to indicate where her trail might have continued. The only disruption in the snow, other than the random tracks of wild animals, occurred from places where clumps of ice had dropped from the tree branches overhead. Reddevek reached up to one of the branches and used it to hang a moment, stretching out the cramp of muscle in the small of his back.

As he did so, no snow dropped to the ground. He leaped up to hang from a higher branch, and immediately a shower of snow and bits of ice dislodged to the ground.

Clever girl. . . stupid monk and very clever girl.

He studied the branch that she must have used and tried to see the possible places where she might have leaped to another tree.

Unless that little gnat can fly, she must have gone north.

Sure enough, the connecting branches leading to the north had very little snow on them. Over the next three hours, he worked back and forth across the timber, constantly climbing higher and higher into the Moorlok, checking any possible trail signs against alternate zenith patterns from other animals.

Sometimes Ranika's trail dropped to the ground, mainly in places bereft of snow. Other times she used rocks or trees to navigate higher into the ancient wood. A wave of vertigo washed over him, warning that he was beginning to strain his tolerance for channeling. He suppressed the flow of zenith and focused on the most likely path she might have used. The trail led him around the broad base of a pine, and his breath caught.

The snow under his feet plummeted down into a steep ravine, and he hung over the edge, supported by a single overhead branch. His weight bent the tree limb, which snapped once. A blanket of snow sifted down on his head and under the back of his collar.

"Grinded, grinding, grinders twice baked in a steaming pile of grind!" he shouted at the sky.

He tried to reach his feet back to solid ground, but more snow gave away, and the overhead branch snapped a little more.

"That's a fair bit of grinding you got going on there, Red," said Ranika from a branch far above him. "A girl could get jealous of all that grinding.. . what is grinding anyway?"

He hung there, trying with tremendous effort not to start chuckling, for that would surely loose his grip and cause him to plummet down the ravine to a painful death. His fingers grew numb, and the muscles in his forearms burned with fatigue. "Help me get back to solid ground, and I'll gladly tell you."

Snow sprinkled from above him as she scurried down the tree. A particularly large dollop landed on the nob of bone at the back of his neck. The frozen glob hung there a moment, then slid all the way down his back down to the crack of his ass. He ignored the sensation until another larger clump of snow landed directly on the top of his head.

"Ranika, my paybacks are double," he growled.

"Sorry, Red, I really didn't mean to," she giggled.

A moment later, her hand grabbed at the back of his belt. She grunted and shifted his weight only a little. "Red, you need to lay off Della's flat cakes." She pulled again. "Now! Put your feet down now!"

Reddevek extended his knees and felt his feet gain purchase. With deliberate care, he walked his footing back. Eventually, he was able to push off from the tree limb. He windmilled once, then staggered back as Ranika pulled hard at his waist. Together, they tumbled back into the snow.

He rolled her on top of him. "Come here, you little gnat!" He rippled stiff fingers into her ribs, making her squeal in laughter. His tickling torment lasted so long she began to kick.

"Red, stop, you're gonna make me pee!" she cried. He tumbled her off into the snow, then sat up and reached overhead to remove another offending glob threatening to run down his back. With a mock growl, he mashed it into her face, causing them both to break out into laughter.

After a few minutes, the aching in his forearms eased, and the numbness in his fingers improved. They sat there at the edge of the ravine, letting the sun warm their leathers. A light breeze carried the crisp aroma of conifers up the gorge. Reddevek turned to his young companion. "Alright, tell me how you do it."

"Do what?" she asked.

"Hide your zenith, your trail," he said. She tilted the brim of the oversized hat back and wrinkled her rosy nose. "How do you hide yourself, so I can't track you?"

She pulled a bit of snow and ice from a wild sprig of straw-colored hair. "I don't know. When I want to hide, I pull my shadow into myself, and people don't see me. They ignore me. Unless I bump into them, then I have to try real hard, or they might see me, you know?" She squeezed her arms up against her side and clenched up her face in an expression of concentrated effort.

He studied her expression and found no sign of deceit. "Is it hard for you to hide from me?"

"Lutney's dice is it ever," she huffed. "It's one thing to pull in my shadow for a short time, but with you, I have to hang on tight for as long as I can. It makes me feel like I could burst. Once on the way here from Callish, I held my shadow in so long my head started to buzz like a beehive, and I couldn't sleep the entire next night, which was alright since you was on the move. But I didn't like the way that made me feel, so I try not to do it that much."

"Is it . . . can you show me now, or have you held your shadow in too long already?" he asked.

"No, I think I can show you," she said. "If you promise to take me with you to Aarindorn."

"Nika. You might not like it there, and once we return, I won't be able to stay with you all the time."

She shrugged. "That's alright. I been on my own most of my life and managed fine. I still want to go with you, Red. So will you take me?"

Ranika met his gaze, looking him straight in the eye . . . in one eye, without wavering. Something in her fearless, sincere intensity inspired him. It reminded him of himself. So he smiled and crossed both eyes, then stuck out his tongue, causing her to laugh. "What kind of man would I be if I broke my word to you? I'll take you. Now, show me the way you . . . pull in your shadow."

She stood and dusted the snow off her coat, using her hat to swat at her backside. "Are you ready?" she asked.

Poised on his knees, he channeled zenith once again, attuning to her pattern. The resonance of her zenith trail sung to him. He nodded. "Go."

Ranika took a breath and squeezed her eyes shut. Reddevek watched with undivided attention as she appeared to shimmer, then waver, like a layer of water separated them. In seconds she disappeared, and he stared at the two empty columns in the snow where her legs had been. He strained, casting the full measure of his gift back and forth across the area, but couldn't see any trace of her zenith trail.

"Alright, Nika. I'm impressed. Don't set yourself to buzzing on my account. Come on back."

The light rippled, and in seconds, she reappeared, zenith pattern and all, standing in the same place. His arca prime fell dormant, stifled by the wonder of watching her materialize before him. And that's when his world changed forever.

As her silhouette came into focus, shiny black rivulets and oily onyx streams slithered down her face and then her torso, finally coalescing on the ground as her shadow.

For the first time possibly ever, Reddevek remained immobilized by utter confusion. He stared with a mixture of raging emotions. His simple, purpose-driven mind struggled to right itself in the raging sea of awe, which surrendered to fear, which then receded to pure fascination.

"Red, you look like Mogdure breathed on ya. What is it?" she asked.

"Nika, I . . ." he swallowed. "Honey, I think you're an abrogator."

Chapter Eleven: The Making of an Abrogator

As a girl, Volencia Lellendule first learned to channel zenith through her aqua rune. The delicate silver veining on her forearm shaped zenith into tactile extensions of her awareness and made water feel like warm clay responsive to her urging. Whenever she channeled, she became aware of water in all its locations. Whether drawn from the aqueduct or residing in living tissue, her gift allowed her to sense its presence.

She had often frequented a shaded cistern a short walk from her family's estate in an affluent district of Stone's Grasp. Glacier melt from the Great Crown funneled through the aqueduct system and kept the deep pool full even during the hottest of summer months. She would lose herself staring into the depths of the clear waters. Sometimes a blue king carp, so named for its azure dorsal fin, fluttered from the shadows.

One day, she crumbled the crust of a piece of toast into the water, hoping to catch a glimpse of the skittish fish. The bits of bread floated on the surface until they became waterlogged, then drifted into the shadows. Something moved in the depths, and sunlight glinted off the edge of a blue fin. She channeled zenith and, ever so gently, caused the crumbs to float back up, enticing the carp out of the shadows.

With breath held, she leaned over the ledge with anticipation. A lone king carp darted up through the cloud of bread crumbs. Soon, two others joined in a frenzy of activity. The fish swirled around one another, momentarily oblivious to her presence.

"What are you smiling at, Vol?" asked her friend, Bartoll. The Lentrell boy lived two blocks down, and the two often played together.

Volencia remained transfixed on the display of dancing fish and lifted a finger to her lips to garner his silence, then pointed into the water. Bartoll leaned over in time to see one last flurry of the carp before they dashed back down into the shadows.

"Moons, Volencia, three at once!" exclaimed the boy. "Can you use your gift to pull them out of the water?"

Volencia thought about the question, then allowed the strands of her gift to pass over the fish. As one swam closer, she swirled the water, causing the creature to spiral up toward the surface. Sensing that the fish struggled, she released her command of zenith. The fish righted itself and swam back into the shadows. "I suppose, but why would I want to do that?" she asked.

As the carp retreated, she withdrew her focus to the surface of the water and flared her gift, dissipating the ripples. In the glassy reflection, she could make out Bartoll's freckles. Her lips drew up in a generous smile, and they stared at one another a moment. With sudden alarm, his eyes widened in an expression of panic, and he splashed into the water.

Volencia pushed back from the edge of the cistern to find Bartoll's older brother, Drevan. The older boy held Bartoll by the neck, keeping him underwater. Drevan glared at Volencia with a strange expression on his face. It was the first time she could recall seeing contempt.

Bartoll thrashed, trying to free himself. Volencia wrapped her small hands around Drevan's wrist to free her friend, but her gesture only made the stronger boy plunge his brother deeper into the cistern.

"What are you doing? Stop it!" she screamed. An old couple on the far side of the cistern looked in their direction but said nothing.

"Lentrells don't associate with Lellendules, at least not the scum of Elbare," said Drevan. "This is what he gets for muddling about with you."

Drevan leaned one hand on the edge of the cistern in casual defiance to her plea and kept his other on the back of Bartoll's head, holding him fast underwater. Volencia grabbed a stone from the ground and held it up in a threatening posture, but the bully cocked his head to the side, unimpressed by her gesture.

She slammed the rock down, smashing two of Drevan's fingers. Blood splattered into the water from the mangled meat of his hand. Drevan released his brother, who fell back coughing and sputtering water. After a strange delay of several seconds, the older boy began to howl and swear. He clutched his injured hand to his chest and hopped about, then ran home.

Once she felt sure he was unlikely to return, she dropped the rock and squatted down to check on her friend. "Are you alright, Tolly?"

Bartoll considered her through tear-brimmed eyes. He blew his nose into the elbow of his sleeve and nodded once as she helped him stand.

"What did you do to make him stop?" asked Bartoll.

Volencia shrugged. "I yelled at him and tried to pull his arm away. When he wouldn't stop, I smashed his hand with this." She squatted to retrieve the stone she had used.

Bartoll's eyes widened in surprise. "Thanks, I think."

"Tolly, why does Drevan pick on you like that?" she asked.

Bartoll shrugged. "That's what brothers do."

"Not in my family," she said. "My brother, Aldrik, would never do that to me." Her words caused Bartoll to shrink, and she realized her error. "Cheer up, Tolly. My family's not perfect. Your father is still an upstanding member of the royal guard, whereas mine got tossed out months ago on account of his love for resco."

"One sip cures the rot," said Bartoll.

"If two makes you brave, I wonder how much a man has to drink to become stupid because . . . well, that's about all Father is these days," said Volencia.

An awkward silence fell upon them. After a time, Bartoll sighed. "I don't know who is worse, your father with his drinking or mine with his temper."

Volencia grunted in agreement.

"I should get home," said Bartoll.

"Me too. See you tomorrow maybe," she said.

A few nights later, Volencia sat with her mother and two older brothers at the dining table. A knock at the door interrupted their meal. Volencia's mother, Shalla, answered the door to find Drevan and Bartoll accompanied by their father. Mr. Lentrell, dressed in the uniform of the royal guard, dipped his head.

"Good evening, Lady Lellendule," he said politely. "Might I step in for a quiet word?"

"Certainly," said Shalla. She welcomed the visitors into an anteroom. "What can I do for you this evening?"

"I find myself in the strange position of asking to speak to your husband. Is Elbare about?" asked the soldier.

"I'm afraid I haven't seen him in . . . no . . . he's not here this evening," said Shalla.

The guard nodded in understanding. "I see. Well then, I would like to speak to your daughter if I could."

Volencia stepped from behind her mother and looked across the room to Drevan and Bartoll. The boys both seemed preoccupied with the floorboards. Neither looked up. Drevan's left hand was wrapped in fresh bandages, and he sported a new bruise across his cheek.

"Are you Volencia, child?" he asked.

"Yes, sir," she replied.

"My boys here tell me that you smashed a rock onto Drevan's hand because he scared away some fish you were feeding at the cistern two days ago."

"Volencia," hissed Shalla.

The guard held up his hand to suppress Shalla's outrage. "I would like to hear what you have to say about the matter."

Volencia stared long moments at Bartoll. In the evening light, she hadn't noticed the welts he now carried on his cheek. She knew Bartoll's father could be a harsh man and wasn't sure how to proceed. If she told the truth, it looked like Drevan and Bartoll were in for a bad time. But if she took responsibility for the attack as the boys explained it, then she was likely in more trouble than she cared. The silence in the room drew out and became a palpable presence as they stood there, considering one another.

"Well, Volencia, go on. Tell Mr. Lentrell what happened," said her mother.

"Tolly and I were watching the king carp in the cistern. Drevan came over and dunked Tolly's head underwater and wouldn't let him up. He said he was teaching him a lesson and held him underwater for a long time. I yelled, but nobody came for help. That's when I smashed Drevan's hand with the rock so that he would let Tolly out of the water."

A dark furrow formed between his eyebrows, and Mr. Lentrell gripped the handle of a baton strapped to his waist. "That doesn't sound like my boys. They know better than to carry on like that. Maybe you're not remembering everything correctly?"

Volencia looked across the room to her friend. "Tell him, Tolly. Tell him how you could have drowned if I didn't help you." But Bartoll remained silent. "Mother, Drevan said he was teaching Tolly a lesson that Lentrells shouldn't be with the scum of Elbare."

"Liar!" yelled Drevan. "I never said nothing like that, and you know it!"

"You're the one doing the lying, Drevan!" she shot back.

"Alright, alright, that's enough!" said Mr. Lentrell. "Shalla, my boys don't lie. And we had to pay a healer from Callinora to mend Drevan's fingers."

The two stared at each other for long moments, Shalla with her arms folded across her chest and Mr. Lentrell with his hand gripping the baton. Shalla grabbed Volencia by the elbow, and they retreated to the dining hall.

"I'll only ask you this once, child. Did you smash that boy's hand to save your friend or simply out of spite?" asked Shalla.

"I spoke true, Mother, every word," said Volencia.

Shalla relaxed her grip on Volencia's arm. "Giver's mercy, I believe you. Was there anybody else at the cistern that day?"

"Yes, there was an old couple on the far side. They might have seen what happened."

Shalla walked back to the entryway and held the door open, gesturing for the Lentrells to leave. "It sounds like you think my daughter is lying. But my daughter doesn't lie. And a couple enjoying the shade at the cistern that day bore witness to the events. If you want to petition the courts for compensation, I'm sure they would be interested to hear what an unbiased witness has to say. When they corroborate my daughter's explanation, we'll demand compensation for the false accusation, judicial costs, and time. If you have a desire to pursue this matter further, we'll see you there. Otherwise, I bid you goodnight."

Bartoll's father drew his lips to a thin line, the creak of leather from the handle on his baton the only sound between them. He leaned in as if he might say something but instead growled at his sons, tossing each out into the street by the back of the neck.

Volencia didn't realize it at the time, but she would never get to see Bartoll again, at least not as her friend. That year visited several misfortunes on her family. Her father succumbed to his misery and addiction. Volencia turned eight and understood that her family could not lightly escape Elbare's disgrace. Neighbors who once considered them friends avoided social contact. Her mother barely managed to keep the family estate, but only by dismissing all their servants and selling most of their belongings.

Later that summer, Volencia and Shalla returned home from the market to find the front gate to their estate swinging open on its hinges. "Mother, the front door is open as well."

They rushed across the front garden to find blood smeared on the threshold. Shalla withdrew a small paring knife from one of her bags and whispered to Volencia. "Stay here. If something goes wrong, run, and find a magistrate."

A moment after Shalla stepped inside, she cried out. "Dear Giver, Volencia, come here fast!"

Volencia rushed inside to find her brothers brutally beaten. The oldest, Aldrik, cradled mangled hands in his lap, and Veldrek held a bloody cloth to a disfiguring gash across his face. Something that looked like apple jelly was leaking over the top of the rag just above his eyebrow. Bruises and welts marred most of their skin.

"What happened?" asked Shalla as she inspected their injuries.

"It was Drevan and Bartoll and a few of their Lentrell cousins. They attacked us at the cistern," explained Aldrik.

"Volencia, run to the House of the Moons and fetch a healer. It's the building with the blue slate roof a few blocks away. Run fast and be careful," said Shalla.

Volencia ran out the door and found her feet taking her along familiar paths. The House of the Moons stood a block past the cistern. As she ran, she turned to see five boys splashing in the waters. Bartoll, Drevan, and three of their cousins were carrying on in a rowdy game. They didn't notice her until she got close enough to see fresh bloodstains on the stone edge of the cistern.

She stood transfixed by the casual way they carried on when the evidence of their brutality still lingered at the pool's edge.

"Grind off and don't sully the waters with your Lellendule taint unless you want some of what your brothers got!" said Drevan when he finally noticed her.

Volencia looked around to call for help, but they were alone, five rowdy teens in the cistern and Volencia standing just at the water's edge.

"You deaf? He said get out of here!" yelled Bartoll.

She stared at Bartoll, searching his face for any sign of the friend she'd rescued just months before. The boy scowled back at her with more venom than any of the others. His complete surrender to anger caused something inside of her to withdraw, and a cold tranquility settled in her core. At that moment, she set aside the fear she carried for her brothers' injuries.

Drevan swam over and pulled himself out of the water to his elbows. "Looks like you need to learn the same lesson." The older boy prepared to hoist himself out of the water, but Volencia raked her fingernails across his face, and he fell back in.

Before any of them could react, she opened herself to zenith and channeled. A surge of power greater than anything she had ever released plunged into the depths of the cistern. The waters churned into a tight cyclone. The power she demanded pulsed at the constraints of her rune, and burning pain lanced across her forearm as she compelled the currents of zenith to her will. Once the five boys were gathered in the center of the cyclone, she directed the water to churn down, plummeting the group of them into the depths. She could feel them struggle against her current, trying to slip up to the surface, but she would have none of it.

There was something satisfying and peaceful about sensing them thrash about for life-sustaining air, only to surrender with silent, panicked agony. At the very end, Bartoll floated up at the edge of the cistern. His body rolled, exposing his face ever so briefly to the surface before being pulled back into the depths. He looked so peaceful without the influence of hatred marring his brow.

The whole task took only a few minutes of dedicated, zenith-powered churning. When she allowed the water to still, she cast her awareness down into the depths to discover only the gentle fluttering of a few king carp. Her head swooned, and she staggered forward, then vomited into the pool. That was when she heard her master speak for the very first time. A gentle hand rested on her shoulder, and he offered her a handkerchief to wipe her mouth.

"Lellendule taint?" asked Tarkannen. "Did that Lentrell boy really string those words together in a sentence? Strange times we are in."

She struggled to make sense of his expression, but the ground shifted under her, and she turned and retched again.

"Oh dear me, you seem to be well into the draft. I can't say I'm surprised. That really was some impressive channeling for one so young, but you can't allow your emotion to leach into the effort. Here, allow me," he said.

Tarkannen grabbed her forearm in his hand, then made a motion as if he were drawing something out of her. Delicate black webs attached to his fingertips tickled her skin as they trailed over her aqua rune. Something . . . not nausea, but a cold dizzy feeling shifted through her, leaving her shivering. When the unpleasant sensation subsided, she felt much better.

"My name is Tarkannen. I'm a cousin to your father, Elbare. If you care to tell me what all of this fuss was about, I might be persuaded to teach you about real power."

Chapter Twelve: In the Crown's Timber

Ksenia cinched the drawstring around the neck of her riding cloak to ward off the morning chill. At this early hour, she passed by only a few others on her way out of the main castle. Apples bumped against her leg from the inner pocket of her cloak as she beat a quick descent down two sets of stairs. She rounded a corner into the stables and saw Winter looking eagerly out of her stall.

The albino cocked her head, a posture Ksenia had come to recognize as irritation. She allowed zenith to awaken a part of her gift and opened herself to communicate with the Aarindin. *"Good morning, Winter. Let's get you out of here for a bit."*

"Yes. I need to pee outside, not in my stall."

Ksenia stifled a giggle as images of Winter fretting about and splattering her stall with urine flashed through her awareness. She made quick work of the gate, then held a welcoming hand toward the entrance to the stables. *"Don't wait for me."*

Winter trotted out and relieved herself at the edge of the pasture surrounding the stables. The Aarindin straightened her front knees and leaned back, stretching her shoulder and rump muscles. *"Ahh, much better. The stall is too small. I miss the fields back home."*

Ksenia sighed in agreement, then called out. *"Come meet me by the Timber Gate."*

"Why is it called Timber Gate?" asked the Aarindin.

"Because it leads off into the Crown's Timber, the woods around the castle," Ksenia replied.

Ksenia led them through the gate and into the forest surrounding the western side of Stone's Grasp. Without asking, Winter kneeled, allowing Ksenia to throw a leg over. Just as soon as she had her weight situated, Winter linked their innate zenith stores, gripping Ksenia, then lurched forward and onto a trail into the wood. This close to the castle, the paths were wide and well-worn. After ten minutes of a purposeful walk, they managed to find a stretch of timber that felt like something closer to home.

Morning songbirds chirped overhead, and rabbits scurried across their trail with carefree activity. A fat marmot with a grey topcoat and yellow belly waddled onto their path and yawned. Ksenia welcomed the animal to their conversation.

"You should be asleep for the cold," she said.

The marmot scratched the yellow fur of its underside and yawned again but offered no response. Instead, a brief image of a warm, dark burrow flashed through Ksenia's awareness.

"None here can speak like me," said Winter.

"You are smarter than most, and you have had practice," said Ksenia. Her attention focused on the lackadaisical manner in which the marmot made its way across their trail and into the undergrowth. *"The animals here are not afraid of us, not like the animals back home."*

"These woods are small, and there is nothing to fear here. No wolves," replied Winter.

They left a copse of trees, and Winter galloped across a field of tall grasses to find a small stream. Ksenia dismounted and allowed the Aarindin to stretch her legs. *"Don't wander too far. I need to return soon."*

Winter galloped along the stream back and forth a few times, then contented herself to nibble at the grasses. Ksenia wandered behind her. This time of day, before her responsibilities began as one of the regent's scribes, had become her favorite. Back home, she often lingered in the countryside, waiting for the sunset. But in Stone's Grasp, finding solitude proved challenging even in the late evening hours. Morning rides provided her one escape.

A light fog rose as the late autumn sun warmed the ground, draping the meadow in a blanket of white mist. A fawn jumped over the stream and stumbled into view, surprising them both. Ksenia used her gift to soothe

the creature, sending a feeling of safety, but she failed to break through the fawn's fear. In a panic, the creature bounded away, but not before sending a frantic medley of images laced with shadow and blood.

"Winter, come here. We need to leave." Ksenia sent the message with a tone that brooked no question, and Winter trotted over. In a choreographed sequence they had perfected, Winter knelt just long enough for Ksenia to throw a leg over, then hopped back up. They trotted back across the field and had nearly entered the cover of the timber when a dark figure stepped out from the undergrowth.

The person wore a hooded cloak and sighted them down a crossbow. After a few tense moments, the figure lowered the weapon. A muffled voice said, "You're a long way from home, Balladuren."

Something familiar nibbled at the edge of her awareness. Her brother had always frowned on the crossbow, finding it too heavy and short-ranged to be of value to an Outrider. The only people to routinely use them were among the city watch. And then that voice. "Mullayne, is that you?"

The young woman trudged farther into the clearing, pulling the dressed carcasses of three rabbits by a small rope. She wiggled her head forward and popped her face out of the hood. Ksenia shivered at the close resemblance Mullayne had to her siblings. As a triplet, all three appeared common enough: dark curly hair, long noses, and a deep slash of dimples in their cheeks when they smiled. But the way they each seemed to look past a person unnerved most who encountered them.

It's like they are always looking somewhere else or paying attention to something else.

"What are you doing out here, Ksenia?" asked Mullayne.

"I like to ride here in the morning. It reminds me a little of home, and . . . wait, are you hunting the Crown's Timber?" she asked.

"I picked up a contract to cull the deer and rabbits," said the sender.

"I don't understand. The woods are here specifically to provide a natural habitat for such creatures," said Ksenia.

"Yes, but as all three hundred acres sit more or less inside the walls of Stone's Grasp, they aren't really natural." The two women stared at each other as Ksenia considered her words. "Don't tell me that the animal whisperer hasn't figured it out by now? There are no apex predators in here. No wolves, no bears, very few hawks."

"So, now you're the apex predator? For what purpose? Sport?" asked Ksenia, her voice flavored with a bit of scorn.

Mullayne pursed her lips and shook her head. "You know, it's a good thing you and Craxton didn't work out." The woman disarmed her crossbow and casually allowed it to rest over her shoulder. She walked past Ksenia toward the Timber Gate.

Ksenia realized her temper was clouding her judgment and loosening her tongue. "Wait, Mullayne. I didn't mean—I'm sorry. Tell me why you do it then; why do you hunt the woods?"

The woman stopped and looked at Ksenia with her eerie expression. A long pause spanned out before them. Eventually, Mullayne mumbled to herself something unintelligible, then addressed Ksenia. "Do you like the flowers that grow in this glen in the spring or the way hummingbirds nest here every year? How about the fact that beavers created a marsh west of here?" Mullayne looked to Ksenia expectantly.

"I think I understand. No wolves and no mountain cats mean too many deer and rabbits eating all the plants and young trees," said Ksenia.

Mullayne winked. "Now you're getting it. The huntsman manages the timber with all of this in mind, and I only fill the tickets he gives me. Besides that, the meat serves another purpose."

Ksenia turned her head to the side in irritation. They had already been down the windy road of this particular conversation. Only others gifted with the ability to communicate with animals ever understood why she chose to be a vegetarian. Mullayne held her hand up in mock surrender. "Relax, I'm not starting another debate. I donate all the meat to the orphanage in the Sprawl."

Ksenia nodded, gaining a full appreciation for the actions of the woman before her. *That's . . . about what I would expect from the smartest in your trio.*

"Are you done for the morning? Winter could carry us both back."

Mullayne seemed to consider the offer for an unusually long time. Just when Ksenia thought she needed to repeat the question, the hunter nodded once and placed the rabbit carcasses inside a burlap bag. Ksenia directed Winter to stand along a fallen tree trunk. Mullayne hopped onto the fallen timber, then easily situated herself behind Ksenia, and they started back to the castle.

"Were you just talking to him? To Craxton?" asked Ksenia.

"Why do you ask?" said Mullayne.

"Sometimes you seem . . . preoccupied, like you're giving attention to something other than what's right in front of you. I'm not complaining. My brothers tell me I do the same thing with animals. Kervin says it's why I have trouble making close friends in Stone's Grasp. Anyway, I wondered if it was something like that for you—for all three of you."

"Mother tells us the same thing," said Mullayne. "It's hard. All I've ever known is being a sender. It used to be that any time I needed, I could reach out and have two other people give me advice. Lately, though, I'm the one counseling Craxton with his complex guild responsibilities. Dexx tries to filter out what he sends to us, but we can tell the Outriders are in a tense situation these days."

Winter pushed through undergrowth, then trotted down and back up a natural bend in the trail, eventually finding a well-worn path heading back to the east. Ksenia lifted a supple branch over their heads.

"Why didn't things work out with you and my brother, Ksenia? Is it because we're senders? Or because he failed entrance to the Outriders?" Mullayne finally asked.

Ksenia turned to look over her shoulder. "Am I talking to you or all three of you?" asked Ksenia.

Mullayne smiled, giving definition to the slashed dimples in her cheeks and looking ever more like her brothers. "No, it's just me, Giver's truth."

Ksenia took a breath and decided that Mullayne deserved an honest explanation. "It wasn't really one thing, but a lot of little things. In the end, I think it felt like Craxton was trying to shape me into something I didn't want to be instead of taking me for what I am. I don't know if I'm explaining it well. I care for your brother, Mullayne, but I found myself resenting his suggestions to act this way or dress that way. In the end, I don't think we would have made each other happy. Does that make sense?"

"Mmm . . . yes, that sounds like Craxton," said Mullayne.

They continued east along winding wooded trails until the Timber Gate came into view. A muffled thump made Winter nicker. Mullayne had dropped the burlap sack of rabbits to the ground, and Ksenia felt the young woman slump forward into her backside.

"Oh, Giver," mumbled the sender.

"Mullayne, what is it?" asked Ksenia.

"Dexxin; he's ranging in the Great Crown with a flank of Outriders. Karragin Lefledge has the lead. Your brother's quad is there with them. Ksenia, get me to the Overwarden Kaldera. His offices are on the far side of the Stone's Grasp. Something terrible has happened, and I need to relay a message."

Chapter Thirteen: Trimming the Fat

BRYNDOR SAT ON THE steps outside the gathering house finishing a small bowl of fruit. He watched Boru devour a generous portion of breakfast pastry with concern. The wolvryn sniffed eagerly at Bryndor's hands, then licked his palms with interest, searching for more food. Since their arrival less than two weeks ago, both Boru and Neska had doubled in size.

At this rate, you'll be pulling the wagon by spring, but not if we don't find something to feed you both.

The laughing voices of children interrupted the normally serene village, and through the distant clouded mists, Lluthean approached with Neska shadowing him. His brother had required a full week to recover from the lingering effects of the strange healing Laryn had carried out. For that matter, Kaellor and Laryn had secluded themselves nearly as long recovering from what they called a second wave of the draft. The malady seemed like a severe hangover mixed with a case of flux. All three of them had started to emerge from their huts in the last few days.

He and Lluthean had begun to hunt small game for the wolvryn but never strayed far from the central village. They kept their forays short, mainly out of respect for Lluthean's weakened state. This morning though, Lluthean had taken Neska on an early hunt. He returned through the village with the carcass of something resembling a small deer slung over his shoulders.

He stopped before the gathering house and shrugged the carcass to the ground, then took a knee, panting lightly. Someone whistled low and long in appreciation from behind Bryndor. They turned to see Laryn leaning on the doorframe to the gathering house.

"Lluthean, how did you manage to take a gendek?" she asked. "They're so swift."

Lluthean squinted to see her through shafts of sunlight, then nodded to the Logrend bow. "Neska found the herd; only I didn't realize it until we rounded a copse of trees, and they spooked. I barely managed the shot, but King Vendal didn't lie. There is something special in the making of these bows."

"Logrend bow or not, Llu, I can't say I'm surprised," said Bryndor. He handed Lluthean the rest of the fruit wedges in his bowl, then bent to retrieve the carcass. "I'll get this parceled out inside."

He bent to lift the carcass by the legs, finding it lighter than he anticipated. Lluthean had already field-dressed the animal, removing the organs and guts.

"What did you do with the kidneys and the heart?" asked Laryn.

"Neska snatched those and most of the liver. I figured it was fair payment for services rendered," said Lluthean. Bryndor spied Neska lounging a few feet away, cleaning the remnants of blood from her muzzle and front paws. Boru sniffed eagerly at his sister, then the carcass, tail wagging with excitement.

Laryn smiled and uncrossed her arms. She strode forward and placed a hand on Lluthean's forehead, pushing back matted, sweaty blond hair. Blue light danced across the portions of her runes visible at her neckline, and a faint murmur emitted. After a brief time, she dropped her hand, and the humming sound dissipated.

"You've made a full recovery. How does your left arm feel?" she asked.

Lluthean shrugged his shoulders, and the V-neck of his shirt shifted, revealing the edge of the silvery scar. He flicked a coin into the air, catching it between the fingers of his left hand, then rolled the silver across his knuckles. "It's . . . as good as ever."

He fumbled the coin to the ground, and she bent to pick it up. "Out of practice?"

"Maybe a little," he said.

"Well, next time, take someone with you," said Laryn. "The mountains hold a variety of dangers you've never seen outside. Now go get yourself cleaned up, and Bryndor and I will see to this."

Laryn flipped the coin, and he caught it again, then nodded his acceptance of her direction with exaggerated agreement. "Yes, ma'am!" He hopped to his feet and quickstepped down the path toward his hut. "Come on, Neska!"

"Is he always governed by whimsy like that?" asked Laryn.

"You don't know the half of it," said Bryndor. "Llu isn't really *governed* by anything. Mostly he likes to see where the wind blows him, but somehow he always manages to land on his feet. I'm not surprised he bagged one of these. Let me guess. They are hard to find, harder to track, and still harder to kill?"

Laryn took hold of the gendek's hind legs. "They are. Come with me. We can make quick work of this at the counter on the backside of the gathering hut."

Bryndor hesitated a moment, feeling a little awkward. Other than the times Laryn spent healing Lluthean, they had not really had the opportunity to become acquainted. She and Kaellor spent most of their time sequestered in their own huts recovering. Something about relying on her to help butcher a carcass felt like a strange way to begin the relationship.

Her words rescued him from further indecision. "Come on. It's not my first time getting a little blood on my forearms."

She led them to a sturdy table, clean but stained with blood and marred by countless gouges from prior knife work. They set the carcass down, and Bryndor withdrew a knife. He considered the height of the table and grimaced as it barely rose to his knees. "Something tells me this was made by Cloud Walkers for Cloud Walkers."

He flipped his knife into the surface of the wood and considered the task. The morning was cool, but he would rather suffer the cold than soil one of his only remaining tunics. After removing the garment, he knelt alongside the table. Once situated, he made neat cuts around the ankles and legs of the carcass. Next, he dissected through the connective tissues holding the skin to one of the hind legs, making quick work of the process. "Can you hold this leg for me, Laryn? With just a little traction, I can get the skin off in one piece."

Laryn stepped forward and held the leg firm. "You've done this before. Did Kae teach you that?" she asked.

"Yes, though in the Bend, Journey's Bend, most everyone knows how to field dress and butcher animals. We had to be quick about it in the Moorlok. Linger too long, and wolves or a bear might steal your kill," said Bryndor.

Together, they completed the work of skinning the carcass. Bryndor set the skin to the side and considered how to best quarter the segments. All the while, Boru whined with anticipation.

"I hear you, Boru, just . . . give me a moment," he said.

Moons, how do you quarter an animal with a skinning knife?

An older villager rounded the gathering hut and gestured with his fingers, communicating something to Laryn. She nodded once and traded the skin of the gendek for a stone tool, which she handed to Bryndor. He held the awkward tool in his hand. The dark wedge of stone, oddly rounded, fit into his palm and tapered into a sharp edge.

"Bakloh will see to the curing of the pelt," said Laryn. "The stone axe doesn't look like much, but mind the blade. It's sharper than you think."

It took Bryndor a moment to figure out how best to use the new tool. Eventually, though, a few forceful chops allowed him to section out the hindquarters and shoulders. He tossed the smallest portion to Boru. The wolvryn turned his head once, looking at the remaining pieces on the carving table.

"That's enough for now, Boru. Next time you and I can try our luck, then maybe you'll get more," said Bryndor. The wolvryn retrieved his portion and retreated under the broad leaves of a nearby bush to devour his share.

"Moons, I think he understands you," said Laryn.

Bryndor lifted his eyes from the carving table and glanced to Boru, then shrugged. "Sometimes maybe, but other times I think he hears what he wants to hear. Do you think Kae is right about how fast they seem to be growing? We never kept a dog and don't really have anything to compare to."

Laryn gathered sectioned hunks of gendek meat onto a large wooden platter. "Hmm . . . my experience is limited, but now that you mention it, I don't recall them growing so fast at such a young age. You and Lluthean should take them deeper into the valley to meet Mahkeel, the handler."

"What's a handler?" asked Bryndor.

Laryn held the platter at her hip. "He trains most of the wolvryn here in the valley. He doesn't speak much of the Kindred tongue, but I can send Ellisina with you. She is well-versed in the speech and loves a visit to the pack. She could show you the way and make introductions if you like."

"That sounds like a great idea," said Bryndor.

Laryn walked the butchered pieces inside, then returned with the empty platter. "How is Kae?"

Bryndor set down the stone axe and loaded up the patter with more hunks of meat. "I think he's alright. It took him longer than he expected to recover from the draft, but I expect we'll see more of him in the next few days."

Laryn nodded to herself. "What about how he's feeling? How you're all feeling? You had a home in the Southlands somewhere. Did you leave people behind?"

Her question gave him pause, and he reflected long enough to feel the sting of tears threaten his eyes. Rona's absence still left a vacancy inside. He inhaled a deep breath to dissipate the sensation. "We did. Journey's Bend was as good a place as any other, I expect. Have you . . . talked with Kae much about . . . any of that?"

Laryn shook her head, indicating that she had not, and something in the way she knelt at the carving table with her hands folded on her lap made her appear hesitant.

Bryndor didn't like the thought of being the first one to talk to Laryn about Kaellor and Rona. "Maybe I shouldn't be, I mean . . . I don't want to say anything that might cause trouble."

"I understand. I didn't mean to put you in an awkward position. I just have so many questions," she said. "What was your home like, how was it raising you, what was Rona like, how did you ever make ends meet?" She tucked strands of hair behind her ears, and Bryndor became momentarily lost in the unique, varied color of her eyes. "The Kaellor I knew had the same conviction of responsibility but knew nothing of making his way in the world without the backing of the kingdom."

"There's a lot to cover there," said Bryndor. "All I can tell you is what I know about Kae now. I don't think Llu and I have a good sense of what life was like for him outside of the Bend. Kae has always been pretty serious, covering all the angles, looking for stray threats. He was always . . . on alert, protecting us from . . . well, from anything that might have to do with abrogators, I guess. Aunt Ro's death just sort of focused all his intensity into one goal: to return to Aarindorn for answers."

"What happened to your aunt?" asked Laryn.

"A group called the Lacuna from Aarindorn sent an assassin. He was supposed to kill Lluthean and me, maybe Kae as well, only he arrived when Aunt Ro was alone. Kae and a fella named Reddevek, an Outrider from Aarindorn, managed to kill the assassin, but they were too late to save Rona," Bryndor explained.

An awkward pause settled between them. Bryndor began to wonder if he said too much when Laryn spoke again. "What was Reddevek doing in the Southlands, and who are the Lacuna?" She squinted and seemed to be posing the questions more to herself than to him. "I think you might have been right when you suggested that there was a lot to cover."

"Journey's Bend definitely left its mark on us," said Bryndor.

"In more ways than one," she said and pointed her chin to the pink patchwork of scars on his neck and shoulder. "How did you come by those scars? They look recent."

Bryndor felt his cheeks flush with heat and tried to explain the complex string of events that led to his injury, but he found himself stumbling over words and phrases. Once he began, it seemed like stepping onto an ice-slicked hill. One step onto the slope, and it was all skipping feet and windmilling arms in a sloppy attempt not to end up on his ass.

"Llu and I stumbled across this wolvryn that . . . it was Boru and Neska's mother. She was trying to protect her pups and, it all happened so fast; we would never hunt something like that on purpose, it was just that—"

Laryn held a hand up. "I have no doubt that you were lucky to live after an encounter with a feral wolvryn protecting her pups, but are you saying that a wolvryn wounded you and caused those scars?"

"Well . . . yes," said Bryndor. The admission of it all in a village where wolvryn seemed revered left him uncertain how to proceed and thankful he could avert his eyes and continue chopping up the gendek.

The words caused Laryn to rock back from her knees. She stood abruptly and dusted herself off, then held a hand on her hip and seemed to contemplate something. He began to wonder if she was angry.

"Tell you what," she said with a crispness that differed from her hesitant questions only moments before. "Bring the rest of the gendek inside once you trim the fat, then ask for Ellisina. Tell her I want her to escort you and Lluthean, and your wolvryn, to the handler. The trip will take you at least three days, but she knows how to provision you for the journey."

"What about Uncle Kae?" asked Bryndor.

"Your uncle and I have a lot to talk about. More, I suspect, than even he is aware of just now. We'll join you with Mahkeel by week's end."

What will Kae think of a delay? Shouldn't we be on our way to Aarindorn?

Bryndor stood a moment, bloodstained hands clutching the platter of gendek meat, and chewed on his lower lip. Laryn's shoulders relaxed, and she gave him what appeared to be a knowing smile.

"Look, Bryndor, you are right to want to counsel your uncle. I suspect he is accustomed to keeping close track of you both all these years, but this valley is completely isolated from the abrogators. The only way in or out requires a ritual that the elders perform. It's the only safe passage past the striations of zenith and nadir, and the way can only be opened twice a year when the moon of Baellen draws closest. The next opportunity to get in or out won't be for another six months."

He glanced to Boru. The wolvryn was using his forelegs to steady a thigh bone while he gnawed at the remnants with his back teeth. *If we are going to be here for a while, it would be good to learn more about you and Neska.*

"Ellisina, that's the girl who comes around looking to play with Boru and Neska?" he asked.

"Yes. She's wanted a wolvryn of her own for a long time now, but she doesn't understand everything about the choosing."

Bryndor turned her words over in his mind and gave her a quizzical look.

"If you hadn't figured it out by now, the wolvryn chooses first whether or not to be a companion and second who to bond with," Laryn explained. "Other than being available, we never could figure out why a wolvryn would choose to bond with a specific person."

"Kae mentioned something like that," said Bryndor. After a pause, he asked, "Do you think Kae will mind if we take some time to see the handler?"

The tiny lines on her forehead smoothed, leaving him with a foreboding feeling. "It isn't like you have anywhere else to go, Bryn. But don't worry, leave Kaellor to me."

Chapter Fourteen: Intimate Communion

Laryn returned to her hut and tidied up, then exchanged the warm smock for a form-fitting long-sleeved top. Three steps outside her hut, an autumn breeze cut through the thin garment, and she stopped and sighed.

What are you doing? He's not even a season removed from the death of his wife; he's certainly not going to pay attention to what you're wearing.

She returned to her hut and wiggled into the warmer smock, then made her way over to his hut, only to find it vacant. A quick search of the gathering house revealed that no one had seen Kae for hours. She found Bakloh at a table with the gendek pelt, busying himself scraping away the excess connective tissue.

"Bakloh, have you seen the longstrider, Kaellor? He is the oldest one of the three," she signed.

"Not since he left with Elder Miljin this morning," signed Bakloh.

His words gave Laryn pause. *What could the two of you have to discuss, and why didn't you include me? I suppose Miljin does know the common tongue well enough to manage without me.*

Feeling a strange mixture of urgency and curiosity, she stepped out of the gathering house and folded into the clouds. Mist and cloud rushed under her smock and made her shiver. She emerged at the footsteps of the spirit house and climbed up to the door. Just as she prepared to barge inside, a pleasant vapor wafted up through the chimney: the faint fragrance of freshly brewed kevash flower tea mingled with the sweet, woody aroma of burning moonwood.

Something in those calming scents allowed her to take a breath and slow down. She tapped a soft knuckle on the door a few times. After a moment, Miljin slid the door open. The wizened man tipped his head. *"Many blessings and honor to your house, Laryn,"* he signed.

She repeated the familiar greeting but found herself looking over the elder's shoulder and into the spirit house. Kaellor was sitting with his back to her, near the central hearth.

"What is . . . is everything alright?" she signed.

"Everything is as it should be. I am needed elsewhere, but it would be rude to leave a guest unattended," signed Miljin. For just a moment, she caught the glimmer of something mischievous in his expression, but the elder hurried down the steps and folded into the clouds before she could voice her growing sense of bemusement.

Laryn stepped inside and slid the door closed. In the time it took her to pull her smock overhead, Kaellor stood and turned. He motioned for her to take a seat and wiggled something with his fingers. It took her a moment to recognize his clumsy gestures.

"Kae, what exactly is going on here?" she asked.

Kaellor hand signed again, slower and with emphasis so that she could understand. *"Many blessings and honor . . . to your house . . . my Laryn."*

"Many blessings and honor to your house, Kaellor," she signed back. Her fingering felt stiff, betraying her surprise.

"Would you like tea? We have a lot to discuss this morning," Kaellor signed.

"Yes, we do. For starters, when were you going to tell me about Bryndor's scar? How long ago was he wolvryn-marked? Are you worried about the prophecy, and when did you learn their hand language?" The signed response danced across her fingers with more intensity than she intended.

"Whoa, whoa, whoa," said Kaellor, holding both hands palm up in mock submission. "That's more than Ellisina and Miljin could drill into my thick head. I missed that last part. How about we sit and use the voices the Giver granted us?"

Ellisina and Miljin? That explains why you called me, "my Laryn."

Laryn took a seat opposite him across from the hearth. The clean, sweet aroma of the burning moonwood wafted up through a small opening in the roof of the hut. Kaellor poured them each a bowl of kevash flower tea.

"How long have you been coming here, Kae?" asked Laryn. She studied him through the steam coming off her tea as she blew across the hot liquid.

"Only two or three days now, but I had the girl start to teach me some of the hand language before then. It could come in handy, you know. We should take it back to Aarindorn." He sipped at his bowl of tea and peered at her from the top of his eyes.

After a long draw of the calming drink, she considered what she knew about the man sitting across from her. *Not half as much as I would like and even less than I should.*

"You seem as far away as the moons, Laryn," said Kaellor.

"I'm just caught off guard. I don't know what to think," she replied.

"Fair enough. Let's start with something simple. I'll tell you what I remember about the woman I left behind in Stone's Grasp, and you tell me what you remember about me. Then we can work forward and fill in some of the gaps."

"That kind of strategy sounds very much like the Kaellor I remember," said Laryn with an arched eyebrow. "I remember you were always the planner, thinking three steps ahead and yet, at times, fairly rooted in your convictions."

Kaellor nodded in agreement. "Some things remain, and some things change, I suppose. My turn, then. I remember you as the responsible, open-minded, and optimistic woman who convinced me of the soundness of the binding when I couldn't see past the need to defend my brother."

"Hmm. That didn't turn out as we expected," said Laryn.

Kaellor sighed but offered her a soft smile. "Most things in life don't turn out as expected. I've . . . chosen not to live with regret about that decision, Laryn. It was the only way to raise the boys beyond the reach of the abrogators. I know that now."

It was her turn to smile ruefully. "If we knew then what we know now?"

They sipped in companionable silence for a time. Images of important events in her life flickered in her mind: their private exchange of vows, completing the binding ritual, that night in the Abrogator's War, awaking in the Sanitorium among the healers at Callinora, her counsel with the regent Therek Lefledge, and embarking on the long journey to the Cloud Walkers.

"You changed your hair," he said off-handedly. His words pulled her back to the room. When she tilted her head to the side in question, he continued, "The white streak, it's distinctive."

"It's a holdover from the war," said Laryn. She fingered one of the white locks of hair draped on her cheek, then tucked it behind an ear. "After the Abrogator's War, Therek found me. I'm told I was buried under a mountain of rubble. I don't remember any of that. Venlith and the healers at Callinora had to place me in a dozenth to suspend my body, giving them time to mend all my injuries. Venlith thinks the effect of being so close to the Drift for so long left its mark on me."

"The war left its mark on all of us, I expect," said Kaellor. "Tell me about your life since then, Laryn. How did you end up here? What gives you purpose to rise every morning?"

After adjusting a pillow behind her back, she took a moment to settle into a comfortable position. "I lost about two years after the war. For most of that, I was suspended in the cocoon. I don't have many scars to show for it on the outside, but Venlith says the tangled lines of zenith on the inside tell a different story. Anyway, I needed the next year to regain my stamina. The simple act of walking was exhausting.

"The recovery was difficult for other reasons. I knew that you had to leave with the heirs, but Therek used all his influence to hide and protect me. In those early days, as reparations for the war took hold, the name Lellendule was a death mark. My parents, my brother, all of my family were killed either in the war or the conflict in the weeks afterward. My cousins, Chancle and Hestian, fled into the high places of the Great Crown. They were able to return only after a few years with the help of Therek."

"Giver's tears, Laryn. You were alone that whole time?" asked Kaellor. His eyebrows lifted in bewildered disbelief.

"I managed with the help of good friends, Venlith, and other healers at the Sanitorium. I spent the next few years returning to Stone's Grasp. I resumed ownership of my family's holdings and the manor in the high district. Chancle, Hestian, and I pooled our resources and rekindled the family businesses in textiles and mining."

"I think that must have been a lot more complicated than you make it out to be," said Kaellor.

She allowed herself to dip briefly into the well of memories from those times, and a half-smile drew up her cheek. "It was . . . challenging. But overcoming those challenges was its own reward. I searched for you. Moons, did I search for you."

Tiny flakes of kevash flower swirled in the bottom of her bowl. "The binding was one thing, but that mantle crafted by your brother was . . . impermeable. Even Therek found his gift unable to ascertain where to begin to look. I considered employing scouts from the Outriders, but Therek assured me he had been searching for you ever since the war ended. And then, about six years ago, he had another vision and convinced me to come here, to the Cloud Walkers."

They spent the rest of the day sharing stories about her life among the Cloud Walkers and his in the Southlands. As much as she loved hearing about his experiences raising the boys, a small part of her awareness remained detached and observant, watching to see how she felt about this man before her, trying to determine how he might feel about her.

Long ago, she had shuttered-up the door to her inner self, to her vulnerability. As the hours wore on, without realizing it, the attentive way he prepared to meet her today, his patience in listening with engaged interest, his laughter when she shared humorous stories, and his genuine empathy when she shared her struggles . . . all of it slowly wedged open the doorway to that long-forgotten corridor.

In the middle of a throaty laugh, as Kaellor shared the story about Lluthean swallowing a large gulp of Malvressian honey-cut, she realized how the hours had melted in what felt like only minutes and how much she truly enjoyed his company. They took breaks, and Miljin organized the delivery of food and drink. The conversation lingered into the evening.

Kaellor stood to stretch and gazed up into the night sky through the opening in the roof of the spirit house. "By the Giver, the stars are close up here. I swear I should be able to pluck one right out of the sky." He closed one eye and tried to pinch one of the twinkling lights between thumb and forefinger.

She stepped close to share his view, allowing her body to brush against the warmth of his. They remained there for several moments. "Careful, Kae. When I arrived, I spent the first few days nursing a stiff neck from doing the exact same thing," said Laryn. "I thought it was strange that the stars were more or less the same as back home, only closer. It sort of makes the world feel a little smaller, you know?"

Kaellor withdrew his gaze from the sky and settled deep blue eyes on her. The smile lines melted from the corner of his eyes, and he withdrew a moment.

"What is it?" she asked.

"You just said something that sounded like someone I used to know," he said.

"Who?"

"Rona." As he uttered her name, something in the hard edges about his shoulders softened.

"I'm sorry. I didn't know, Kae." She stepped back slightly, giving inches of separation that felt more like the division between Aarindin and the Southlands.

"Wait, Laryn . . . don't, if you don't mind, don't step away," he said with a soft tone and had to swallow to clear his throat. "I married Rona, it's true. But we were never like man and wife. Rona fancied other women and loved children. I needed help raising the boys, and ours was a relationship born out of necessity but grew into something more like brother and sister. Anyway, I haven't felt like this since the night before our binding and . . . it's nice, you know?"

Laryn swallowed to dismiss the warm fullness that gathered just above her arca prime. She searched his expression, finding only genuine vulnerability there. After a moment, she stepped in, and they entangled their arms in an embrace twelve years in the making. They stood there so long that she had to shift her weight to keep her feet from tingling.

She found her hands massaging the muscles in the small of his back and along the sides of his torso and took pleasure in the shared warmth where their bodies connected. His strong hands grasped the nape of her neck, and she craned back a little, relishing his intimate touch. Eventually, she became aware of the rhythmic contractions of his quiet sobs, and she felt her chest constricting, then releasing with her own need to weep.

They stood there, alone in intimate communion in the spirit house among the fragrant wisps of moonwood smoke rising from the hearth, crying for a time that lingered so long she lost track of herself. Eventually, she leaned back to look up into those azure blue eyes that, years ago, had eroded the last of her resolve. They smiled, then laughed . . . and then kissed.

Chapter Fifteen: Moonstruck

"WHAT DO YOU MEAN, SHE'S down there, Nolan?" Karragin asked. The intensity of her clipped words lacked much emotion, but Nolan paled and swallowed. She considered handling him with a softer tone, but his revelation had surprised her more than a little.

Her brother took a knee, then gave his report. His words tumbled out in a frenzy of scattered emotion. "We followed the not-zenith, the skip trail, to this cavern, and this thing was excavating holes in the side, then wedging-in planks to make a ladder, only it wasn't a real ladder. It looked to be ready to climb out, so we shot it; I shot it with arrows, but they had no effect. Amniah sent in a column of air and caused the creature to tumble back down. We thought maybe it was injured, so I ran back to signal you. After I started the signal fire, I ran back here, and she was gone, but . . . her signature leads down there."

He turned a vacant expression to the dark cleft in the ground. "She's down there, Karra, alone with that thing and the Giver only knows how many grot. We have to go get her!"

Karragin placed a hand on his shoulder and grabbed his chin, lifting his eyes to meet hers. "Breathe, Nolan. Stop and take a deep breath. Remember your training." She held him there a moment, waiting. Eventually, the panicked wide-eyed expression on his face melted, and he blinked a few times then nodded.

She released her hold on his chin, then motioned for Kervin and a few other primes to step closer. "Tell us more about this creature. What do you recall about its strengths or weaknesses?"

Nolan explained his encounter with more detail, describing the flat-headed thing from the cavern and his belief that it had communicated with a good number of grotvonen far below. After he recounted the event, she turned and walked a few paces to stand alone. She siphoned zenith and attempted to direct the force into her rune of premonition, but as usual, the rune remained dormant. A frustrated sigh escaped her lips, and she turned to address her small council of primes.

"What do you make of it?" she asked.

Most of them stared with haunted eyes into the darkness. Eventually, Kervin spoke up. "If I didn't know better, I would say Nolan's been sneaking vivith."

Karragin cocked her head to the side, resisting an urge to throttle her friend and toss him into the hole after Amniah. Kervin held up his hands in surrender. "Easy, Karra, I said if I didn't know better. Levity, you should try it sometime." She kept her unwavering gaze settled on him, and his face flushed. "Right, anyway. It sounds . . . like Nolan might have encountered an umbral."

"That's the most intelligent thing you've said since this expedition began, Kerv, and I agree," said Karragin. She turned to search the small crowd of Outriders who ringed them in a semicircle. Her gaze landed on a young man with shallow, slashed dimples in his cheeks.

"Dexxin, you're the only sender on this mission. I have an important message that needs to get to the regent and Overwarden Kaldera immediately. Do you know if your siblings are in Stone's Grasp at the moment?" she asked.

The young man stepped forward. The focus of his eyes drifted to something internal for a moment, and then he seemed to return his attention to Karragin. "Craxton can get to your father in perhaps ten minutes. It will take a little longer for Mullayne to reach the overwarden."

"Relay this message with a dark moon priority. Secrecy is paramount to avoid panic in the kingdom." Karragin waited for the young sender to acknowledge the gravity of the situation.

After a moment, he saluted thumb to thumb and finger to finger in obedience. "We understand. What is the message?"

"Relay to the regent and the overwarden only that we have reason to believe that an umbral has been spotted in the Great Crown. Give them our location. Tell them we are going to investigate further and confirm Nolan's observations. More information will follow this evening."

Dexxin nodded, then retreated into himself, sending the message to his siblings. Karragin returned her attention to Nolan. "Alright, how long has Amniah been down there?"

"Maybe a half-hour now. I tried calling down, but there was no answer, nothing. Not even any more of the weird clicking noises."

Karragin tongued the scar of her upper lip. She tried to calculate the risks and benefits of infiltrating the warren. *We don't have enough information. What do they want with Amniah? How many are down there? What if there is more than one umbral?*

Kervin cleared his throat. "Karra? Don't tell me you're considering going down there? We don't have surprise. We have no idea about the numbers and don't have proof of life." He seemed to realize his words might have been a bit harsh. "Sorry, Nolan. But we have to acknowledge the possibility at least."

"Amniah is my responsibility. She's in my quad, and I sent these two up here on reconnaissance," she said with a straight, calculated response.

Kervin studied her face a moment, then shook his head. "At least consider leaving Nolan here, then," he pleaded. He stepped close and pitched his voice low so that only she could hear him. "Elbiona asked me to make sure that the regent's children were not placed in unnecessary danger. It doesn't take a sympath to see that you plan to go down there. Perhaps only one of you should go?"

Karragin waved off the rebuttal. She knew full well that this expedition, overprovisioned with a full flank, was Elbiona's attempt to remove her and Nolan from immediate jeopardy. *It's rather fitting that we found something more dangerous than grondle just when the warden moves to insulate us. Moons, at least we're consistent.*

"I appreciate the difficult position you are in, Kerv," she said, softening her tone. Then she cleared her throat to address the group. "We all knew the risks when we joined the Outriders. I'm taking my quad and one other into that hole to find out what happened to Amniah. Savnah, your quad is with me."

A stout, short Outrider hooked her thumbs under her belt, made a guttural noise, then hocked a thick glob of spit onto the ground. Savnah Derrigand wore twin moonblade axes, one on each hip. She winked, twitching a scar-streaked eyebrow. "It's about time the toughest bitch in this flank saw some action. Dex, Argul, Runta . . . form up!"

There is that, and I want your sender along so he can relay any real-time information back to our leaders. Giver knows we might even need Argul's munitions expertise.

Karragin dipped her head once to acknowledge the prime's enthusiasm. She turned back to Kervin. "Kerv, I want you to garrison here. Fortify a defensive position around this hole. If anything other than an Outrider tries to crawl out of that warren, apprehend and isolate. Scout the rim of this valley. If it's clean, drop ghost protocol, then pick the fastest rider to relay all of this to Warden Elbiona straight away."

Kervin looked past her, appearing to search the barren valley for alternative answers. Eventually, he relaxed his shoulders and seemed to accept the inevitability of the plan. "Alright. Just get back here in one piece. Don't make me have to deliver bad news to the warden."

Karragin pursed her lips. "Better that than a long conversation with my father." She raised her voice one last time. "Kervin has the reins while I'm away. I'm ordering all of you to treat the events around this valley with dark moon secrecy. Warden Elbiona will decide what information, if any, can be shared with others."

Within minutes, the two quads had staked ropes into the ground for rappelling down into the darkness. Karragin double-checked her rigging and made quick work of the knots on her line.

"Ruck up, riders. Make sure you have easy access to a few hot-tops. I'll drop in first to be certain it's safe. We don't even know if our ropes will reach the bottom, and I can climb back up easy enough if we need a different plan. Wait for me to ignite the blue torch, then follow. Double-check your harness, and don't grind up on the drop. We don't know what might be waiting down there, so don't announce yourselves." The seven members of the descent team gathered around the warren. She leaned back over the hole and worked her way over the edge.

"Eyes to the horizon, Karra," said Kervin.

"Eyes to the horizon, Kerv." She bounced and wriggled in the harness, testing the security of her hips in the rigging, then kicked back. On the way down, she passed countless wood planks, some bent and others broken as if a large boulder had careened down the fissure. The thought brought back memories of the first time they discovered the grotvonen den.

Moons, if Amniah did this, she's getting stronger.

Occasionally she had to move left or right, avoiding planks of timber still protruding from the inside of the cave. The air grew stale and warmer than the surface. A strange combination of musty, damp soil and sweet musk permeated the cavern.

The stone walls seemed to veer away from her, and she hung in midair, unable to secure her feet against a solid surface. *Right . . . so wider at the base than the top. I should have expected that I suppose.*

A gentle swing of the feet carried her side to side as she tried to determine the space available in the dim light and shadows. Eventually, she resorted to igniting one of the hot-tops. The small torches burned bright but lasted less than ten minutes. A quick strike of the cap against her hip ignited the sparking light.

A small cascade of sparks showered down into the depths, well below the end of her rope. The burning embers smoldered out on top of the boulder she had tossed down the shaft the last time she was here. Next to the large rock, the remnants of several tree trunks appeared to lay splintered on the cave floor. *At least Amniah isn't there.*

The bottom seemed too far for any of them to drop. Karragin held her position there a moment.

How did that umbral climb out?

Staring back up into the shaft revealed the latticework of planks. On the wall opposite her, they continued, undamaged, where the cavern receded. She swung her feet again, making herself a pendulum until she drifted close enough to grab one of the makeshift rungs. The damp wood held solid, and she tested her weight. The rung vibrated in its strange mooring but held firm.

She dropped the torch and moved with haste. The dim light allowed her to find purchase for her feet and wedge herself against the wall. After securing the rope around her waist, she used the meshwork of rungs to climb down. Twenty feet from the bottom, her rope drew taught. Karragin removed the tie from around her waist, secured it to a wood plank, then scrabbled to the bottom.

The last of her hot-top flickered out as she reached the cavern floor. She took a knee and drew her saber with one hand while feeling for any tremors in the ground with the other. Long moments passed in which her eyes and ears strained to sense anything in the vacant darkness. Humid, fetid, musky air was all she could sense. The oppressive nature of her descent, the thought of over a hundred feet of rock overhead, and the palpable silence threatened to overwhelm her resolve.

She shook off the feeling and slammed the cap of her second hot-top on her hip. The bright flare burned away the darkness, and a chorus of shrieks shattered the silence. For a moment, it seemed like shadows on the floor rippled out from her, and she was the lone pebble dropped into a very deep, very dark pond.

As her eyes adjusted, countless grotvonen scurried about in the darkness. Some ran directly at her, chancing the blinding light. Instinctively, she ignited her gift. Currents of zenith cascaded across her runes and funneled through her arca prime.

Karragin held one hand high and whipped her saber in quick crossing slashes, deflecting the jab of a spear and the arc of a club. She leaped to the side, taking one grotvonen at the knee and another in the throat, then spun low, feeling the blade swipe through at least three others.

There was no time to assess her enemies, so she continued to spring back and forth, severing limbs, spilling entrails, and occasionally decapitating the creatures. The flurry of her activity was met with discordant howls, guttural clicks, and shrieks of pain. The cavern became a confusing echo chamber of bestial conflict. The flashing, scintillating sparks of the hot-top reflected like a strange strobe light from the eyes of the grotvonen horde.

A familiar whistle announced the descent of an outrider munition. Karragin whirled about with a violent cleaving swing, then wedged herself against the boulder, protecting her eyes. Two sunbursts flashed overhead, followed by a single shatter-bite. The last of Argul's munitions detonated in a wide ring of shrapnel.

The cave erupted with screeches of panic and pain. Karragin leaped from her crouched position and took the offensive, stabbing, slicing, and cleaving through the bodies of her blinded foes. But more grotvonen poured into the cavern.

More than once, a spear tip tore at her leathers, and she caught the shaft of several on her forearms. She felt something jump onto her back, immediately followed by the sensation that several more of the creatures were piling on in an attempt to subdue her. More rushed in and grabbed for her arms and legs.

Acting more out of instinct than anything tactical, she dropped the torch and continued to swing her blade one-handed. Reaching her free hand overhead, her fingers plunged into what she guessed was a snout. When she pulled forward, the tissue broke away, and hot fluid splashed onto the back of her neck, but the weight on her shoulders remained unchanged. A few grubby hands reached in to snuff out the light, but she sliced back and forth, removing digits and limbs.

The diversion allowed still others to climb onto the growing pile of grotvonen on top of her. Karragin crouched a little, then jumped up. She felt several bodies tumble away and struggled to maintain her footing on the writhing hill of grotvonen. Ignoring the crunch of bones vibrating through her boots, she flailed about with her sword, slashing at anything moving in the fading light.

The fading light; Giver, grind me for a fool!

She looked down through the wriggling pile just in time to see the torch snuff out. Utter panic overwhelmed Karragin's orientation. Fear drowned out any resemblance of an ability to think of a plan. She grabbed what felt like an ankle in one hand and her saber in the other, then spent the next few moments slashing both in a windmill of expended zenith.

She sensed that she struck into the grotvonen horde with her first few turns, but then it was just her whirling wildly into the darkness. In her disorientation, she tumbled from the grotvonen pile but kept her sword arm spinning in wild slices. After several more turns, vertigo set her off balance, and something truly massive smacked the side of her head. Sparkly white lights skittered at the periphery of her vision, and she dropped to both knees panting heavily. Solid rock braced against her shoulder, and she realized with chagrin that she had dashed her head against the stone in her wild flailing.

Something she hoped was sweat burned her useless vision and ran down her face. In her struggle, her cheeks had begun to flush from the body heat trapped by her thick Outrider leathers. She considered shedding the heavy outercoat, then realized it must have been protecting her. Her arms and back throbbed in pain from countless places where a spear shaft or club had landed a glancing blow, and her head throbbed from the impact, but based on the number of times she'd been hit, she knew it could have been worse. Shifting her weight, she turned to rest her back against the stone.

Over the next several minutes, she kept waving her blade back and forth. The futility of slicing aimlessly at the darkness started to make her angry, then defeated. "The Giver take you all! Get on with it then!" she yelled.

As if in answer, the grotvonen horde began making clicking noises. The clacking seemed to come from all around her, echoing through the cavern. Then, a strange hissing noise brought an abrupt stop to the cacophony of clicking grotvonen. It descended from somewhere overhead, followed by a clatter and the familiar eruption of torchlight. She looked up to realize that her back was resting against the same boulder she had pushed into the cavern. A hot-top torch, dropped from far above, landed on the boulder and flooded the cavern with light.

Another torch landed not three feet from where she sat, and a third one ten feet away. Her eyes adjusted only a moment before the grotvonens'. She rose to her feet and sidestepped a spear arcing through the air. A group of four larger grotvonen approached her, clicking and growling. These four fanned out in a coordinated formation, and each wore oddly fitting armor. Bushy hair sprouted from the joints where boiled leather and plates fit poorly.

The fear that shrouded Karragin's mind lifted, and she felt her ability to strategize return. Without taking her eyes from the approaching grotvonen warriors, she reached down with her off hand and retrieved a stout club. A moment later, the group of four rushed her from all sides.

All the years of sparring and training kicked in, and she carried out attacks of precision. She hurled the club at the grotvonen on her left and charged directly at the same beast. It batted away the club, but the distraction allowed her to sweep under its spear tip and slice deep across its chest and into the soft crease under its arm. Sliding to a stop, she pivoted and deflected a thrown spear.

Without waiting, she quickstepped in a zigzag fashion and took out the unarmed grotvonen who'd thrown the spear. The two remaining grot charged, and she prepared to meet them. Instinct gave her insight into where she could take advantage of the weakness in their approach. As she crouched in preparation for her strike, something heavy throttled into her back, knocking the wind from her and crushing her to the ground.

Her saber slid across the cave floor, just out of reach. The muscles in her core seized up, preventing her from drawing in a breath. A firm, clawed hand wrenched her head back and up using her hair. She couldn't see the one that held her, but in the torchlight, the last armored grotvonen lifted a heavy club high.

The beast shifted its weight to smash the club down, but a shiny axe blade sliced clean through its knee from back to front, and the grotvonen toppled. Savnah stood behind it with a feral grin on her face, wielding twin moonblade axes. The stout woman cleaved through the backside of the grotvonen warrior's neck, then surged ahead, taking the other who held Karragin.

Once released, Karragin dropped to all fours and struggled to draw a full breath. She blinked away sweat and gore to watch as Savnah completed a turn whirling her axe blades, chopping through three others. The prime wielded the crescents with expert precision, hacking into feet and legs, spilling entrails, and making a bloody mess of things. She kicked Karragin's blade back across the floor and continued her assault.

"Karragin, can you fight, or do we retreat?" she yelled while she continued her dance.

After a moment of breathing like a fish out of water, Karragin's muscles relaxed, and she finally sucked in a full breath. Her hand gripped her saber, and she stood, infused her strength rune with zenith, and surged to Savnah's side. Together they fought back-to-back, meeting one last wave of armored grotvonen.

Karragin leaped forward, spinning her saber through the belly of one warrior and ending her surge with a two-handed swing that went clear through another grotvonen warrior's shoulder and into its chest. The creature's oversized eyes glazed over as its sundered body fell to the ground, nearly divided in two. She spun, searching for the next attacker, but found none. The two primes stood there panting. Gore, sweat, and blood stained the leathers of both women. The echo chamber fell silent but for the panting of the two Outrider primes.

"Grind me sideways, Lefledge," Savnah giggled through panted breaths. "I might be the toughest bitch this side of the Great Crown, but you're definitely moonstruck." Savnah gestured around the cavern floor at the countless dead, then craned her neck and howled up into the cavern like a wolf.

The echoes of Savnah's howl dwindled as the last light of the remaining torch flickered out. In the darkness, a cold sensation settled into Karragin's core, and she gripped the leather binding of the hilt of her saber with a mixture of dread and anticipation. *Giver, not again.*

Chapter Sixteen: A Measure of Peace

KAELLOR AWOKE IN HIS hut, surprised to find himself alone, but the depression where Laryn had slept next to him remained warm to the touch. A kettle emitting fragrant steam sat with a mug on the bedside table. He dressed, poured himself a serving of the tea, and stepped outside. The potent infusion awakened his senses, and he gulped the entire mug down, then turned to grab a refill just as Laryn appeared from behind the hut.

"Good morning," she said.

"It's possibly the best morning I've had . . . well, ever," he said.

She stepped close and wrapped her hands under his outer coat, and they embraced. "You shouldn't show your teeth when you smile at me, Baellentrell. The village women will gossip."

The skin around his ears tightened, and he realized he couldn't help himself. He had not felt this happy since living in Aarindorn all those years ago. With effort, he relaxed the muscles in his cheeks and enjoyed the warmth of her embrace in the cool morning air.

"Where did you wander off to, anyway?" he asked.

"I folded into the clouds and checked on the boys," she said. "It took only a moment to find them. They made good progress toward Mahkeel. Bryndor was relieved to hear that you approve of them spending time with the handler, while Lluthean seemed preoccupied with something he called a billow seed."

"Don't let his apparent complacency fool you," said Kaellor. "Llu has a nimble mind. He might appear to be preoccupied with whatever his busy fingers are doing, but he notices everything. And I mean everything." Kaellor went on to explain Lluthean's unerring ability to recall mapping details from memory.

"That makes sense. I found them practicing the Damadibo hand language. Lluthean seemed much more confident with it. I can't believe how grown up they are, how much time has passed," she said. "They seemed completely at ease. Their camp was tidy, and the wolvryn were fed. You've put a lot of good things into both of them."

"I used to regret that my brother wasn't able to be around more. But I have to admit, my life would have little meaning without them," said Kaellor.

"I understand. Do you still want to make the journey to Mahkeel?" she asked.

"I'm no stranger to light travel, and I can't miss the chance to see a pack of wolvryn," said Kaellor.

"Would you mind some company?" she asked.

"I know you can blink down there with that cloud-walking thing you do," said Kaellor. "But, I was sort of hoping you might join me. It could be kind of fun."

"Why do I get the idea that the kind of fun you are talking about is hard to enjoy surrounded by your nephews and a crowded village of Cloud Walkers?" she asked.

"Why, Ms. Lellendule, you offend my royal sensibilities," said Kaellor, playing along. "As a prince of the realm, I have only the noblest of intentions."

"Hmm . . . you can have your noble intentions. I think we're due for a bit of fun," she said.

He chuckled. "Agreed. When do you want to leave?" he asked.

"Would it be alright if we waited a few days?" she asked. "You could always leave early, and I could join you. One of the villagers is due any day to deliver a child, and now that I have command of my gift, I would like to be there to ease her labor."

He wrapped his arms and pulled her in for a reassuring embrace. "I think that sounds perfect."

After a moment, they separated and walked toward the gathering house. Laryn turned to him. "There's something I meant to ask about the other night. Bryndor's scars, on his chest and shoulder."

"I wondered when you would get around to that," he said.

"I know you never put much credence in old prophecy, but Kae, it's just . . ." She shrugged as her voice trailed off.

"It feels like more than coincidence. I'll grant you that," said Kaellor. "I know my brother and Nebrine studied the old texts. They held strong convictions about the abrogator derivation."

"Is that the one that referenced the death of a sibling?" she asked.

"It is," said Kaellor. "When the wild wolvryn scars the highborn one, the channelers of nadir will rise. And then a few lines later, something like 'Seek the bearer who carries the burden, then look to reveal the Eidolon, but only after the sibling passes to the Drift.'"

"I thought so. What are you going to do?" she asked.

He scratched the grey chin hairs of his beard. "I don't know. The more I try to guide the boys on one path, the more circumstances seem to conspire to place them on another. I told someone once that sometimes you just have to get out of a Baellentrell's way, and maybe that's true enough. But I'll spend my last breath to keep that particular fork of prophecy from becoming their reality."

"Now that sounds like the Kaellor I remember," said Laryn.

After a light breakfast, they returned to Laryn's hut, where three villagers waited, seeking her counsel and advice regarding different ailments. In the short time since the return of her gift, the Cloud Walkers had become impressed with her skill at mending broken bones, curing sickness, and easing pain.

Kaellor took his leave to give her the space to practice her ministrations. He returned to his hut and considered rereading *The Book of Seven Prophets*. *I don't imagine the words will tell me anything I don't already know.*

He tossed the book into a chair, and the hilt of the Logrend blade caught his eye. The raspy hiss of the sword releasing from the scabbard sung to him. The feel of the grip seduced him to test his control. *Not just a Logrend blade anymore. Now you're my guardian sword. So we might as well get acquainted with one another.*

He sheathed the blade and strode to the edge of the village to a small glen. In relative seclusion, he withdrew the sword, gripping it first with one hand and then two, rolling his wrists to test the weapon's balance. He pivoted, arced the blade over his shoulder, then brought it to rest at his side and stood there long moments. To an onlooker, he appeared to be staring aimlessly at the grasses. But Kaellor's mind was recalling lessons long ago left behind in Stone's Grasp.

I'll have to start with foot speed and balance, then incorporate jab, riposte, and simple parry maneuvers.

He began his retraining in earnest. Nobody asked him why, and he never asked the question of himself. Perhaps the exercises were a way to keep himself busy. Maybe he needed to feel something more of the man he left behind in Aarindorn. Since reuniting with Laryn and breaking their binding, his gift certainly called to him, enticing him to allow zenith to suffuse him and usher forth his power. He didn't voice a reason, not to himself. Instead, he acted on the need to sharpen skills that had dulled long ago. And so he began.

Laryn found him several hours later, alone in the glen. He had created a circuit of exercises designed to challenge his quickness and balance. After completing these stations, he jumped up and back down on several boulders of various heights. Next, he used the sword to practice offensive and defensive forms.

He concluded by stringing several of the elements together in a flurry of motion. A pivot led to a swing in which he rolled his wrists, bringing his longsword around, jabbing, slicing, recoiling, turning, and finally slashing the blade through the tall grasses. The labor and exertion left his body panting, but his mind felt at peace.

Her applause brought him up short. His heavy breathing steamed the air between them, but he thought he recognized a glint of appreciation in her expression.

"Those are some unlucky reeds there. I shudder to think what grievance they caused you to suffer such a fate." She walked forward, holding a waterskin.

Kaellor sheathed the weapon and accepted the drink. "I might have overheard a village elder talking about how these particular stalks here are in league with abrogators."

"Is that so? Abogators in our valley?" she echoed. Stepping closer, she reached forward and pushed back the sweat-dampened hair that draped below his eyebrows. "Thank the Giver we have you to protect us."

He chuckled, and something about the sound felt right . . . unfamiliar, but right nonetheless.

"Have you finished stamping out disease and pestilence for the day then?" he asked.

"As a matter-of-fact, I have," she said. "I thought we could see how much of your gear is travel-worthy. The Cloud Walkers have no use for tents."

"I imagine that's true. I think at least one of the tents made it here with us," said Kaellor. "Let's go have a look."

They left the glen and walked back toward the village at a leisurely pace. Kaellor sensed something rustling just beyond sight through the misty clouds. Something or someone seemed to be shadowing them. They turned to walk down a beaten path, and whatever made the disturbance turned as well but remained just beyond his sight.

He drew in zenith and thought to awaken his arca prime, but the guardian rune accepted the power with a sluggish nature. A sense of alarm heightened his awareness, and he grabbed Laryn's wrist, stopping her in mid-stride. He put a finger to his lips and stepped forward, keeping a wary hand on the hilt of his sword.

"What's gotten into you, Kae?" she whispered.

"Someone is following us, just over there," he said and pointed to their right.

Laryn pulled her head back, searching his eyes. After a moment, her expression softened. "Kae, we're safe up here, in this valley." She placed a hand on his, enticing him to release his grip on the sword hilt.

With flushed cheeks, he nodded understanding and released his weak hold on zenith, mastering his apprehension. Laryn understood the simple gesture and concentrated on something in the way the clouds eddied for a moment. "It's just Senda. She's an herb gatherer. Come, I will introduce you."

"How can you tell?" he asked.

"Most of the Cloud Walkers gather the mists underfoot with unique patterns. See how the vapors swirl in a knot there at her feet? I've spent enough time with Senda in the high places to recognize her signature," she explained.

Kaellor strained his vision into the grey vapors but struggled to identify any meaningful pattern. *Still, I do sense something different. Otherwise, I never would have known she was there.*

Laryn spoke soft words in the strange whispering tongue of the Cloud Walkers. A small, olive-skinned woman stepped forward. Rows of neat, tidy braids circled her head, and red face paint swathed in a band across the top of her face masked her eyes. She spoke to Laryn using their hand language. Instead of the delicate dance of finger-play, her gestures were swift and sharp. Kaellor found himself unable to follow her meaning, but her intensity conveyed a sense of alarm. After a few exchanges, Laryn sucked in her breath.

She grabbed him by the wrist and pulled him forward. "Quickly, I'll explain when we get there." Together, they jogged down the trail toward the spirit house. Laryn led them up the outer steps and slid the door open without waiting for an invitation.

Inside, a Cloud Walker man lay on the same mat Lluthean had occupied. Elder Miljin stood beside him, fanning fragrant fumes from a hand brazier over the man's face. Laryn approached and knelt beside the two of them but waited for the elder to finish his ritual. Elder Miljin set the brazier down, and they exchanged heated gestures.

Kaellor watched Laryn retreat into her gift. In moments, the room hummed with her song as she assessed the source of the man's ailment. Abruptly, she pulled her hand back, and the healer song stifled.

Kaellor stepped forward. "What is it, Laryn? Can I lend you my strength like we did with Llu?"

"No, he isn't . . . he's not there anymore," she said.

To Kaellor's eye, the young man seemed to be asleep, drawing in shallow and infrequent breaths.

Elder Miljin interrupted the strange silence. "If you can not sense Ahben with your gift, then it is as I feared. He strayed too long in the high places."

"And that's a bad thing, right?" Kaellor asked.

Laryn explained, "At the summit of the Korjinth, wild currents of zenith and ribbons of nadir run in concentrations dense enough you can actually see them. Well, some of them. They surge back and forth against each other. Sometimes they cancel each other out, emitting an eerie keening wail. It's easy to become entranced by the sight and sound of it all. Sometimes in their collisions, a tight vortex forms, and one source is deflected to the ground. If anyone is standing at the summit under a nadir strike . . ."

"That's what happened to him then?" asked Kaellor. "So, what's to become of him?"

"There's nothing I can do for him," said Laryn. "It's as if all trace of zenith was burned out of him. His body will linger a day perhaps, maybe two. But I can't repair this kind of damage."

Kaellor scratched his beard, contemplating the situation. "Is this common knowledge? Why would anyone hike up there in the first place if it's so dangerous?"

"I did once," said Laryn. "I needed to retrieve some rare ingredients to invoke the ritual that allowed me to find you and then bring you back here. Ahben is an herb gatherer. I suspect he became entranced by it all and lingered too long."

"If that much pure nadir strikes a man, is the effect sudden? I mean, how did he get back here?" asked Kaellor.

"One of the wolvryn brought him to us in the condition you see now," explained Miljin.

"Is there anything we can do?" asked Kaellor.

The elder pulled a blanket up, folding it neatly under Ahben's chin. "No. His family will arrive soon, and I should make preparations for the ritual of release. But we should speak in a few days. There is much I would share. The ancestral spirits are aware of a dark presence in the Drift, one that retains a foothold in this world."

"And why exactly is that information we need to know?" asked Kaellor.

"Because the spirits revealed his name to me with guarded whispers," said Miljin.

"Tarkannen," grumbled Kaellor.

Before Miljin could say more, the door to the spirit house slid open, and three somber-faced Cloud Walkers appeared: an elderly couple and a young woman.

"Come on, Kae," said Laryn. "Let's give Ahben's family a measure of peace."

Chapter Seventeen: Dark Passages in the Deep

Karragin's forearm vibrated with zenith-infused strength as she prepared for another assault in the darkness.

"Well, that's no good. Give me a moment. I got it," said Savnah, and she lit the cavern with another hot-top. The prime held the torch high. "Karra? Karra, are you alright?"

Karragin searched the shadows expecting the shifting light to reveal another wave of grotvonen. Savnah looped her axes onto her waist and stepped close. Only then, when the two women stood eye to eye, did Karragin realize she was crouching in a defensive posture anticipating another attack. Understanding and reason eventually allowed her to muscle down her lingering fear, and Karragin stood to her full height.

"I'm fine. Thanks for . . . coming when you did," said Karragin.

"Us moonstruck have to stick together," said Savnah. She fingered a bit of fur and debris on the edge of one of her moonblade axes. "How about we light that blue torch of yours and signal the others that it's safe to come down?"

Karragin nodded and retrieved the signal torch from an inner pocket of her leathers. She held it forward, and Savnah used the hot-top to ignite it. Blue flames bathed the cavern in a sterile light. Karragin wedged the torch into a crevice on the boulder resting in the center of the cavern, and they waited.

"How did you know?" Karragin asked. Savnah cocked one eyebrow in question. "How did you know to drop munitions and hot-tops or follow me down?"

"Argul sort of made that decision for us. We all heard the grot screeching and clacking, but Argul took it upon himself to drop in the flash-bangs. Then there is your brother," said Savnah. "That boy is about as moonstruck as you are. Right after you dropped in, he eased back, fully intending to follow you down. He didn't even have the safety rigging of his harness cinched up. Kervin stopped him and suggested I follow. I was going to wait for your signal but could see Nolan wasn't going to have it. Poor boy looked about ready to blow mud, so I came down."

Man of no knowledge. Thank the Giver that my brother is as big of a monk as I am.

The dissipation of zenith allowed fatigue to settle into her muscles. As they waited, Karragin leaned back against the boulder while Savnah prowled the perimeter. "Mind a little bit of advice, Karra?" asked the prime.

Karragin lifted her placid gaze toward Savnah, then waved as if beckoning her forward.

Savnah hocked spit into the shadows. "You took a stupid risk coming down here. I get it. Amniah is in your quad. You sent her up here and feel responsible. But you've got a great team here with you. Next time, let's do this together?" Savnah suggested.

Karragin exhaled a deep breath of self-recrimination. "I didn't intend for it to go this way, but thanks all the same, Savnah. Anything else?"

The woman knelt beside one of the larger grotvonen and called out over her shoulder, "No. I'm not one to toss salt into a wound. Come on over here and take a look at this. Where do you suppose they get the armor? It wasn't crafted for them, all mish-mashed and poorly fitting."

Karragin watched her comrade then decided she should use the opportunity to learn as much about their enemy as she could. With an effort, she rose to her feet, grunting in pain. In the short time she sat, the muscles in her arms and legs had begun to stiffen. Something beyond stiff muscles in her back throbbed and caused her to breathe in splinted shallow breaths. She tried her best to ignore the pain and joined Savnah in the inspection of the grotvonen.

Thick, dark grey skin stretched over muscled hands and forearms. Coarse hairs of grey and black covered the upper arms and torso. Their legs resembled those of a large hound and seemed suited to bounding and running more than standing.

Savnah held up the hand of a grotvonen corpse. "It's a good thing these can't fight to their potential. They're all hair and muscle. Look at how the tops of their knuckles are calloused."

"Sometimes they run on all fours. The smaller ones do that; they're quite fast," said Karragin. Despite her pain, she bent to retrieve one of the spears and considered its make. It felt too heavy to make an effective missile. The haft was too thick, and the balance felt off. She compared several of the weapons, finding each a unique marriage of haft and blade. Some ended with sharp fluted stone, and others had a dagger or similar knife repurposed to the spear tip.

"They must not have the ability to shape metal," said Karragin. She offered the collection of spears to Savnah, who considered their shoddy make.

"I doubt they complain much about crappy weapons when they can see in the dark," said Savnah.

Karragin glanced down to consider the face of one of the grotvonen. Savnah flicked a finger at the lens of a large eye. A bony ridge encircling the globe gave the grot an appearance of eternal surprise, even in death. Wrinkled ridges with deep, furrowed slits appeared where the nose should be, and large, angular ears sprouted from the coarsely-haired head.

"A little help, maybe?" Tovnik's voice echoed from up above. He dangled awkwardly at the point where the column opened up into the cavern.

"Use the tethered rope to pull yourself to the side, Tovnik. You'll see a sturdy scaffold of planks wedged into the cave. Use those to make the rest of the drop," said Savnah.

Tovnik followed her advice. The medic dropped to the floor and set his pack down, then rolled his shoulders. He curled a lip as he considered the two primes and the gory scene.

"Are either of you injured?" he asked.

Savnah hocked another glob of spit into the shadows. "I'm fine, and Karra won't say otherwise, but I think her leathers are hiding more than she's letting on."

Tovnik walked over and handed Karragin a small flask. "It's tea of spiritwort. It will ease some of the stiffness without making you drowsy like bandle root."

Karragin sniffed at the flask, took a small sip, capped the container, and handed it back. "Thanks," she said.

"Mind if I have a look . . . inside?" asked Tovnik.

Karragin drew her head back slightly. She knew what he meant. Healers could discern more profound injuries, but the connection always felt slightly intrusive and a little too intimate for Karragin's comfort. At the moment, though, she ached from too many places to offer protest and nodded her consent.

Tovnik rolled up his arm sleeve, slid a hand along Karragin's forearm, then lightly grasped the back of her neck. He closed his eyes, giving his attention to the full measure of his gift. Zenith illuminated the runes on his forearm, accompanied by a low-pitched whir.

After a few minutes, he popped his eyes open. "Moons Karra, is there any part of you not welted or bruised?"

She looked past him to the pile of grotvonen bodies. "There was a bit of a welcome party. My low back on the right side hurts the most. If you can do something about that, I'll manage fine."

Tovnik shook his head in disbelief. "That's because you've got a collection of blood around your kidney. The bruise there rivals the one on the backside of your head. Give me a moment."

Over the next several minutes, while the rest of the expedition team descended, Tovnik mended what he could. He let go of her neck and forearm and stumbled back a few steps. Karragin reached forward to steady him. She suddenly felt much better. Her breaths pulled in full and easy. She didn't realize how severely her pains had limited her until they were gone. Now all she sensed were minor bruises on her arms and legs, no worse than what she might incur from a rough day of sparring.

Tovnik blew air through his cheeks. "I'm fine. Just don't count on that again until we get out of this place."

Karragin quickly ran through what she knew of Savnah's other quad members. Dexxin was a capable archer and invaluable for his ability to send. Argul had mastered alchemics and possessed some skill with munitions. Runta had studied at Callinora, but Karragin had seen her bungle more than one healing, leading to more harm than good among some of her fellow Outriders. Thankfully the medic made up for her ineptitude in her skill with the bow.

"You're the only real healer down here, Tov." Karra pitched her voice low so only he could hear. "Save your strength for Amniah, in case she needs you."

Over the next twenty minutes, the rest of the expedition descended through the cavern. Nolan arrived shortly after Tovnik. He jogged over in obvious concern looking first to Karragin, then Savnah.

"We're fine, Nolan. There are several tunnels out of here. See to finding Amniah's trail, and we can head out when everyone is here," said Karragin.

A marble bobbed up and down in Nolan's neck as he swallowed, but he didn't give voice to his concern. He shook his head and followed her order. After activating his gift, he wandered around the cavern in a strange serpentine pattern. Eventually, he squatted down at the corpse of one of the armored warriors, retrieved something, then made a frantic search among the other grotvonen.

"Nolan, what is it, what have you found?" asked Karragin.

Nolan turned from his squatted position, holding a handful of thick, black hair. The locks were crudely twisted through fluted bone. "It's Amniah's, all of it."

Karragin examined one of the strange fetiches a moment, then gathered the rest and placed them inside one of her inner pockets. "Did you find anything more? Anything with skin or blood?"

Nolan curled his lip in reflexive revulsion. "No, thank the Giver. Her trail leads down that tunnel."

"Good. Savnah, you mind holding the rear guard?" asked Karragin.

"This is your mission." Savnah shrugged. "Besides, the grot are as likely to come from the rear as the front." The Outrider smiled. "I think I might have to use that one."

Karragin frowned in confusion.

Savnah rolled her eyes. "Grots from the rear, you know like blow mud, barbarians at the gate . . . churn brown butter?"

The usually reserved Dexxin chimed in. "How about sink a slug or birth a brown snake?"

"Ew Dexx, that's just . . . ew," said Savnah. "No, I think, 'drop a grot' sounds about right."

"Alright," Karragin interrupted the banter with a harsh tone. She understood how some Outriders needed the strange humor to deflate the trauma of Nolan's discovery. At the moment, though, she intended to make the grot pay for any harm that might have come to Amniah.

"We can discuss the finer points of defecation when we find Amniah and get out of here. For now, Nolan, you are on point with me. Tovnik will follow on torch. Savnah, your quad has the rear guard. Let's skin out."

Nolan led them to a ten-foot-wide channel off the side of the main cavern. Torchlight reflected off silver flakes in the coarse rock. As they descended the winding path, rivulets of water streaked down the walls, gathering as a small stream on the cave floor. Over the next several hours, Nolan led them through winding tunnels and enormous caverns. The first several channels they passed were irregular and naturally occurring, but the farther they traveled, the more pronounced the influence of the grotvonen became.

The creatures had straightened and reinforced the walls with blocks of stone. Trenches cut into the edge of the rock diverted water in streams, which trickled along while keeping the central path dry. They crept along a wide arc of stone that acted as a rock bridge spanning a craggy cavern. Light from Tovnik's torch dimmed before reaching the ceiling or the floor below.

At the far end of the bridge, Karragin drew them to a halt at a small landing before another tunnel. She unstopped a flask of water and passed it around. Everyone except Nolan took a moment to kneel or sit. Her brother stared with purpose out into the darkness, then turned back.

"Something's not right," he said.

"Grind me three times in each hole, tracker. You're brilliant!" scoffed Savnah. "We're five miles deep into the grot, and you're just now noticing that something's not right?"

Nolan flushed. Karragin knew he was uncertain how to address the gruff prime but waited to see how the situation would play out. To her surprise, Savnah elbowed him in the shoulder and handed him her canteen in apology. "Sorry, all this mucking around in the dark has me scratchy as burlap panties. I keep waiting for another wave of grot to rush in from the shadows, you know?"

Nolan took a long draw of water. "I know what you mean, and I don't think you're going to like what I was going to say."

"What has your gift revealed, Nolan?" asked Karragin.

"The grot tracks . . . they're everywhere, and they're hot," said Nolan. He waited for a response. When nobody spoke up, he continued, "So, where are all the grot? For more than an hour now, the grot sign has been fresh. It's almost like they're running away from us."

"What about the skip trail? Have you seen any of that down here?" asked Karragin.

"Yes," said Nolan. "It runs along Amniah's trail down this next tunnel."

"Alright then, let's change things up," said Karragin. "Savnah and I on point, then Nolan and Tovnik with Runta. Dexxin and Argul, wait here five minutes, then bring up the rear guard."

They assumed the formation Karragin suggested and began the descent into the tunnel. The path dropped in a tight spiral that wound in at least three complete turns as far as Karragin could tell.

"They might not be able to smith metal, but the little grinders can sure dig. There's no way this is a natural formation," said Savnah.

Karragin found herself nodding agreement but chose not to say anything. If there were grot or worse waiting at the bottom of the spiral, she intended to give worse than she got. She and Savnah crouched low and fanned out when the tunnel opened into a long cavern. They formed up and crept ahead. The leading edge of the torchlight flickered over something lying on the ground.

"That's Amniah, her signal is hot, and she's alive!" said Nolan. He stepped forward, but Karragin grabbed him by the collar of his leathers and pulled him back.

"Everybody wait!" she hissed. "Form up in a perimeter, and we'll move slowly. Light yourselves up and watch the shadows."

Everyone in the group channeled zenith into their respective gift. Even the healer song whirred as a faint murmur. They formed a rough circle facing forward and yet attentive to the shifting shadows to the sides. With slow purpose, they moved toward the mass lying on the cavern floor.

"Karra, I think we're in for a muddle," said Nolan. From just beyond the radius of the torchlight, something shifted in the shadows. Karragin raised her saber in time to deflect one of the crude spears.

All at once, the grotvonen charged. Tovnik or Runta ignited another hot-top, and the sparking torch rolled on the ground in front of Karra. Somewhere between eight to ten armored grotvonen recoiled from the light, roaring in guttural growls of surprise and pain. Karragin used their momentary blindness to surge ahead.

She built momentum and punched forward, catching a warrior low on the breastplate with a fist. The grotvonen's guttural roar pinched off in a painful squelch as the armor caved in, and it flew back, toppling several blinded grotvonen into a heap. She turned, prepared to slash out when an arrow took the next grot in the cheek. Running past the fallen enemy, she circled around, slashing at knees, elbows, and armpits, removing limbs with each zenith-enforced blow.

The tumbled pile of grotvonen warriors rose to their feet in time for her to take one at the neck while shattering the thigh bone of another with a snapped kick. The rest crumpled forward over fatal arrow wounds. With her side of the cavern secure, she turned to see Savnah take a spear through the thigh. The prime head-butted the grotvonen warrior, then clapped her moonblade axes together at the beast's neck. Its head lurched back, bubbling and frothing fluids in a death fountain.

Karragin ran over and watched as Savnah casually tried to remove the spear but could not get enough leverage. "Karra, mind helping me out? Seems a grot fancied sticking me with its wood and left some behind."

"You really don't feel that at all?" asked Karragin.

"You have your gifts, and I have mine," said Savnah. "I told you I was the toughest bitch out here."

Karragin sheathed her blade, placed a hand on Savnah's shoulder for leverage, then jerked the crude spear back. It released from her outer thigh with a crack, and blood welled up in the wound.

"Runta, see to Savnah's wound. Tovnik and Nolan, check on Amniah," Karragin ordered. She held a firm hand over the wound on Savnah's leg until Runta took over, controlling the bleeding. After the whirring murmur of the healer song escalated, Karragin made the rounds, ensuring the final death of the grotvonen. By the time she returned, Tovnik was preoccupied with his ministrations of Amniah.

"I count nineteen. That's a reasonable force, I suppose, but I thought there would be more," said Karragin. "And where is the umbral?"

"I have a better question. Where are Dexxin and Argul?" asked Savnah. "They were supposed to trail us by only a few minutes."

"Taker's breath," Karragin cursed, then ran back up the spiral tunnel. She emerged onto the platform in time to see Dexxin shoot his last arrow.

The sender yelled at his companion. "Argul! It's too late. Come back!"

The munitions man crouched on the rock bridge ahead of him. On the far side, a wave of grotvonen surged toward the stone bridge. Leading them across the stone walkway, a tall creature with a flat head lumbered forward on legs that bent at odd angles.

The umbral's body sprouted three arrow shafts, but it seemed unaffected. With casual ease, the creature produced a globe of murky blackness in its hand. Karragin watched in horrified fascination as the umbral threw the globe at Argul. It landed just beside him, hissing like a cracked egg plopped into a hot iron skillet. The munitions man recoiled, and Karragin saw a hole where the substance dissolved the stone.

Grind me. That's a nadir strike for sure.

Karragin's attention drew back to Argul. He sparked a hot-top to life and wedged it into a crevice in the bridge, then popped up and sprinted back toward them, yelling, "Get back! Get—"

BOOM!

A massive detonation threw Dexxin into Karragin, and they landed several feet inside the spiral tunnel. Violent shaking and rumbling vibrations followed the initial explosion. The tunnel's natural curve blocked most of the flying rock and debris, but a heavy cloud of smoke and dust roiled over them. Karragin buried her face in her leathers and blinked to clear her eyes.

The smell of sulfur and ash lingered in the thick air. A pressure settled into her ears, and they hummed with a strange ringing. Dexxin lit a torch, but it was minutes before they could see out of the tunnel and to the platform through the thick haze in the wake of the devastation.

She sensed Dexxin tap her on the shoulder. He seemed to be yelling something, but the trauma of Argul's explosion had rendered her deaf. Karragin took the torch and crept forward out of the tunnel. Argul's munition hadn't just left a gap in the bridge. The entire bridge, Argul, the umbral, and a good number of grotvonen were gone. . . and so was their only way back across the massive cavern.

Chapter Eighteen: Pithing the Gourd

"Not like that," said Tarkannen. "Sloppy. You waste the flow of nadir. You can accomplish the same task with far less and avoid the frenze. Tighten up your control and compress all those loose fibers into one cord."

A young Volencia looked up from the haze created by the unorganized, wispy fibers of nadir that billowed out from the sigil on her forearm. Tarkannen stood, leaning with one shoulder against the stone interior of the wine cellar of her family estate. Lamplight flickered over the myriad of black sigils painted on his face like moonlight over a slick of oil on water.

Most people regarded him with fear and suspicion. But from the first time they met, Volencia felt intrigued. After the "incident at the well," as her mother, Shalla, called it, the abrogator had earned Shalla's trust. His coin paid for the best care from the healers from Callinora, and his unique gift allowed her sons to recover with almost no pain.

Volencia labored to focus her control as her master directed. After a struggle, she ignored the cold, stinging sensation of nadir as it channeled through the new sigils on her forearms. Where zenith vibrated with warm currents, nadir flared across her sigils with a cold, tingly sensation. The discomfort of channeling the reductive force was nothing compared to the pain she'd endured in stripping away her aqua rune. She ignored the frigid sting of the power coursing through the black sigil on her arm and bent the nadir to her purpose. The loose black strands that blossomed from her forearm gathered as one prehensile extension of her will.

"That's better," said Tarkannen. "Now, see if you can lift this goblet without breaking it. Precision and control are far more important than simple force. With zenith, you were restricted to the manipulation of water. Through the accurate control of nadir, you can accomplish a far wider range of tasks."

Tarkannen held the goblet forth on an open palm. Volencia felt the coil of nadir wrap around the goblet. The onyx tentacle gripped the glass and conveyed the sensation of ice sliding over ice. She perceived the pressure of the goblet, but nothing more. When she employed zenith, the currents of water became palpable and malleable in a much more textured and tactile manner. Holding anything through the filter of nadir reminded her of coming inside from the cold with ice-numbed fingers.

With delicate purpose, she lifted the goblet, swung it across the room, and set it down on a small table. The task complete, she released her command of nadir. The sigils on her forearm rippled once, then settled into a dormant state. She realized that she panted a little, not from exertion but from elation. She felt invigorated.

"I can do more. Give me another task," said Volencia.

Tarkannen studied her a moment, then retrieved a small green gourd from a shelf and placed it on the table. "Alright. This time, try to summon just a sliver of nadir and focus it into a tight blade or even a needle, then pierce this gourd."

Volencia placed all her concentration into her forearm and felt nadir chill the sigil, causing it to wriggle on her skin. Wispy black tendrils extended from the sigil, then fused into a thin dart. She directed the black barb forward but struggled to make it pierce the gourd. Instead, her prodding caused the gourd to spin and wobble as her projection failed to skewer the object.

"That's close, but instead of forcing the nadir into the gourd, let it slide in, feel it . . . reduce away the resistance," said Tarkannen.

Volencia directed the tip of the nadir pick to settle on the gourd's surface and waited. She resisted the urge to push the pick forward and instead coaxed the nadir to remove any resistance. Her eyes widened in fascination as she felt the sliver of nadir melt into the gourd, burrowing a perfect hole.

She stopped channeling and stepped forward to inspect the new defect in the husk. "It was just like you said, Master. You don't push the nadir in; you let it eliminate the resistance. Let's do something else!"

"No. That's enough for today, lest you develop the frenze. We have a difficult enough time keeping your new gift secret without that," he said.

"But—"

"No Volencia, I insist. Unless you want your mother and everyone else to think you're addicted to vivith, you must learn to pace yourself. Your will is strong. That's why I chose you. But even you can't hide the signs of the frenze."

Volencia folded her arms to hide the subtle tremor she felt in her fingers, but the action only made her aware of her thrumming heartbeat. "I don't understand why I can't claim the sigils of nadir as you did."

Tarkannen inhaled a deep breath and seemed to require a moment to master his frustration. "I know. But I don't think it's possible. The way I went about it was even more difficult, and mistakes were made. The pain you felt when we stripped away your runes was nothing compared to that. You might have the capacity for that kind of sacrifice someday, but not today. I know that you are frustrated, but be patient. As you learn control, I can engrave more sigils, and then you will safely command more and more nadir. Until then, be sure that your eyes aren't bigger than your stomach. Understand?"

"Yes, Master," she said. "If I try to channel too much nadir before I am ready, it will send me into the frenze."

"And?" he pressed the lesson further.

"And the world isn't ready to see all that we can become and will move to stop us," she replied.

The cellar door at the top of the stairs opened, casting daylight onto the steps. Volencia unrolled her shirt sleeve to cover the dark sigils on her forearm as Veldrek descended. Her brother carried a steaming loaf of bread. The right side of his profile showed a handsome face. As he reached the cellar floor, Veldrek turned to approach them. A purple scar disappeared under a patch over his left eye and puckered up his cheek, making him appear to squint under the eyepatch.

"Mother thought you two could use some sustenance," said her older brother. "How go the history lessons?"

"Your sister is a quick study. Come here, boy, and let me inspect your injury again."

Veldrek set the bread on a small table and approached Tarkannen. Long fingers embellished with delicate black sigils lifted the patch covering Veldrek's face. Smooth skin had sealed over the unnatural crater marred by an angry purple scar.

"The healers seem to have managed their work very well. Does it cause you any more pain?" asked Tarkannen.

Veldrek offered a soft smile. "No, not since you helped me, my lord. It only itches a little. And Aldrik comes out of his splints in a week."

Tarkannen hoisted a satchel over his shoulder. "That's good news. Volencia, study hard but mind what I told you about pacing yourself."

He turned to climb the stairs. "Are we done for today?" she asked.

"Yes, I have other students I need to check on this evening. I will return in a week to check on your progress. Until then, remember today's lesson: bring your intention into tight focus, and you can accomplish more than you could with simple unbridled strength."

Volencia awoke from the dream and stretched her feet inside her bedroll. Frost gathered on her eyelashes and brows, an unavoidable effect of the dark veil she wore across her marred face. It took a moment for her to orient to her surroundings. Though she remained self-conscious of her disfigurement, the dead man lying beside her would never comment. She considered removing the silky shroud while alone, but her scars were sensitive to the elements, so she kept it in place.

Turning to her side, she looked at the body of Vecks, her guide into the mountains northwest of Dernegia. "There never was much of a chance that I was going to let you walk out of here alive. You were a good grind on a cold night, but you talked too much and snored even louder."

The dead man lay with his head listed to the side, exposing a pinprick at the back of his skull. The black defect marked the point of entry from her nadir pick. Over the years, she'd perfected the technique, directing the nadir through a tiny opening, then expanding it to dissolve any resistance once inside.

There was something elegant in the way the weapon had ended him in the early morning hours. *No mess, no blood, no sign to anyone but an abrogator that you didn't die of exposure. Neat and tidy.*

After extricating herself from her bedroll, she pulled on her boots, then searched through his pockets and belongings, looking for anything that might tie the two of them together. Finding nothing, she retrieved the coin she had previously paid him, then chewed on a piece of salted meat. She sat beside the corpse in quiet contemplation, reflecting on her prior month of travel.

Her journey to the mountain range's craggy base had proved arduous. Mounts bore her west from Callish across the Southlands. Then she'd negotiated passage on different merchant vessels north to Vargast, then Beskin, and finally to a small port town southwest of Dernegia. That much of the journey took three weeks.

More time than I cared to lose, but still faster than slogging through the untamed wilds of the Northlands.

An artisan in Dernegia had paid her a fair price for a few trinkets and a gemstone necklace. The extra coin provided for a day to rest in suitable accommodations. The next day, she'd solicited Vecks and provisioned herself with supplies and two high-quality mounts. She pushed her guide and the animals hard, using nadir when necessary to diminish their fatigue. Several days ago, she began to rely on stilben root tea to dampen the early stages of the frenze. The calming tincture allowed her to keep her mind focused, or so she thought.

They'd arrived at the foothills of the mountains last night, and Volencia's patience withered under the weight of the malady. She didn't just feel restless or edgy. She suspected that Vecks was going to try something in her sleep. "You were going to kill me and leave me here for the wolves, weren't you?"

Even as she spoke the words, some deeper part of herself knew that channeling too much nadir had made her paranoid. She used her restless, nervous energy to good purpose and broke camp. With the horses tethered together, she led them along a narrow game trail that wound along the ridgeline, climbing up through the frost line and into a gap between two mountain peaks. After several hours of hiking, the path dropped into a rugged canyon lined by craggy cliffs.

She remounted and descended through a winding ravine left from a dry stream. The twisted path ended at a small lake bed with a patch of ice at the gorge's center.

Dead end. Well, now that was a grinding waste of time. . . or was it?

Loose rock and rubble scattered from a ledge ahead and to her right. Her mount curled back its lip, inhaled, blew air out through its nose, and tightened the muscles around its eyes. A glance back revealed that the other horse stood tense as well, with tail tucked down. Their vigilant behavior lasted several minutes, then passed.

Volencia dismounted and stroked the horse along its muzzle and neck in reassurance. "If I'm right, they know we're here but won't show themselves until it's dark. So you have until then, my friend."

After collecting two armloads of wood, she made a small fire. She left the horses to nibble at the dried scrub along the banks of the lakebed. As the sun dipped behind the ridgeline, shadows swept over the canyon, plunging the area into frosty darkness. She continued her patient vigil. The horses returned, and she tethered them to a stake. Several hours later, after turning the embers and adding wood to the fire, clacking noises echoed distantly across the canyon.

Finally. Let's get this over with.

She grabbed two rocks and struck them together in rapid succession five times. The harsh sound echoed into the night, followed by a chorus of clicking and clacking noises, high pitch hoots, and guttural howls. Eventually, at the edge of the firelight, restless shadows shifted about. Several grotvonen lumbered forward, shielding their eyes and squinting. Some paced back and forth on their knuckles. A group of larger warriors adorned in ill-fitting armor and wielding spears approached with a swaggering gait.

Volencia stood and slammed the stones together again, repeating the same challenge with five harsh strikes. The largest of the grotvonen pulled its lips back to reveal curved fangs that protruded up from its lower jaw. The beast almost seemed to chuckle based on its clipped ululations and sharp hoots. It scratched casually at its groin, then raised a spear to the masses gathered in the darkness. A thunder of clicks and howls erupted.

Without warning, the beast crouched and leaped in an arc while holding the spear with considerable finesse. Volencia had already summoned enough nadir for the task. A tentacle of her power whipped forward with a killing edge. The lash passed through the warrior, snuffing out its battle cry in a squeal of surprise. The beast landed a few feet short of her and stood puzzled for a moment. A burbled cough escaped its lips before the top third of its chest slid off like a plane of ice sheared away from a cliffside.

All the distant ululations and clacks muted to a murmur of low-pitch hoots. Volencia picked up the two rocks and cracked them together in the same challenge. Through the shadows, something larger approached, announcing itself first by the scatter of loose rock and then by an even louder roar. A grondle strode forth, black curved horns reflecting the firelight. The beast pushed through the pack of smaller grotvonen. On its back rode the largest grotvonen she had ever seen.

The rider hopped down. It wore fitted armor plating and held a heavy double-bladed axe in one hand. The warrior lifted the weapon with ease, bouncing the haft on a muscled shoulder. It raised its chin and grimaced, pulling thick pale lips back in a snarl, then spoke as if the words caused it pain. Speech, thick with a guttural accent and originating from an unnatural place deep in its throat, came forth stuttered but understandable. "I, Grasdok of Brognaus. You walk on Brognaus land."

Volencia raised her voice to speak over the clamor of noise. "I do! Tarkannen sent me!"

Grasdok sauntered around the inner edge of the firelight a few steps. Her horses whinnied and bucked, tugging at their tethers in frantic efforts to escape. The warrior cocked its head, then lunged forward with alarming speed and agility. He cleaved the axe through the spine of first one and then the other horse in two easy swings.

"Brognaus eat well tonight!" said Grasdok.

Volencia watched as several grotvonen scurried over the carcasses, collecting the blood into gourds. She knew the horde would likely take her mounts, and the loss did not affect her. Instead, she schemed over the best way to demonstrate her superiority without causing offense. Fortunately, the Brognaus leader decided for her.

"You raise challenge. Meet Guldek!" Grasdok pointed to the grondle that had acted as his mount. The half-man, half-bull roared in acceptance.

Volencia summoned more nadir and nodded once. She waited for the beast to rear back, then attacked without delay. Thick, shadowed coils erupted from her palms and lurched forward, strangling around the grondle. In a show of force that pressed her stamina, she thrashed the grondle around, scattering the smaller grotvonen. She tangled its legs, slammed it onto its flank, then forced the tentacles to constrict. The grondle grunted in pain, eyes widened either by fear or surprise as it searched for an escape. With all the grace and casual disregard of a lazy house cat, she sauntered forward, keeping her eyes fixed on Grasdok.

One hand controlled the nadir coils. With the other, she produced a single onyx shard of nadir. She directed the blade to sink into the creature's muscled shoulder, removing any resistance to its passage. The beast snorted and thrashed in panic, but her coils of nadir held it firm while the probing shard continued to burrow. She sensed the tip of the blade approach the grondle's quivering heart and cocked her head to the side to give Grasdok a chance to save his mount.

The grotvonen chieftain leaned forward with what could only be construed as a look of fascination. With a flick of her finger, the nadir blade plunged into the grondle's heart. In but moments, the beast grunted once, then lay still. She withdrew the tentacles, then, for appearance more than anything else, slashed the nadir blade through the grondle's neck, decapitating the head.

Volencia stifled the flow of nadir and resisted a strange urge to craft more of the deadly tentacles and lay waste to everything around her. Her heart thrummed, and she held tremulous hands on her waist. She felt certain that if this Grasdok gave her reason for violence, she would be unable to restrain herself.

Instead of summoning more nadir, she lifted the grondle head by the horns. The weight of the piece surprised her. With a grunt, she tossed it toward Grasdok. The head rolled a few times, coming to rest staring directly at the Brognaus leader.

"Tonight, the Brognaus eat *very* well!" shouted Volencia. Grasdok pulled his lips back in a savage mockery of a smile, jutting his lower jaw out to accentuate his sharp tusks. He raised his axe in acceptance and roared.

Chapter Nineteen: Follow the Wind

Nolan stood at the edge of the rocky outcropping where the rock bridge had previously connected. Zenith infused his arca prime, and he cast a wide probing net out into the cavernous darkness. On Karragin's order, he repeated the survey several times an hour, searching for any new signs of grotvonen or the umbral. Both above and far below, the resonance of their passing sung through his gift, but all the signals felt cold.

He kicked a stone over the edge and listened, expecting to hear it clack against the bottom of the cavern. After nearly a minute with no sound, he walked back down the spiral path to the cave where the others waited.

"Find anything new, scout boy?" asked Savnah. Sarcasm flavored her words more than usual, an indication of their collective fatigue and frustration. The harsh, rhythmic rasp of a whetstone over a crescent moonblade echoed in the chamber.

Nolan gazed across the room at the others. Their faces and uniforms, splattered with gore and cave dust, bore evidence of the prior battle. In the shadows of the cave, Savnah and Karragin, in particular, looked almost like one of the dark-skinned people he imagined from the western coast. He had read about sailors from Besken and Vargast and wondered if his sister could pass among them. Only Savnah's palms, rubbed free from much of the grime, betrayed her true skin color.

What's to become of us down here?

"There's no sign of the umbral or the grot returning," said Nolan. "So, we have that at least. How is Amniah?"

Tovnik sat with his back resting against the cave wall near the young woman. The medic nodded his head from side to side to indicate that her condition remained unchanged. Amniah lay curled in the fetal position, awake but staring with a vacant expression. A hood covered her bald head. Without her thick, black hair, she appeared somehow withered and small.

Nolan watched her breathe in and out slowly; she rarely blinked. His attention lingered on her bandaged feet. Where the limbs should naturally extend to the toes, they tapered to unnatural, short stumps. He surmised that the umbral had cleaved off the long bones of her feet, using them to adorn the fetiches of the grotvonen warriors. After the explosion that destroyed the land bridge, Runta and Tovnik had applied their gifts to her injuries, only to find that she didn't have much that they could mend.

Her wounds, if they could be called that, ended in strange withered, blackened flesh. The grotvonen had shaved her hair to craft trophies from her bones. Nolan suppressed a pang of guilt. *We were too late.*

Tovnik was able to encourage new flesh to grow over the end of the stumps, and Runta relieved most of the pain Amniah experienced, but nobody had an answer for the woman's apparent mental trauma. If they were stranded in a cave deep in the Great Crown, Amniah seemed lost down an even darker chasm.

Karragin had spent hours whispering to the guster, trying to both draw her out from her dark shadow and learn anything valuable from the attack. The guster had yet to say anything more than a few mumbled words since they found her, and that was four days back. "Follow the wind" was all she could utter.

His sister had ordered a thorough search of the cave. After scavenging all the equipment from the grotvonen corpses, they'd dropped the rotting bodies into the cavern. Between the clubs and spear shafts they collected, they had enough material for several small cookfires. Most of the warrior types had carried pouches of some kind of dried tuber. Nolan employed his gift to ascertain that the food was edible, but that ran out yesterday.

Karragin rationed the rest of their provisions, but they were running low on water. Argul, their munitions colleague, had left a pack full of random munitions, torches, and candles. The first day stuck in the cave, they'd burned through several tapers while searching for an alternative way out.

His sister had tried to climb up into the massive cavern by the remnants of the rock bridge on three occasions. Each time, she returned frustrated by her inability to continue in the dark. Now one of the last tapers burned, casting a dim light into the chamber.

Nolan gazed absently at the small flame. "Any word from the surface yet?" he asked.

The sender, Dexxin, sat cross-legged near the candle. He lifted his head to speak with his strange, almost ethereal tone that always made Nolan wonder if Dexxin was talking to the people around him or the ones in his head. "I relayed our circumstances to my siblings, but they are both in Stone's Grasp. Your father and Overwarden Kaldera ordered immediate reinforcements, and an emergency assembly has been called to muster an army. Warden Elbiona should be able to send help, but that might still be a few days away."

"All of that is about as helpful to us as a kiss from the Taker's puckered asshole," said Savnah.

Nolan watched the edgy prime but chose not to say anything. Nobody did, not even Karragin. His sister had long ago lost her desire to correct Savnah's breaks in decorum, and Nolan couldn't help but wonder if she felt responsible for their current predicament.

Eventually, Savnah sighed with exaggeration. "Don't mind me; hunger sharpens the tongue. Moons, the next time a cave rat scampers by, I'm going to club it and eat it raw—bones, tail, and all. It can't be any worse than those grot tubers."

Nolan's stomach growled, but he didn't think he was hungry enough to eat raw cave rat. *Still, if it comes to that, wouldn't it be better to have the option at least?*

"Grind it," Karragin cursed. "That's brilliant."

"I didn't really mean I would eat raw cave rat, Karra," Savnah retreated.

Karragin waved off her explanation. "I understand, but if cave rats have a way in here, then maybe there's a different way out. Nolan, you're up. Search for any sign of things other than grot and umbral."

He walked the perimeter of the cave, casting a wide net, searching for any signs of cave rats or other living creatures. At the back of the cave, high up on a ledge, his gift thrummed with a hot signal. It was a cave rat trail that led up to a high crevice, well beyond his reach. *Somewhere up there, the resonance is strong.*

Amniah mumbled once again behind him, "Follow the wind."

Nolan turned to consider his friend. Karragin knelt beside the guster, trying to understand the meaning behind the strange mantra. Amniah stared up into the shadows of the cave, in the direction where he sensed the rat tracks. Karragin retrieved the candle and held it up high against the wall of the cave.

They stared at the guttering flame, dancing in a gentle current of air. "Follow the wind," said Karragin. "Nolan, anything? Can you sense anything at all?"

"Actually, yes. I can sense an active cave rat trail up there, over the ledge. It's higher than I can reach, but maybe you could climb up?" Nolan suggested.

Without words, she retrieved several of the makeshift spearheads from the grotvonen. She centered herself, then lunged with zenith-infused strength. At the apex of her jump, she slammed one of the spearheads into the cave wall, then used that as a handhold to hoist herself up. She plunged in a crude dagger and then another spearhead. Within minutes, she scrambled more than thirty feet up the cave wall.

"Move to your right a few feet. The signal is hot there," said Nolan.

Karragin plunged the last spearhead into the wall to create a handhold, then navigated to the area Nolan indicated. She pulled herself up and peered into a crevice. After a moment, she turned back. For the first time in several days, his sister spoke with a sense of urgency. "Nolan, there's a slight breeze up here. I can see a crevice in the wall. Toss me one of the grot clubs."

"Right here," said Savnah. The prime stood just behind him, watching with interest, and flipped up one of the heavy clubs. Karragin caught the weapon, then turned and bashed at a shadowed alcove. The first several strikes caused a sharp echo in the cave as the stone resisted her excavation attempt. On the fifth swing, Nolan exhaled at the sound of rock and rubble giving away.

He turned to look at Savnah. The woman arched an eyebrow at him. "Scout boy, if you found a way out of here, you can slap my ass till it shines like the moon of Lellen."

"Umm, thanks, I think." Nolan felt the tops of his ears burn and couldn't help but grin. His voice cracked as he yelled to check on Karragin. "Karra!" He cleared his throat. "Karra, what's up there?"

He watched as his sister pulled herself up and over the edge of the wall into the shadows. When she returned, the smile beaming back from her blood, grime, and dust-covered face made his hopes flare. "I broke through. I think this leads to one of the carved channels the grot made to carry water, only it's dry. We can use it to crawl out of here. Toss me some rope."

Over the next hour, they packed up what they could scavenge and prepared to climb out of the cave. Eventually, they all stood circled around Amniah. None of them spoke, but Nolan sensed that none of them would leave without the guster.

"Have you tried to give her an order?" asked Savnah. "Maybe she'll respond to a military command."

"I don't think battle shock works that way," said Karragin.

Karragin knelt beside the guster and grabbed her shoulders, pulling her to a sitting position. Amniah's haunted eyes stared out from the dark recess of her hood. Karragin folded the edge of the hood back and waited.

"Amniah, Outriders stick together, and we never leave a person behind. I can carry you up and out of here, but it won't be easy, and it won't be pretty. Besides, I smell like yesterday's chamber pot. So, what do you say we get out of here and follow the wind?" Karragin asked.

Nolan knelt beside his sister. "Niah, we are so close to leaving this place. Once we make it topside, maybe you could show me Stellance and teach me how to make crown beetle pockets. What do you say?"

Amniah blinked and turned to Nolan. "I . . . I would like that very much."

"Alright then, let me help you stand," said Karragin.

The slight woman rose with her help and stumbled a few steps, then seemed to find her balance. She pulled her hood forward over her face, and a muffled voice said, "I'm ready. Let's leave this place."

They formed up at the base of the makeshift ladder Karragin had made. She began to strip off her Outrider gear to expose the runes on her arms and chest, leaving on only her smallclothes. As she tied the top around her waist, she explained her strange behavior.

"Alright, listen. When we get to the top, you have to crawl through the hole I made. It's dark, but there is only one way forward, and it opens into a crude tunnel. It's only three feet high, and we only have one candle and two torches, which we should save. I think the only light we'll have to see will be the dim illumination from our runes. Don't channel more than you have to. I have no idea how long we will have to go. As long as you don't release the zenith, the draft should not affect you for a long time. We are getting out of here, and it's still winter topside, so keep your gear with you. Any questions?"

Nobody spoke as they each began removing the layers covering their torso. Nolan shivered, but once he began to climb the wall, he forgot about his discomfort. In short order, he followed Karragin up the staked-out handholds to the shadowed alcove. They used the rope as a safety aid in case anyone dropped, which proved critical, as Amniah lacked the strength to make the ascent. Once he reached the nook, he could see where Karragin had broken through a crevice and onto a dry groove cut into the side of a three-foot-high tunnel. Rubble had long ago collapsed the passage to the right.

"Alright, brother, I'm placing you on point. I need you to use your senses to make sure we don't stumble into the grot or worse," said Karragin. "I'll be right behind you, then Dexxin and the others. Savnah has the rear guard and will make sure Amniah follows."

Nolan lifted his chin toward the cave-in. "Left it is, I guess." The pale light emitting from his runes allowed him to see only three or four feet ahead, but after a few minutes, he settled into his gift and cast his awareness forth, scanning the tunnel for any signs of grotvonen or the umbral. In this fashion, he crawled on hands and knees, searching for a way out.

The stone leeched the heat from his hands, and he stopped to tear off material from his uniform to wrap around the pads of his palms. They each took a moment to rest and reproduce Nolan's trick, then continued. After more than an hour, he developed a crick in his neck, his arms ached, and his knees burned. But somehow, he felt better. Something about the act of moving, of making progress, seemed to lighten his mood. He recalled the rhymes he used when training with the alchemist's guild.

Nettle tea will make you pee: crush six dried leaves, steep and wee. Berry of lammen for winter famine. Kaliphora settles the tum but take too much and get the runs. He smiled to himself, recalling better days when all he had to worry about was passing Master Gwillion's daily alchemy quiz.

"Karra," he said softly.

"What is it?" she asked.

"Have you noticed that this tunnel seems to be leading . . . well . . . down? I think it's taking us deeper under the Great Crown."

"I know, but what else can we do? That cave was becoming our coffin," she answered. "Have you sensed anything yet?"

"No grot or umbral, but cave rats use this channel, lots of cave rats," said Nolan.

Karragin grunted. "How are you holding up? You're the only one actually channeling. The rest of us are just infusing our runes with zenith. Any sign of the draft? Nausea? Dizziness?"

"Nothing like the last time on the Borderlands," said Nolan. "Believe me, I learned my lesson."

"Let me know if anything changes. Hold here a moment. I'm going to check on the others." With that, she pivoted on a knee and crawled back into the darkness. After a few minutes, she crawled forward and took her position behind him. Coils of rope were wrapped around her shoulders in a figure-eight pattern and trailed off into the darkness.

"What's going on, Karra?" he asked.

"It's Amniah. She doesn't look . . . she can't continue, so Savnah and I tied our Outrider tops together to make a sled."

"You're pulling her? How long can you keep that up?" he asked.

Karragin looked at him without responding. He knew from experience that his sister rarely betrayed any of the things she was feeling or thinking, but sometimes her resting asshole gaze was maddening.

"Well?" he pressed.

"Well, what?" Karragin asked.

Nolan sagged his head forward. "How long do you think you can manage it, Karra?"

"Who can say? She's much lighter than she looks, and I will channel only when I have to. Push on for now, and I'll tell you when I need a rest."

"Is she going to be alright?" asked Nolan.

He saw Karragin's shoulder shrug slightly in the dim light. "She's been through a lot. We got her moving, and this is working for now. Focus on getting us out of here and worry about Amniah if we get to the surface."

"When."

"When what?" asked Karragin.

"When we get to the surface," he said with a smile, then turned and cast his gift down the tunnel. They continued another hour, his senses able to identify the random trails of cave rats, spiders, and some kind of giant cave snail. Fortunately, the signs of grotvonen remained dormant, and there were none of the skip trails he associated with the umbral.

The tunnel eventually opened into a natural shaft that dropped into darkness. Nolan reached a hand down into the void, hoping to get a sense for the passage below, but found only emptiness. The light from his runes showed that two other channels emptied into the shaft, both within reach. He pushed back and turned to Karragin.

"This tunnel drops into a shaft but also connects with two others. Cave rats have the run of the place, but I can't tell where to go now," he said.

"Any sign of grot or umbral?" asked Karragin.

"No. Those tracks ran cold a few hours ago."

"Alright, let's stop here for a break." Karragin cleared her throat and spoke loud enough for the group to hear. "We're at a crossroads up here. We'll rest a bit, then determine the best way forward."

Nolan needed no encouragement and flopped onto his back. He thought about crawling to check on Amniah, but exhaustion overtook him. The muscles in his arms throbbed, and his legs burned from knee to ankle from the relentless crawling. He unwound the wrappings around his hands and placed them under his armpits for warmth, then donned his topcoat. After discharging the little remaining zenith coursing over his runes, he allowed his eyes to close. He awoke some time later feeling as cold and stiff as the deep mountain stone on which he lay.

A lilting voice spoke his name, and he rolled his shoulders a few times. Dexxin's face appeared in the dim light of the sender's runes. The sender waited for Nolan to get his bearings, then pointed at Karragin. His sister crouched near the shaft, the telltale signs of zenith playing across the runes on her right forearm. Nolan looked over her shoulder to see three sets of beady red eyes staring at her from one of the connecting tunnels.

"Got yourself a few admirers, I see," he whispered over her shoulder.

Karragin spoke without turning, keeping her focus attuned to the trio of cave rats. "Can you get a fix on the one in the middle? The fat one? I think he might know the way out. I can only get a sense for what they have been eating."

"How does that help us exactly?" asked Nolan.

"The fat one has been eating from the marrow of a dead carcass, maybe a mountain goat. The last time I checked, mountain goats lived on the outside of the Great Crown, not the inside," said Karrragin.

"Oh . . . right! Can you entice the fat one to come closer, then maybe pluck a hair? Without some kind of direct connection, I'm not sure I can separate its trail from the hundreds of others in these tunnels."

A low growl of frustration rumbled from his sister. "This might take some time."

Nolan watched as Karragin sat in silent communion with the creatures. The other two rats sniffed at the air and wandered off, but the larger one remained enthralled. Several minutes passed, and the rodent lifted its snout into the air and began to sway. Zenith flared as a scintillating azure light from Karragin's runes. Sweat beaded on her brow, and she reached forward, then plucked a tuft of fur from the rat.

"Will that do?" she asked through gritted teeth.

Nolan awakened his gift and sent a probing tendril through the hair follicles marking the creature's unique pattern. He cast his awareness into the passages and easily found the residue of the rat's passing among all the other crisscrossing trails. "Perfect. I have it, Karra."

Karragin lingered a moment longer, laboring with her gift, then seemed to push at the rat with a gesture of her hand into the air. The creature blinked a few times, sniffed at the air, then scurried down one of the connecting tunnels.

"Tell me you can follow that thing out of here," said Karragin.

"I have him. What did you do?" asked Nolan.

"First, I had to enthrall him with images of food. That one is really fond of dead goat. You can't imagine how hard it is to make a rat see and smell dead goat. I might never get that taste out of the back of my mouth. Anyway, then I made him think he was hungry for more."

"You think it will work?" asked Nolan.

"We can only hope. Sometimes the Giver gives," said Karragin.

Nolan rewrapped his hands and awakened his gift to follow the fresh trail from the goat-fattened rat. He scrambled across to the other tunnel without delay. After another hour of labor, the passage spiraled, then sloped down and spilled into a proper tunnel large enough for them to stand. The trail from the cave rat led off to the right.

He waited for everyone to gather. Karragin lit one of their last remaining torches to reveal distinctive chisel marks in the stone, a sure indication of another crude grotvonen tunnel. Nolan sucked in a breath at the sight of Amniah. The dim torchlight accentuated the shadows of her withered cheeks and sunken eyes.

They each took a moment to pull on their soiled Outrider tops. Karragin hoisted the guster onto her back, and they carried on. He shared a look with his sister and prepared to offer to relieve her burden. But she cut him off with a simple nudge of her chin as if to say, "The Giver smile on you, brother. You have your job, and I have mine; now see to it."

And so he did. Nolan alternated between sifting for the cave rat trail and any fresh grotvonen signs. The tunnel opened up into an enormous cavern, and he led them across to a connecting chasm. The hours blurred together in a series of dark tunnels and twisted caverns, all faintly outlined by his tenuous connection to the rat.

Just as he started to doubt that the creature was leading them out of the cave system, a chill breeze of humid air wafted past his face.

Nolan turned back to the group. "I think I hear a waterfall."

None of them spoke. Instead, they pushed on with an urgency spurred by excitement. Finally, he stumbled out into the night air, boots crunching on fresh snow. They stood to the side of a small waterfall cascading from high overhead. The current had long ago cut a channel through the mountain rock.

Smooth mounds of ice, like massive pearls, lined the sides of the stream and reflected the pale light of the blue moon. The descent down looked like no easy task, but from this height, he could see that they would reach the plains. The crisp alpine air and bright stars overhead brought tears to his eyes.

He surrendered his hold on zenith and considered dropping to his knees, but his shins still burned from all the hours of crawling. He watched as each of his fellow spelunkers left the tunnels with different expressions. Karragin stepped forward with Amniah asleep on her back. His sister hitched the guster higher on her shoulders with ease, then winked. "Well done, brother."

Dexxin exited and seemed both preoccupied with the stars filling the night sky and attentive to an inner dialogue. Runta walked out, weary but smiling, followed by Tovnik, who patted him on the shoulder. Savnah stepped forward and knuckled the small of her back.

"Ahh, now that's a better sight than any I've seen in a long while," said the prime. "If I ever volunteer to go underground again, somebody grind me sideways with something very stabby or pointy."

Nolan couldn't help but giggle, and in short order, they all seemed to chuckle.

"What now, sir?" Nolan asked Karragin.

Karragin frowned at the panoramic scene before them. The light of the moon of Baellen shone full and bright, illuminating the plains before them. "We still have quite a climb and then a hike to get out of the Great Crown, but, wait—"

She turned and searched the night sky. "We're not in Aarindorn anymore. Baellen should sit inside the summit of the Great Crown, not behind it. Taker's breath; that's the Borderlands. We've come out the other side."

Chapter Twenty: A Message Left in Stone

Ksenia lifted her eyes from the ancient tome and pinched the bridge of her nose. She sighed in frustration and released her pull on zenith, allowing her linguistic rune to fade to dormancy. The tedious, persistent application of her gift produced a headache and frustration but no clues to the ancient language.

Not yet anyway.

When she began to work with the text left by Weckles, the steward of the archives, she'd looked upon the task as a mundane burden. Then she considered the tome's age and possible significance to Aarindorian history. Penned at a time just before the Cataclysm, the words might reveal insights into the founding of Aarindorn and the ancestors who laid the foundation at Stone's Grasp.

Aside from her rides with Winter, her time struggling with the archaic language was the only moment she didn't feel confined or manipulated into position by her mother. Now that she actually wanted to unravel the mysteries of the text, her failure to do so only amounted to more frustration. Written in High Aarindorian, the basics of the language still eluded her.

Why couldn't our ancestors just speak Kindred like the rest of Karsk?

She stood and walked around the library table, one of many in the royal archives. It felt good to stretch the muscles in her neck and back. The clatter of stiff-soled shoes on the stone floor announced the approach of someone from the far end of the archives. The steps grew louder until, at last, Vinnedesta rounded a bookshelf.

"There you are," said the scribe. "Are you still at it with that thing? I don't know why you bother."

"It's a form of self-masochism," said Ksenia. She tapped at a small, weathered book sitting beside the ancient tome. "This one came easy. It's in Low Aarindorian. I think the artisans and stone masons from long ago used it."

"How so?" asked Vinnedesta.

"It uses a lot of figures and numbers. That's how I was able to figure it out, I think. But from there, it goes into the weeds detailing the placement of a fulcrum relative to the lever strength and payload . . . the whole thing made my teeth ache."

"Why did you bother with any of that at all?"

"I was hoping I could cross-reference something to unlock the secrets to High Aarindorian. That's what's in Weckles's ancient tome," said Ksenia.

"I'm guessing that you didn't get very far. You look exhausted. Why put yourself through any of it?" asked Vinnedesta.

"I suppose it's my chance to make a difference. There's so much going on in the kingdom. Maybe I can find something that unites us instead of divides us."

Vinnedesta offered a rueful smile. "Was it that bad?"

Ksenia sat back in the chair, elbows on the table, and plopped her chin onto her hands. "We started with the routine slate of petitioners. But then we went into a closed session. The regent and vice regent sent formal declarations to the noble houses and duchies regarding their intent to muster an army. Then they debated over the best way to engage the ungifted who are, apparently, organized and in control of two minor trade guilds." Ksenia sat back and rubbed at her temples. "Maybe I shouldn't be telling you all of this, confidentiality and all."

Vinnedesta shrugged her shoulders. "I understand. But if it makes you feel better, I already knew about both of those issues from a similar session yesterday." She patted a reassuring hand on Ksenia's, then leaned in with a hushed voice. "How did the old lynx seem to you today? Yesterday, the vice regent tried to get him to consider meeting with representatives of the noble houses to discuss abandoning the monarchy in favor of democracy."

"He seemed fine, but they never spoke of anything like that. What do you mean, exactly?" asked Ksenia.

"I was in the middle of recording the session when the vice regent indicated I should stop writing, but he didn't dismiss me, which seemed rather strange. Then they began to speak about the strategic value of entertaining the group. The regent expressed concern that the meeting would only legitimize the issue. While Chancle agreed, he thought it might be the best way to get the noble houses to be more agreeable to support the efforts to raise the army."

"When I took this assignment, I don't think I realized how many times we would bear witness to those kinds of conversations," said Ksenia.

"I know, right? The two of them never seem to catch a moment of peace," said Vinnedesta.

"How did the regent react to Chancle's proposal?" asked Ksenia.

"Not well, at first. But then he seemed to retreat into his gift for a time. I swear, it's like he can sense when someone is duplicitous. Anyway, he said he would consider the meeting. Then they discussed the reinforcements to the Outriders in the Great Crown."

The conversation stalled as Ksenia considered everything her colleague revealed. Eventually, Vinnedesta leaned in further. "Can you even believe it? I mean grondle, the grot, and an umbral reappearing after all these years, and so close. Have you heard any new details today? Is your brother safe?"

"The latest sending this morning indicated that they have the entrance to the warren secured. And the team that descended into the caves emerged somewhere out on the Borderlands. That bit of information did seem to ease the regent's mind. I can't imagine what that man must go through navigating the stresses of his office, all while wondering if his children are safe."

A scholar waddled past carrying a bulky collection of texts and sat at an adjacent table. Ksenia pushed her chair back, bursting the bubble of their intimate conversation. She closed the ancient text and patted her hand on the weathered cover. "Well, I've struggled about as much as I care to for today. I found a phrase similar to my last name in here and can't even place its syntax or meaning."

"What phrase is that?" asked the scribe.

"*Balladur Cor Delledence*," said Ksenia. "It sounds so similar to Balladuren, and it feels vaguely familiar, but I can't place the words."

Vinnedesta stood, her round face beaming. "Come with me, Kess. I might know where we've seen that before."

Ksenia returned the ancient tome to the head archivist, then followed her friend through twisted bookshelves. They exited the archives and walked through hallways bustling with activity. The second tier of Stone's Grasp housed many of the administrative offices and buildings. With all of the kingdom's changes, from the initiation of trade routes to the south to mustering an army to combat the grotvonen menace, the clerks and officials bustled about with frenetic energy.

They meandered through the crowd, eventually finding an exit to the outer courtyard. The brisk mountain air nipped at her nose and cheeks. Ksenia wasn't prepared to spend much time outside, but Vinnedesta hustled up the broad flight of stairs to the third level. They stepped inside for a moment. Vinnedesta paced with her hands under her arms, and Ksenia blew her breath through cupped hands.

After a few minutes, the round-faced scribe seemed to settle herself. "Sorry, we should have grabbed our coats. I was just so excited to show you something. I promise it will be worth it. Are you ready?"

"Where are you taking me?" asked Ksenia.

"You'll see. Have patience, Ms. Balladuren."

Vinnedesta pushed the thick outer door open and scurried up the next staircase to the fourth tier of Stone's Grasp. As they climbed the broad, curved stone steps, Ksenia held her hands under her arms and chanced a glance back toward the city. Citizens milled about outside the curtain wall. Far beyond, to the southwest, the sun reflected off Lake Ullend. While she preferred the solitude of a mountain stream or forest trail, the grandeur of the sight gave her pause. She had to admit, something about the view from their position was captivating.

She stood transfixed at the edge of the cantilevered structure jutting out from the Great Crown. A frigid gust of mountain wind caused the blue pennons to snap at the apex of the parapets. The cold brought tears to her eyes, and she blinked once, then hurried to follow after Vinnedesta.

At the top of the stairs, she rushed back inside to the warmth of the castle structure. She and Vinnedesta huddled for a few minutes near a zendil. Currents of zenith streamed across the spiral heating element, emitting constant warmth.

Ksenia's teeth chattered, and she giggled. "We could have just taken our time and come through the inner passages, you know."

"That would have added an hour to our walk this time of day, and you know as well as I do that we could be pressed into service for someone in the administrative wing."

"You're right, I suppose," said Ksenia. She glanced down a long hallway to the desk where Bextle stood guard. The man paid them no attention, a fact for which Ksenia was thankful. "At least you brought us through a door far away from him."

"Agreed." Vinnedesta took a moment to secure some errant strands of hair into her bun and straightened out her scribe uniform, being particular that the regent's insignia on her shoulder remained visible. She turned to consider Ksenia and tsk'd, retrieved a few hairpins, and made quick work of Ksenia's unkempt brown hair, sweeping it up and off her shoulders and pinning it back. Next, she brushed along Ksenia's shoulders and down the front panel of her uniform. "That will have to do, I suppose. Look and act like we are supposed to be here, and none of the staff should give us a hard time. Let's go, then. We have a lot of steps to manage."

Vinnedesta led them through several halls and doors, always walking deeper into the castle. The scribe pushed through a door set into a round column of stone, and they stepped out onto a platform at the top of a massive spiral staircase.

Ksenia peered out over the railing. "Are you taking me to the inner sanctum? Vin, what is this all about? If we get caught down there, in that holy place—"

"Stop worrying. Nobody comes here unless it's for a Rite of Revealing. Now come on, I promise, this will be worth it," said Vinnedesta.

They began the descent down through the levels of Stone's Grasp. After a time, the front of Ksenia's thighs began to burn from managing so many steps. At the bottom, Vinnedesta peered around the corner. "It's just as I thought, nobody here. Let's go."

The women approached a set of twelve-foot-high stained-glass doors. Intricate shards of colored glass formed serpentine dragons in each door, one red and one blue. Vinnedesta pushed, and the doors swung open on silent hinges. They stepped into the chamber, and Ksenia felt the skin between her shoulders tingle.

At the far end of the great sanctuary, the oversized statue of Eldrek Baellentrell stood holding hands outstretched. Several paces in front of that rested the life-sized figures of Japheth and Nebrine Baellentrell. A reflecting pool lay between them. Currents of zenith meandered through the stone walls' veining, emitting a blue light that reflected off the pool's calm surface. The effect gave the room a strange, otherworldly appearance.

Vinnedesta led them forward. As they passed the petrified remnants of the last Baellentrell monarchs, Ksenia stopped. The king and queen stood in a position identical to the statue of Eldrek, eyes trained on something far ahead, hands outstretched with palms up. While the statue of Eldrek appeared crafted from the same white stone of Stone's Grasp, these two appeared covered in a translucent, shimmering patina of light. Through the scintillating film, she could still see the queen's long eyelashes and the coarse hairs of the king's beard.

"Coming?" asked Vinnedesta.

Ksenia stepped toward the statue of Eldrek but kept her gaze trained on the monarchs. "When you stand close, they seem to be looking at something in the distance. But a few feet away, it's like they're looking right at me."

"I know, it's strange. They say the last thing these two saw was the flight of the abrogator and his horde of grot. But that's not why I brought you here. Come on, this way."

Vinnedesta led Ksenia around the reflecting pool and to the statue of Eldrek. Carved into the base, in scrolling text, rested the words, *"Balladure Cor Delledence."*

Ksenia looked up at her friend, back to the words, then to her friend again, who smiled triumphantly. "How come I never knew about this?" Ksenia asked, feeling more than a little bewildered. She crouched and ran her hand along the engraving.

"How many times have you been down here?" asked Vinnedesta.

"Just the once, for my Rite of Revealing. You?"

The scribe shrugged. "A few times. It's quiet, but the long trek to get here makes it an impractical place to retreat to very often. Anyway, I thought maybe this would help you with your work on deciphering that old tome."

"It could, I suppose," said Ksenia. "Have you any idea what it means?"

"No, but someone in the archives might, maybe one of the historians. We could ask later."

Ksenia stepped back a few paces to better assess the towering figure of Eldrek. In one hand rested a small serpentine dragon, and in the other, a hawk. *I don't recall seeing that when I was here before either. I think I was too excited to notice many of the details of this place the last time.*

She trained her gaze across the room, noticing details she'd missed before: the scrolling veining along the walls woven in intricate patterns, the small benches cast from stone sitting along the perimeter of the sanctuary, and the mural of stained glass resting on the ceiling above the reflecting pool. A man's voice echoed through the hall, startling Ksenia and sending a shaft of ice down her back. "Finding everything to your liking?"

Chapter Twenty-One: The Sense of the Wolvryn

" *Look for the bird, find the bird,"* Lluthean signed to Neska. The wolvryn cocked her head to the side, appearing to consider his command, then either sniffed in disdain or sneezed. The uncertainty made him giggle. He reached into his pocket, retrieved a piece of dried meat, showed it to her, and then closed his fist around the treat. The wolvryn huffed out a breath then trotted off into the grasses.

Mahkeel sat a few feet away and craned his neck back with a nod of appreciation. *"You learn faster than the wolvryn but will need a patient hand. That one is strong-willed and cunning,"* he signed.

Adopting the hand language of the Cloud Walkers came easy for Lluthean. Ellisina had taught them new phrases every night as they traveled to the southwestern stretches of the valley. Where Bryndor required review and repetition each day, Lluthean sat prepared to absorb and incorporate the next lesson.

A significant part of the hand language's emotion and context required attention to posture, body language, and facial expression. One sign delivered with a bowed head indicated a welcome greeting. Yet the same signal gestured with chin out issued a challenge. With a simple lift of the chin, the greeting, "welcome friend," became instead, "hello, why are you here?"

More than once, Ellisina had broken into uncontrolled laughter as the brothers labored to marry their longstrider notions of typical body language to the subtle meanings of the hand signing. Bryndor grumbled that his performance of the sign language must be truly awful to make any member of the stoic community express their emotion in such a loud manner. After the third night of suffering Ellisina's laughter, the brothers had decided to limit their communication to the silent hand language. That was three weeks ago, and their immersion had given them more than a rudimentary command of the language.

Lluthean waved his head from side to side and signed, *"You are wise, Mahkeel. Thank you for your teaching. Neska is more cunning, but Boru is more . . . persistent."* He labored to recall the sign for the last word.

"Boru is more what?" asked Bryndor. His voice sounded garbled and raspy. He cleared his throat and hocked spit to the side.

"Persistent." Lluthean re-signed the word for his brother. "And you broke the silence first, brother. That means you get to cook dinner tonight."

Bryndor waved him off and nodded in agreement. "I like my cooking better anyway. What on Karsk made you think to learn the sign for persistent?"

"Ellisina taught me. She said Neska is cunning and Boru is persistent," Lluthean signed.

"Dammit to the Drift," Bryndor cursed to himself and sucked at his teeth. *"Again, please. Show me again, slower."*

Lluthean repeated the sequence of gestures, waited for Bryndor to mime the signs, then signed approval. Their conversation gave the handler reason to smile. *"You both learn fast, and you are correct. Neska is like most females. That is why they lead the pack. Ghetti is the wisest among them all and leads the pack in all things."*

The silvered matriarch stepped through the grasses and crouched belly to the ground beside Mahkeel. Even lying in this fashion, the ridge of her spine still obscured the Damadibo man, forcing him to walk around the wolvryn to see Lluthean. The handler stroked the underside of Ghetti's chin, and the wolvryn turned her head to offer her ear, which he rubbed with affection.

Ghetti panted and drew her lips back in a smile, then huffed something between a low rumble and a stifled bark.

"One returns," signed Mahkeel. *"Ghetti tells you which one. Can you understand her yet? Is it Neska or Boru?"*

Lluthean turned to the silver wolvryn. *"Who comes?"*

Ghetti huffed the same strange sound, a rumbled growl ending with a stifled bark.

"I do not know that sound, so I guess Boru?" Lluthean signed.

Mahkeel stepped his right foot forward and tilted his head in a gesture Lluthean understood as agreement or possibly consensus. He signed, *"You gamble well."*

Boru trotted through the grasses and dropped the training decoy, a piece of wood with the red and yellow feathers of a game bird wrapped around it. The wolvryn trotted over to Bryndor, who signed for Boru to sit and wait, then rewarded him with a bit of dried meat and praise.

"Boru is getting better. He finds the bird almost half of the time," Bryndor signed, then turned his attention to Boru. *"Where is Neska? Find Neska."*

Boru rose to his feet and loped to the other side of the clearing in the grasses just as Neska bounded forward. She dropped the fresh carcass of an actual game bird at Lluthean's feet, then spent a moment pushing her tongue against the roof of her mouth. Lluthean took a knee, concerned that she might have something stuck in her teeth. As he reached to assist her, she spit out the red and yellow tail feathers from the training decoy.

Lluthean knelt, placing his knee on the evidence of her triumph. *"Clever girl, you win!"* He smothered her with affection and a treat.

"Clever indeed," said Bryndor. He walked over and retrieved the game bird by the feet, but Lluthean didn't think his brother saw the feathers from the training decoy.

"Our secret for now," whispered Lluthean.

Bryndor prepared a small cookfire and began to dress the game bird. Lluthean turned to Mahkeel, who signed, *"The respect you show each other is a kindness, but Bryndor should know when his wolvryn is not first."*

"Wise words. I will not hide her success next time."

Boru and Neska began another round of games chasing each other around Ghetti. For her part, the matriarch tolerated the romping pups until Boru tried to leap over her to reach Neska, who huddled against Ghetti's flank. He didn't quite have the necessary body control, and somehow his hindquarters flopped over before his front feet.

Boru tumbled down Ghetti's side to plop on top of Neska. She seemed to have been waiting for this very occurrence and snagged her brother by the neck, using his uncontrolled momentum against him and rolling him into a position of submission. She leaped back, barked once, and they started the romp anew. Ghetti yawned and hopped onto a boulder, apparently tired of acting like a piece of furniture for the brawling pups.

"Mahkeel, will Neska and Boru grow as big as Ghetti?" asked Lluthean.

"They walk a different path. This is why I have been teaching you both to hunt with them."

"I do not understand," Lluthean signed and cocked his head to the side.

"Passing over the mountain changes them. Something in the currents of zenith makes them grow big," the handler gestured.

"Bigger than Ghetti?" Lluthean blurted the words out loud, then signed so that Mahkeel could understand, *"How big?"*

The handler altered his posture and expression, reflecting concern. *"I can not say. When a wolvryn slides through the mists in the high places, it changes them. If they are struck by nadir, they become feral. This is what happened to their mother, Vencha, I think. But I think they can also be affected in ways I do not understand."*

"Does Ghetti go to the high places? She is the largest," signed Lluthean.

"Rarely. She is smart enough to know the dangers. You came here under the guidance of the ancestors and will leave through the same path someday. That way is safe but also thick with zenith, and something in the currents makes the wolvryn grow larger. When you leave, that process will continue." Mahkeel stopped and waited for Lluthean to process the gestures. Lluthean asked him to repeat the sequence, finding it a bit more complicated than he anticipated.

He thought a long moment about asking his next question. He knew the gestures but worried about the response he would receive from the handler. *"Should we leave them here with the pack? Would it be better for them?"*

Mahkeel watched the pups in silence. They broke apart, panting. Neska sauntered over to Lluthean then settled onto her belly, while Boru loped over to Bryndor and plopped down directly on Bryndor's feet, causing him to stumble. The handler studied them all with a placid expression and seemed to be wrestling with indecision.

Eventually, Mahkeel pinched his lips and sighed. *"No, this would not be a good thing. It is too late. These two have chosen you both. If you leave them now, they will try to follow. Neska might have the cunning to remain, but Boru would persist until nadir struck. They will grow beyond Ghetti, so you will need to know how to provide for them."*

Lluthean exhaled with relief and busied himself combing fingers through Neska's fur. Something about the stillness of the valley, the ever-changing cloud formations, and the feeling of safety behind the Korjinth allowed his usually frenetic mind to feel settled. He withdrew three billow seeds from his pocket, then reconsidered and replaced them.

He sat in contemplation, listening to the sound of the gentle river and remembering the Shelwyn. Winter fell as a mild damp season in the valley, and waterfowl yodeled in the distance. He sifted through memories of their home in Journey's Bend, of Aunt Ro's smiling face in the kitchen window. The sounds of the valley made him recall how the Shelwyn had meandered out of the Moorlok. Unbidden, flashes of the conflict with Vencha, mother to Boru and Neska, flickered in his mind.

Regret gathered in his throat like a smothering, heavy sensation. He swallowed hard to dissipate the unwanted emotion. When they had arrived at the handler's camp weeks ago, Mahkeel received them with a reservation beyond the stoic Damadibo. After several visits with Laryn acting as both interpreter and mediator, the handler had concluded that Vencha was feral.

Mahkeel never spoke forgiveness of the event, but indicated that the brothers were lucky to escape with their lives. From the wolvryn's perception, they were a threat to her pups. The reunion of Boru and Neska with the pack seemed to mollify any further anger on Mahkeel's part. Now that Lluthean had borne witness to the intimacy with which the handler lived with the wolvryn, a feeling of guilt welled up whenever he thought about that day.

A low, moaning howl echoed from the horizon. The call gave Ghetti cause to stand, stretch, then hop down from the boulder. She huffed once and rumbled a soft growl. Boru and Neska ran over to sit at attention. The silvered matriarch held them there a moment, then led them off through the grasses.

Lluthean knew from prior experience that the pups were safer with Ghetti than anywhere else. The summons from another in the pack indicated that she was leading them to a fresh kill. They needed to learn as much from her and the pack as from Mahkeel during their time in the valley.

A trembling hoot mimicking the whippoorwill of waterfowl carried from the cookfire. Lluthean looked over to see Bryndor cupping his hands together, emitting the sound. Once he had their attention, he signed, *"Dinner is ready."*

The three of them shared the meal in silence. As they finished, Ghetti returned with the pups, then bounded off again into the night. Boru's purple tongue rolled forward with an exaggerated yawn, which soon infected them all with stretches and yawns. Lluthean resisted the urge to crane his neck back but couldn't help himself, and even Mahkeel started to yawn. The shared experience made them all break into laughter.

Mahkeel brought forth a small pipe flute, and they settled around the cookfire for the evening. As the sun waned behind the Korjinth, both wolvryn rose to their feet, attentive to the mists. They trained their attention to the northeast.

Mahkeel stopped playing and observed the pups. *"Not idly do sleepy pups awaken. Ask them what they sense."*

"What do you sense?" signed Lluthean to Neska.

For her part, the wolvryn looked briefly to Lluthean then back to the mists.

"I've told you before, not that way. You need to be one with her to sense as she does. Lay your hands on her, then close your eyes and wait," signed Mahkeel.

The brothers did as the handler directed. Lluthean sighed. They had tried this exercise nearly every night under the handler's training. The practice never yielded anything meaningful. Once again, Lluthean strained to hear beyond the gentle bubbling of the rushing waters. He inhaled a slow, deliberate breath, searching for anything on the wind.

A peaceful stillness settled across his mind, and he focused on Neska, on her warmth and the way her fur laced through his fingers. He felt her respiration slow into synchronization with his, and a moment later, something warm rippled from Neska and into his hands. The sensation traveled up his arms and into his chest, where it settled as a pleasurable tingling just above his breastbone.

That's something . . . new.

His next breath pulled in humid and rich as a complex tapestry of sensations surged into his awareness. The char of the cookfire lingered sharp on the back of his tongue and mixed with the fragrances of dormant grasses and wet soil. In various shades of blue, he could see through the twilight far into the distance, well past the limits of the campfire. There, Kaellor and Laryn walked toward them in conversation. Lluthean could smell the horses they led and hear the shuffle of the pack animals through the grasses. The unique commingling of the otherworldly senses captivated him.

He directed his focus to Bryndor, who was kneeling beside Boru across the campfire. The two of them, human and wolvryn, seemed to blend into each other's silhouette in the amber light. Faint ripples of blue light traveled through Boru's fur and into Bryndor's hands. A wispy filament of blue thread merged with the nimbus of light around his brother before undulating up and away into the darkness like an errant strand of spider silk.

Lluthean drew his attention back to his uncle and Laryn. Something of the sounds she made changed. Her breath caught just before she released a throaty laugh. Some undertone of his uncle's scent emitted a sensation of peace, and Lluthean thought he could also taste a hint of desire permeating from both of them.

The thought made him feel intrusive, and he opened his eyes to the amber light of the campfire. Mahkeel continued to pipe a melancholy tune, and the world became stifled. The complex interplay of what he could see, taste, hear, and smell all muted back to his dull human senses.

Who needs vocal speech when you can sense all of that all the time?

Eventually, Bryndor tilted his head toward the campfire. He lingered in that strange pose a moment, then opened his eyes. *"Did you finally see it, Llu?"* Bryndor signed.

"Yes. Seven gods and all the blessings of the Giver, yes! Saw it, smelled it, even tasted it," said Lluthean with a laugh. He ruffled both hands through Neska's fur, and she rolled onto her back, encouraging him to rub her belly. He obliged, then looked up to his brother. "Wait, how long have you been able to do that?"

"Not as long as you have been able to master Damadibo sign, but more than a week," Bryndor signed.

Lluthean kept both of his hands entangled in Neska's fur and spoke over the campfire. "You cheeky grinder. Why didn't you say anything?"

"The only way to receive the wolvryn sight, their perception, is to still your mind. You're so competitive. I thought if I told you we could do it, you might struggle all the more. Besides, I knew you were close and that all you needed was more time," said Bryndor.

"You couldn't sign all of that to me?" Lluthean asked with a challenging pitch.

"Maybe if I practiced . . . a lot." Bryndor laughed and stirred the coals, then added a bit of wood. The flames offered a welcoming beacon, and several minutes later, Kaellor and Laryn wandered into their camp.

With thick and clumsy fingers, Kaellor addressed them all. *"Blessings and honor to you three. We brought sweetbread and honey-chunk and would share for a spot next to your fire."*

"You two were supposed to be here weeks ago?" Lluthean lifted his chin to the side, adding the connotation of a question to his signing.

"You needed time with Mahkeel and . . . more than one Damadibo benefitted from Laryn's ministrations," signed Kaellor.

Lluthean leaned back in surprise. *"You've been practicing!"*

Kaellor grunted agreement. "So I have. Now, are you two going to sit there or give Laryn and me a proper welcome?"

Lluthean beat Bryndor to his feet and embraced Laryn, then Kaellor. Laryn made introductions while the brothers settled the mounts and unpacked Kaellor's tent. They gathered around the campfire just as Mahkeel finished a story. Something in the handler's telling and Laryn's translation to Kaellor left Lluthean a little suspicious that the humorous part of the tale came at his expense.

Laryn arched back, laughing so hard that when she rocked forward, she had to wipe tears from her eyes. "Oh, Giver! That's rich. Lluthean, you didn't tell me that you asked Ellisina for her hand in marriage."

Lluthean's head jerked around. "I did no such thing . . . did I?"

His question caused all of them to laugh again, but none more than Mahkeel after Laryn signed his response.

"Dear child, show me how you sign the greeting to Ellisina whenever you see her," said Laryn.

Lluthean wiped sweaty palms on his pants, then moved his nimble fingers through the pattern signing. He spoke out loud as he carried out the gestures. "Blessings and honor to your house, Ellisina."

His signing made them all erupt in laughter again, even Bryndor and Kaellor.

His uncle recovered. "I'm no expert, but even I can see we have a royal scandal on our hands. What is the dowry of a Damadibo firstborn anyway?"

"Alright then, show me what I'm really saying," said Lluthean.

Laryn regained her composure and stood up. She waved her hands to quiet the group, then signed and spoke. "This means blessings and honor to your house. See the difference? My small fingers are not interlocked, and my feet are parallel. When you lock your pinkies and step forward, you are saying," she cleared her throat and said, "it would be a blessing for you to join my house."

Lluthean thought back to how many times he must have ground up the greeting to the girl. The sour look on his face made them break out in another round of laughter.

The first to sober, Kaellor asked, "What is it, Llu?"

He giggled, allowing himself to enjoy a little of the humor of the moment. "Well, by my count, I've asked that poor girl to marry me no less than fifteen times."

"Oh, Giver," Bryndor laughed. "Do you suppose she ever said yes?"

"I don't know," said Lluthean, "but I think her grandmother and at least two other village elders did."

Chapter Twenty-Two: Challenge Accepted

The musky, sweaty reek of grotvonen wafted into Volencia's chamber, and she found the odor a welcome departure from the sulfurous fumes that lingered in the deepest recesses of the Torgrend Range. Deep underground, hot springs bubbled up from the center of Karsk in pools that frothed and boiled. The grot had excavated a clever set of canals and reservoirs to filter and siphon off the water.

Shallow pools housed an entire forest of mushrooms, whose gills filtered the water's toxins and impurities. From these underground lakes, channels cut along the walkways carried drinkable water to the Brognaus horde.

There was biodiversity in the "Underdark," as the grotvonen called their home under the mountains. Different mushrooms hunkered low against the periphery of pools and were harvested for food. Luminescent mosses and lichen clung to the yellow sulfur-stained rocky outcroppings above the pools, bathing the cavern in a pale light of green and purple hues. Stranger still were the schools of tiny fish that darted along the filtered channels of water. The fingerlings emitted a brilliant blue light when startled and often scurried ahead of anyone, illuminating the paths.

None of the natural beauty made up for the overwhelming reek of rotten eggs that hung in the air. *And if you think the stink of that grot is a welcome relief, then you've been here a bit longer than you imagined.*

She turned to regard the frail creature. It wore a tattered shirt over one shoulder, a gift she'd bestowed more to assist her in keeping track of the clever beast than out of any sense of kindness. The garment's frayed edges, stained dark with soiled material, hung just low enough to cover its groin.

Mottled tufts of unkempt hair sprouted at random angles from under the shirt. The creature bowed low, then lifted its saucer-shaped eyes and pursed its lips.

Some quirk of inheritance left it without the oversized bestial fangs commonplace among the horde. The absence of the visible signs of its virility might have given other grotvonen cause to ridicule the creature. Instead, they treated the slight beast with deference for its ability to speak with Volencia and with the score of umbral that lived with the horde openly.

"Why have you come into my chambers, Eguma? I did not send for you," said Volencia.

Eguma bowed even lower, ears twitching. He paused with forehead almost to the floor, then slowly lifted his eyes. A sibilant voice purred, "Eguma begs the pardon of Death's Mistress. One of the shamans requests your presence. The Consort of umbral and the shamans seem at a . . . disagreement."

Eguma sneered, his mouth in a grimace, the task of forming human speech accomplished only with significant effort. Three-syllable words, in particular, gave him trouble, and Volencia strained to knit his strange speech together.

"I would advise your shamans to adhere to the dictates of the umbral. The Consort's tolerance for opposition is limited. They do not follow reason as you would expect and will not hesitate to enforce Tarkannen's will. Yet," she sighed and continued more to herself than the slight grotvonen, "we will need the full might of the shamans if we are to succeed in the days ahead."

"I have said as much more than once, mistress. Though they have learned much from the umbral, the shamans seek their own path out of the darkness."

Years of training in abrogation, and I'm reduced to this—no more valuable than a nanny to bickering schoolchildren.

"Let's be quick about it then. Lead on," said Volencia.

Eguma turned and loped forward, leading Volencia through the twisted tunnels. She cast thin filaments of nadir forward using the tendrils to probe and guide her through the darkness. The images she perceived were incomplete, but the technique allowed her to keep up with Eguma. Occasionally, she stamped a foot to startle the school of fish lingering in the channels carved along the pathways. Faint blue light zipped forward through the water, showing her the path ahead with more clarity.

Eguma led her into a large, familiar cavern. The air flowed cool through the spacious chamber, and the oppressive humid rot of sulfur lifted, if only a little. The shamans had gathered in this location to prepare for Tarkannen's return and carry out the horde rituals. Usually, a group of five or six chanted in unison. As Eguma and Volencia approached, a bickering chorus of clicking teeth interrupted with hisses and growls greeted them.

Three umbral, their flattened heads inscribed by the arcane symbols of enslavement, sat along one side of the chamber. The way they crouched with overlong and oddly jointed limbs reminded her of strange albino stick creatures more than anything humanoid. The entire host of shamans, at least twenty, gathered opposite, a shifting mass of angry grotvonen prowling on all fours. The clamor among them silenced as she stepped forward.

One of the shamans lay crumpled on the floor in the center of the debate. Volencia nudged the corpse onto its back with a boot. The fat shaman's large head rolled to the side, its mouth unhinged, and a thin tongue flopped forward. A perfect black hole was seared into the grotvonen's chest. *Nadir burn.*

Volencia sighed. "Where is Grasdok? This seems like the kind of thing he should be attending to."

Eguma pointed a clawed finger up into the dim green nimbus at the ceiling of the cavern. "He directs the . . . excavation of the channel to the surface to prepare for our master's return."

"Someone explain to me why this shaman lies dead. We will need the combined power of the Consort and the shamans to carry out Tarkannen's plans."

Eguma translated her words and waited. One of the umbral responded with a rapid succession of clattering teeth and screeches. A shaman similarly made a rebuttal, then Eguma held up a clawed fist to garner their silence.

"The Consort think the shamans should prepare to retrieve the vessel that ties our master to this world. For some reason, they think it might be in danger. They . . . demand a stop to training for the Rite of Sundering to accomplish this new task. The shamans voice concern that if they are not fully prepared for the ceremony, then Tarkannen will not be able to return."

Intrigued, Volencia turned to the umbral trio. "Explain what you mean about the vessel. This is the first I have heard of this."

The center umbral cocked its neck, tipping its flat head. Using a combination of gestures and the clacking speech of the grotvonen, it offered a response. As the monologue clattered on, several of the grot shamans perked hair-tufted ears forward. When the umbral stopped, at least half of the shamans cooed and hooted softly.

Eguma turned to face Volencia. He took a deep breath and shook his head, staring briefly at his feet. "These words will be hard for me, mistress."

Volencia nodded but waved her hand for him to continue.

"Tarkannen has long . . . monitored the safety of the vessel. It is housed and safe, in a place called . . . the Sanitorium in Callinora." Eguma rubbed the muscles at the side of his face and unhinged his jaw. "Until the layers of the binding weakened he did not know its location but now desires that it should be recovered and brought here. The Consort learned this and need the shamans to open the way. The Consort desire to teach them how to bend nadir to this task."

"Did Tarkannen communicate anything else to the Consort?" asked Volencia.

Eguma chattered with the umbral, then nodded and returned his attention to her. "For now, dark lady, that is all."

"Explain to the shamans that their progress in the Rite of Sundering is important, but if Tarkannen has a new task for them, they should change to his purpose."

Eguma chattered to his audience; his explanation was met with restless acceptance. One of the shamans raised a furred palm then spoke in harsh guttural tones, concluding with a gesture to the corpse of the shaman at her feet.

Eguma held up a fist to garner the shaman's silence, then turned to Volencia. "They will do what must be done for the sake of the Brognaus. But they demand that the Consort stop spilling shaman blood."

The center umbral sprang up to its full height on its oddly jointed and lanky limbs. It clacked and gestured a short response. Volencia didn't need Eguma's interpretation to understand the creature's intent.

The thickened ridge of skin around Eguma's saucer-shaped eyes thinned, making it appear as if something massive had gripped the slight grotvonen around the waist, and only by his exhalation did his eyes remain seated inside his skull. "The umbral says, you, dark lady, and the shamans must comply with Tarkannen's wishes, and that nothing else matters. If you resist, you will only meet the same fate as the one at your feet."

Finally. I expected this challenge weeks ago. So be it, flat-head.

Volencia paced a serpentine pattern, using the distraction to pull long and hard on the currents of nadir. Without warning, she turned and unleashed a shaft of power that erupted forth and throttled the umbral against the cave wall. The other two umbral scattered away, but she held the offending creature pinned to the stone.

"You respond to power. Let me show you mine!" She bent the nadir to her will for several moments, crushing the umbral's limbs and causing its joints to pop and buckle. The creature tilted its head back and forth, emitting a harsh scream that echoed into the cavern. It tried to lash out, flailing errant tendrils of nadir wildly into the air.

Finally, she tightened the black fibers into a dense shaft, then focused on the umbral's flat head. She allowed the nadir to surge in its raw form for several seconds, then stifled her flow. The body of the shadowed man crumpled to the ground. Its neck ended in a blackened taper, a smoking void where the head used to rest.

Volencia panted, enjoying the sterile nothingness created by the release of so much nadir into a confined space. Light, sound, and even vapors were consumed by the torrential surge. For the first time in weeks, she allowed herself to inhale deeply, unfettered by the reek of grotvonen and the stench of their underground home. From the shadows, the other two umbral stepped forward, tilted their heads, and bowed in silence.

Chapter Twenty-Three: Runes Unshackled

Bryndor tugged stiff leather gloves over bruised knuckles and gripped sore fingers around the wood stave he used for a practice sword. Winter in the valley had felt like a wet wool sweater, heavy and grey, and for the first time in weeks, the sun fell across the village full and bright, reflecting off the white crystals coating the ground.

He stepped onto the pasture that served as their sparring and training arena, aware of the crepitous grind of iced grass underfoot. The sensation reminded him of Journey's Bend, but only emptiness and sorrow greeted him when he wandered down those particular corridors. He forced a deep breath in and held it, waiting for the hollow feeling to lift from his chest.

An unusual clamor of giggles and hushed voices drew his attention back to the edge of the clearing. Many of the younger Damadibo had never seen ice or snow, and the soft-spoken, olive-skinned children pulled oiled leathers tight around their necks to ward off the unusual cold. He watched several of them reach out to touch the prickly shards of ice, only to giggle in amazement as the crystals melted at their touch.

"There's something you don't see every day," said Lluthean. He wandered over to the children and signaled a greeting in the hand language, then gathered up a fistful of hoarfrost from the broad leaf of a bush. Bryndor watched his brother make a show of crushing the thin layer of ice in his fist, then melting it on his tongue for all to see.

"*Cold water is,*" Lluthean signed, then stopped and turned back to Bryndor. "I don't suppose you know the sign for ice or snow?"

Bryndor shrugged. "I don't imagine it's a word that gets much use here."

Lluthean scraped up more of the thin layer of frost and molded it into a small snow shard, then handed it to one of the adolescent boys. *"Cold water is hard. Make it warm to make it . . . water."*

One of the girls sucked in a breath and juggled the ice from one hand to the next, uncertain how to proceed. Lluthean repeated the demonstration, gathering up a shard of ice then melting it on his tongue. Caution finally gave way to curiosity, and she placed the snow in her mouth. The olive skin around her dark eyes radiated pure exuberance and amazement. The group of young Cloud Walkers busied themselves with gathering and eating the hoarfrost.

Kaellor walked out of the mists that shrouded his hut. The excitement of the villagers caused a smile to reach his eyes. He signed a greeting then crunched across the pasture, a hand resting on the pommel of the guardian sword at his hip.

Without further words, his uncle began a routine of morning stretches and exercises. In the last month, the three of them had spent their morning hours sparring. Kaellor taught them the basics of footwork, parry, more footwork, riposte, jab, and . . . more footwork. In the previous week, they had learned to combine these basic moves with thrusts and slices, but always the drills started and ended with footwork.

Bryndor drew his lips to a thin line and cinched the gloves tight but didn't bother complaining about the discomfort of the bruising on his hands, ribs, and legs. Kaellor trained Lluthean with a lighter stave, and his brother managed the forms with uncanny agility. Bryndor preferred the feel of the two-handed grip on a longer, heavier length of wood. On occasion, his strength overwhelmed his brother's defenses, and Bryndor still lacked the control to pull his blows gracefully. Three matches in the last month had ended with a bloody retreat to Laryn's hut to heal an errant whack to the noggin.

Bryndor bounced the stave on his shoulder and chewed on his inner lower lip, thinking about why Kaellor had demanded they begin training in earnest. *What kind of home are we returning to that a man has to be able to defend himself with the sword?*

He watched as Lluthean rehearsed some of the basic stances and maneuvers. His brother performed several isolated steps in slow motion, then repeated the combination, chaining the moves together faster and faster. All at once, he dropped to a knee, spinning, then rolled to his feet while slicing with an overhead arc. The whirling effect certainly looked impressive, though Bryndor wasn't sure how successful the maneuver would be. No doubt his brother's imaginary foes fell by the dozens. *I'm pretty sure I would manage to twist a knee if I tried that.*

Lluthean rose to his feet and walked over, tapping the stave against his boots. Already, the thin layer that blanketed the open pasture had melted. He pitched his voice low. "I think we can work the frost to our advantage against Kae."

"I don't know. It will likely hinder us as much as help us. We're the ones attacking his defensive stances. It seems to me it would be easier to be the one standing in one place." Bryndor watched his uncle continue his warm-up on the opposite side of the pasture.

As Kaellor stretched and began to practice different stances, several more Cloud Walkers joined to watch. "I wondered if the colder weather would keep the looky-loos away, but it only seemed to attract more attention this morning," said Bryndor.

Lluthean looked up and waved at a group of older boys who had just arrived. "I asked those fellas to join us," said his brother.

Something in Lluthean's sly bearing gave Bryndor pause. "Why do I get the feeling there is more than you are letting on? Don't tell me you started some kind of betting pool."

Lluthean assumed the expression of someone with wounded pride. "And with what would a Damadibo bet? Kevash seeds?"

Bryndor observed the Cloud Walkers through shuttered eyes. Kaellor's voice interrupted his thoughts. "Line up for drills. We don't have all morning before Ghetti returns with your wolvryn."

Several times a week, Boru and Neska hunted with the pack in the evening and usually stayed out until late morning. When they returned, the wolvryn demanded their undivided attention. The brothers made sure to reconnect with the creatures, following the lessons Mahkeel taught them. Just like learning the sword, training with the wolvryn required patience and a significant investment in time.

The brothers walked forward and assumed defensive stances before Kaellor. Their uncle nodded, and they began the dance of footwork and slow maneuvers of combat. Kaellor backstepped, turning and twisting to avoid the exaggerated strikes but focusing more on their feet or the position of their shoulders and hands.

"Good, again, only mix up your attacks somewhat," said Kaellor. They retreated several steps and began the dance again. After several passes, Kaellor held up his hand.

"Alright, now face each other. Bryn, start with offensive passes. Half speed, touch contact only for recognition. Let's see if we can get through a morning without disappointing Laryn. Five exchanges, then switch. Begin," said Kaellor.

The brothers moved as instructed, back and forth in exchanges that churned the frost into mud. Eventually, Kaellor called them to a stop. Even though they drilled at half speed, Bryndor's shoulders and forearms burned with mild fatigue.

"That's not bad. Llu, rotate your wrist after a parry, and then perform a simple thrust. You're fast, but the thrust is quicker and deadlier than a slice. Bryn, don't fall into the same rhythm. Part of combat is being unpredictable and reacting to new opportunities and weaknesses in your opponent's defense. If you overcommit to a pattern in your mind, you will miss an opportunity to react to an opening. Again, this time Lluthean initiates."

After several consecutive passes, Kaellor called them to rest. Bryndor set the tip of his stave on the ground and loosened his gloves. His sweat made the leather supple, but his fingers still ached from the previous day's training. "Tell me again why this is so important," said Bryndor.

"Learning the sword is valuable for several reasons. The discipline and structure involved are themselves worthwhile endeavors," said Kaellor. "But more than that, I want you two to be self-reliant. You may be called upon to travel the kingdom without my constant protection. But for now, I want you to be able to push me in our drills, and so far, you have yet to land a single strike."

Bryndor bounced the stave on his shoulder again, considering his uncle, but Lluthean gave voice to his thoughts. "That sounds rather like a challenge, Kae," said his brother.

"I'm not above a little taunt if it brings out your best," said Kaellor. "Tell you what, if either of you lands a solid strike on me this morning, I'll shave my head and face as smooth as the day the Giver welcomed me into the world. But if you don't, then you both have to do the same."

Lluthean lifted his stave and twirled it once, then lightly poked Kaellor in the abdomen. "I hope Laryn loves you, old man, because you are not going to look very pretty by the end of the day."

Bryndor sighed and tightened up his gloves. He took position beside his brother, and they waited for Kaellor. The guardian sword remained in its scabbard, but he untied the weapon from his belt. Instead of holding the blade raised in a stance for attack, Kaellor inverted his grip, point down, in a passive posture intended for defense only.

"Alright, begin," said Kaellor.

Bryndor thrust while Lluthean attempted a slice from the other side. Kaellor blocked Bryndor's attack, stepping into the lunge and just out of reach from Lluthean's swing. Bryndor sidestepped, placing himself on Kaellor's opposite side, and the two of them attacked at once again. They each attempted random combinations of strikes, thrusts, and swings. Lluthean even tried to drop to a knee, spin, and swing. Kaellor managed to block, shift, dance back, and turn . . . always at the last moment. Bryndor became more determined and tried to be conscious of varying his strikes but eventually gave in to instinct and placed all his strength into his swings.

Lluthean moved with equal purpose, but had to dance back, giggling every time Kaellor thwarted his attack combinations. Their uncle moved with an economy of motion, deflecting a swing from Bryndor then rapping him on the back of the head with the flat of his scabbard as Bryndor tripped past.

After several minutes they separated, panting. Bryndor finger-combed long strands of matted hair back out of his face. Kaellor stood tranquil, breath unlabored.

"I don't suppose you managed to land a touch on him?" asked Lluthean.

"No, but I think we might have a better chance if you could stop laughing for a bit," said Bryndor.

"I can't help it. It feels so strange to try to whack him a good one," said Lluthean.

"Llu, every time you get a fit of the giggles, I catch the flat of his sword. We accepted a bet. I don't intend to shave my head, and let's be honest; it will take you a year to grow back the scruff you consider a beard."

Bryndor's words sobered Lluthean's expression. "What do you have in mind?"

"We charge in from opposite sides. I'll attack high, and you go low. I'll try to keep him busy with slices and swings. Those take more time for him to block and parry. See if you can land a fast jab or thrust. All we need is one," said Bryndor.

They separated and turned to face Kaellor. He cocked his head and waved them forward. As one, they surged ahead. Bryndor barely managed to keep his feet on the slick ground but began to swing for Kaellor's head and upper torso. Time and again, Kaellor twisted or deflected their attacks. Several times during the exchange, Lluthean's stave punched forward, striking air but never landing a blow on their uncle. From the periphery of his vision, Bryndor realized their disadvantage: quick as a glint of sunlight on a bird's wing, blue light flared across the runes visible at Kaellor's neck.

Bryndor gritted his teeth in frustration and increased his attacks, mixing thrusts and swings with a frenzied pace. The frantic nature of their attacks increased until Kaellor turned on one foot, leaned back, and deflected a wild swing from Bryndor. The errant stave careened overhead and struck Lluthean on the shoulder just as Lluthean's jab lanced forward and thunked into Bryndor's abdomen.

Bryndor crumpled forward over the blow. His muscles constricted, and it took a moment for him to draw breath. Steam billowed around him, a mixture of his breath and the heat rising from his collar. He rose to his feet and looked at his uncle. Kaellor made a mock scissor motion through his beard but remained silent and waiting.

Lluthean walked over, rubbing his shoulder. "I've had enough. Listen, this time, we do it my way. We charge in and get him to turn his back to the fellas standing behind us. I'll give a signal, and they will hurl stones at Kae's backside. That should give us the distraction we need to land at least one blow."

Bryndor pinched the inside of his cheek between his teeth. "That doesn't seem right."

"Grind it, Bryn. What's right about all the welts we've received this morning? He's channeling zenith. What's right about that?" Lluthean challenged.

Bryndor looked past his brother to the group of older boys standing in idle chat. He turned his gaze to his brother's grey eyes. "You're right. I'm in. What makes you sure they won't hit us? Lutney hasn't really smiled on us this morning."

"You surprise me, brother," said Lluthean. He arched his back and stretched. "You should know by now that Lutney's a Southland god, and we're of Aarindorn. It'll be the Taker's knuckles or the Giver's bright smile, but never Lutney." Lluthean moved close to Bryndor to obscure his intention and signed to the youths. "Don't worry about their aim. I've seen a few of them sling a rabbit on the run. Just work to the far side of Kae and make a good show of it, then be ready. We'll likely only get the one chance."

They strode forward together, then launched their attacks at the same time. With aggravating ease, Kaellor blocked, sidestepped, dodged, and maneuvered away from the strikes. Bryndor worked his way to the right while Lluthean circled the left. Bryndor thrust as a feint, then pulled up to catch his uncle under the arm, but his stave deflected off the scabbard. He adjusted his feet and set to deliver an overhead slice.

Four stones arced through the air, set for Kaellor's head. Bryndor heaved on the stave in preparation for another thrust and fleetingly wondered if his uncle was in danger. Before the stones landed, Kaellor's head snapped up. Zenith blazed from the pommel of the guardian sword and suffused his eyes with an azure flare. Kaellor punched a fist into the air, and a concussive blast erupted in a sphere around him.

Bryndor felt the ground vanish from underfoot as a tremendous force hurtled against him. White clouds swirled overhead, and he flew back, landing on his side in the mud. He lay there stunned, ears ringing and unable to draw breath.

He strained to lift his head from the mud and found his brother in a similar state, clutching his abdomen. Kaellor staggered forward on clumsy footing with a wild, panicked expression. His eyes had faded to their usual dark blue, and the guardian sword seemed dormant in the scabbard.

Kaellor yelled something and was reaching to check on Bryndor when a blur of black and grey swept over him. A snarling, gnashing flurry of claw and teeth grabbed Kaellor by the arm and tossed him several feet away. At the same moment, Bryndor felt his abdominal muscles unclench enough to allow a sweet breath of air to rush in.

He rolled up, utterly confused by the scene before him. Kaellor knelt more than ten feet away with one arm bloodied. His uncle's wrist was bent at a strange angle, looking more like a dinner fork than the muscled forearm he knew. Blood splattered onto the frosted ground. Neska and Boru paced around the man, teeth bared and ears pinned back.

Kaellor looked at Bryndor with a pleading expression and seemed to yell his name, but Bryndor's ears registered only a muffled noise. He strained to bring his thoughts into focus as Boru gathered himself and prepared to leap forward. Kaellor sighed and looked down for a moment, then lifted his head with a rictus snarl of pain. Zenith played across the runes on his arms and chest, skittering about like blue lightning, looking for an opportunity to release.

He clutched the guardian sword in his good hand, holding it close to his chest. A tight blue sphere of shimmering, translucent light erupted around him just as Boru and Neska leaped in to attack him. Each wolvryn careened off the shielding without harm only to gather themselves and prowl the perimeter of the protective orb.

Understanding finally penetrated the haze of pain, and Bryndor pushed to his knees. He yelled, "Neska, Boru!" The wolvryn persisted in their search for a weakness through the blue nimbus surrounding Kaellor. Bryndor ushered a shrill whistle followed by a hand signal to the wolvryn. *"Heel to me, now!"*

At once, Neska trotted over and licked the sweat from Bryndor's forehead, then settled onto her haunches, panting, her purple tongue lolled to the side. The larger wolvryn continued his prowl around the blue dome. Bryndor threw an arm around Neska's thick neck. He felt the vibration of the wolvryn's growl, but his ears remained muffled. He allowed his focus to meld with Neska's, sinking his awareness into the wolvryn's.

It took longer than usual, but eventually, their breathing synchronized. Through Neska's senses, he smelled Boru's intent. The wolvryn prowled Kaellor's protective perimeter with a strange conflicted mix of curiosity, anxiety, and fear. But more than all of that, he smelled of intensity. "Boru, come. All is safe now, no more danger. Come to me."

Boru paused in his search and looked over to where Bryn knelt with Neska. The wolvryn cocked his head in apparent confusion. "Call him, Neska. The game is over. Kaellor is no threat."

He wasn't sure if Neska understood. Lluthean moaned and rolled to his back but remained in no condition to help. Neska wagged her tail, rumbled a low growl, then issued a deep bark.

Finally, Boru trotted over to sit beside Bryndor. He ran a hand across his muzzle with affection, singing praise to them both, then sat back in relief. The cold wet of the muddy ground seeped through his pants and into his awareness for the first time. He moved to stand when a firm hand pushed back down on his shoulder. He looked up to see Laryn saying something.

"My ears, I can't hear you," he signed.

She surveyed the scene, making a fast triage of the three men. Looking more like a disappointed field commander than a medic, she folded her arms, shaking her head in disbelief, then ruffled the muzzle of Boru and Neska for good measure. Laryn signed to him with curt gestures. *"Lluthean first, then Kaellor, then you. Stay down if you know what's good for you."*

Chapter Twenty-Four: Uncommon Grace

Therek strode across the inner sanctum, passing under the towering statue of Eldrek to stand beside the preserved remains of the last king of Aarindorn, Japheth Baellentrell. The regent stared a moment, looking past the translucent, shimmering veil of preservation that held his friend in stasis. Though he had visited the sanctuary once a week, he never became accustomed to seeing the king without a tapestry of runes adorning his neck and weaving up across his jaw and to his temples. Without the accentuation of the runes, Japheth didn't appear naked. Instead, he appeared . . . unburdened.

The regent turned his attention back to the two young scribes standing nervously at the base of the statue of Eldrek. "It's quite a hike down here and back again. What is it, I wonder, that draws two of Aarindorn's brightest?"

Ksenia, the Balladuren daughter, cleared her throat. "I've not made much progress deciphering the text left behind by Archivist Weckles, but I came across a phrase that seemed familiar. Vinnedesta realized the same words are scrawled across the base of the statue of Eldrek."

Therek considered the young woman. Her posture struck a formal tone, and she spoke without dissembling. He peered at the phrase engraved at the base of the statue. "*Balladur Cor Delledence*; I can understand why that might interest you in particular. My loose understanding is that it means something like 'Without condition, wield your greatest power.' If you could source that in any of the ancient texts and give context to its meaning, that would significantly contribute to Aarindorian history. We lost so many of our records after the Cataclysm, as you know."

The girls stood in polite silence. At last, Ksenia spoke up. "If I might ask, what brings you down here, Your Grace?"

Therek gestured to the still forms of Japheth and Nebrine. "I like to see my friends, though of late I am reminded of how much I have aged since the Abrogator's War and how much they remain unchanged. I tell myself I'll stop coming when the climb back to the top becomes too much of a burden. The old knees aren't what they used to be, but I still manage."

"Well, we didn't mean to intrude," said Ksenia. The girl appeared ready to wrench off her own hand at the wrist.

"Nonsense," said Therek. "I know the sanctum is a sacred place, but I've often wondered why no one else ventures down here. It seems a shame not to pay our respects more than during the occasional formal ceremony or Rite of Revealing, don't you think?" His words seemed to place them both at ease.

"I guess so," said Ksenia. She and Vinnedesta stepped forward to assess the king and queen. "The only other time I was here, for my rite, I was so nervous. I didn't take the time to appreciate . . ." her voice trailed off as she scrutinized the monarchs closely. "Moons, they were preserved with the blood of innocents staining their boots. People never talk about that."

"It's an ugly truth that some would prefer to leave in the shadows, I'm afraid," said Therek. His back ached, and he wandered over to recline on one of the stone benches.

Vinnedesta cleared her throat. "I beg your leave, Your Grace. I am committed to scribing transactions for the vice regent this afternoon."

Therek looked up and smiled through his wispy brows. "Most certainly, don't let me keep you. Chancle's work is more valuable than my ruminations."

Vinnedesta turned to Ksenia. "I'll see you after. Perhaps we can research the phrase more this evening."

Ksenia waved and continued her inspection of the preserved monarchs. After a time, she wandered over to appraise the statue of Eldrek. She tilted her head to the side, errantly finger-combing through hair that tumbled over her shoulder. "Do you think he really had all those runes, all the way down his legs? I'm not sure I've ever seen anyone so densely marked."

"That is actually a matter of scholarly debate among historians. Some believe the runes reflect artistic license. Others find the very notion sacrilegious and assume that the runes must be an accurate representation," said Therek.

Ksenia walked over and took a seat on a small stone bench next to him. "What do you think, Your Grace?" she asked.

Therek crossed his gangly legs and folded his hands under his arms in an uncharacteristically casual posture. It felt good to just . . . relax. He was tired of the power struggles among the noble houses and the constant worry about his children, the competing guilds interested in profiteering from the new trade roads, and the looming threat of grotvonen and their ilk.

"I think that when we are in this place, you can call me Therek, or Master Lefledge if you prefer."

"Your Gra—I don't understand," said Ksenia.

Therek sighed and offered her a wistful smile. "This is one of the few places in the kingdom I can come to escape the stresses of the regency, if only for a short time. We all need an escape. If this is to be mine then, we can drop the formal titles. Unless that makes you uncomfortable?" he asked.

"Not at all," said Ksenia. "It's nice. Back home, on the ranch, we don't stand on ceremony. If a mare struggles to foal, it doesn't matter who's in the barn. You roll up your sleeves and pull whether you're a Balladuren or one of the ranch hands. Keeping track of people by their titles is exhausting. It seems that life would make more sense if we all treated everyone with equal respect and dignity. All those titles do is separate people."

Therek chuckled at the woman's reductive but not inaccurate reasoning. Out of habit more than genuine suspicion, he kindled a flicker of zenith across the runes on his forearms. His abilities of sapience and discernment rippled under his sleeves. "You have lived a life of unusual adventure, well beyond the average royal scribe, I should think. You must miss it."

Ksenia's shoulders slumped, and she stared across the room, attentive to a memory. "I do. I don't mean to sound ungrateful, but there's nothing like taking a wild ride across open fields or along the foothills and bluffs of the Great Crown. It's not the adventure of an Outrider, but for me, it's . . ."

"Freedom," he answered.

"Yes." She lifted her eyes to regard him, unfettered by formal propriety or title for the first time. She reminded him of Karragin at that moment: honest and plainspoken. Her ease and comfort with herself made their interaction feel like the first genuine discussion he had carried out since his children left for the Borderlands. His gift remained quiescent, absent of any of the telltale vibrations of obfuscation or dissembling.

"What is it?" she asked.

"In some ways, you remind me of my daughter," he answered with a reassuring smile.

Ksenia flushed, then squinted, considering his words. "Karragin? That's either very flattering or possibly confusing."

"How so?" asked Therek with a friendly, challenging tone.

"I met Karra when she trained with my brother. They were in the same Outrider class, and we're all sympaths. She is one of the most driven people I have ever met. So . . . serious."

Therek chuckled out loud. "I can understand why most people find her reclusive. But once you get to know her, she's like anyone else."

Ksenia bopped her head in agreement. "Anyone else who can talk to horses at least. Have you heard any more news of their progress in the southern range?"

Therek sighed. "I apologize. I don't always pay attention to which scribe rotates on which day. You are aware then of the latest discovery?"

"I brought Mullayne to you and then sat as your scribe the next day while you received updates from Dexxin in the field," said Ksenia.

By the light of both full moons, how did I forget that?

"That's right, forgive me. I've had a lot on my mind of late. I haven't heard anything since this morning. I should probably climb the steps soon to see if Craxton has anything new for me."

At the mention of Craxton's name, a discordant vibration resonated back through his gift, indicating turmoil or possible conflict. "Since you know Mullayne, I assume you know her brothers, Dexxin and Craxton? Quite a rare trio, those three; a true blessing to the kingdom."

Ksenia sighed. "I know Craxton better than most. We were . . . involved last year, but let's just say things didn't work out."

"Apologies, I didn't mean to salt a wound," said Therek. "If I'm honest, I miss these kinds of conversations with Nolan and Karra."

"I don't imagine that anything I have to tell you is as important as what Karra and Nolan are going through," said Ksenia.

"It all depends on your perspective, but most parents find the welfare of their children more important than anything else. While your struggles might seem trivial to others, I'll wager they are of particular interest to your parents."

At the mention of her family, a cold, dissonant ripple traveled back through his gift. He couldn't help but investigate the sensation. "How are Elbend and Madola?"

"It's complicated. Father is happy. He has sons in the Outriders and the city watch. The demand for Aarindin is high, so business is good."

"And your mother?" asked Therek.

"Mother is Mother." She held her hands up in exasperation. "She won't let me join the Outriders, where I know my experience with Aarindin would be a benefit. We don't see eye to eye on that particular topic."

The disharmony conveyed by his gift lingered a moment, then settled as Ksenia thought about her mother.

"Ahh," said Therek. "Well, if Madola had a hand in your arrival to my staff, I'm grateful. You've already proven yourself an exceptional addition to the office. Just think of how you could shape the history of Aarindorn if you unlock the secrets of the book left by Weckles."

They sat in companionable silence for a time. Ksenia placed her hands on her thighs in preparation to stand. "Without condition, wield your greatest power? It's a place to start, I suppose."

The stained-glass doors to the inner sanctum swung open, and Craxton Endule stepped forward. He startled when he made eye contact with Ksenia but quickly regained his composure. "Your Grace, apologies for the interruption. I have news from Dexxin and didn't think it could wait."

Chapter Twenty-Five: On the Nonmedical Uses of Embertang

Karragin stretched her neck and pulled at the collar of her Outrider gear. Dried grotvonen gore had stiffened the leather, and now it chafed, but the cold temperatures made the outerwear necessary. Tugging on the jerkin made her aware once again of the lingering taint of the creatures from the cavern. Human blood left an iron, mineral scent. The cloying scent of grotvonen blood stained the back and sides of her tongue with something that reminded her of rancid garlic.

She scraped at her sleeves and front panel with the edge of a knife to remove as much of the dried blood as she could manage. Her labor didn't yield much improvement, and she wrinkled her nose in revulsion.

Savnah laughed at her discomfort. "Glad to see I'm not the only one that smells like the Taker's puckered asshole. When we get back, the first thing I'm going to do is burn all this gear, then bathe in a vat of survivor's essence."

Karragin grunted in agreement, then hunkered over their small campfire. She didn't often agree with Savnah's expressions, but this time the woman had the right of things. A few green spruce sticks placed onto the hot coals smoked, and she waved the vapors forward.

If I can't clean my gear, perhaps I can cover up the reek.

After a few minutes, she sat back, teary-eyed. A quick dip of her nose revealed that the smoke did a poor job of covering the worst parts of the grotvonen funk.

"That's maybe a little better," said Karragin.

"I'll try anything at this point," said Savnah. The woman leaned in, repeating Karragin's smoke bath, then sat down. Savnah ran her nose along a sleeve and inhaled. "I don't know. I think I smell like smoked grot, and that's a combination that might make me averse to meat. What would Father say?"

Karragin didn't follow Savnah's last comment and turned to regard the woman. They stared at one another for a few moments. Eventually, Savnah sighed. "Listen, Karra; you don't have to pull that resting asshole face on me. If you want to know something, just ask. I'm an open book."

"Sorry, old habits," said Karragin. "What do you mean about your father?"

Savnah bobbed her head up and down and poked a stick into the fire. "Have you ever made the trek to Callinora and stopped at Midrock? There's an inn, with a big taproom. They serve the best smoked chop in the kingdom."

"You're talking about The Wolf's Maw," said Karragin. "It's a nice place, cleaner than most. I'll have to take your word on the food."

"The next time you pass through, ask for Savnah's plate," she said as she jabbed a thumb at her chest. "It's a platter of four different cuts. It's not on the official menu, but Father would make sure to take good care of you."

"Your father the pitmaster?" asked Karragin.

"When he was younger. For about a decade now, he's been the sole proprietor of the inn. Anyway, I don't think he would know how to react if I swore off meat all on account of a little grot blood."

"We'll be back to base camp soon enough, and I'll join you for a ceremonial coat burning," said Karragin.

She looked through the haze of smoke at her fellow Outriders. Dexxin sat on an ice-glazed rocky outcropping inspecting the fletching of a few borrowed arrows. Tovnik and Runta were carrying on a quiet conversation near Amniah. The guster stared with vacant eyes into the campfire. They had all tried to engage the young woman in conversation but met with little success. As if in answer to her thought, Tovnik looked back and sighed with a defeated expression.

"I've seen battle shock before, and she's got it bad," said Savnah.

Karragin stared at the hooded guster. After exiting the grotvonen caves, they'd hiked a few hours to a defensible part of the ravine. There they agreed to set up a temporary camp, mainly to allow Amniah to rest.

Nolan had foraged game and sought out lammen, a bush that dropped red fruit in early winter. While it proved tart, they all knew of its restorative properties. Her brother made sure to portion out generous shares to Amniah. While the guster regained some of the color in her face, she still appeared lost. *All because I sent them ahead into the valley on a scouting mission. Taker's breath, how did she fall down that hole in the first place?*

She swallowed back the mounting sensation of regret. "I was hoping that the journey back might give her time to come out of it. She's regaining strength, but I worry she won't be able to return to the field."

"Well, if anything like that ever happens to me, just dust off my axes, get them into my hands, and point me toward danger. I'll either come around or make a messy end to talk about," said the prime.

Just then, Nolan hiked up the steep ravine, panting. A large game bird bounced over his shoulder, and he trudged with his head bowed. He tossed the carcass to the side and took a knee.

Karragin allowed him a moment to catch his breath, but Savnah broke the tension. "What's got you so muddled, tracker?"

Nolan raised his head. Instead of answering Savnah's question, he tossed handfuls of snow onto the campfire embers. He watched the smoke trail follow the wind and swirl up the mountain in the direction they had come from.

"That wind is the Giver's blessing. There are at least eight grondle about a mile down this ravine making slow progress this way," he said.

"Do you think they saw you?" asked Karragin.

"No. After I shot dinner, I took a moment to search the valley for any sign of the grot or umbral. On a whim, I searched for grondle, and that's when I found them. I watched for a time. They don't seem to be in any hurry, but the ravine leads naturally back to the falls where we exited the caves. As long as the wind holds out, they won't sense our campfire."

Karragin tongued the scar on her upper lip. She spoke in a soft voice meant for Savnah. "I was hoping we might be able to try something, but not against a crush, not all at once, and not when Amniah is so . . . damaged."

"What did you have in mind? I'm willing to test my blades against those things. Besides, it's not as if they can make me smell any worse," said Savnah.

"You might be able to manage one or two of them, Savnah, maybe. But the one we encountered back at the base camp was surprisingly strong. I don't think our group would fare too well against a crush."

Karragin rubbed involuntarily at the fading bruises on her neck. As her fingers ran across the patches of bronzed, course skin, she felt no pain. Instead, she felt an intense desire to charge down the mountain ravine.

And do what exactly, Karra? Extract some measure of revenge against one, only to have the others fall on your friends?

She stared a moment at Savnah, then Nolan, a plan forming in her mind. "I need a moment. Let me see if I can get a sense for anything with these." She tapped at her forearm.

"Are you sure we have time?" asked Savnah. "No offense, but you didn't learn anything the last few times you tried that trick."

"I know, but I have to try," she said.

Karragin knelt in the snow and withdrew into herself. She forced out the awareness of her tainted Outrider gear, the nip of winter on her nose and ears, and focused until the gentle rushing of the nearby river was the only sound that occupied her thoughts. Zenith flowed into her runes, unbidden and easy. She directed the flow into her rune of premonition and waited.

In her mind, she brought forth an awareness of their camp, the high ground on which they stood, and the enemy approaching. To her surprise, heat flared across the rune on her forearm, and a myriad of images flickered as possibilities of a future yet to be cast. She envisioned a retreat to the caves, but those images were overshadowed by cries of agony.

Next, she imagined a direct confrontation with the crush, but the brute force of the grondle overwhelmed their group. The images blurred and shifted, leaving her struggling to make sense of the best way forward. At last, her perception focused for a brief instant, revealing a possible successful outcome. She worked to recreate the scene in her mind, but the images faded, and her rune fell dormant.

"Taker's breath," she cursed and opened her eyes, bringing her awareness back to the group. They all looked at her, waiting. Even Savnah fingered the top of a moonblade axe with an expression of anticipation.

"That didn't take very long. Did you learn anything useful?" asked Nolan.

"Perhaps. The crush has a leader, some kind of alpha. It will be the first to reach us. There is a ledge some thirty feet up this cliff. We can hide there until the full crush arrives. Everything else will rely on Amniah," Karragin explained.

May the Giver absolve me if this goes sideways.

Karragin stepped around the fire and took a knee in front of Amniah. "Tov, I need a spot of embertang," she said.

Tovnik rummaged through his pack and found a metal vial. The medic turned back and regarded her with a concerned expression. "Karragin, if you're injured, you should let me see if you really want this applied. It's nasty stuff. Have you even handled it before?" Karragin just tilted her head and held out her hand. "If the wound is in an . . . awkward place, I assure you it's nothing I haven't seen before. Or if you'd prefer, Runta could examine the . . . region."

"It's not for me, Tov, and nobody is injured," said Karragin.

"Well then, what is it for?" asked Tovnik as he handed over the vial.

"We are not going back into those caves; we won't survive there, and the only way out of here leads through those things. Savnah and I could likely take a few grondle, but not a crush. For that, we need Amniah."

Karragin waited for her words to provoke a reaction. Tovnik shouldered his pack and began to string a bow, while Runta counted then divided the leftover arrows between them. She watched, hoping for some response from the guster. The frail woman retreated into the shadows of her hood. Karragin reached forward and rolled back the front edges, exposing Amniah's face and the scabbed abrasions on her shaved head.

"Arrows will only announce our intention and cause the grondle little harm. There is only one person here who has a chance to harm most of them all at once." Karragin waited, but Amniah looked back with the same empty expression.

She unstoppered the flask of embertang and applied a single droplet onto her own forearm.

"Karra, that's undiluted. You shouldn't handle it without gloves or at least—" Tovnik's protest withered as Karragin took Amniah's forearm and pressed their flesh together, sealing the single drop of embertang between them.

The tincture seared into her forearm, and Karragin sucked in a breath. Amniah registered the pain and frowned, finally drawing her focus to Karragin. The younger woman tried to pull her hand back, but Karragin held tight, gritting her teeth against the pain.

"I know you've been hurt, Niah. I know you have wounds I can never mend. But I also know you are still here. And as long as you can feel pain, you're alive, and you can choose. Either accept the pain or do something about it."

Amniah stood, attempting to wrench her arm back, but Karragin flared her arca prime and held fast. The guster snarled a lip, and a torrent of air began to spin bits of ice and snow around them.

"That's it! There you are," said Karragin. She raised her voice above the roar of the wind rushing past her ears. "Now imagine how much pain you could inflict if you used the rest of the embertang to thread the needle right into the gill slits of those grinders!"

The torrent of air swirled a few seconds more, and shards of ice strafed against Karragin's cheek. Abruptly, the maelstrom stopped, as did Amniah's attempt to remove her arm. Something alive and . . . dark flickered in Amniah's eyes, something that gave the normally cerulean blaze of her gifted eyes a darker midnight blue hue. Amniah nodded once.

Karragin shook her forearm in pain. "Grind me. Tov, have you got anything to stop the burn?"

The medic produced a flask of what looked like resco. He liberally doused their forearms, then rubbed ash over the embertang welts. In moments, the burning faded to minor discomfort. The skin of her arm drew taut in goosebumps, cooled by the volatile liquid.

"I didn't know you could neutralize embertang," said Nolan.

"You learn a few things in training when you mishandle the stuff," said Tovnik.

Savnah cleared her throat. "You know, I could have managed to get through to Amniah without so much as a shiver."

"Maybe. But it's kind of hard to convince someone that you understand something of their pain unless you feel it too," said Karragin. Amniah met her eyes in silent agreement.

"So, what's the plan then?" asked Savnah.

Karragin turned her gaze to the steep rocky walls of the ravine. "The advantage of high ground will be lost as soon as the grondle close the distance, and I don't think we can outrun them if things grind sideways. First, we need to create false trails in the snow to make it look like we are hiding close to the river. Then we have to climb the cliff of the ravine. We have a chance if we can reach that shelf thirty feet up. I will explain the rest once we are up top."

"If we hurry, we should have time," said Nolan.

They marched across the ravine, making several unmistakable trails in the snow and underbrush. Satisfied with their work, Karragin ordered a retreat back toward the cliff face.

"Start climbing. I want all of us up there. I'm going to rebuild our campfire, so the smoke draws them in. Tovnik and Runta, gather all your embertang. I want Amniah to thread the needle straight into their gills. Hopefully, it will send them back to whatever abyss they came from."

"How do we know that will hurt them at all? Maybe it will just turn the oversized bulls into raging monsters," said Savnah.

"Maybe," Karragin conceded. "But Venlith said something that makes me believe these things are not from the Drift, not strictly speaking, anyway. And if they are flesh and blood, not just constructs of nadir, then I have to believe the most caustic substance we own can cause them harm. I'll tell you the rest up top."

They stood in a small circle, each considering the plan Karragin had outlined. The climb alone looked difficult, and if the plan didn't work, they would be trapped. While the grondle might not be able to reach them, there was no way off the shelf except down.

Savnah hocked phlegm and spit to her side, then approached the wall of the ravine. "Right then, you heard the lady. Last one up sucks the Taker's salty balls. Except you, Amniah. No one expects you to be first with your injuries."

Without words, Amniah bent to retrieve a coil of rope and slung it over her shoulder. The guster pulled back her hood and stared at the steep wall of the ravine. Swirls of snow and loose rock gathered under her stunted feet, and she sprinted headlong at the rocky wall with unnatural speed. From three strides away, she leaped, and a puff of air carried her in a high arc. She hopped, scrambled, and surged up the thirty-foot cliff with bursts of air, eventually landing on the shelf in a flurry of snow.

Savnah waved her hand at the falling ice, pebbles, and debris. "Well, tickle me straight in the asshole with a feather duster. Have you ever seen such a thing?"

"I've never even held a feather duster," said Nolan.

Karragin looked up at Amniah and tilted her head in a gesture of respect. For her part, the guster turned and secured the rope, then tossed it back down for the others. Karragin rekindled their campfire then made her way up the rope to the shelf. After retrieving the line, they all sat back against the wall.

"Right then, listen up," said Karragin. "Once the crush arrives, half of them are going to charge our false trails toward the river."

Karragin turned to Savnah and held her gaze a moment. "My premonition ability is . . . unreliable. I can't control when I receive visions. But I did see you, Savnah, standing at the end of our trail. Half of the grondle will charge and fall into the gorge. I saw what you can do, but it's not my place—"

"You want her to be bait," Dexxin interrupted. "That's just crazy."

Karragin waited for the woman from Midrock to comment. But Savnah turned her attention to the river. "I'll do it. It tests the limits of what I can do, but I think I can manage. Still, that only rids us of half the grondle."

"I know," said Karragin. "That's where Amniah comes in. She's going to thread the needle with embertang right into the remaining grondle. Any questions?"

She took their silence as an acceptance of her command. They spent the next several minutes making obvious tracks through the snow. After marking false trails toward the river gorge, they retreated to the safety of the ledge where Amniah perched. And then the waiting began. The next half-hour drew out in painful stillness and wound her up tighter than a bowstring.

Hurry up and wait. This must be what the docent meant. . . Makes me wish I had her rocker up here.

Karragin double-checked the security of the ropes she and Savnah would use to rappel down the cliff face. Next, she fingered the edge of her saber and the spare dagger on her hip. A kick of her heels together dislodged a fragment of mud from her boots. She considered another assessment of the ropes then realized how that might look to the others under her command.

With an effort, she sat down and studied the remaining members of their expedition. The medics huddled in quiet conversation. Nolan alternated between scanning the canyon for grondle and attempting to make conversation with Amniah. To his credit, the young woman responded to him in words too soft for Karragin to hear. Savnah fingered her moonblade axes and leaned back against the cliff in uncharacteristic silence.

"Nolan, any sign of them yet?" asked Karragin.

Thick locks of cinnamon hair jostled on his shoulders as he shook his head. "Nothing yet."

Dexxin stood and approached, clearing his throat. "In case this fails, I took the liberty of making a full report of our progress to Mullayne and Craxton. My brother is with the regent. Your father says the plan is flawed and explains that embertang is an oil. By that, he means it will scatter into droplets. He advises that Amniah should practice before the grondle arrive. If she can't hold the embertang together, we should wait for reinforcements."

Dexxin usually abstained from making comments whenever they gathered for idle chat. Something in his tone sounded almost pleased that her plan was less than perfect. Perhaps he was as nervous as the rest of them. She squashed the notion and considered his news.

I don't know if we can hold out for the five to seven days it would take the others to get here. "Tell my father his counsel is appreciated, but unless he can fly us the food, water, and supplies to remain on this shelf a week, we will have to try something unorthodox."

Dexxin stared back at her, uncertain how to proceed. "You want me to say all of that?"

"No, I suppose that snark won't get us through this any faster. Relay to him that we appreciate his advice, but needs must. Tell him we'll send word once it's all over."

She turned to the medics. "Tovnik, do you have a basin or a bowl, something to hold water?"

Tovnik removed a mortar and pestle from his pack, set the pestle to the side, and filled the mortar with water. Karragin watched and waited. "Niah, see if you can gather up the water in the mortar and . . . do whatever it is you gusters do," she said.

Amniah sat down beside the medic and appeared to collect herself, looking more like the unfettered young woman from base camp than she had in days. A small dust devil whirled about the mortar, the only sign of her channeling. The water churned in a vortex then rose from the bowl. The guster reached both hands forward and appeared to shape the air before her, narrowing and tightening the currents into a long funnel. The water responded, swirling into a thin tube.

"Give me a target," she said without taking her eyes from the liquid.

"There's a winterberry bush crawling up the far side of the ravine. Can you hit that from here?" asked Karragin.

Amniah cocked her head to the right, considering the request, then released the column of water. It shot forth, slower than an arrow, but with a similar trajectory, arcing slightly then splashing onto the purple berries of the bush.

"That settles it; Amniah's on my team the next time we throw darts," said Savnah.

"Alright, good. This could work," said Karragin. "Tov, I don't want to waste the embertang. Do you have any tinctures made of oil that she can practice with?"

Tovnik nodded once, removed a different flask, and poured a strange dark purple liquid into the mortar. Some of the liquid splashed right out of the shallow basin, landing on the ground and breaking up into small globs of oil. When the individual spheres bumped into one another, they coalesced into a larger ball.

Nolan whistled in appreciation. "Is that Eldrenol's solution?" he asked. "That stuff is supposed to cost a small fortune."

"It is, and it does," said Tovnik. "But it's the closest liquid I have to embertang. Both have the strange property of being less cohesive than water. It breaks apart into tiny beads when jostled."

To emphasize his point, Tovnik poured a tiny amount of the purple oil into his palm and blew a puff of air at the substance. It broke apart into small spheres and misted into the air. The cloud of Eldrenol's solution wafted toward Savnah, and she backed away. "Dammit to the grindin' Drift, Tov!"

"I assure you it's not dangerous, Savnah. You can breathe it in, and it's quite inert unless you're an abrogator. Then you might want to hold your breath." To emphasize his point, Tovnik leaned forward and inhaled some of the purple cloud with an exaggerated sniff. He sneezed once and wiped a faint purple mist from his nose. "There, see? Nothing to worry about. It's the opposite of Veramanth's decoction."

"You mean stiller's powder? Do you carry that too?" asked Nolan.

"Yes, I can brew it into a tea to prevent anyone from channeling zenith," said Tovnik.

"Why would you ever need that?" asked Nolan.

"Channeling zenith has the strange property of causing fractures to mend quickly. On the rare occasion that an Outrider suffers a long bone fracture in the field, I can set the injury first, 'ranth them up, then arrange definitive care without having to worry about the bone mending in a crooked position."

"Huh, I didn't know that," said Nolan.

"All the same, keep all that stuff away from me," said Savnah.

Karragin waved a hand, dispersing the rest of the vaporized solution. "Focus. I don't know how much time we have left. Amniah, try again with this. See if you can thread the needle to that bush again."

Amniah dipped a finger into the mortar and rubbed a bit of the oily solution on her thumb. She sighed once, seeming to resolve herself to the task, and began. The bowl wobbled as air currents swirled about, and the Eldrenol's solution vaporized into a fine mist. Amniah pursed her lips tight enough to kiss a spider and labored to bring the tiny particles back together. Several moments passed, and the amorphous cloud undulated and changed shape in the air. Misted particles merged into small beads that joined into small balls only to break apart into mist again.

She hovered the strange cloud of vapor in place for a moment, then slowly migrated the haze to the far ravine. It fell apart, splashing against the winterberry bush, and landed in a three-foot diameter area around the target.

Amniah shrugged, and she panted a moment. "I think I can do it, but your father was right. If embertang is like that stuff, the grondle might see it coming, and I can't move it very fast without having it all break apart."

"Sometimes the Giver gives, and sometimes the Taker takes," said Karragin. "We'll have to bait them in, get them close together, then you could hit them all at once," said Karragin. "Moons, here comes the alpha."

Chapter Twenty-Six: An Elder's Counsel

The fragrance of something delicate and slightly floral drew Laryn from a deep slumber. She rolled to her side under a heavy fur blanket and tried to return to sleep. With a tentative, probing foot, she stretched out, expecting to find Kaellor's leg. His side of the bed felt cool and empty.

Where have you gotten off to this early in the day, love?

The aroma of kevash tea wafted under the blanket, and her empty stomach gurgled. She popped her head above the edge of the fur to discover Kaellor fanning the steam of fresh tea in her direction.

"I see you've got your range of motion back then?" she said and stifled a yawn.

With an exaggerated motion to demonstrate the function of his newly mended wrist, Kaellor poured her a mug of tea, then set the wood carafe down. He inspected the ruddy flesh stretched over his wrist and forearm, clenched a fist, then slowly uncurled his fingers.

Healing the wound caused by the wolvryn two days ago had taken her most of the morning. After she set the fractured bones, she had to mend the damaged muscle fibers. Controlling his pain while completing the weaving was a labor of tedious intensity and had left her with a headache that only lifted this morning.

"I know this woman," he said wistfully. "She's a healer, you see, and quite gifted."

She looked at him over the mug of tea. "Mmm . . . she must think a lot of you. I know cutters who would lop the hand off at the wrist and be done with it."

"I can only imagine," said Kaellor. "If not for the Giver's luck and her skill, I would be known as Lefty by those at court. She even managed to weave the runes back together."

"No, your gift did that. I could feel the lines of zenith fusing through the mended tissue, but that was an act of the Giver, not me," said Laryn. She scooted back in their bed to a comfortable sitting position. "Come here, let me see."

Kaellor sat down on the edge of the bed and offered his wrist for inspection. The only sign of the wolvryn bite was the smooth, hairless, and pink skin under the runes. She turned his forearm and inspected the motion of his wrist and elbow. Finding no limitations or blemishes, she brushed her lips across his knuckles, then made a playful snarl and snapped as if she would bite him. He didn't pull back but instead cupped her cheek, so she turned in and kissed his palm.

"It seems I've put you back together, but let's not make a habit of that. My headache only just left in the night. I've experienced enough of the draft this season to last me a lifetime."

"I know, and I promise to be better," said Kaellor. "It all happened so fast. I had no idea the wolvryn would appear from so far away."

"They've learned to fold into the clouds. All wolvryn in the valley manage it. Which one bit you, anyway?"

Kaellor rubbed at his beard with the back of his hand. "I think it was Boru, and it's a good thing too."

"How so?" she asked.

"Boru is formidable, all muscle and fang when he gets worked up. But Neska is . . . crafty. I think Boru acted out of basic instinct to protect Bryndor. Neska studied me, looking for any weakness in my defense. If she had found one, I don't think she would have settled for an arm. Boru used his strength to toss me away, separate me from the boys. Neska would have found something more . . . final."

"Never trifle with a woman given to protect something she loves."

Kaellor held his hands up in mock surrender. "I've been humbled and brought to task."

She arched a single eyebrow. *The sun has yet to set on the day when a lone act brings you to heel.* "Have you seen either of them this morning?"

"The wolvryn? Yes. It's as if nothing happened. Neska padded right up to me when I first left the hut wanting a scratch behind the ears, and Boru licked the grease from my hands after breakfast. Mahkeel says they're no danger to anyone, as long as they don't threaten the boys."

"Is that going to interfere with your training?" asked Laryn.

Kaellor sighed. "Mahkeel suggests we involve the wolvryn in the drills, make them watch and keep them engaged, then we can continue, but I don't think I can ever let things get out of control like that. I was . . . caught unprepared. I think it was the sword. Somehow it magnified my defenses, heightened my awareness, made me . . . eager."

His words gave her pause. "What do you mean when you say eager?" she asked.

"I didn't realize it at the time, but the sword intensifies my gift, makes me crave confrontation. It was like I wanted the boys to try to hurt me so that I had a reason to summon and release my gift. When they orchestrated a sneak attack, the flood of zenith overwhelmed my ability to hold it back. After Boru threw me, it was all I could do to resist the surge. My gift . . . beckoned me for release. There was a moment there when . . . I could have killed them all—"

She studied his haunted face. His cheeks flushed, and tiny beads of sweat gathered on his forehead. She reached for his hand once again to pull him back to the room. "But you didn't. Despite the pain of a broken and mangled arm, you kept it in check, Kae."

"That's a kindness if ever there was one," he acknowledged.

The years have eroded so much of the carefree man I once knew. "Why do you do it? The drills."

She interlocked her fingers in his, the gesture releasing his tension like the turning of a valve. Kaellor puffed out his cheeks then exhaled. "I started, I think, because it gave me purpose. But if I'm honest, it's Aarindorn."

She waited in silence, holding space for him to continue. His gaze lingered on the guardian sword resting at the foot of their bed, then withdrew to someplace distant. Eventually, he continued, "I can't shake the feeling that our return isn't the end of our troubles, but the beginning of it all, and we're planning to walk right into the grinding thick of it. I don't know if it's the drills or the sword or just the distraction, but for a few hours every day, I feel like I'm doing what I can to prepare for what awaits us."

"Well, it will be the Taker's kiss for anyone who stands in our way . . . together then, we'll manage," she said.

"Together," he echoed.

She wrapped both hands behind his neck and fingered a lock of hair. "Now then, tell me more about this mysterious healer woman that dared to lay hands on you."

Her words drew forth a soft smile on his face. He tilted his head back to consider her with an appraising eye. *There's the man I fell in love with, resting underneath all that guilt.*

He reached forward and pulled her into an embrace. "Oh, she's a crafty vixen. Some would say she plies her witchery to beguile and fool the unsuspecting. Others fear her ability to make brave men wilt under her gaze."

The muscles on her forehead tightened in a challenge. "And what do you say, brave guardian?"

He pulled her closer, pressing a hand to the small of her back. The simple intimacy of how easily he lost himself in her gaze narrowed the entire world down to the breath between them. He swallowed. "I say—"

A rap on the doorframe to their hut announced a visitor. Kaellor dropped his head onto her shoulder, and together, they released a groan of frustration. Something about being in that moment, of being needed and needing him, made her giggle. Laryn whispered into his ear. "That's not a Cloud Walker. They don't announce themselves with a knock."

He nodded in understanding and cleared his throat. "Good morning, Bryn."

Bryndor pushed aside the door reinforced with furs and tilted his head inside. "How did you know it was me?"

"The Damadibo don't knock, and your brother is never awake before you are," said Kaellor.

"Oh, that makes sense, I suppose," said Bryndor. "Anyway, Elder Miljin wants you up at the spirit house when you get the chance."

Laryn pulled Kaellor close to stave off the chill of the winter air. She lifted her chin over his shoulder and winked at Bryndor. "Did he happen to say what he wanted?"

"Not exactly, but if I'm reading him right, he wasn't in a rush," said Bryndor.

"That man doesn't know how to rush," said Laryn. "How are you today? Any lingering effects from the other day?"

"I'm fine. We're both fine, ma'am," said Bryndor.

She tsk'd. "Ma'am again, is it? Off with you now, you're letting out all the warmth. Tell Miljin we'll be along in a little while."

Bryndor nodded and made to remove himself when a puzzled look creased his face, and he grunted. Boru's broad head pushed under his arm and caused the door to flap open. The wolvryn filled up the doorway and considered them all with what appeared to be a sloppy smile. Kaellor reached out and caressed his broad snout and forehead.

"Sorry—come, Boru," said Bryndor, and he extricated himself and the wolvryn.

Laryn leaned back to Kaellor. "Was it just me, or was that wolvryn smiling at us just now?"

"You tell me. You know more about those creatures than I do," said Kaellor.

She made quick work of sliding into a set of warm leather breeches, wrapped a warm hide skirt around her waist, stepped into boots, and grabbed her outercoat.

Kaellor sat back on the bed. "What do you suppose the elder wants this morning?"

"I don't know. It could be he's considering the very bad example you are setting for all the young people by shacking up with me in this hut." She stomped her heel into the bottom of her boot.

Kaellor's brow furrowed. "Really? But we are wed, even though the ceremony was rushed . . ."

Laryn gathered her hair back into a tight ponytail. "Aren't you charming? But no, silly, the Damadibo don't cater to such silly notions. Walk me to the gathering house so I can grab a bite, then we'll go see."

He reached into a pocket and produced a small package wrapped in cloth. She opened the bundle to find a ball of sweet bread, still warm from the ovens. The rich aroma caused her stomach to gurgle.

"Prince Baellentrell, if I didn't know better, I might believe you are trying to curry favor with me. First, you ply me with my favorite tea, and now this. What aren't you telling me that I should know about?" She pulled the bread apart and popped the smaller half in her mouth.

"No false agenda here. I'm just . . . making up for lost time, I suppose," he said.

She swallowed and washed the bread down with the last bit of tea. "Well then, pace yourself. We have the rest of our lives. Come on, to the spirit house."

A short time later, they sat around the warm hearth of the spirit house, watching Elder Miljin grind dried butterfly wings into a fine powder. He collected the orange powder into a small earthenware container then turned, dusting off his hands.

"I asked you here this morning because I received a visit from an ancestral spirit last night," said the elder.

Laryn sensed Kaellor's eyes on her. He looked as surprised as she felt that the wizened man had chosen to speak in the common tongue and not the hand language. "The elder enters communion with the spirits several times a month. Usually, it's to reconnect, to share memory. But sometimes they impart advice or answer questions," Laryn said, answering Kaellor's unspoken question.

"Not sometimes," Miljin corrected. "Almost never . . . maybe two or three times in a full transition of the moons do the spirits concern themselves with the things we find important."

"I understand. So, what did you learn?" asked Kaellor.

"We shared brief words before of a dark presence lurks in the Drift, just the shadow of one who used to be, but who remains separate from the spirits, isolated. The ancestors have never concerned themselves with the being before."

"What changed?" asked Laryn.

"Someone," he paused, then reverted to signing. *"Forgive me, my words are not the best to explain what I mean, and this is important."*

"Go on, I will translate," signed Laryn.

"Someone crafted a barrier of unnatural zenith. It binds this creature in the Drift. Something in the resonance of that barrier matches your gift, Kaellor. However, what was once a wall of stone has diminished to a thin shroud. As a result, the spirits can sense this presence."

"His name was Tarkannen," said Kaellor.

"Yes," said Miljin. The elder studied their faces for long moments in contemplative silence. Something in his bearing appeared drained, exhausted. Laryn held her breath, waiting to see the playful wrinkle of skin at the edges of his eyes. This morning he remained grim, and darkness steeped into his expression.

Miljin dipped his head, attempting to speak the right words. "The creature that dwells in the Drift is not the man who was banished there years ago. What was done to him, has . . . he has been altered."

"What was done to him was the least he deserved for his atrocities," said Kaellor. The beard along the angle of his jaw flared a moment until he unclenched his teeth. "I'm sorry. Please, continue."

Miljin nodded. *"Kaellor speaks an earnest truth. But what was done to the man was not just of the Baellentrell gift. It was torture of his own making. He pulled himself into the Drift to escape a permanent end, and while there, he has become something darker than anything else the spirits have encountered."*

"None of that really matters as long as he remains there," said Laryn.

"That is, in part, why I asked you here," signed the elder. *"The spirits can sense his presence and have revealed four things."*

The elder adjusted to a more comfortable position, smoothed out his robes, then began to sign again. *"First, the barrier keeping him there is thinning. Second, he has become something of significance, a power, or they would not bother to mention him at all. Third, most troubling, he is somehow anchored to this world and not of the Drift."*

"What do you mean?" signed Laryn.

"The spirits can sense that he probes for a way through the barrier, but his efforts seem directed at a return to the living and not a merging in the Drift."

Laryn finished the translation, and they sat in silence more than twenty heartbeats. Eventually, Kaellor cleared his throat. "I suppose that none of that should surprise us. Do the spirits know how Tarkannen is anchored to this world? Is it a . . . lashing that we can cut?"

The elder smiled for the first time and tilted his head to Laryn. *"I see why you were attracted to this one in the first place. He has a sharp mind."*

Laryn looked to Kaellor. *"Not sharp enough to learn all the intricacies of signing."*

"I recall it took you more than a season to learn the language," Miljin signed, then rose and walked with a slow grace to place an earthenware kettle over the brazier.

"What did I miss?" asked Kaellor, baffled at the abrupt hiatus in the conversation.

"Nothing. He's just getting to the good part."

Miljin circled behind them, lit a stick of incense, then returned to his seat untroubled by any part of the conversation. He stretched arthritic fingers, then continued, *"This creature is tied to a body in this world by a tether that sustains him. Find that person and sever the tether before the barrier holding him breaks, and he will be consumed in the Drift."*

Laryn translated the elder's words, and they sat in silence again.

"Is such a thing even possible?" asked Kaellor.

"I don't know. The Damadibo are not given to embellishment. I don't think the ancestors would make any of this known to Elder Miljin unless it were true," said Laryn.

With clumsy fingers, Kaellor signed for himself. *"Do the spirits know who this person is?"*

Miljin's face, unwrinkled by expression, looked down at empty palms.

"I see," said Kaellor. He pulled at the silvery tufted stripe at the chin of his beard and cast a sideways glance at Laryn. "What do you think?"

"I think . . . that there is actually a way someone could be kept alive, nourished even, despite the strain of supporting a parasite from the Drift. In Callinora . . ." Laryn stood and walked a slow circle. As she worked through the details in her mind, she felt as if the room shifted.

"By the Giver's blessings, have we undone ourselves?" Laryn said to nobody in particular.

She turned to find Kaellor at her side, his brow darkening the light behind his eyes. "What is it?"

"The healers at Callinora can craft a dozenth. It's a way to preserve a patient in a cocoon of zenith. It allows the body to heal without the ravages of time. It's how they mended my body after the Abrogator's War."

"That sounds a lot like the construct placed around initiates who sit for their trial of revealing," said Kaellor.

"Those are minor creations by comparison, but the principle is the same," said Laryn. "A patient is suspended and fed a constant flow of zenith."

"Would anyone at the Sanitorium act to aid the Usurper?" asked Kaellor.

"Not willingly, but when I awoke from the dozenth, there was an entire wing of patients in similar states of stasis recovering from injuries more grievous than mine."

"And you think Tarkannen could remain connected and sustained by a person in such a state?" asked Kaellor.

"It's the only way I can imagine someone could survive something like that," said Laryn.

Kaellor turned back to the olive-skinned elder and signed a slow question, *"What was the fourth thing?"*

"You see, sharp mind," he signed to Laryn. *"The fourth thing is that the barrier is fading fast. You can not afford to wait until spring to dance with the spirits. You must take your wolvryn and cross the summit of the Korjinth."*

Chapter Twenty-Seven: Guster's Last Stand

Karragin and her fellow Outriders crouched in silence on the shelf high in the ravine. The sound of hooves clopping up the canyon announced the arrival of the first grondle. Karragin's premonition proved accurate; the beast climbing up to their campsite made the grondle from the Outrider camp look immature by comparison.

Broad hooves, lifted with casual grace, plunged into the snow. Steam rose from the grondle's muscular back, and all nature stilled as the predator approached. Faded red and blue fetiches of hair and bone dangled from a thick rope worn as a necklace over the upper torso. The grondle twisted to survey the campsite, and sunlight glinted off a metal breastplate fitted around the fleshy gill slits. Gouts of steam billowed out from the fenestrations in the lower torso.

The alpha stopped short of the camp and furrowed thick ridges of hide over black beady eyes. A crude battle axe rested on its shoulder, and it casually tapped the massive blade against one of its curved ebony horns. In its other hand, it held a thick spear that it jabbed into the snow, using the spearhead as a spoon. After sniffing and tasting the snow, the beast craned its neck back and bellowed a deep, grinding yowl that echoed down the canyon.

Then the alpha rocked its weight back onto its hind legs and waited. In moments, overlapping higher-pitched yowls carried up the canyon. Several minutes later, the rest of the crush stampeded up the ravine. None of the grondle matched the alpha's size or adornment. They each carried thick hafted spears, but only the alpha wore any semblance of armor.

Thank the Giver for small victories.

The company remained hidden and observed as the leader snorted and grunted commands, drawing the others to attention. The crush spread out in two lines, with four in front and three behind, leaving the alpha to stand at the rear. After a muffled snort, the crush plodded forward along the false trails toward the river.

Karragin turned to Savnah and nodded, then whispered to Amniah, "After Savnah lures them out, I need you to whip up the snow to obscure our drop. Give us maybe thirty seconds, then save yourself for the embertang. Got it?"

Something feral passed over the guster's expression, and she nodded once.

"Tovnik, get the embertang ready. The rest of you harry them with bow fire when I call for it."

Karragin spared a look to the other prime. Savnah was holding a fist forward and scrunching up her face in concentration. The air around the woman rippled as if she were giving off heat. At the far side of the camp, a version of Savnah walked out from the cover of trees and stood just in front of the drop-off to the river.

The crush drew to a halt. The lead line appeared eager, pawing at the snow and snorting, but they didn't charge. Karragin leaned forward and whispered, "Almost, Savnah. Just give them a reason to charge."

The prime wrenched her neck to the side in pained focus. Her apparition clanged the moonblade axes together and yelled a challenge. A derisive snort escaped the alpha's snout, and it gestured the crush forward. The first wave charged, churning up clods of snow and mud and howling in rage.

Karragin turned to Amniah. "Now, Niah, churn the snow." She shook Savnah's shoulders to bring her out of the trance. "That's enough. Time for us to drop."

The air around the prime lost its strange, lustrous halo, and Savnah opened her eyes. They each grabbed ropes and began to rappel down the cliff face. Over the rush of wind and snow drafted by Amniah, the fearful mewling of grondle falling into the river gorge echoed across the camp. Karragin kicked back to rappel down and thought she heard Savnah mutter, "Nice!"

The two primes reached the bottom before Amniah's cloud of snow dissipated. They stood their ground, weapons drawn, and waited. Amniah allowed the torrent of winds to subside, and the grondle came into view. The alpha and its second line of three turned in agitated circles, searching for their prey.

"Loose arrows!" Karragin shouted. "Fire at will!"

From above, Nolan, Dexxin, and Runta took aim, releasing arrow after arrow. The three lesser grondle formed up before the alpha. Arrows found their mark more often than not, but the grondle seemed annoyed more than injured. Several arrows sprouted from meaty arms and torsos, and a few even lodged near the bony snouts. Those that struck the lower torso careened off into the snow.

We need them to charge. Amniah can't affect them from there.

Karragin stepped forward and yelled a challenge. "Come at me already!"

From behind the rank of three, the alpha hurtled the thick spear. The shaft flew as if on a rope, and Karragin had to deflect the weapon overhead. It vibrated as it wedged into the cliffside above her. Still, the crush remained in place.

"Now what, Karra?" asked Savnah. "Time for a muddle?"

Karragin stared at the dead-eyed alpha. "Let me try something, see if I can get them to charge."

Before she could think better of it, Karragin shifted the flow of zenith into her sympath rune and reached out to the grondle. *"Hey grinders, can you understand me?"*

The alpha seemed immediately drawn to Karragin and brandished its battle axe in two hands. The other grondle ceased their agitated movements despite the continuous barrage of arrows. The beasts stood momentarily still. Then, as a unified chorus, they howled an angry roar.

Images overwhelmed her senses as the grondle pushed back through her sympathic connection. She witnessed them tearing living people apart and became immersed in the tactile nature of the vision. Somehow, the grondle communicated not just images but also the sensations of their brutal feast.

She felt the sinewy texture of tendon and muscle pull through their teeth as they ate raw flesh. She sensed the pleasure they experienced in gorging on fresh liver, laden with salty, hot blood and the spongy way the organ meat chewed, the mineral tang at the sides of her tongue. Something in the brutal, total immersion of the sensation of eating another person overwhelmed her. To break the connection, she dismissed the flow of zenith, then promptly dropped to her knees, retching.

Savnah was immediately at her side, hoisting her up by the arm. The woman from Midrock shouted with a hint of fear behind the tenor of her voice, "Giver's tits, Karra! Move your moon-kissed ass!"

Karragin shook her head and swallowed back her bile in time to see the grondle charging. She summoned zenith into her arca prime. "I'm fine. Ready yourself. Work in a circle; stay on the outside!"

Two lesser grondle charged first, slipping and sliding before colliding into the cliff wall. The beast closest to Karragin slid on its side, and she took the opportunity to hack at the exposed limbs with two-handed, zenith-fueled, overhand swings. In three chops, she cleaved away one leg and left another severed and useless.

She stepped to the side in time to see the alpha swing its massive battle axe in a downward arc toward her. Her saber deflected the oversized blade, and it bit into the frozen ground, but the haft of the weapon struck her side. The alpha roared, pulling the weapon back without slowing. With blinding speed, the battle axe swung over her head. She ducked and lunged to the side, sweeping her blade in a slicing arc. Her saber clanged against the metal cuirass covering the beast's chest, and a burning throb vibrated up her arm.

She switched hands with the saber and danced back as the alpha charged her. The beast mixed attacks, swinging the deadly battle axe, rearing back to trample her, and even trying to throttle into her with its mass. Each time Karragin parried, ducked, or dodged back out of the way. The grondle struggled with the snow-slicked ground more than she did, and she worked her way to the side.

The alpha exhaled a roiling, fetid breath, and fleshy folds of purple tissue billowed at the edge of the metal breastplate. Karragin lunged forward to impale the gill slit, then realized her mistake, as the grondle seemed prepared for the attack. The great battle axe cleaved down, slamming her saber into the snow. A massive black hoof clopped down over the hilt, and the grondle swatted her with a meaty fist.

She stumbled back several steps despite her gifted strength. An unmistakable chuckle rumbled from the alpha, and its massive torso shuddered. Behind them, another grondle mewled in pain, and sunlight glinted off Savnah's moonblades.

Karragin spat into the snow, tasting salt and iron. "Clever, but that makes two of you grondle. Two left of your filthy crush!" she yelled, then pivoted and ran to the edge of the camp past several trees.

The alpha growled and snorted, then gave chase. Karragin waited for the beast to pick up speed. The trample of its hooves felt close, and at the last moment, she grabbed the trunk of a tree to swing around and sprinted back toward Savnah. The grondle tried to repeat the same tactic, but its weight snapped the tree, and it slid in a clumsy arc, losing its footing.

She raced back and dropped to her knees, intending to find her saber. Her hands sifted back and forth through the snow for several seconds and came up empty. In the distance, the alpha howled. Karragin turned in time to see the beast kick at the snow with its hind hooves, rear, and charge.

She turned and sprinted back to the cliff face to call for Nolan's sword when she spotted a discarded spear left from the grondle she had incapacitated. She hoisted the weapon under her arm and set her back to the cliff wall just as the alpha closed the distance.

Zenith thrummed through her arca prime as she set the butt end of the spear against mountain stone. The alpha tried to stop, skidding forward across the snow. She held the spear high, but at the last moment, stepped to the side and directed the tip down. The spearhead sheared off against the beast's metal armor, but Karragin's strength held the weapon fast. She wrenched the shaft to the side and into the beast's fenestration. The splintered haft sheared through sinewy tissue, and the alpha shrieked a cry of pain.

With all her effort, she held the spear in place, preventing the alpha from closing. The battle axe clanged forward once, twice, and a third time as the grondle raged. The swings missed her each time, but always landed a little closer. A flailing front hoof caught her on the hip, and she nearly dropped the spear haft.

"Now Niah, release the embertang on me, now!" Karragin yelled.

Karragin labored to hold the spear shaft in place while dodging the wild swings from the grondle. Any moment now, she anticipated feeling the terrible rush of embertang burning her skin. What would happen to her if she inhaled the caustic substance?

Something firm throttled into her, and she flew to the side, rolling more than ten feet away. She looked up in time to see Savnah with a wicked grin on her face. The brutal woman from Midrock stood in her place. Savnah ducked once to avoid the alpha's battle axe, then heaved both of her moonblades in an arc to attack the last standing lesser grondle. Her blades clanged off horn and hoof, causing no damage. Then the vaporous cloud of embertang painted the three of them in an oily mist.

The effect was immediate . . . for the grondle. The alpha dropped its oversized battle axe and mewled in pain, rearing back and stumbling to its side. Massive clawed hands scrabbled over its purple fleshy fenestrations to remove the source of the pain. The other grondle threw itself into the snow in an attempt to smother the searing pain it appeared to endure. After several seconds, they both seized up. When each one gasped a final breath, dark fluids bubbled out through their gill slits onto the snow.

Savnah walked out of the cloud toward Karragin, holstered her moonblade axes, then dropped to her knees and exhaled. Karragin lay stunned on her side, staring at her equal. A puzzled expression must have played across her face.

Savnah panted and leaned forward with one hand in the snow, sucking in air. With the other hand, she pulled at the collar of her Outrider gear. Blue and silver light streaked across the top of her arca prime. "Like I . . . said before, Lefledge . . . you have your gifts . . . and I have mine."

"You don't feel any of it? No pain at all?" asked Karragin.

"Only . . . if I want to . . . and right now . . . I don't want to," said Savnah.

The two primes shared a chuckle that became throaty laughs.

"Smart thinking, holding your breath," Karragin grunted.

Nolan was the first to drop from the protected shelf. He trotted to Karragin's side. She lifted her eyes to meet his. "I'm fine. We're both fine, Nolan." But she couldn't seem to make herself forget the vivid images the grondle had forced through the connection of her gift.

Tovnik approached next with a look of concern. "Help me get her to her feet," said the medic.

She didn't resist as Nolan and Tovnik stood her up. The familiar murmur of his gift hummed as he carried out an inspection of her injuries without waiting for permission. He tsk'd as he assessed deep bruises and welts. After a few minutes, the sound of his gift dwindled. "Well, nothing's broken. Let me see to Savnah."

Together, Tovnik and Runta donned gloves, then helped Savnah strip down to her smallclothes. Tovnik assessed her for injuries while Runta liberally bathed the prime in resco to neutralize as much embertang as possible.

When they finished, Savnah rolled in the snow for good measure. She popped up, blue-lipped and shivering, then brushed off the slush. "What? I don't feel pain now, but I can't keep channeling through my arca prime forever. Better safe than sorry when it comes to embertang, no?"

"I guess but, Giver's tears, what were you both thinking?" asked Tovnik.

Savnah took three steps back, reached into the snow, and retrieved Karragin's saber. Karra inspected the weapon, dried it off, then replaced it in her sheath. The woman spoke with her usual cheeky nature but kept her gaze trained on Karragin. "*I* was just thinking that I'm glad I rolled over the hilt and not the blade. *She* was thinking about how miserable it would be to remain stuck on that ledge with you lot for a week while we waited for rescue from those grondle."

Nobody responded to Savnah, so she pressed on. "What? Don't look at me like I'm the only one uncomfortable with dropping a grot over the edge with your friends only steps away. That's downright uncivilized, isn't that right, Karra?"

Karragin blinked and tried to make sense of Savnah's words.

"Are you sure Karra's alright, Tov?" asked Nolan. "She didn't hit her head or anything?"

"She's fine. At least, she will be, after we get back to base camp, get out of these grimy uniforms, and settle down to a nice hot meal. Roast boar and taters, I'm thinking," said Savnah.

Karragin's brow twitched, and she exhaled through pursed lips to dismiss another wave of nausea. "Sure. But maybe just soup and bread for me, for a while anyway."

Chapter Twenty-Eight: Out of the Sanctum, into the Sprawl

Ksenia sat forward on the stone bench in the inner sanctum. A slick of sweat gathered under her palms where she gripped the polished edge. She waited with the regent in strained silence for Craxton to withdraw from the trance he always slipped into when receiving communication from one of his siblings.

"Maybe I should go, Your Grace," she offered in a hushed voice.

Therek stood patiently, hands clasped behind his back, waiting for an updated report. In the time it took Craxton to cross the room, she had watched the sagacious man change from a relaxed father to the clinical and calculating regent of Aarindorn. Now that hawkish tactician turned his gaze to her. "No. Stay. If I need to relay messages quickly, your services might be needed. Just bear in mind that anything Craxton relays to us needs to be considered confidential."

"Absolutely, Your Grace," she said.

Craxton stood staring with a vacant expression into the shadowed alcoves of the inner sanctum, entranced. She had never seen him linger so long in communication. His mouth parted, and he sucked in a breath. Long moments passed until, eventually, he blinked and sharpened his awareness to the room. Finally, he turned to address the regent directly.

"They're all safe, all of them."

Ksenia gasped out loud with the release of nervous joy. Something in Therek's bearing changed, and his shoulders relaxed. The older man tilted his head in her direction. The hint of a smile creased his eyes.

"That's good news, Craxton. You can relay the particulars to me here. Ksenia is acting as my historian in these events."

"Of course, Your Grace. The embertang trick worked exceptionally well, and they managed to take out a full crush of grondle." Craxton then relayed the details of the skirmish.

"If the Giver bestows a limited number of second chances, Karra better start keeping track," said Therek. He paced a slow circle. "I assume your sister has informed Overwarden Kaldera of these events as well?"

"Yes, Your Grace," said Craxton.

"Craxton, please relay a message through your sister to the overwarden. Tell him that I will requisition the production and dispensation of all stores of embertang from Callinora at once. Advise the overwarden that he should implement training strategies in the safe handling of the substance. Ask him to look into ways to deliver the oil as a weapon. We don't have enough gusters among the Outriders to deploy the embertang in similar fashion."

The regent turned to her. "Ms. Balladuren, if you would be so kind, please draft an immediate requisition of all embertang stores from the sanitoriums across the kingdom. All stores to be sent to Warden Elbiona at the Pillars of Eldrek. The crown will, of course, provide fair market compensation.

"I shouldn't have to tell either of you to keep the specifics of embertang's success against the grondle in strict secrecy. The cost will rise because of this requisition. If anyone asks, we will indicate that the stores are in preparation for medical needs on the front line. If word gets out about its use as a weapon, the cost will escalate beyond our ability to manage."

Ksenia nodded her agreement while she penned the last line of the regent's order, then held the paper for his inspection and signature.

"Yes, see that this gets disseminated at once," said Therek.

"Of course, have you need of anything further?" asked Ksenia.

Her question seemed to pull the regent from complex thoughts. He looked to her, and his gaze softened. "What? No, thank you, that should be all for now for both of you. See to the timely delivery of that."

Ksenia gathered up her folio and stored the zeniscrawl and document, then began to exit the inner sanctum. Craxton's voice reached her just as she set foot on the first step.

"Kess, hold a moment. I'll walk with you."

His familiar use of her name gave her pause. In times past, it had made something swell inside of her. Now, it felt like a greeting someone would use before they asked her for something. She turned and waited for him, and they ascended the long flight of spiral steps together. After the second spiral, he hopped a few steps ahead. He took a moment to look past her, then spoke.

"Can I ask you a question and not have you assume the worst?" asked Craxton.

Ksenia felt her right eyebrow arch involuntarily in suspicion. "You can ask, but I'll reserve the right to decide."

He dipped his head and said in low tones, "I wanted to ask if you are going to formally join us."

Ksenia looked around the stairwell; finding it empty, she tilted her head in question. "Join who, exactly?"

He arranged his hands in the symbol of a circle, thumb to thumb and forefinger to forefinger, then deliberately popped his fingers apart as if a spring released. Ksenia slapped his hands with her folio and stared at him.

"Where did you learn of that, and why would you think I have any knowledge of what it means?" she asked.

"Kess, come on, relax. I'm pretty sure I recognized Kervin's voice when he introduced you at your first meeting. It didn't take too much to figure it out. So, are you going to join?"

"I'm not, I didn't . . . you, Kervin, ahh," she hissed in frustration. She stepped back to make some space between them and studied his face. Craxton waited for her response with what appeared to be genuine interest. She climbed the steps until she could turn and face him eye to eye. "I haven't decided yet."

They continued the ascent but took the steps slower. "What's to decide? We have a chance to be part of a movement that will shape the kingdom for generations."

She sighed. "Are Dexxin and Mullayne members? Never mind, they must be. It's complicated. First, there are my parents. I can't imagine what either of them would say."

"I understand. It's not an easy choice, but I'll bet you come around."

At his words, she felt a strange sensation of being penned in, so she clasped her folio to her chest and pulled ahead of him on the stairs. Craxton stopped climbing and sighed with exaggeration. "That's not what I mean, don't get like . . . look, Kess. Wait . . . moons Kess, stop a moment. I owe you an apology!"

She turned on the next step to face him. He stood several steps behind her, staring at his feet a moment, then looked up with a rueful expression. "Mullayne told me what an ass I was before. I'm not looking to control you or make you somebody you don't want to be. I know I messed that up. I just think . . . you could really be part of something important."

Thanks, Mullayne, I think. That wasn't what I thought he was going to say. She nodded once and waited for him to join her, then they continued the slow climb.

"All that we are working for is a departure from the monarchy in favor of a government that works for everyone. You like the regent, right?" he asked.

She nodded in tentative agreement.

"Well, that's a good start. Our first initiative after dismissing the monarchy will be to have Therek named the first sovereign over the country."

More silent footsteps followed. "Craxton, I appreciate your enthusiasm. Let me deal with the delivery of this message and then—" she shrugged her shoulders.

"What if I could show you something the Lacuna are doing right now to make a difference in the lives of common people?"

She considered his words as they continued their ascent. Eventually, she answered, "What did you have in mind?"

"Hawker's Row is a wide road off the west side of the market district. Follow it west, then turn south just before the Sprawl. There's a tavern on the corner, The Kettle and Pot. Meet me there in two hours?"

They reached the top of the stairs, and she felt slightly winded. She took a deep breath and agreed. "I know the place. I'll see you there, but you're buying."

"Yes? Alright, dinner's on me," he said.

Ksenia delivered the regent's mandate to the offices on the second tier of Stone's Grasp, then stored her folio. Overseeing the delivery of the order to the proper people took more time than she imagined. There was just enough time to return to her quarters, where she changed into warmer outerwear.

A short time later, she urged Winter along the paved roads of the elite neighborhoods just beyond the curtain wall. A flash of zenith kindled her sympathic gift and settled her mind from the stress of the last few hours.

"We should run the timber," Winter insisted.

"Not tonight, Winter, perhaps tomorrow. I have to meet someone. It's still better than the stables."

"Who are you going to meet?" asked the Aarindin.

"Do you remember Craxton?"

"You don't like Craxton. I like Craxton. He gives me apples."

"Now you sound like my mother."

"Does she like apples?"

"Never mind, turn here, Winter."

They rode around the market with its mostly empty stalls. The sparse foot traffic on Hawker's Row allowed Winter to proceed at an easy canter. Even in the cold, the odor of too many humans assaulted her senses, and Ksenia resisted the urge to encourage Winter to gallop. A short time later, they arrived at The Kettle and Pot. Craxton was leaning against a sturdy wood frame supporting the awning over the boardwalk.

He stepped forward and offered Winter a small apple. She nickered in pleasure and accepted the treat. "I thought you might get her out for a stretch," he said to the Aarindin.

Craxton blew between two fingers, emitting a harsh whistle, and a boy walked from the backside of the tavern. "Kess, he'll stable Winter out of the wind if that's alright?"

Ksenia gave her consent and directed Winter to go with the groom, then followed Craxton inside. The warm, humid air inside the tavern caressed the sting of the cold from her cheeks. The aroma of fresh bread and savory stew filled the taproom, and her stomach rumbled.

Patrons sat in clusters around tables in idle chatter, sharing round loaves of bread that they dipped into bowls of stew. She started to remove her gloves and outercoat, looking for where they might sit in the crowded hall.

Craxton placed a hand on her shoulder and spoke over the din. "Leave those on. We aren't staying. Follow me."

He led her to the back of the tavern and through a swinging door to the kitchen. Where the taproom was a cozy, warm retreat from the cold, the kitchen was a massive, sweltering nest of activity. Cooks busied themselves kneading dough balls for bread or preparing ingredients for stews. Four huge cauldrons simmered over hearths. A small army of workers scurried about in concert, making more food than they could ever hope to sell in the small taproom.

A short man with ruddy cheeks and a cherubic nature yelled over the clamor, "Crax, your order is ready!" The cook looked past Craxton and seemed to size up Ksenia. "Think she can handle it? I can have one of the boys help you."

Craxton smiled and leaned in. "Don't let the fine clothing fool you. She's no stranger to hard work."

"Alright then, m'lady, if you'll come over here." The cook placed meaty hands on Craxton's shoulders then positioned Ksenia three steps behind him. The odd man placed a stout wood beam on their shoulders. A thick hook hung from the center of the beam.

"Are we all sorted out then?" the cook shouted.

Craxton reached into a pocket and paid the man a handful of coins. The cook waved over, and two assistants hoisted one of the cauldrons from the hearth, clamped a lid over the bubbling stew, and secured it to the hook on the beam.

The cook handed Craxton a burlap sack full of fresh bread. Ksenia adjusted her footing under the weight but found the cargo manageable.

"Kess, are you ready?" shouted Craxton.

"Yes, I suppose!" she answered, then stepped forward as the weight of the beam shifted.

Craxton led them out the back door. They walked down a gentle ramp and across a yard surrounded by high stone walls. Long tables occupied most of the real estate, where more people huddled together, sharing bread and stew and conversation. She timed her steps to remain synchronized with Craxton, and they approached a locked door at the back of the yard. A burly man winked at Craxton and opened the door to let them through.

As they stepped beyond the doorway, she heard a heavy lockbar drop in place behind them. They walked down a walled alley shadowed in the fading light of day. Her shoulder started to ache from the weight of the cauldron.

"It's just up ahead," Craxton grunted.

He approached a door on the opposite side of the alley and pounded a fist three times. A young girl with a dirt-smudged face opened the door. She tipped her head and welcomed them inside.

Rolling her shoulders to relieve a cramp, she surveyed the room. The clamor of no fewer than twenty children filled the space as they chattered around an oversized table. Craxton led them to a sturdy side table, and they set the cauldron down.

Her hair was matted to her forehead, and she found relief in removing her gloves and coat. An older woman, the only other adult in the room, removed the heavy lid and ladled stew into the children's bowls.

"There's a peg on the wall behind you for your coat. You and Crax are welcome to join us."

Ksenia hung her coat up and turned to see Craxton waving her to the far side of the table. She sat down beside him and watched. The disorganized chatter of the children settled as the portions of stew arrived. One of the older children, the girl who answered the door, divided the loaves of bread evenly between the kids. In minutes, the loud clamor became a strange chorus of "mmm" interspersed with the staccato of wooden spoons in wooden bowls.

Eventually, a generous portion of stew was set before them both. The older woman finally retrieved a bowl for herself and sat down beside them.

"Hello, my name's Suvi. Welcome to the Giver's Blessing," said the woman.

"Is this the orphanage Mullayne donates meat to?" Ksenia asked.

"One of four in the Sprawl," said Suvi. "There used to be just the two, but thanks to the support from the Lacuna, we've been able to open up two more in just the last few years."

Ksenia sipped at the warm broth and scooped up a chunk of potato. "Where do they all come from?"

Craxton waved his spoon toward the children. "Most of these kids are runeless. Some come from families that fell on hard times."

Ksenia made herself look closer at the children around the table. Most looked more than ten, old enough to start to manifest runes, should they inherit them. Yet the only marks adorning their forearms and faces came from smudges of ash and dirt.

She leaned closer to Craxton. "Are you saying that families give up their children if they are runeless?"

Craxton swallowed a generous spoonful of stew and nodded. "That's the number one thing all of these kids have in common."

Ksenia finished her portion then sat at the table, watching as the children gathered their bowls and acted in concert to clear the table. Several of the kids approached Craxton and demanded a hug. More than a few shared unique handshakes or tried to engage him in games of chase. He obliged each of them.

A thin, straw-haired girl skipped with exuberance from the table and collapsed onto Ksenia's lap. Ksenia allowed a hand to drop onto the child's head and shoulders. Her fingers ran across bony edges. The girl hugged her thighs a moment, then lifted bright eyes. "Thank you for the food, m'lady!"

Ksenia swallowed hard and widened her eyes to dissipate the subtle sting of tears forming. She offered a soft smile and nodded once. The girl skipped away. A short time later, she sat beside Craxton in the empty dining hall.

"Well, what do you think?" he asked.

"It's not what I expected," said Ksenia.

"This is the kind of place, these are the kind of people, that the Lacuna supports, Kess. I knew if I tried to tell you about it, you might listen, but until you sit down with these kids and see them for who and what they are, it doesn't sink in. I suppose I owe you an apology."

She shook her head in confusion. "Apology for what?"

Craxton rubbed his palm on the table. "I know you. You're . . . just a good person. It's not possible to come here and not be changed. You came with me tonight with questions. You might not be ready to commit to the Lacuna. But I'm willing to wager you won't be able to walk away either. This place, these kids . . . they pretty much make the decision for you."

She squinted at him in mock frustration. He held up his hands in surrender. "Well, it is definitely something to consider."

Chapter Twenty-Nine: The Warden's Flight

As reddevek and Ranika returned from a day in the Moorlok, the scent of smoked boar billowed out from the chimney of the Bashing Ram, marinating the appetites of anyone within three hundred paces.

And just in time. I don't know whose stomach rumbles louder, mine or hers.

Ranika rode behind him astride the Aarindin and remained seated as long as Zippy didn't make any sudden changes in direction. They followed a winding road into town, and Zippy had to sidestep an approaching mule pulling an empty wagon. He sensed her slide to the side, then use the back of his belt to hoist herself back to a neutral position.

She rested her head in the middle of his back. "I still don't get how you manage to stay on Mr. Zip without being tossed off. Seems to me it would be much easier with a saddle."

"I told you, horses are easier with a saddle. Aarindin are not," said Reddevek. He turned his head and pitched his voice low. "You know how you can channel nadir? Well, Aarindin use zenith to sort of . . . grip their riders, the ones they choose anyway."

They continued in silence. "Why doesn't Zippy grip me then? I slide off as easy as a stick of butter."

"I think it has to do with your gift, Nika. Zippy likes you well enough, but he can only grip those that can channel zenith. Even then, an Outrider needs to work with the same Aarindin for weeks before the creature will choose to trust him enough to grip him. There are exceptions, but usually, it takes a month or longer."

She bobbed her forehead against the small of his back several times. "Do you suppose the Taker strikes out looking for folks like me? Cursed people like . . . I mean . . . abrogators?"

The warden answered her with a formal but lighthearted tone. "No, I do not, and don't you busy yourself worrying about it."

He brought the Aarindin to a halt, twisted, and hoisted Ranika to sit in front. Once she was situated, he nudged Zippy forward at a comfortable walk.

"I imagine I'm the first person you ever trusted enough to show your gift, Nika. And I need you to listen to me now like it's something important, because it is. Are you listening?"

"Yes, Red, always."

"You're gifted. Not dark, or tainted, or cursed. Gifted." He let the words settle a bit. "Do you know anyone else who can sneak up on a sleeping boar, attach a snare, then deliver a single chop with one of my axes to dispatch it?"

"I suppose I don't."

He chuckled. "I know it's not really something most girls your age aim to be good at, but Nika, you didn't even need the snare. Anyway, the thing that makes you different . . . it's allowed you to hide, but I've been training you this last month to see that it makes you strong. You can protect people. You can do all sorts of things with your gift. Making people see that might take some time. Until then, I promise you, I'll always stand at your side, even if you can't sit on an Aarindin any better than a stick of butter."

He watched her head bob side to side and knew she accepted his advice. *Getting it to sink in, though, always seems to be the hard part. I don't know how you got under my skin, grind me for a monk, but you did.*

She clutched her hands over her stomach with exaggerated hunger pains. "I think Ingram's outdone himself with that boar. The smell from his smokehouse has been tugging on my stomach since we left the Moorlok."

"I'll drop you off out front. Take the sack of pepper lichen in for Miss Della. I'll see to Zippy and meet you inside." He directed the Aarindin to the front boardwalk of the Bashing Ram. Ranika swung a leg over and hopped down, retrieved the goods, and disappeared through the front door of the inn.

The murmur of happy patrons spilled out of the doors as she entered. "Looks like a full crowd in the taproom tonight, Zip. Let's get you sorted out."

The Aarindin wandered to the back of the inn, stopping a few feet before the entrance to the stables. "Feth? You there, boy?"

He waited a moment, but the stableboy never appeared. A moment later, the Aarindin flared its nostrils, grunted a muffled sound, and perked its ears forward. Reddevek clicked his tongue and felt the Aarindin release its grip. He summoned his gift as he dropped to the ground, then lingered there a moment, rubbing a hand along the Aarindin's withers and up his neck.

Unseen to all but the tracker, wispy filaments powered by zenith surged forward, probing the dark corners of the stables. A resonance vibrated back through his gift. Feth remained in a back corner, unconscious. Five common horses remained in their stalls, three of them emitting the same nervous aura as Zippy. Nobody else entered his awareness until he searched the rafters. Three figures perched high in the shadows: two just inside the door and one near the opening to the only empty stall.

He sighed. *I was just getting used to this place.*

He considered running in the back door of the inn to check on Ranika. *But I would never know who is waiting, and I can't abide the notion of being chased.*

Reddevek cleared his throat. "Well, looks like I get to see to your feed tonight, Zippy." The warden led his mount by the reins, making assessments of the three foes in the rafters. All three were men, he guessed. They cast vibrations of anticipation through his awareness. Heartbeats pulsed with rapid fervor, and their patterns echoed through his gift with the familiar savage intention of predators.

The warden loosened the leather strap over the axe on his left hip and allowed his forearm to brush against the hilt of the large knife on his right. He led Zippy into the empty stall, stepping fast under the Aarindin's neck to the center aisle.

A storm gathered in his chest, and he used the rage to fuel his attack. He retrieved a pitchfork stabbed into a hay pile, tossed the straw into the air, then stabbed up with the crude weapon. The center tong punched through a boot with a satisfying rasp as the metal bit deep into the meat of the man's foot. The man cursed with a yelp that sounded more girlish than brutish, then fell to the ground.

A loaded crossbow clattered beside him, discharging a bolt into a post. Reddevek stepped to the side just as the twang from another weapon warned of another bolt. The missile careened along the floor.

The warden pivoted and thrust the pitchfork out, jabbing the first man with two of the tongs in the hip and thigh. He followed by stomping forward, crushing the man's arm just below the elbow.

"Stay down, and you'll survive. Move, and I'll spit you like the pig you are," he growled, then cast his gift back to the other two men. They remained hidden in the shadows.

"You haven't killed the stableboy, so you can still leave. But the folk of the Bend don't take too kindly to outsiders attacking one of their own."

The two other figures dropped from the rafters at the front of the stables. One tossed a spent crossbow to the side, and both held stout cudgels. The larger man rivaled Reddevek in size. He cocked his head and spoke out of the side of his mouth.

"See, that might make sense, except the only man in these stables that didn't grow up in these parts is you. Strictor said you were a crafty grinder. You alright, Heff?"

The man on the floor behind him grunted but remained curled in a ball. "Yes!"

Reddevek recognized the name. "Heff? That must make you another Hawklin. Bruug, I'm guessing? Is your father about? The constable will be eager to see you boys. Your brother is out of the fight. Without medical attention, he won't survive the night."

The burly thug slapped his cudgel in a meaty palm and stepped forward. "Let's get him!"

As they rushed forward, Reddevek stepped back and jabbed the pitchfork into Heff's lower leg, eliciting the expected scream. Bruug faltered and threw out his arm to stop the last man, but he plowed forward.

"Wait, grind it, Ozhen, he's got Heff," yelled Bruug.

But Ozhen blundered forward, a gleam of hungry commitment in his gaze. The man swung his cudgel back and forth, and Reddevek had little difficulty predicting his crude attacks.

Each time Ozhen attacked, the warden sidestepped or backtracked just out of reach. When the thug overextended, Reddevek turned. In a fluid motion, he unholstered his axe, swung it in a tight arc, and twisted his wrist at the last moment to bring the butt of the weapon down against the back of the man's head. Ozhen crumpled facedown into the ground.

Reddevek cocked his head to consider the last man. Bruug took a menacing step forward, but Reddevek lunged back to Heff, who lay whimpering. The warden held the tongs of the pitchfork just above Heff's ear, then looked back to Bruug in question.

The thug stopped two paces away. He glared with dark eyes and panted, a nervous uncertainty crossing his expression.

"Who sent you, and why are you here?" asked Reddevek.

"Give me my brother," Bruug demanded.

"Give me answers, and I'll think about it. Play games with me, and it will be the end of him. Then I'll let the blade of my axe finally taste Hawklin blood."

For emphasis, Reddevek twisted a single prong into Heff's back. The young man screamed out.

"Alright! It was Strictor. He knows about the girl. She failed the test. She's a reacher, a thrall!"

"The fat man in the white suit? What does he want with Nika?" asked Reddevek.

"He's a member of the Immaculine. They're spreading all over the Southlands. My father is an envoy in the ranks and has the ear of Margrave Rolsh in Riverton. We're weeding out any reachers. When they hear of this, there won't be anywhere you can hide. But give me my brother, and they might go easy on you."

Reddevek considered the news without surprise until he studied the emanations from Bruug through his gift. *The way this lad speaks, full of conviction, belief . . . now that's a danger.*

"One last thing. What do the Immaculine want with a simple girl?"

Bruug sneered. "I told ya, she's no simple girl. She's a thrall. She can't help but reach into the Drift to pull out power that isn't hers. Strictor discovered her a few days ago. He's found plenty of thralls that use zenith, but she's the first one he ever come across to use something he calls nadir. And by the way you spotted us in the dark, I'll bet you are too. It doesn't matter. They're coming this way, moving up the coast. You might get away tonight, but they'll catch you. And I'll be the one to see you purged."

Reddevek almost laughed. "Are you that dumb, boy? Threatening me while I stand over your brother?"

Bruug paced back and forth but never approached, immobilized by indecision.

"I'll make this easy. Your brother can't run. He's lame until he heals. You can either come at me and take your chances or run. I've no quarrel with you yet, but take another step into this barn, and it will be the last time you see Heff alive. Otherwise, I'll give you five minutes before I inform Whirik."

Bruug stared at his brother. Heff whimpered, "Bruug? Don't leave me!"

The brute threw his cudgel against the rafters in anger and ran out of the stables. Reddevek tracked him for several minutes. Once he felt sure the young man would not circle back, he checked on the other two assailants.

Ozhen remained unconscious and was easy to tie up with a coil of rope. An inspection of Heff's wounds showed nothing life-threatening. Congealed blood oozed from the stabs on his foot and leg, and he cradled a broken arm in his lap.

The warden squatted down and cast a glance across Heff's injuries, then looked him in the eye. "Sorry about that. None of those wounds are lethal, but you'll need some mending. I imagine Mr. Strictor can see to that. Is he inside with any others?"

Heff flared his nostrils and grimaced but remained silent until the warden pressed a thumb along the deformed part of his forearm. The young man cried out in pain.

Reddevek grabbed a fistful of his hair to pull him to attention. "I don't have the Giver's . . . the All-Mother's mercy, boy. Tell me what I want to know, or I'll break more than your arm."

Heff panted and blinked back tears. "Strictor told us to find him inside when we finished with you. He's waiting with two others of the Immaculine. That's all I know."

Reddevek tied Heff's good arm behind him, then secured his feet. Satisfied the young man couldn't escape, he checked on the stableboy. Feth lay tied up in the back of the barn, gagged and awake.

Reddevek made quick work of the bindings. "Can you stand?" he asked. The boy responded by smiling up through a freshly split lip but seemed otherwise unharmed.

"Good. I need to speak to Miss Della. Stand guard over these two. If either of them tries to move, jab him in the leg with the pitchfork."

Feth nodded, and Reddevek stalked across the yard to the back door of the inn. He listened at the door and cast his awareness inside. Ingram and Della were busying themselves in the kitchen, but he sensed no others.

He crept inside and closed the door behind him, then waited. Ingram turned a spitted boar over smoldering embers while Della portioned out generous slices of bread onto platters. She glanced up from her work with a look of irritation more than surprise, eyeing him down the length of the bread knife.

"Just because you brought us this boar, don't mean—" Her words trailed off as he placed his finger to his lips to signal silence. He waited a moment longer, and she waved him forward then continued sawing through the bread.

Ingram glanced over his shoulder, nodded once, then stepped over to his sister's counter. "Why do I get the feeling that you've got the look of Lutney's mischief about you?" asked the pitmaster.

"I can't say I know all about the Southland gods, but I'll wager it's Mogdure more than Lutney that has anything to do with what's going on in these parts."

His words caused the pitmaster and his sister to draw back. Della set her knife down, and Ingram wiped nervous hands on his apron.

Reddevek continued, "I don't have time to explain it all. The newcomer, Strictor, is a representative of a group that calls themselves the Immaculine. They might have the margrave's ear, so don't go causing trouble for them on our account. For reasons I can't say, they mean to capture and kill Ranika. They recruited Heff and Bruug Hawklin and a local lad named Ozhen. The three of them tried to ambush me in the stables just now. Ozhen and Heff are tied up. I have Feth keeping an eye on them, but Bruug escaped. I don't imagine I have much time to skin out of here, so I need you to get Nika back here without raising a fuss."

"I can do that easy enough. I'll tell her I need help back here," said Della. "Give me a moment."

The warden stepped behind the door as she backed into the taproom with a platter full of piping hot bread.

"What can I do, Red?" asked Ingram.

"You and your sister have been nothing but kind to Ranika and me. Don't get yourselves tangled up in this business until you have clear sight of how much influence this group has with the margrave. Let Whirik make all the decisions about the Hawklins."

"I understand. Are you planning to leave tonight?" asked Ingram.

"I don't see any way around that. Bruug will be back here soon with more members of his group. It will be less trouble for you all if we are gone before he gets back."

"Maedra's mercy, Red, it's the middle of winter. Where will you go?" asked Ingram.

"Southeast. Bruug said the Immaculine are working their way up the coast. We'll find somewhere they aren't and hole up for the winter."

Della returned through the door with Ranika behind her. Both carried empty plates on serving platters. Through the door crack, the warden caught a glimpse of Strictor. The man sat in the center of the room adorned in his strange white attire in conversation with two others. His white-gloved fingers were wrapped around a goblet of wine.

In that brief moment, Reddevek learned all that he needed to know of the newcomers. Where Strictor wore an ostentatious white suit, his companions wore tailored black uniforms. Two white stars graced their left shoulders. Otherwise, their gear lacked any other embellishment. Each man sat with a vigilant posture. While Strictor rambled on in conversation, these two professionals sat at attention and studied the room like hawks perched in the timber.

Nika walked to the bread counter and snatched a slice of bread for herself. She peeled away the edge of the buttery crust. "So, when do we leave?"

"How did you . . . wait, what did you learn in there?" the warden stammered.

"Not much. But that fat man in the white suit's been looking at me strange, like one of the drunk sailors in Callish that wants more than directions. I learned a long time ago to avoid his type, and he's sitting with two others that have a serious look about them."

Reddevek relaxed an elbow on the hilt of his axe. "Right. Nika, can you use your talent to sneak upstairs and gather our things? Then climb out the window and come around to the stables?"

The girl wolfed down the slice of bread and mumbled a sound of agreement.

"Are you sure, Red?" asked Ingram. "Maybe I should see to that, and you two wait here."

Reddevek sighed and patted the pitmaster on his burly shoulder. "Like I said before, you and Della have done enough for us already. It's time we leave before you get into any trouble on our account."

Ingram studied the warden's face for a moment as if to argue, then nodded and hurried to wrap up generous portions of meat for them. Della took his cue and loaded another platter with bowls of stew. The stout woman turned to Ranika, her nose congested and rosy.

"Come here then, and be quick about it," she said to Ranika.

The girl stepped forward, and Della smothered her in a bear hug before pushing her back. She pulled wisps of Ranika's straw-like hair to the side and grabbed her by the chin. "You listen to Red and get as far away from these parts as you can. Stay safe. And if you are ever in the Bend again, I expect you to come see me straightaway."

"Thank you, Miss Della. I will," she said.

Della studied her face a moment, then sniffed back a tear and hoisted the platter. "Alright then. If you think you can get to your rooms, follow me out."

Ranika stepped close to Della. Reddevek watched as shadows seemed to flow across the room like thick smoke to enshroud the girl. In seconds, she vanished from sight. Ingram stood wide-eyed and poked a finger forward. Ranika giggled when he pulled back.

The door swung open, and Della stepped into the taproom. Reddevek then took the parcel of meat from the bewildered pitmaster.

"So. Uhh . . . the blessings of the Seven be upon you, Red."

"Thanks, Ingram. And on you and your sister as well. Pass along the same to Steckle if you could. Eyes to the horizon, my friend," said the warden. Then he crept back to the stables and off into the night.

Chapter Thirty: Cresting the Korjinth

Bryndor adjusted thick leather straps across his shoulders. The warmth of the pack in the small of his back reminded him of days gone by when computations of distance and notations of a headland or river gorge had possessed all of his attention.

A chill air gusted across their temporary camp high in the Korjinth. They had climbed to the high places and spent the last four days acclimating to the thin air. The first few days provoked a strangely exhilarating malady: headaches and tingly fingertips mixed with palpitations and labored breathing just from mundane activities like walking. Finally, this morning his body seemed not to betray him from the simple task of managing the pack.

He gazed back across the sweeping stands of timber to the distant Valley of the Cloud Walkers. Thick clouds and mist swirled above and below them, offering only passing glimpses of the small smudge on the valley floor where the Damadibo village stood.

Another gust of cold air dissipated the mists enough for him to observe Kaellor in quiet conversation with Laryn and the wizened elder of the village. He followed part of their conversation, a mixture of common speech for Kaellor's benefit and the signing hand language of the Damadibo.

"What do you suppose they have to discuss that hasn't already been reviewed five times this week?" asked Lluthean.

"From what I can tell, and knowing Kae the way we do, our uncle is trying to pry more explanation from the elder regarding the plan to send us over the mountain," said Bryndor.

Lluthean rotated three perfectly circular stones in his palm, their soft, rolling clatter making more noise than the conversation with the elder. "He's never been one to trust to someone else's planning or strategy. What kind of odds do you give us?"

Bryndor gave his brother a sidelong glance. "It seems like you're asking me to make a bet when I only hold two cards. I think I would rather make my wager after the dealer hands me the other three, and even then, I should like to see Lutney's gambit."

Lluthean shrugged. "Fair enough, though I never like to rely on the last open card, especially when anyone can add it to their hand."

"Tell you what. We make it over the Korjinth, together, whole . . . and I'll buy the first round and stake you in any game of cards at the first tavern we can find," said Bryndor.

He continued to observe his uncle. Laryn stood at his side, waiting and occasionally signing. She must have melted Kaellor's resolve because his shoulders softened. His uncle looked north to the mountain range, nodded once, then bowed his head and uttered what appeared to be something respectful to the elder.

Thick grey and white clouds rolled between them. Bryndor inhaled deeply, sensing the moisture in the vapor. A gust cleared the mists, and his aunt and uncle stood but steps away. Elder Miljin must have taken the opportunity to fold away into the clouds.

"Learn anything more?" asked Bryndor.

A slight crease furrowed between Kaellor's brow for a moment. He rubbed his chin hairs and sighed, then smiled. "Your aunt has convinced me that I can't control everything on this journey of ours, and while it has taken me the better part of a week to understand it . . . she is right."

"By the Seven in the south, the Giver, and both moons," said Lluthean. He beamed a smile at Laryn. "If you can bend him like that in just a short time, I've no doubt about our chances!"

Laryn pulled an errant lock of white hair behind an ear and smiled. "Kae is right to be cautious. The peaks are treacherous. But I trust the spirits. If they told the elder we could make it, then I believe we will. But it's all on you and the wolvryn now."

Kaellor lifted his gaze to the summit. "I admit I don't like pushing ahead without knowing more, but needs must. We have to have faith in Miljin's sources, and they believe we must push on. Tarkannen has a link to this world. We need to return to Aarindorn and the scholars at Callinora to understand how to stop him. But that mountain range and the storms of zenith and nadir stand in our way."

Laryn took his hand in hers. "Ghetti will lead us up to the summit. We'll have to travel several days overland in harsh winter climates. You two will use your unique connection to the wolvryn to scout out the knots, since Kae and I can only see a vortex just before it discharges. And if that happens, we've allowed it to drift too close."

"We can see them easily enough. I checked again this morning," said Bryndor.

Kaellor continued his search of the north skyline with a wary eye. "What do they look like?"

"Nadir ripples across the skyline like shiny black cords. It buckles and wriggles like it's trying to break free, don't you think, Llu?" said Bryndor.

"Yes," said Lluthean. "And zenith looks more like a ribbon of blue or sometimes purple. When they start to spin around each other, they make these dark swirls that gather and tighten into a knot. Last night I practiced with Neska. A vortex took the better part of an hour to dissipate into a strike of dark lightning to the ground."

"I saw one erupt in only a quarter of an hour this morning. And they drift, they . . . swivel around. The knots don't appear to remain in place," explained Bryndor.

"The elder thinks it will take us three days of steady travel before we can descend," said Kaellor. "We won't be able to stop for long, and even then, one of you will always have to keep your guard up."

Bryndor chewed on his lip and nodded. "We can do it. When do we leave?"

"Mahkeel is supposed to arrive with Ghetti any moment now. It's a shame we had to leave Scout behind, but there's no way the old boy could manage."

Bryndor blinked a few times, then drew his gaze once again back down into the valley. "He has a good life there. All the grasses he can eat, kids who fawn over him, and he never has to pull the wagon again."

"Agreed. It's a just reward for all of his service." Kaellor looked past them and down the valley. "Alright then, get your cold-weather gear on. Mahkeel is here with the wolvryn."

The handler approached with hand gestures and a silent smile that reached his eyes. He stood back as Boru and Neska raced forward, tails wagging. The pups, if they could even rightly be called that, enticed Ghetti to play by nipping at her chin and scampering about. The frenetic activity carried on a few minutes until the matriarch released a single muffled growl. Then both Neska and Boru sat in calm attention.

Going to have to remember that trick.

Mahkeel offered a formal greeting, then added, "*I wish I could come with you, but mine is a different path.*"

"*Good morning, Mahkeel, many blessings to your house. I hope that this is not the last morning we share,*" signed Laryn.

The handler nodded in agreement. "*Ghetti can take you to the summit, but she will not leave the valley. The pups are large enough to carry the boys.*"

"Your help is a kindness all the same, and it's much appreciated," said Kaellor.

Mahkeel turned to Laryn, who signed in translation. They embraced in one last farewell, then gathered their travel gear and packs. As the largest of the three wolvryn, Ghetti strode to Kaellor and lowered her belly to the ground, waiting for him to approach.

"It's not like riding a horse, Kae. You sit farther back, and you have to lean forward. It's more like you lay on top of her," explained Laryn. "You can grab the fur around her shoulders or neck but don't try to steer her like a horse. It's . . . not the same. Just be a passenger. Let Ghetti ferry you up to the summit."

Kaellor seemed to know enough not to argue or complain. He leaned forward and looked the matriarch of the pack in the eye a long moment, then smiled and offered her a strip of jerky. She sniffed at the offering, then devoured the morsel.

"*Is good,*" signed Mahkeel. "*Now mount and go.*"

Bryndor watched as his uncle labored to throw a leg over Ghetti's back. The wolvryn grunted a little until Kaellor settled his hips back and cautiously leaned forward, appearing to embrace the creature.

"Now what?" His words whooped out in a yell of surprise as Ghetti lurched forward and bounded twice, then hopped into a dense cloud bank and disappeared.

"I better attend your uncle. See you at the top." She winked and stepped back, folding into the clouds, there one moment and gone in a swirl of mist the next.

Mahkeel looked at the pups one last time, a look of disbelief as he signed, *"When their mother took them out of the valley, she must have been affected by zenith. Pups never grow so fast or so big. They will be larger than Ghetti. Larger than your Scout, I think."*

"Thank you for everything you taught us, Mahkeel. If we can, we'll come back someday. Eyes to the horizon, my friend," signed Bryndor.

Mahkeel gestured, and the pups lowered their bellies to the ground, panting in expectation. Bryndor mounted with ease and leaned forward. Boru's coarse fur tickled his nose and smelled faintly of the grasses of the valley. Just as Bryndor signaled for them to go, he felt his stomach lurch as Boru bounded into the clouds.

Cold clouds and vapor stung his face and ears. He blinked away tears and strained to see through the grey and white mists. Occasionally, the clouds parted, and he spied a flicker of sky or the ground below him. The way the wolvryn folded through the clouds reminded him a little of the dizzying effect of the shadow chaser hound.

He felt weightless astride Boru—then they lurched to a halt, and his weight returned. His boots scuffed the ground, and he felt it was safe to dismount.

Ice-covered snow crunched underfoot, and the bitter air froze the moisture in his nose, stirring him to action. After pulling a covering over his face, he stomped his boots into the ground to test his footing. His breaths came short and rapid, provoking the same exhilarated feeling that the thin air had caused when they arrived at their base camp earlier in the week.

"Thank you, Boru," he gestured.

Emerging from the clouds, Kaellor and Laryn stepped forward. Kaellor's forehead appeared pale above his face covering, and he stumbled on unsteady legs.

Laryn supported him for several steps. He staggered to his knees, wrestling to remove his face covering like it was a caustic material. After a few splinted breaths, he abruptly and violently emptied his stomach.

"Stupid, stubborn monk," cursed Laryn. "I asked you if you needed my help. I could have dissipated the motion sickness in seconds."

Kaellor continued to retch and heave until Laryn activated her gift. A soft murmur hummed under the howling wind, the only indication of her channeling. In only a few breaths, the color returned to Kaellor's face, and he sighed, nodded, then covered back up.

"Next time, I'm climbing up the mountain the way the Giver intended. None of that folding into the mists for me . . . ever," growled his uncle.

Bryndor ran a mitted hand over Boru's head. The wolvryn appeared unlabored by the trip. In another moment, Lluthean joined them with Neska trotting in his shadow. Ghetti watched the group of them with head cocked. Laryn embraced her one last time. The matriarch huffed once, a warm sound, then loped back down the mountainside to a dense cluster of clouds.

The view at the summit of the Korjinth arrested them each in place. Stretching out across the horizon were miles of snow-covered peaks erupting through a billowy, white carpet of clouds. Gentle currents of air swirled and whipped the vapors in roiling waves. At the highest places, wisps of snow washed over the craggy, black, angular peaks, creating reflective facets that gleamed until another current of snow obscured the summit.

Posed just above it all, the blue moon of Baellen appeared as a large saucer hanging like a piece of art above the peaks. He imagined it could topple into his hands and became lost in the clarity of the surface details of the celestial object.

"Eyes to the horizon . . . indeed. Have you ever seen those . . . marks on the blue moon before?" asked Bryndor. His words came clipped between short breaths. "On the surface . . . of Voshna, Baellen, there are dark . . . pits and areas where . . . the blue seems to shift about. It's not one uniform color. It's like it's alive. It's . . ."

"It's beautiful," uttered Kaellor. His steaming breath plumed out in unnatural, rapid succession. "The Giver take me . . . for a monk for doubting . . . but it's the most . . . beautiful thing . . . I've ever seen."

A harsh scraping sound tore across the sky, interrupting their communion. A dark splinter of lightning slammed into the ridge only a few hundred paces away as zenith and nadir collided in a violent discharge. White flew into the air, and an eerie moan echoed across the canyon.

"Boys, give us a sense of things and fast," said Kaellor. "I can see one knot . . . far to the east."

Bryndor gestured, and Boru walked over. He attuned himself to the wolvryn, then cast his enhanced awareness north across the mountainous terrain. What he saw caused him to drop open his mouth. Spread out before them hovered not just one or two knots but countless spirals where zenith and nadir collided in a stormy vortex.

"Well, Bryn, what do you see?" pressed Kaellor.

"They're everywhere. I thought . . . I expected maybe a few, but there are—"

"Hundreds," finished Lluthean. "The entire horizon . . . it's full of knots. There isn't a patch of normal sky . . . not anywhere."

Bryndor drew his attention to his uncle and nodded once in acknowledgment that this time, for once, Lluthean did not embellish the findings. Kaellor looked once to Laryn and seemed at a loss for words. She considered them all for a moment. She alone appeared unlabored by the high altitude and spoke with a calm voice of authority.

"Right then, boys. Look at me. Nobody on all of Karsk has ever seen this. And together, we are going to take this story back to the rest of the world. Bryndor, I believe your uncle asked for a heading. We can only see a vortex that is about to erupt, but we knew there would be a lot more. Can you sense a path forward?"

Bryndor tucked his nose under his face covering. "Yes, ma'am. Where that last one discharged . . . two others look about to go. We should be fine . . . if we follow this . . . ridge to the north."

Laryn's eyes creased slightly behind her face covering, and he could tell that she was smiling. "North it is. Keep your delicate bits covered, fellas, and your eyes to the horizon. Since I have the most experience up here, I'll lead. Bryndor, you follow. Lluthean, you'll be our lookout in a few hours. Kae brings up the rear. If I walk too far or too fast and you need to rest, speak up. I don't expect you to keep pace with me today, but we need to push at the limits of what you can tolerate. Let's go."

She tightened her face covering and pulled a dark gauze cloth over her eyes, jabbed a hiking stick into the snow, then plunged north along a ridgeline.

Bryndor fell in step, thankful for the way his aunt had pulled them from their moment of shock and awe. Something about the simple act of moving in a direction, any direction, allowed him to subdue his fear. As he labored to keep pace with his aunt, he held a hand on Boru and studied the churning currents of nadir and zenith as they tangled in violent knots that drifted before them.

Chapter Thirty-One: Empty Goodbyes and Embertang Eggs

Nolan sat on the edge of a boardwalk outside the command post. The new three-story timber building rose as a beacon in the center of the forward base camp. A whetstone rasped along the blade of a long knife, keeping his hands busy while his sister and Savnah held council with Warden Elbiona.

All around him, the frenetic activity of woodcutters and builders continued as the Aarindorian forces mustered between the Pillars of Eldrek. A cacophony of mallets, axes, and hand saws echoed across the camp.

A shadow obscured the morning sun, and he looked up to see Amniah sitting on an Aarindin. The sunlight silhouetted her lean figure and cast a strange halo through the stubble of hair on her scalp. In the week since they returned from their misadventures in the Great Crown, she had recovered something of herself. She joined the quad for meals once a day but preferred to remain under the watchful care of the medics. While her bruises and abrasions had mainly healed, he suspected other wounds had left deep scars and would require more time to mend.

Whenever his duties allowed, he visited her in the medic tent. After muddling through an hour of one-sided conversation in which he asked questions in an attempt to fill the silence, he opted for a new approach. They spent several hours each day playing King's Crown and other strategy games in silence. While Amniah rarely volunteered much conversation, she engaged the games with tactical prowess. To Nolan, that seemed like a significant first step in her healing.

He sheathed his knife and stood up. "So, you're off to Stellance then."

Amniah nodded. "The warden and Docent Venlith believe it's for the best."

"You'll be missed, Niah. I will miss you. Hurry back when you . . . just come back as soon as you think you can."

His words sounded hollow, and he struggled to think of something to fill the space between them. "Are you making the trip alone?"

"No. Runta is coming too. She has family in Stellance, and I still need treatments to my stumps for another month or so."

"Stumps?' he asked, then realized his error as she pointed at her boot. "Oh. You're getting around so well; it's easy to forget."

"It's not that easy to forget," she said.

"I didn't mean . . . what I meant was that you're recovering so well that—"

She rescued him with an uncharacteristic smile. "Relax, tracker. I know what you meant. I'm just having a little fun with you before I go."

He blew out a breath of air through pursed lips. "Well, consider me good and truly tendered. Is there any chance you could convince your mother to send you back with some of those meat pockets? I've had a craving for crown beetle hiccups, and I hear that's just the thing."

Amniah bopped her head, and he couldn't tell if she agreed to his request or not. "I'll see, Nolan. The Giver keep you." And just like that, she tapered the conversation, directing her Aarindin to leave.

"You too. Eyes to the horizon." He watched her depart across the camp.

When her silhouette became lost in the crowd, he made his way across the boardwalk and found Tovnik working at a table under a broad tent. A concentrated scent of pine resin cut through the air, wafting up from a black cauldron sitting over hot coals. He peered over Tovnik's shoulder as the medic frowned in concentration.

Nolan pinched his nose and blinked away tears. "That's the first time I've had the rancid stink of grot blood cleared out of my head, but moons that's potent."

Tovnik pulled back and glared through a heavy set of goggles. Wax plugs filled his nostrils, giving his voice a comical nasal intonation. With a resonant pop, he removed the goggles to reveal circular indentations rimming reddened eyes. "I know what you mean. It's a bit much, but it's better than grot funk."

Nolan thought back to that first night when their haggard group had returned to camp. None of the other Outriders, not even Warden Elbiona, had approached closer than ten feet. Even after they burned their uniforms, bathed, and dressed in clean fatigues, the taint of grotvonen blood stained his awareness. *I can't imagine how Savnah and Karra put up with it.*

"What are you doing, Tov?" he asked.

"Making embertang eggs," said the medic. Tovnik replaced his goggles, then dipped a small cup into the cauldron. From this, he drizzled the heated pine sap resin into small, rounded depressions in a stone tray. Into each recess, he cautiously spooned a small quantity of embertang. The oily liquid coalesced in the center of the resin, and the medic quickly poured more of the sappy pine mixture over the caustic substance.

Out of curiosity, Nolan infused the runes along his forearms and made a quick assessment of the resin. "So, that's a mixture of heated pine sap, a catalyst, and some kind of hardener? Moons, that's brilliant, Tov."

"I can't take credit for it. The docent, Venlith, assisted a few of the alchemy guild adepts with the formula. They call it brittle amber. When it cools, the eggs are safe to handle as long as you're careful. Here," said the medic, and he handed a cooled egg to Nolan.

The oval mass filled his palm with the weight of a skipping stone. He pressed his thumbnail into the surface, leaving a crease, but the shell remained intact. Holding the egg up to the light revealed a swirl of dark embertang inside the glassy casing. "How much force is required to break it?" asked Nolan.

"Let's just say you shouldn't drop it on the ground. I think we'll be able to store four or five in a well-insulated pack. The warden has Outriders trading bows for slings. I suppose that means we can lob these from farther away, but I'm not sure how accurate anyone will be."

"Oh, I don't know," said Nolan. "A lot of us grew up with slings before being trusted with the bow. It's still the best way to take a rabbit or small game. As fast as the grondle fell to Amniah's embertang cloud, I think I would rather store my bow and throw the egg. Can I try one?"

Tovnik reached into a basket on the ground and handed an egg to Nolan. "It's a void, for practice. No embertang inside, but the unbound sap will stick to your hands."

Nolan walked out to the edge of the camp and hurled the egg at a tree. The missile struck the trunk and shattered, splashing its resinous contents across the bark. *Not bad, and I'll bet it's flammable as well.*

He returned to Tovnik's side, hiding his nose under the front of his tunic. "Do you need help with any of this?"

Tovnik replaced his goggles, then continued to drizzle sap into molds, his response delayed by his concentration. "This is the last batch, thank the Giver. But if you could retrieve some kind of packing material from the munitions tent, we can secure the eggs for safe travel. Argul was a master of packing up his fragile alchemics and explosives."

Nolan took two steps toward the munitions tent, then stopped. "Are we headed out then? What are our orders?"

Tovnik set down the pitcher of heated resin, then shrugged. "Search me. Your sister said to be ready to leave by midday. I assumed you knew more than me."

"No. I'm still the closest thing to a tender in this group. Who do you suppose will replace Amniah?"

The medic scratched errantly at his flank. "I think the warden is shaking things up a bit. I don't know what's in store for us, but I think what's left of Savnah's quad is joining us."

"Hmm, with Dexxin and Savnah, that'll make us what, a five-er? A . . . pint? A pent?"

"A quint," said Tovnik.

"We've never drilled as a group of five. How do we range? Who's even in charge?"

Tovnik shrugged, then pointed behind Nolan. "I'll wager those two have the way of things."

Nolan turned to see Karragin and Savnah approaching along the boardwalk of the command post. The brutal woman from Midrock sauntered with her casual stride, axes strapped to hips, toes high, and heels to the ground. She muttered something to Karragin, then laughed at her own comment.

For her part, Karragin cocked her head to the side, listening. His sister didn't seem to register the humor of Savnah's words as she prowled forward with quiet precision.

"What's the status of those embertang eggs, Tovnik?" asked Karragin.

"All set. Nolan was just going to retrieve some packing materials. They should be durable enough for us to handle on a ranging."

"How do they work?" asked Savnah.

"The embertang is housed inside a brittle amber shell. They are safe enough to handle so long as you don't drop them. They shatter on impact, delivering the embertang," explained the medic.

Savnah grabbed one of the eggs sitting in a basket on the table. She massaged the missile in her palms, then tossed it in the air a few times. "It's still warm, and it doesn't feel very brittle to me."

Tovnik and Nolan both stepped back from the table. The medic clutched a neutralizing flask of resco to his chest. Savnah dropped the egg back into the basket, where it clacked against the others.

"Moons, relax boys. I wouldn't waste good embertang," said Savnah.

Both Nolan and Tovnik watched to see if the egg had cracked or leaked its caustic contents. Savnah picked up the egg and shook it near her ear playfully. "See? Not a drop wasted."

Karragin stepped to the table and ran her hands across the strange creations. "If I hadn't seen the devastation Amniah created with the cloud of embertang, I would never imagine these might be useful. How many will we each be able to carry?"

"I had enough time and materials to make four apiece, assuming we travel as pint . . . a pent, a quint!" said Tovnik. He sighed and removed the nasal wax plugs while casting a sidelong glance at Nolan.

"The overwarden issued new orders. Our quads are to double up into groups of eight. We will join Savnah and Dexxin. Savnah has agreed to ride as my second, but the rest of you, follow her orders with the respect given to any prime," said Karragin.

"What's behind the changes?" asked Tovnik.

Savnah hooked her thumbs over the broad leather belt at her waist. "Quad formation works best while accompanying a person of interest or ranging in stealth. After learning more of the danger of the grondle, the overwarden thought we needed to beef up our units."

"Are we going to travel as a double quad then?" asked Nolan.

"Not exactly. We are still the exception," said Karragin. "On Overwarden Kaldera's orders, we're to push farther into the Borderlands to make contact with Voruden. It's a town along the north face of the Korjinth Mountains."

Nolan whistled low in appreciation. "How long has it been since anyone pushed that far south? Do we know anything about the people there?"

"Nobody has ventured that far into the Borderlands and returned since the Abrogator's War," said Karragin. "However, while we were mucking about in the grot warrens, another quad rescued a couple fleeing the region. They lived on an isolated farm north of Voruden. Grondle and grotvonen had raided their livestock. From what they describe, it's a decent-sized city and might be able to defend itself. Our mission is to make for Voruden, determine its defensive capabilities, and offer an alliance."

They stood around the table in silent contemplation of the mission. Nolan wrestled with two emotions: excitement and trepidation. He intuitively understood his skills would be pressed into service to keep them safe from any grondle and grotvonen threats.

Savnah eventually broke the tension. "Dexxin will relay messages back to Aarindorn. His sister is riding here to enable the warden to coordinate from the forward camp. I'll be any extra muscle we might need. It's not a garden stroll, but I'll take a range under open skies any day compared to that crawl through the dark side of the Taker's asshole."

Karragin cleared her throat. "We leave in two hours. Gear up for a long haul under ghost protocol."

Nolan's chin plopped to his chest for a moment, and then he peered up at Tovnik, who nodded toward the mess tent. *Right. One last hot meal before we slog off into who knows what. Count me in.*

Chapter Thirty-Two: Enticement of the Lacuna

The afternoon sun hovered just above the curtain wall as Ksenia navigated the streets of Stone's Grasp. The nip of winter stung her nose as she stepped beyond the royal grounds and into the city. Within a block, she became aware of the smell of wood smoke. Every shop, tavern, and residence that lacked a zendil was burning timber harvested from the Great Crown for warmth.

Inside the royal grounds of Stone's Grasp and among the affluent estates, zendils emitted only sterile vapors. The rich scents beyond the curtain wall reminded her of home, and something in the tension of her shoulders relaxed. She considered turning left to make her way toward the Delve, a district of elite shops carved into the stone of the Great Crown. However, the meeting she planned to attend there wasn't scheduled for a few hours yet, so instead, she turned right, deciding to visit the royal stables.

Metal rails rasped as she unhinged an oversized door, the clamor of the hasp and lock clunking back into place announcing her arrival. The heads of several common horses and two Aarindin leaned out to investigate. *But not you, Winter. Giver help me if I don't visit you every single day. Let's hope a few dry carrots from the larder change your mood. Grind it, Kess. Why do you let an Aarindin cause you so much guilt?*

She raised her chin and stepped forward. As she approached Winter's stall, she spied the Aarindin's tail, its strands of silver-grey her only resemblance to the breed standard. Ksenia rested both arms on the gate and waited, watching the steam of her mount's breath billow up into the rafters.

"Hello, Ksenia," said one of the grooms from a few stalls away. "Watch yourself. She's got a bit of an attitude today. More nippy than the weather, she is."

Ksenia turned to regard the teenager. "Thanks, Munts. She forgets how nice these accommodations are and how frigid the winds were on the ranch."

The stableboy tossed fresh hay into a stall and walked over, dusting his hands on his breeches. The young man peered past the Aarindin. "She hasn't touched her feed today."

"She doesn't likely need it. She's used to grazing on grasses at the ranch. That's how they generate enough heat to endure the cold nights."

Munts wiped a runny nose on his sleeve then sniffed. "The stables aren't heated. By the Giver, I wish some days that they were."

"I should think not. You care for what, forty or more horses? Stagnant air breeds the flux. An enclosed stable with so many would have the royal mounts drowning in bloody froth within a few weeks," said Ksenia.

"Mmm . . . that's true enough," said the groom. "Say Ksenia, seeing as your family near enough wrote the book on the care and grooming of horses, could I get your opinion on one of my charges?"

Ksenia opened herself to her gift and channeled. "*I'll be right back, Winter.*"

The albino turned to regard her with a pale blue eye and snorted. Ksenia laughed. "*Oh please dear, be more dramatic. The Giver knows I don't get enough of that in the castle.*"

She severed their connection before Winter could offer a rebuttal and the Aarindin stomped her front hoof in what Ksenia knew was a moment of consternation. "Sure thing, Munts, lead the way."

They walked to the end of the aisle, then turned into the adjacent row of stalls. A blue roan mare stood passively in the back of the enclosure. Munts nodded toward the horse and cleared his throat. "She's been here a week, the mount of a highborn Endule visiting on some business with the vice regent. The last few days, I can't get her to show much interest in anything."

Ksenia studied the mare. A thin silk saddle cloth adorned with red tassels was draped over the horse's back. Despite the ostentatious covering, something in her bearing looked withered. "Does she answer to a name?"

"Annan," said Munts.

"Give me a moment." She rekindled her gift and opened herself to the mare. *"Annan, look at me. I'm Ksenia."*

She waited for the horse to return some indication that she understood. A moment of silence passed between them, and just when Ksenia began to wonder if she had mismanaged her gift, the horse relayed a strange image. The vision of a dead horse entered her awareness, lying on its side on frozen ground, legs erect and stiffened, a patina of frozen lather smeared over its nose. The cloying scent of decay accompanied the images.

"So detailed," Ksenia mumbled. She thought she sensed something more from the image, a sense of hopelessness.

"Giver's mercy, you poor thing. We'll need to show you that you are not so broken," she whispered and unhinged the gate to the stall. Soothing emotions rippled out through her gift, but no further response came, so she stepped forward.

Ksenia caressed probing hands under the mare's jaw and neck, searching for any sign of swollen glands. Finding nothing unusual, she examined each leg and ran her hands across the horse's body, then laid her ear flush to the mare's ribs to listen for its breathing and heartbeat. While the horse emitted clear sighs absent of any popping or gurgling, its breathing rate and pulse seemed very slow. In the cold stall she couldn't be sure, but the animal also felt unusually cool to the touch.

A search of the mare's feed bin revealed cracked corn but no straw. "What have you been feeding her?"

"Strange you would ask. Her owner demanded the staff feed her cracked corn," said the groom.

"So all week she's had cracked corn, nothing else?" asked Ksenia.

The stableboy shrugged. "Who am I to tell a highborn anybody what to feed their horse? He asked what feed cost the most and demanded that be the only thing she was allowed to have."

"Alright, I think I understand what might be going on. See . . . horses need high-quality hay in the colder months, like what you've been feeding Winter. Believe it or not, the hay gives them the stamina to survive and endure the chill. Cracked corn is fine in small amounts, but it doesn't give her what she needs, and I'll wager she doesn't digest it all anyway. If the corn is moldy, that can cause a lot of other problems. Regardless, Annan senses something about the feed and won't take to it."

"That's a truth right there, she hasn't finished but half of what we bring her for two days," said Munts.

"There is still a chance you can nurse her back to health. She's cold, and her idiot of an owner shaved off her winter coat. See her tail? She's a rare curly; they are supposed to have thick, lush coats in the colder months. She might also benefit from stabling with another. Move her to an interior stall. In fact . . . let's place her with Winter for a few days. Socialization would do both of them some good. Then get her some blankets and swap out the corn for all the hay she can manage. Be sure she gets plenty of fresh water, and you might see her through. Anything less, and I honestly don't think she's going to make it."

"Really?" Munts paled. "Moons, are you sure Winter will accept her?"

"Yes, I'll speak to her, but we need to move them to a double stall. Come on. I have enough time to help you."

They made quick work of coaxing Annan out of the stall and into a double pen on the stable's interior. Ksenia turned to retrieve Winter. "Munts, do me one favor? Be sure to charge that Endule the full amount for the cracked corn. It will be our secret. Your reputation as a groom and this mare's health shouldn't suffer the stupidity of a noble."

The stableboy nodded, then busied himself, bringing in fresh hay. Ksenia walked back to find Winter poking her proud head over the gate, looking about with interest. *"Are we speaking again?"* Ksenia asked.

"Did you bring treats?" asked Winter. *"I smell treats."*

"When did you get so clever as to answer a question with a question?" said Ksenia. She plunged a hand into a deep pocket and retrieved a thick carrot.

"I missed you. I'm sorry I haven't been able to ride this week. I will make it up to you in two days." Ksenia stroked Winter's jaw and muzzle.

"Yes," said Winter.

"Yes? That's all I get? A yes? Did you miss me too?"

Winter dipped her nose low and under Ksenia's arm, enticing a massage of her snout. Ksenia giggled. *"You're incorrigible,"* said Ksenia.

"I am Aarindin. You are my human."

Though Winter's response seemed simple on the surface, Ksenia's connection with her allowed a deeper understanding. The message rippled with memory and emotion. Ksenia saw flickered images of times when they played games of chase, rides along the foothills of the Great Crown, and simple conversations. Ksenia lay her forehead against the Aarindin's, sharing the intimate moment. *"Yes, I'm yours. I need your help, Winter. There is a mare who is alone and cold. I want you to look after her, encourage her to eat, remind her how to be happy. Make her your friend."*

Winter conveyed curiosity and followed Ksenia out of the stall and down to the larger double pen. The Aarindin appraised the lethargic mare a moment, then turned a pink-lashed eye to Ksenia. *"She is like the others, simple. Leave her with me and bring treats. Lots of treats."*

Ksenia crossed her arms. *"Because I love you, I will come back tomorrow with more."*

"Not for me, for her. I think treats will help her stop thinking about giving up."

Ksenia sensed a sigh escape from Winter. *"Will you be alright?"*

Winter sauntered around the double-pen stall, assessing the accommodations. She sifted through a fresh amount of hay and sniffed at the water trough, then turned back. *"Of course. Leave her with me. Tell Munts to make sure we have enough water."*

Winter walked over to the roan mare and rumbled a soft huff from deep in her throat, a gentle beckoning sound, then the two sniffed at each other a moment. Annan perked her ears forward and lifted her head for the first time, then turned and walked over to the feed bin and began to nibble on fresh hay.

"Would you look at that," said Munts.

"I'll come back tomorrow to check on them. If Annan gets worse, send for me." Ksenia ran a hand along Winter's neck, then walked out of the stall.

She backtracked along the curtain wall, passing the main gates, and hurried toward the Delve. The wide paved road made a gentle descent as it curved into the base of the Great Crown. Several people passed her without a glance, mostly couples returning with parcels and goods purchased from the various shops.

The Delve housed high-end craftsmen and artisans who sold exclusive wares in the catacomb-like district. While she understood that only shops of the highest reputation could afford the prestigious location, something about seeing the rough-hewn stone walls towering more than twenty feet overhead prickled the skin at the back of her neck.

Deeper into the district, the temperature warmed. The crisp smell of lamps burning survivor's essence opened up her stuffy nose, and people mingled in and out of shops speaking in lighthearted tones. She stopped to peer through a large window displaying the wares of a gilder.

Three small armies of horse figurines, one leafed in copper, another in silver, and a third in gold, stood poised on a triangular board. Next to that, a mobile with replicas of the twin moons oscillated around a golden model of Stone's Grasp. She lost herself in studying the intricate details.

The shopkeeper approached from inside, waving and beckoning her in. Before he could engage her in conversation, she dipped her head and continued deeper into the shopping complex. At the fourth intersection, the road leveled out. She chanced a glance up to the night sky. At least forty feet overhead, the walls disappeared into the shadows, and lamplight obscured the stars.

The aroma of spiced bread made her stomach growl and distracted her from the feeling of being caged. Two right turns brought her to a dead end. A set of lamps gleamed off a burnished metal sign that read *"Bekson's Fine Restoratives."*

After stepping inside the threshold, her eyes adjusted to a surprisingly spacious lobby well-lit by lamps. Several customers waited in chairs while sipping on beverages and holding quiet conversations. A thin, well-groomed man in a grey tailored suit stood beside a wood podium with an open ledger. Behind the man, rows of shelves housed ornate decanters of resco and other liquors. Opposite the manager, a chest-high bar topped with polished wood displayed several dishes: plates of savory meats, tureens of stews and vegetables, and platters with bread and cakes.

Ksenia swallowed down her hunger. Without words, she held her hands before her: thumb to thumb and finger to finger, forming a circle. Making sure that none of the patrons paid her any attention, she created a gap between her fingers. The manager nodded and pointed to a hallway off to her right. Ksenia dipped her head and walked the length of the hallway, passing several small rooms large enough to hold tables for small groups. The hall ended at a door where another man stood.

She hesitated a moment and looked back to the lobby. The light clamor of patrons put her at ease. *You've come this far; might as well see it through.*

After repeating the hand sign of the broken circle, the doorman nodded once and granted her passage. Once inside, her eyes adjusted to the dim light. A short walk brought her to the back of a large semicircular room ringed with rows of benches. She took a seat and stared long moments at her feet.

Over the next ten minutes, the room filled with no less than thirty members. Most kept to themselves or whispered in quiet conversation. As the pews filled, the whispered voice of what she guessed was an older woman spoke from her right side. "Apologies, is this seat saved? I'm to meet my son here."

Ksenia kept her face shadowed. "No, please, have a seat."

"The Giver's peace to you, my dear," said the woman. The greeting should have put Ksenia at ease, but her stomach tightened, and she remained vigilant.

As they waited, the woman unwrapped a basket. A hunk of cheese, half a loaf of bread, and dried sausage lay inside. The woman broke the bread in two and offered a portion to Ksenia.

"The Giver's peace to you as well, ma'am," said Ksenia, and she accepted the gift. As she chewed through the buttery crust and into the meaty center of the bread, she allowed her gaze to drift across the room. Most of the other members sat in huddled conversations sharing small bits of food and drink.

"This your first time here?" asked the woman.

Ksenia swallowed and nodded, feeling awkward engaging in the small talk that she often avoided among the gifted in Stone's Grasp. "What gave me away?"

"I spent as much time staring at my feet as you the first several meetings I attended. Trust me, it's not worth the sore neck, and nobody cares about your identity. We're all just friends, sharing a bit of food and listening to the wise counsel of the Aspect."

From her left, a familiar voice spoke and made the skin on her forearms tingle. "I wondered if Kervin would be able to get you here. Seems my younger siblings have more sense than most."

She turned so quickly that her hood fell back, exposing her face. "Rugen?" she whispered.

Her brother held a finger to his lips and smiled. A thick, black, well-manicured beard framed his face, and their father's dark blue eyes gleamed from the depths of his hooded cloak. He reached thick fingers forward to adjust her hood, obscuring her face. "Hello, little filly. It's good to see you."

The sight of her brother caused all the tension to drain from her shoulders. She hugged him with enough exuberance to make him giggle. "How did you know to find me here?"

Rugen sighed. "I know Mother. I knew she had plans to get you back to Stone's Grasp. She means well, but all her meddling . . . why do you think I left the ranch in the first place? Anyway, I ran into Kervin before he left on patrol, and he told me to watch for you. Winter makes you a pretty easy mark."

"I suppose that's true. How are you? What have you been up to? I left messages for you after I arrived. Did you receive them?" she asked.

Her brother hung his head a moment, then looked up. "I'm sorry, I did. I wanted to see you, but time slipped away from me. I've been . . . well, my days are busy with the city watch. I'm a subcaptain under Captain Oren. My responsibilities there are one thing, but my involvement with the Lacuna . . ." Rugen blew air through pursed lips and ran fingers through his hair. His face betrayed the same tension as her father after staying up all night to assist a struggling mare to foal.

He lifted his eyes to the front of the room, where an official stood wearing a hooded black robe. "I've been charged with overseeing certain guild interests pertaining to the new trade routes to the south. When I can, I try to attend a meeting. Sitting next to you was the Giver's luck. It's so good to see—"

The official turned and cleared his throat to address the room. Red tassels adorned the cuffs of his robe, and Ksenia nearly snorted. *If this is the kind of person trusted by the Aspect, perhaps we're all wasting our time.*

She wrung her hand around her left wrist in irritation until Rugen settled a calloused palm over her restless fingers. He tilted his head in concern. "What is it?"

Before she could give the matter any further thought, the man cleared his throat. "Welcome all who return to hear the word of the Lacuna and share the good news from the Aspect. I will be your acolyte this evening. The meeting will begin shortly, and we have a large crowd tonight. Out of respect for everyone, please keep your voices low as we begin."

Rugen leaned in and whispered, "We'll catch up after this meeting, Kess."

She nodded and returned her attention to the front of the room, where the acolyte placed a thin metal candle stand. He removed the candle from the stand and replaced it with a palm-sized nut. As the meeting came to order, a nimbus of light emanated from the seed, and a disembodied head appeared. The Aspect of the Lacuna spoke.

"We welcome all who listen tonight. Our members join from all sectors of Aarindorn: from Stellance to Midrock and Stone's Grasp to Callinora. Some gather in large numbers and others in small groups, but all are welcome to share in our vision for a free and prosperous Aarindorn. Tonight I would like our members to share examples of how the Lacuna have enriched the lives of our people."

Ksenia relaxed into the burly shoulder of her brother as she listened attentively. Several different members shared stories from across the kingdom detailing acts of charity supported by the group's generosity. She thought of the orphanage, believing that their story should be shared. To her relief, a familiar voice stepped forward to report on the success of the runeless orphanage. She smiled under her hood. *That's Suvi.*

For the first time since entering the room, Ksenia felt connected to the people around her. As Suvi recounted the brief success of the outreach in the Sprawl, she remembered the straw-haired little girl and all the cherubic faces of the children nourished by the stew she and Craxton had delivered on behalf of the Lacuna.

After the better part of an hour, the meeting drew to a close, with the Aspect issuing a challenge. "We welcome all to shelter under our wings. We need the able-bodied help of all to ensure the prosperity of Aarindorn. For those who want to pursue a formal role in the organization, speak to the acolyte at your meeting to learn more."

The woman seated next to Ksenia reached over and patted her hand. "You should give thought to the Aspect's words, dear. We could use more young people like yourself in the movement. Consider speaking to the acolyte when you are ready. Until then, the Giver's peace be with you."

"I will, and thanks. You as well, and may the Giver smile on you this day," said Ksenia.

She sensed Rugen standing at her side. "So, want to grab a bite and catch up?" he asked.

"Yes, but there's something I need to do first," she said.

As members filed out of the large room, Ksenia approached the acolyte. The man kept his face hooded and offered polite farewell remarks. She stood behind him, waiting her turn. Despite her initial rancor at how he'd mismanaged his horse, the testimonials left her feeling convinced of the rightness of joining the group. For the first time since coming to Stone's Grasp, Ksenia felt like there might be a place she belonged.

Chapter Thirty-Three: Lutney's Last Favor

Forty-four . . . forty-five . . . forty-six . . . forty-seven . . . forty-eight . . . forty-nine . . . fifty . . . grind me, that felt more like fifty thousand.

Lluthean labored to lift his back foot out of the snow and rested his hands on his knees. He pulled deep and rapid breaths, sucking the thin mountain air through the scarf over his face. It didn't matter how fast he breathed; the air never satisfied his persistent need for more. *It's like pouring water into a bucket with a huge hole in the bottom.*

The constant feeling of air famine left him both exhausted and exhilarated. Neska turned to him, tail wagging, and licked frost from his eyebrows and face covering. She and Boru seemed content in the snow, and their weeks of running in the high places with the pack had acclimated them to the mountain air. Her playful manner made him giggle. "Thanks for the kisses, Neska."

He began to count his breaths. Their passage over the mountains relied on staying together, and his uncle could only manage fifty steps, then required thirty breaths rest before moving on. And if he were completely honest, he felt thankful for the excuse to stop.

He synchronized his breathing with Neska and allowed her senses to overtake him. Lifting his gaze to the horizon, he spied four knots churning the skies immediately in front of them. None seemed to spin in the dense spiral that indicated they might discharge to the ground. Two others drifted close behind them for a time, then careened back up the mountain.

The winds dashed searing bits of snow across his forehead, and he suspected the skin there had long ago burned from the frost. He stopped feeling pain and instead felt an odd, dull tapping sensation against his skin. His coat sleeve extended down over his wrist, keeping his bare hand protected whenever he stopped to connect with Neska. Her body heat warmed his fingers, but as they thawed, the return of feeling caused a painful throbbing ache to awaken in his fingertips. He balled the numb fingers of his other hand inside his mitten.

Lluthean had considered walking down the mountain without changing which hand he used to link to Neska, but Laryn thought that would only raise the chance for serious injury from frostbite. So every half hour, he alternated which hand he thawed and which one remained numb.

Twenty-nine . . . thirty. Dammit to the Drift, that was too fast. He stepped in a slow circle to check on those who followed. Bryndor was squatting on both knees and ruffling Boru's coat with enthusiasm, displacing bits of ice and snow from the wolvryn. His brother tossed a chunk of ice into the air, and Boru leaped for the item as if it were a treat. Kaellor was leaned forward, hands on knees, and Lluthean waited for him to signal his ability to continue. His uncle looked up, nodded, and took a plodding step forward.

Lluthean studied the knots in the sky again, then pointed for Laryn to continue along a ridge leading to the north. He replaced his bare hand inside his mitten and started counting steps again. And so, the afternoon of the third day lingered.

On numerous occasions the first two days and twice this morning, they had to stop out of respect for the storms of zenith and nadir. Most of the time, the vortex swiveled off into the distance, but one had discharged only one hundred paces to the east this morning.

The shearing, tearing sound, like a sheet of metal being ripped apart, caused him to shiver more than the bitter cold. The black and purple storm had erupted with a concussive detonation that left his ears ringing for several minutes. And then an ethereal, mournful wail carried over the howling wind.

The Cloud Walkers called it "the death sigh." Both revolting and compelling, the sound rooted him to the spot. He had stared at the horizon entranced, waiting for another eruption until Neska lunged up, placing her paws on his chest and knocking him into a snowbank.

Reliving the memory of that moment made him grateful for her companionship. He watched as the wolvryn cocked her head, attentive to a disturbance in the west. A knot of cascading shafts of black and blue lightning contacted the ground on a neighboring range.

Seconds later, the vibration of a faint death sigh rippled through him. Then a low rumbling sound echoed across the canyon as a massive sheet of snow slid down the mountain, churning a foaming torrent of white death. The wave of snow tossed boulders and shale high into the air. A cloud of white powder obscured the leading edge. When the avalanche settled, an entire side of the black mountain appeared denuded from the white blanket. Strange outcroppings of shiny, black rock glinted in the light.

Lluthean studied the other cliffs around them and the range before them. He realized they had descended onto a level stretch of mountain and were nearly out of danger from any similar avalanche threats. *It might be Lutney's last favor before we cross over, but I'll take it.*

Over the next hour, the mantle of snow covering the ground thinned. The howling winds drove thin wisps of white powder over more shards of black, polished rock. They all found the footing clumsy, and his ankles shifted and turned as he stumbled on the uneven ground.

Forty-nine . . . fifty. He took a knee. Neska had become accustomed to their pattern and sat at his side. He removed a mitten and shifted his sight to hers, thankful for the warmth despite the returning aching of his fingers. His surveillance revealed numerous immature knots meandering all around the tops of the range, but none lingered in their immediate vicinity.

He cast one last glance behind them to be sure that none of the fickle spirals were drifting close and noticed something very odd. A faint ribbon of blue undulated down from the sky, anchored to Boru. High overhead, the blue strip fluttered like a kite ravaged by violent winds. Yet, where it connected to the wolvryn, the streak of zenith appeared placid.

Lluthean craned his neck back from Neska to see if a strand was attached to her as well, but he couldn't be sure. His eyes teared from the cold wind, and he tucked his chin back into the warmth of his scarf. A red cloth waved overhead signaled everyone to gather. Within minutes they huddled in a tight circle.

Three grim faces, strafed red by the wind and cold, peered at him from behind fur-lined hoods and scarfs iced over at the nose and mouth. Each of them wore the dark mask of sleep deprivation. They all stood there long moments waiting. At last, a smile creased the corner of Bryndor's eyes, then Kaellor's.

"What are you three smiling about?" Laryn shouted over the droning winds.

"I've never been so exhausted, and there's something about the air up here," said Bryndor. "It's all I can do not to break out into a fit of laughter. Is it just me?"

A huff of air steamed before Kaellor. "No, I feel it too." He panted. "It's one part sleep deprivation, one part labor, and . . . one part sleepy labor."

His odd phrase hung in the air, and Lluthean began to wonder if his uncle was struggling more than he'd assumed. Kaellor pulled his scarf down over his beard, grinned with an unusual toothy smile, then replaced the face covering. "I can make a joke too, but you two keep your focus. We can't cross safely without you."

Lluthean nodded understanding. "So . . . think bad thoughts?"

The comment made them each laugh for a minute. Laryn placed a mitted hand on Lluthean's shoulder. "Why did you call us together? Do you need a rest?"

"There's something strange going on with Boru. When I look at him from a distance, with Neska's sight, I can see a ribbon of zenith attached to him from the sky," Lluthean explained. "I saw something similar once when I used her sight to watch Bryn and Boru while linked back in the valley."

His words gave them pause. Kaellor and Laryn looked about with curiosity, searching the horizon. Bryndor stared at his feet, shivering.

Eventually, his brother lifted his gaze from the ground. "Neska has it too. I didn't want to worry you and figured there isn't anything we can do about it."

"Have you seen it before? In the valley, did you ever see it there?" asked Laryn.

"No. Well, maybe. It's something new . . . in the valley I could see a thread of zenith connected to them . . . up here it's like a thick ribbon. What does it mean?" asked Bryndor.

Laryn's boot crunched over loose rock as she scuffed her heel back and forth. "It means . . . Giver's mercy. I don't know, but Mahkeel mentioned something about how the concentrated flows of zenith alter the wolvryn. I saw something like it when I healed Lluthean the first time we met. I think . . . I think the wolvryn are absorbing zenith as we cross. We have to get off this grinding mountain as soon as we can."

Lluthean sensed an unusual tension in the pitch of her voice. "Do you think it hurts them? Is there anything we can do?"

Steam billowed out from Laryn's face covering. "Hurts them? Not likely. They are creatures of zenith. But who can say what effect it might have? They were already going to be bigger than Ghetti. This crossing might make them grow larger than Scout, and . . ."

She shook her head, staring at her boots and kicking a toe at the loose rock. "Nobody knows, but the longer we are up here, the more zenith they are likely to absorb. And something tells me that's not what the Giver intended."

She craned her neck, searching the northern horizon. "How are you doing, Kae? Can we push on? I think we can make better progress on this plateau."

"I'll manage. I'm ready when you are," said Kaellor.

They labored across the plateau, stopping on occasion to allow the vortices to pass by or veering course when one loomed before them, appearing ready to discharge. The next several hours melded together in one long, miserable trek.

Lluthean stopped for another break, but Kaellor waved him on. "I think I finally got my legs back. We can keep going if it's all the same. The sooner we drop into the tree line, the sooner we can all sleep."

"I still need to study the knots. One moment." On cue, Neska sat on her haunches, waiting for him to employ her sight. He studied the way forward. Several knots skipped on the horizon where a dark spine of the mountain rose from the plateau.

Lluthean turned to the east and west, finding no threats. But when he looked to the south, from the direction they had traveled, strange black strings, almost like kite strings, intermingled in a weaving pattern on the horizon.

"Bryn, can you link with Boru and tell me what you see there to the south?" asked Lluthean.

His brother turned and studied the south horizon for long moments. "I see them . . . black strings or . . . Mogdure's breath."

"What is it?" asked Kaellor.

"They're getting closer," said Bryndor. "I think . . . it might be like the cords of zenith we see attached to the wolvryn . . . only it's not zenith. It's nadir. And whatever those strands are attached to are coming this way."

Kaellor looked to Laryn. "What do you think?"

"It's nothing I've encountered before, and I don't think we want to. How many of them do you see?" asked Laryn.

"Eight, no nine. There are nine," said Lluthean. Still connected to Neska, he strained to sense whatever was approaching, but they were upwind. Several minutes passed in which he and Bryndor scrutinized the far horizon. Then, finally, the source of the strange phenomenon appeared through their wolvryn sight.

Lluthean withdrew from his link with Neska to pet her neck in reassurance and realized that both wolvryn were releasing low-pitched growls of warning.

"It's a group of mountain cats. Big ones, like panthers or something," Lluthean explained.

Laryn stopped scuffing her boot on the loose rock and cocked her head. "The only thing I know of that might match that description is a spotted cloud leopard. They're supposed to be shy, and I've never heard of such a large number of them together."

"Let's push on," said Kaellor. "I'm better. Stop only for brief moments to study the knots. I can keep up, and we should start to descend within a few hours. Whatever those are, they might have our scent. Let's not linger and make for easy pickings."

"I'm warmer when we keep moving," said Bryndor, and he turned back to the north, assuming the lead. His brother set a grueling pace over the next two hours, making only brief stops to survey their surroundings.

Without a word, Bryndor veered to the west, and they all followed. Minutes later, a vortex discharged several hundred paces to their east. A geyser of powdered snow erupted into the air, followed by the familiar keening of the death sigh across the range. Lluthean stopped a moment, transfixed by the mournful song until his uncle gripped him by the shoulder, pulling him to action.

They caught up to Bryndor, who was hunched forward, hands on knees. "I think I need a break. It's a blessing of the Seven, of the . . . Giver's mercy that I didn't lead us into that last storm of zenith. I can see where the plateau starts to descend. There's a tree line on the horizon. But we still need to navigate around four or five knots."

"I can see us through," said Lluthean. He stepped forward and linked to Neska to study the knots. *Bryn was right, but moons, all four look ready to burst in the next few minutes.*

Lluthean turned back to the south one last time to survey the strange panthers connected to the nadir strings. Five of the creatures were loping toward them. He became lost in studying the serpentine way they wove their path across the rocky terrain.

Neska lunged away from him, causing him to yelp in surprise. Only then did he realize the feral intensity of her growl. In an instant, the two wolvryn had charged across the plateau as undulating streaks of silver and black death.

"Boru! Neska! Come back here," Bryndor shouted. He gestured the commands Mahkeel had taught them, but the wolvryn ran ahead, heedless.

Bryndor sprinted after the pups. Lluthean started after him, but after no more than fifteen steps, they drew up. His brother panted, and his eyes conveyed wild desperation. They focused on the south horizon, watching the wolvryn disappear in the swirling snow.

"Dammit twice to the grinding Drift," Bryndor muttered in resignation. "We can't go after them, Llu, and they gave in to the chase. You were the last to see the knots. I wasn't . . . my head is so foggy I can't even remember where they spun. If you can get us off this plateau, the wolvryn will find us."

"There were too many of those nadir . . . cat things! We could chase them off, recover the wolvryn, then continue with their sight to guide us," said Lluthean.

"Bryn's right, Llu," said Kaellor. "Son, I'm all but spent. Three days with no sleep, the thin air, the effect of those storms . . . I don't think I'll make it if we go back. You've got to do your best and give us a course ahead."

Lluthean searched their faces, hoping Laryn might give him the excuse he needed to recover Neska. The woman lifted those strange eyes, one stained with the color of the red moon, the other a deep blue. He found compassion there and understanding, but not the release he hoped to see.

"Neska is crafty, and Boru is bigger than two of those cats. Together, they'll find us. I know it's a lot, but trust them!" Laryn yelled over the winds.

Lluthean forced his attention back to the north, willing his memory to call forth the last images he viewed through Neska's gift. "We should veer two . . . maybe three hundred paces to the east, then push north as hard as we can. We might make it, but there were four of those storms gathering to discharge."

"The Taker never makes it easy. Eyes to the horizon then, lead on, and I'll keep up," growled Kaellor.

Lluthean set off at a jog, veering to the east. He stumbled over the craggy terrain, his footing made awkward by both fatigue and his concern for the wolvryn. He strained time and again to see any sign of Neska, but the bitter winds made his eyes brim with tears, and occasional glances were all he could manage.

"Llu!" Bryndor shouted. "That's three hundred fifty paces. Should we turn north?"

Lluthean stopped and searched the skies and the north horizon. A vortex appeared several hundred paces ahead of them and discharged. As bits of glassy black rock and snow fell to the ground, the eerie death sigh echoed over the plateau. Lluthean felt the last vestiges of his motivation wither, and he dropped to his knees.

Grind me. Which knot was that? A new one? One of the four? Why did we think we could pass? It's easier to rest here and wait. Neska will find us here as well as anywhere else.

A high-pitched growl caused him to glance to the side. A black panther lunged directly at him, only to be repelled by Kaellor's discharge of zenith. A crescent of blue light surged out from Kaellor's hand, tossing the large cat ten paces back. Something in his uncle's release of zenith broke through the trance of the death sigh.

Lluthean shook his head as if waking and looked around. Laryn and Bryndor struggled to their feet, appearing to have dropped as he did. In moments, his awareness of the danger of their surroundings returned.

The cat his uncle deflected, if it could be called a cat, slowly rose to its feet. The wind rippled over shiny, grey fur, but when the creature flexed, chitinous, glossy black plates along its shoulders and hips sprouted. An overlong tail with a barb whipped back and forth as if tasting the air.

He considered pulling out his bow but didn't think his numb fingers could manage the weapon, let alone string it. He kept a mitted hand on the hilt of his dagger and stumbled toward his uncle. The panther limped a few steps, favoring a front leg and mewling. The creature inhaled, and the fur about its head and throat puffed out with more chitinous plates.

The beast coughed once, spewing a dark liquid on the ground, and limped off. Where the strange ichor fell, the snow dissipated, revealing glassy black rocks.

"Did you know your gift would break us from the trance?" asked Laryn.

"No," said Kaellor. "It's the Giver's blessing that creature attacked when it did. I think it triggered my gift. If not for that, I would have fallen, same as you. Come. We need to be off this plateau. I can see the tree line."

Lluthean noticed for the first time that they stood at the north edge of the plateau. He looked down the steep descent of snow, which lasted perhaps five hundred paces before a line of trees sprouted up. They trudged ahead over rocky ground that gave way to ankle-deep snow and then knee-deep drifts. Bryndor took the lead, making a trail they each followed.

Behind them, another collision of zenith and nadir strafed the skyline, then another. The melancholy songs scraped the air, shearing through the winds. Oppressive, otherworldy fatigue began to settle in, but Kaellor released another surge of zenith. A light blue dome flickered around them for a few seconds, then winked out.

Lluthean looked over his shoulder and nodded once to his uncle. Kaellor had plunged the guardian sword into the snow and was resting on one knee. Azure light twinkled from his eyes and through his face covering.

His uncle grunted once, stood, and growled. "Move! Get to the trees! There are at least three more of those nadir cats following us."

Bryndor rose and plowed ahead, creating a trail through the snow, which had become waist-high. The line of trees came more clearly into view, and for the first time in three days, Lluthean began to feel they would make it.

He followed behind Bryndor, pushing a path through the snow, creeping ever farther down the mountain. His leg muscles ached, and his chest burned from their labor. The sense of air famine returned as they pushed ahead. He caught up to his brother at the tree line and collapsed to both knees. Their sprint down the mountainside had stolen the last vestiges of any stamina.

Like billows spouting rapid gouts of steam into the air, they panted for several minutes. Eventually, Lluthean managed to stand, but he clutched hands to knees, sucking hungrily at the air. Finally, he couldn't stand it anymore and giggled. "The Taker's icy balls, I never thought we would make it off that mountain."

He waited for Bryndor to comment. When his brother said nothing, he looked up. "Bryn? You alright?"

Bryndor stared back up the mountain. Fifty paces back, Laryn stood motionless. One hundred paces back, Kaellor stood in waist-deep snow, brandishing the guardian sword. Prowling between them, three black nadir cats padded across the snow, their barbed tails whipping back and forth.

The creatures appeared unencumbered by the drifts, stalking over the snow rather than through it. The lead panther inhaled, and chitinous black plates expanded through its fur, causing its head and neck to puff out. It spewed oily black material toward Kaellor, the liquid spraying in a mist on the wind. Zenith flared across the blade of the guardian sword, and Kaellor shielded himself in a bubble of zenith. The nadir stain slicked off and hissed into the snow.

The other two cats turned their attention toward Laryn. They rumbled throaty growls, then sauntered down the mountain, eyes trained on their prey.

Chapter Thirty-Four: Swelling the Ranks

The Aspect of the Lacuna retrieved the zenith seed reserved for his inner council meetings. Surrounded by a smooth, leathery husk, the strange flat nut nestled in the palm of his hand. He wondered briefly at the distances covered by the rover woman who had sold him the collection. None of the forests in Aarindorn ever dropped such oddities.

A question for another day, I suppose.

He summoned zenith to his bidding, awakening his ability to funnel air. A delicate current lifted the seed and hovered it before his face. A deliberate projection of his intention laced with just a bit more zenith and emotion brought forth his likeness in a blue nimbus.

Muscles low in his throat relaxed, and the pitch of his voice dropped. "I call to order the inner council of the Lacuna. I trust everyone is in attendance?"

The shimmering field of zenith shifted as different wispy images and voices appeared. "I'm here in Callinora orienting our newest recruit," said Inasia.

"All is well in Midrock, Aspect," replied Burl.

The images became watery as both Valdesta and Kunzie responded, "Here."

The Aspect assumed control of the communication. "Good, all accounted for then. I'll make this brief. I have it on good authority that the regent is entertaining the notion of abandoning the aristocracy in favor of an open republic unfettered by the rules of noble succession. However, still more pressure is needed before the Assembly of Nobles in the spring. If we convince enough influential families to support our cause, Therek will have a difficult time resisting the will of the assembly."

Valdesta's shrouded face appeared, and she cleared her throat. "Our recruitment efforts have brought in many among the common citizens. The lower classes in particular flock to our banner when ours is the sole source of sustenance through the lean winter months. Our latest agreements with the Spicer gang have further solidified our influence in the Sprawl."

"That might guarantee us a hot bowl of soup on a cold winter day, but I should think we need more influence in the high families if we are to bend the will of the regent," said the Aspect. "How have our invitations among the ungifted been received? That group, in particular, should be primed to join us and break away from a country ruled by only a select gifted cast."

Kunzie's likeness appeared. "My son introduced us to their leader, the Dedicant. My sense is that we have piqued their interest, but he wants written affirmation of their place in our new social order if we are to curry his favor."

"That is not an unreasonable request, although the Taker's fingers can tangle the tapestry if the details are not fully understood, as they say." The Aspect paused a moment in contemplation of how to proceed.

"Let the Dedicant know that we are interested in offering a formal place at the table . . . more specifically, this table. We can cover the specifics of how to communicate with an ungifted later, I suppose. Find out exactly what he expects, and then get back to me so we can move to solidify that relationship. There are many closeted ungifted among the noble families. It's possible that their support might be the catalyst for more change among the members of the Assembly."

"Give me a week, two at the most," said Kunzie. "I will bring their demands forth to the inner council," said the man. "If you don't mind my asking, why do you think the regent might be turning to our cause?"

"Our agents inside Stone's Grasp," said the Aspect. "They report that the stresses of the office weigh heavy on his mind these days, especially with his children at no small amount of risk in the field. He seems withdrawn and more . . . preoccupied than usual. On two occasions, the topic came up during formal discussions with petitioners to the court.

"One account has the vice regent working in concert with the old lynx to settle a property dispute between an Endule and a commoner. The petitioner claimed that the regent only sided with the Endule out of obligation to the royal cast. The discussions became . . . heated, according to the scribe, and ended with the regent muttering something about a simpler way to settle disputes. The general mood in the room left many wondering if Therek is ready to abandon the post altogether."

Burl's image appeared in the nimbus. "Our previous attempts to create an accident among one of the Lefledge children didn't work out so well. Do we need to consider another run? If the man is that fragile, it might be worth another attempt. I have one of our strongest field agents installed."

Valdesta chimed in, "It's a risky endeavor. I imagine Lefledge is wiser than he appears. If another attempt is made and fails, he'll surely know someone plots against him. If we do this, we should take out just one of his children. Besides, he doesn't deserve to lose everything, does he?"

The zenith seeds remained silent for long moments while the members of the inner council contemplated this. The Aspect stared at the empty blue nimbus of the zenith seed. *Is this what we've come to, then? Killing an innocent to provoke change for the greater good?*

"Let's not make those moves at this time, but keep your man close," said the Aspect. "Too much pressure, and the old codger might become useless to us. He's not a bad man, after all. He's laboring under an antiquated system. If he demonstrates continued resistance to a dissolution of the monarchy, then we will take more serious steps."

"Are we prepared to support a leader of our own if that should happen?" asked Inasia. "If the regent agrees to support a free republic, his guidance would be just the right thing to steer the wagon over poorly mapped ground."

"There are a number of candidates free from ties to the nobility and able to step into that role. We would need to move swiftly to install our choice. Captain Oren or any of the high-ranked members of the Outriders might suffice," said the Aspect.

The nimbus hovering above the zenith seed remained dormant a moment as they each considered his words.

"Has the seer revealed anything else more meaningful to us?" asked Inasia.

"No," replied Burl. "We monitor him for any revelations. They come on during sleep, unbidden and without warning. His whole body shudders with surges of zenith, and most of the time, he mumbles random phrases like bits and pieces of dreams. We try to record everything he speaks, but mostly it's just mumbled gibberish. He hasn't offered anything substantial for a long while now."

"Does he ever recall the visions? Could he be holding out?" asked the Aspect.

"Not usually. That's why we keep a constant vigil when he sleeps," said Burl.

"What have you been able to record lately?" asked Inasia.

"As I said, it's all random phrases. I have the last two night's recordings here." Burl cleared his throat and recited, "The unbound sentry wards the path on which the lost sheep wander, the ministrations of the daughter of the red moon shape the currents of zenith while the blue moon shines brightly over Stone's Grasp, that kind of stuff."

Actually, that doesn't sound like jibberish to me. The Aspect cleared his throat. "All the same, do whatever we can to keep our agents embedded in the forward staging area at the Pillars of Eldrek. I should not like to think that anything amounts from the regent's folly, but one can never be too careful."

"I have another point of business to bring forward," said Valdesta. "One of our agents, a young man named Skellig, muddled a vivith drop with the Spicer gang. He went to deliver the goods, but the city watch happened by, and the unit just happened to be free of our influence, shall we say. Our man was captured, and the Spicers lost a man in the scuffle. They're looking for compensation and assurances of better security."

"Is the agent close to anyone of importance?" asked the Aspect.

"No. He's a gutter rat from the Sprawl. Nobody will miss him, but he is also ungifted. If we could see to his release, that could help build trust with the Dedicant."

Save face with the Spicers or build bridges with the Dedicant?

"Arrange for his untimely demise while in the royal cells," said the Aspect. "Our relationship with the Spicers is more important just now. Let them know of our controlling interests in the new trade routes to the Borderlands. See if the importation of resco below cost from the next caravan placates them."

The Aspect paused, calculating the benefits of his plan. "Then . . . let it slip to the Dedicant that one of his own, an ungifted, was poorly treated while in royal custody."

"I like it," purred Valdesta. "I'll see to it at once. I'll use one of our agents in the city watch."

"And I can see to the negotiations and reimbursement to the Spicers," said Kunzie.

"I admit that I don't visit the Sprawl," said Inasia. "But I understand that life has become less abysmal and a bit more . . . civil? Our management of the Spicers requires a careful hand. How do you assess their capabilities? If news of their organized activity bubbles up to the regent, we could have a problem. We want them to manage the quarter effectively but also to understand their place."

"At this time, they are effectively managing the vivith trade, black market goods, brothels, and gaming houses. We collect our share without getting our hands dirty," said Valdesta. "Our combined support of the commoners through food kitchens and the orphanages gives a certain . . . nobility to their efforts. Have no fear, when they reach too far, and they will, I'll see to the removal of a few top men to send the appropriate message."

"Very well, keep me apprised of any significant overreaching on their part," said the Aspect. "Now then, I do have some pleasant news to share. I believe we have secured another Endule in the Lacuna. She's from a high family in Beclure and seems poised to join ranks with us. While she might not be able to swing the balance of discussion at the spring Assembly, she has provided valuable intelligence on the political persuasion of her extended family."

"Can we trust her?" asked Burl. "I mean, never mind that she's a member of the aristocracy but from Beclure? That entire duchy has been looking down from their perch in the Great Crown so long that they don't know any other way to consider the rest of us in Aarindorn."

"So far, she has proved her value with reliable intelligence," said the Aspect. "Her family struggled under the reparations after the Abrogator's War more than most. It seems there might be several lesser nobles along the western duchies ready to consider aligning with our cause."

"It's not just the duchies that might prove fertile grounds for our recruitment efforts," said Inasia. "Here in Callinora, the scholars see themselves as operating rather outside the minor concerns of politics so long as their colleges and sanitoriums are supported. It's bred a certain contempt for the nobility, especially among the younger generation. We've seen a significant increase in first-time attendees at our gatherings in the last month."

"That is good news," said the Aspect. "We'll need to be inclusive to the newcomers. The employment of a healer of the third circle might have any number of benefits and . . . uses."

Chapter Thirty-Five: Wolvryn in the Mists

Laryn stared up the mountain at the approaching nadir cats. Her heart thrummed, and she knew she should run, but she remained frozen in place. Farther up the mountainside, Kaellor released a crescent of zenith at the lead cat. His power dissipated as it flashed down the mountain, rippling the snow in its wake. The thrill of his zenith pulsed through her and drew her mind into focus.

She assumed an aggressive posture and took a step forward, waving her arms. "Get out of here! Go on! Back to the Taker with you!"

The two black cats stopped to consider her antics only a moment, then continued forward, tails whipping back and forth. Laryn maintained eye contact but began to backtrack down the mountainside.

The slow retreat seemed to keep the cats at a distance for ten paces. Then her footing slipped, and she felt her ankle wrench to the side, forcing her to spin to avoid injury. When she looked back up, the two cats were bounding toward her.

"Run, Laryn, Come on!" Bryndor shouted. The young man struggled to reach her through the snow, brandishing a knife and a tree branch.

She recovered her balance and began to trudge through the channel in the snow the boys had created. A glance over her shoulder showed the panthers on the move; their unencumbered leaps across the surface of the drifts would close the distance in seconds.

The tree line stood fifty paces away, and Bryndor only half that. She ignored the pain of swollen ankles and frozen feet, ignored the surging throb of her heart in her chest, and focused only on Bryndor's eyes.

Something fierce and determined glared back through his stone-grey gaze. Feeling emboldened, she lifted her knees above the snow and renewed her attempts to reach him.

Over the howling wind, she felt something land just behind her in the snow and heard the soft percussion of the predator padding behind her. Something in Bryndor's expression changed at that exact moment, and he drew up short, appearing confused.

Laryn tossed herself to the side, expecting to feel the claws of the nadir cat. From the corner of her vision, something silver and black flashed across her path, colliding into the panther. A violent cloud of powdered snow roiled up into the air. Savage and guttural growling broke out above the winds, and the great cat howled in pain, then mewled, then was silent.

A soft breeze stirred the snow in eddies, rising from the mountainside and flavored with the spiced scent of pine. The snow cleared to reveal Boru. He stood growling, the dead panther limp in his jaws.

You great, big, beautiful thing.

She rose to her feet and began a slow retreat toward Bryndor. Farther up the mountainside, Kaellor continued to struggle with the lead cat. The predator lashed out with its barbed tail. He managed to deflect the attack, but his sword swing appeared clumsy compared to the speed with which the cat darted about him.

He looked utterly exhausted and heaved his shoulders, sucking in air. Kaellor lunged out with a wild swing and collapsed to a knee. The panther crouched just out of range, prepared to pounce. Before the great cat could lunge, Neska erupted in a flash of silver and black from a swirl of snow. She streaked in front of the panther.

The wolvryn landed beside Kaellor, and the nadir cat stopped only a few feet away, appearing unharmed. A moment passed in which both predators considered one another. Then Neska spat out a chunk of flesh from her jaws.

The meat stained the snow with black and maroon ichor. Neska sat back on her haunches, watching the cat whip its tail overhead. A bubbling froth of the same black and maroon fluid eventually gushed from a rent on the lead cat's neck, staining it with an oily bib. It wobbled, then collapsed without a sound.

The last nadir cat emitted a high-pitched growl, then sprinted back up the mountain, lunging over the snow until it disappeared to the plateau.

Laryn craned her neck around in search of any other dangers. Boru loped over to her side, panting with tail wagging.

"You are a true gift of the Giver," she said and hugged him around the neck. "*Go to Bryndor,*" she signed. The wolvryn looked down the mountainside, then trotted down the channel to Bryndor.

Laryn turned her gaze back to Kaellor. He sat on his heels, slumped forward and leaning on the sword, but upright. "Kae? Kae, are you alright?"

She started the climb back to him, calling every few paces, but stopped when he lifted his head and waved a mitted hand, indicating he heard her. He reached out and stroked Neska on the top of her head, then the two of them walked the rest of the way down the mountainside.

When he reached her, they touched foreheads and embraced. He mumbled something once, then repeated himself with raspy, slurred speech. "I would kiss you . . . but I don't dare . . . remove my face covering . . . Besides, I don't have the breath . . . and my face." He gestured at his chin with a clumsy hand. "Too numb to . . . make my mouth work right."

"It's okay, love. Let's get down into the tree line. We all need a rest and a fire," she said.

Another hour of slogging through the snow left them feeling defeated. The conifer forest blocked the wind but allowed the snow to drift waist-high in most places. After slogging through several drifts, her legs wobbled from the stress and fatigue. Laryn resisted the urge to voice her dismay; she didn't want to contribute to their mutual suffering.

Lluthean made a sharp turn and hollered with excitement. She labored to follow the boys, and they discovered an ancient dead tree. When it fell, the root bulb, which was wider than she was tall, had left a protected natural depression in the ground.

If she had any doubt about their ability to make camp there, her fears melted as Neska and Boru crept under a few of the remaining roots. The wolvryn lowered bellies to the ground, tucked their tails, and slept.

"I guess that settles it. Welcome to our home for the next few days," said Bryndor. Nobody argued.

Over the next hour, the boys made a fire then worked to cover the ground with fresh pine cuttings. Laryn turned her attention to Kaellor. He sat at the edge of the deadfall depression, unusually quiet.

She studied his face and noticed for the first time that blood stained the ice crystals gathered over his face covering. A curse escaped her as she pulled down his scarf to discover a blue pallor to his lips. Without waiting, she unshackled her gift, allowing zenith to infuse her arca prime. The soft murmur of her skill hummed.

"What are you doing?" Kaellor croaked more than spoke.

She shook her head and glared at him. His silent acceptance of her assessment told her as much as her gift. Laryn removed her mittens to place a hand on his forehead and reached another alongside his ribs. Despite the touch of iced fingers, Kaellor tolerated her probing in silence.

Her hands ran along the edge of muscle under his armpit, finding it more defined than usual. *You've lost more than a few pounds on this journey.*

Her gift commingled with his as she assessed the flows of zenith through his vital tissues. Then, satisfied that he remained unaffected by any lingering effects from traveling so close to the strikes of nadir, she drew her focus to his lungs. In more than half of the air spaces, a thin fluid bubbled.

The discovery caused her to open her eyes with a grunt of surprise. He wiggled his chin above his face covering, and she saw that more bloody froth was iced to his beard.

Laryn glared back at him. "When did you fancy you might tell me about this, Prince?"

In answer to his silent question, she withdrew a hand and pinched a piece of the pink ice clustered to his chin hairs. "How long have you been coughing up fluid tinged with blood?"

"Since yesterday," he answered. "We couldn't stop, and if you healed me on the plateau, I knew it might just happen again. Is it . . . serious?" The simple act of speech forced him into a hacking cough, and he spat more of the blood-tinged foam onto the ground.

She turned her head to the side, watching him. *Really?* She left him to the misery of his spasms of coughing for a minute, then pushed him to lean back.

"Seriously, Kae, what is it with you Baellentrell men? Less sense than a monk and twice as stubborn sometimes. This would have been a lot easier if you had let me know the moment it started. Your lungs are overreacting to the thin air. It's like the combination of the high altitude and the cold burned them. To protect itself, the tissue covers the inflamed surfaces in water. If you went another day like this, you would literally have drowned in your own sauce."

To his credit, Kaellor held up a hand in submission and nodded understanding. "What's the cure?"

"Normally, we would need to descend all the way down the mountain, but I don't think any of us are in any kind of shape to do that. Fortunately for you, I'm the best healer this side of the Korjinth."

She stopped when she realized where their camp rested. "Well, one of the best anyway. Hold still. This is going to take a while. Try your best not to cough. Every time you do, I have to start all over. Are you ready?"

He took a few shallow breaths, then nodded once. She replaced her hands against his skin and redirected her focus into the damaged tissues. Over the next hour, she labored to filter thin filaments of zenith into the delicate tissues. First, she relaxed all the blood vessels in his lungs, coaxing them to reabsorb the fluid, then she labored to displace the remaining edema. To his credit, Kaellor didn't cough once, a fact of which she was only peripherally aware.

She finished by soothing the inflamed lung tissues with strands of healing zenith. Sensing she had pushed herself overly hard, she pulled back and made a fast inspection. Blood, lymph, and zenith appeared to migrate through his chest in a normal pattern, so she stifled her gift.

Kaellor sat forward and coughed, but only for a few seconds. Rivulets of sweat ran off his forehead and into his beard. The purple hue under his eyes had vanished, replaced with vigorous ruddy cheeks. His baritone voice echoed as he said, "By the Giver, love . . . that is so much better."

Laryn nodded once, then eased herself back into a reclined position. Bryndor and Lluthean sat opposite a fire, a fat rabbit skewered on a stick. She adjusted herself to better feel the warmth on her feet and face and relaxed. After eating a flank of rabbit, sleep settled swiftly upon her.

They spent the next two days sleeping and recovering in a similar fashion. More than once, she uttered, "Sometimes the Giver gives," when one of them returned from hunting with more than enough game to satisfy even the wolvryn. On the morning of the third day, they began the laborious descent into the foothills that led to the vast rolling plains of the Borderlands.

By the week's end, they emerged from the forests to gaze on a horizon that stretched without end. Wind gusted over tan and yellow grasslands, creating waves despite a thin crust of snow. In the distance, a dark, unnatural structure interrupted the smooth transition of the rolling hills.

"What do you suppose that is?" asked Lluthean.

Laryn felt a slight stinging sensation draw across her windburned cheeks as she smiled. "If we're where I think we are, that's Voruden. It's the only town of any size this close to the foothills of the Korjinth."

Bryndor knelt with his hand on Boru's neck, surveying the region through the wolvryn's gifted sight. "That's not just a town; it's a small city. There's a palisade that stretches a mile or more around and a steady flow of wagons to the east."

"It must have grown a lot in the last six years. Let's hope the Giver sees fit to offer us one more gift. The people of Voruden were suspicious when I passed through by myself. That was what, five or six years ago?"

Laryn combed her fingers through Neska's fur, realizing with surprise that the wolvryn's back rose much higher than when their journey over the Korjinth started. "I'm not too certain how they will react to the wolvryn."

Her other hand found Kaellor's. His warm strength and deep register gave her comfort. "Crossing the Korjinth took all of us, especially the wolvryn. As long as we're together, I'm confident there isn't much worse for us waiting in Voruden."

Chapter Thirty-Six: The Founder's Memorial

Ksenia felt her head swoon and stifled her linguistics gift. She sat back in the padded chair at the archives table and stared at the ancient tome. Dark smudges stained the sides and lower corners of the pages, the leavings of any number of scholars who, like her, had labored to understand the archaic words.

She ran a cloth-gloved finger over the delicate parchment. *I wonder if these are really the fingerprints of someone who knew High Aarindorian and not some recent careless archivist as frustrated as me. All I need is a bit of context. If I can unravel even fragments of the language, I might be able to untangle the whole mess.*

Vinnedesta sat down in a chair opposite her and pried open a new ledger. The bindings creaked as she worked to open the stiff pages. The sweet scent of glue and resco berry wafted across the table. "Still punishing yourself with that old book?" asked the scribe.

Ksenia watched as her friend removed a sheet of paper with names and divided columns, activated her zeniscrawl, and began copying information from the sheet of paper into the ledger.

"Sadly, yes. What started as my opus has become my weekly dose of self-flagellation. The words from Eldrek's statue haven't unlocked anything. Also, why does that new book smell like resco berries, and what are you working on?" asked Ksenia.

"It's the new paper. It's made from a pulp using pressed resco leaf fibers. Everyone knows that."

"They do?" asked Ksenia.

"Well . . . now everyone does." Vinnedesta smiled and looked back at her work. "These are formal death records. First, I list the names, then indicate if any property was passed down, and if so, to who. If a cause of death is known, I document that, then file the whole thing away."

"You've got a whole page of names, Vin. How often do you update the ledger?"

The scribe tapped her chin with her zeniscrawl. "About twice a month. There was a fire in the lower market district last week and an outbreak of flux in the Sprawl, so I have a bit more work on my hands today. But most of those folks don't have anything to pass on, so it's mainly a tedious list of names." She flipped a few pages of loose paper under her thumb, each filled with names of the dead.

"All those people died in the last two weeks?" asked Ksenia.

"Oh, no. The last two pages are birth records. Happy news, but those can get really tricky, especially when it comes to the high families."

Ksenia rubbed the back of her neck and waited for further explanation. Her partner kept scrawling names into the ledger. "Why are the birth records tricky?"

"Well, think about it. There's any number of illegitimate births in the Sprawl." Vinnedesta leaned in conspiratorially. "But the high families? Some of the Endules are so intermingled that it's difficult to tell where one line starts and stops. Last week a baby boy was born to a woman in Beclure, sired by a man who would have been his first cousin instead of just his father."

Ksenia tried to untangle the string of words. "Wait, doesn't that mean that the mother of the baby was the aunt to the father of the baby?"

"Yes, exactly so!" said Vinnedesta. "And they only got properly married after the conception! It makes the Endule family tree look more like a twisted vine."

They both giggled until an older archivist slammed a book closed in annoyance. "Anyway," whispered Vinnedesta. "I've been updating these records at the request of the regent. It turns out that a scholar in Callinora was tracking the lines of ancestry ever since the Abrogator's War. In all that time, there hasn't been a Baellentrell birth in the kingdom. No Baellentrells and only a smattering of Lellendules. It won't be long before the high families become extinct."

"That makes sense, I suppose. The war claimed most of them. It kind of makes you wonder how long the regent will hold on to the old ways," said Ksenia.

Vinnedesta mumbled agreement, returned to her work a moment, then stopped. "Can you even imagine how complex the death records would have been in those days? I mean, all those lives lost, all at once."

Ksenia had a thought. "How far back do you think those records go?"

"I don't know. The death records kept with this level of detail started just after the war as a means to track property inheritance and prevent any abuses from the reparations," said Vinnedesta.

Ksenia tapped the ancient tome that eluded her gift. "Are you aware of any other texts written in High Aarindorian? A birth or death record might give me some insights into the basics of the language."

"No, the only records I'm aware of are in stone—the base of Eldrek's statue in the sanctum and the Founder's Memorial in the regent's private garden."

Ksenia sat up in her chair and propped herself forward on elbows. "There's a Founder's Memorial? Why didn't you ever say anything? Do you think the regent would mind if I asked for access?"

Vinnedesta shrugged. "Sorry, I thought everyone knew about the memorial. I don't see why he would mind. I saw it once when he had me transcribe some letters, but I couldn't make any sense of the dead language."

With a careful hand, Ksenia closed the ancient tome and returned it to the head archivist. "Thanks, Vin. I'll see you later."

"Where are you going in such a hurry?" asked the scholar.

"It's after midday. That means the regent is likely in his chambers, and since it's midweek and you are here, he had a light session this morning. So, he's likely to be in a good mood, making it the perfect time to visit him and see if he will grant me access to the memorial."

"Giver's good fortune!" said Vin.

Ksenia hurried through the library and offices of the second tier. Ignoring the cold, she chose to jog along the outer steps, climbing up to the fourth tier. The winter winds stole the heat from her unprotected face. She pushed inside the heavy doors, panting.

Bextle looked up from his post in surprise. "Taker's breath, Ksenia, you know better than that. Get over here and warm up."

The burly guard motioned her over to the zendil. She obeyed, stepping close to the zenith-powered heating element. Through chattering teeth, she tried to speak, but the cold made the muscles around her mouth and chin numb. "Th-th-thanks."

Bextle turned a valve, and the grill over the heating element flared a brilliant blue, emitting more heat. He pulled a chair over and directed her to sit down.

"You know you can come up through the staff halls and stairwells now, right? It's the Taker's kiss to walk outside this time of year. The winds come off the Great Crown and carry a nasty bite."

Ksenia nodded in agreement. "I w-w-was in a hurry." Tingly, stinging pains erupted on her nose, earlobes, and forehead as the heating element melted the ice from her skin.

Bextle walked away only to return a moment later with a steaming mug of tea. Ksenia looked up at him. An expression of confusion must have played across her face.

"What?" asked Bextle.

She clutched tingly fingers around the warm mug. "It's just . . . why are you being so nice to me?"

The guard looked back down the hall, then turned to her and held his hands in the sign of the broken circle. "Craxton told me, then I made you out at a meeting a few weeks back. I'm sorry I treated you the way I did when you first arrived. You didn't deserve that, and my brother can be a lot. I mean, court one, and you get all three. That has to be some special kind of crazy, right? Anyway . . . accept my apology?"

She didn't know Bextle well but found a certain sincerity in his words matched only by her surprise. "Yes, of course, Bextle . . . think nothing of it."

"If you don't mind my asking, what made you brave the worse part of winter to get up here so fast?"

She sipped at the tea. "I wanted to see if the regent would grant me access to his gardens so I could see the Founder's Memorial. Vin tells me there are words written in High Aarindorian along the base. I've been trying to decipher an old tome for the archivists and getting nowhere. I thought if I could see the words with a different context, on a memorial, maybe I could start to unravel the mysteries of the language."

"You don't need the regent's permission for that. The hall to the garden is just beyond here. I can show you in when you're ready."

"That's . . . moons, that's more than I expected. Yes, thank you, Bextle." She stood, made a rotisserie of herself before the zendil, and allowed the chill to roast away on all sides. "Alright, I think I'm ready."

He led her across the circular entry hall and down a corridor that seemed to cut straight through to the castle's north side. Pale blue light emitted from crystal sconces set every ten paces high on the wall. Bextle stopped before a thick wood door. "It's just beyond there. There's not a lock on the door. Give it a push, and you'll be inside. I should get back to my post, but holler if you need anything."

With that, he retreated back down the hallway, leaving her alone before the door. The change in Bextle's demeanor gave her pause, and she stood a moment to puzzle it out. Before today, she had felt so sure the man hated her that she had tried to avoid this particular entry for weeks. *Is it really the Lacuna? Did Craxton say something, or did I just muddle it all up in my head in the first place? Hmm, well . . . best not to squander the Giver's blessing.*

Inspection showed no handle or knocker, so she pushed on the middle of the door. Something shifted when she applied her weight to the right side. The massive timbers turned in a slow, silent revolution on a strange central hinge. She stepped through, and the door closed behind her with a soft click.

The garden before her made it impossible to be amazed by the craftsmanship of the ancient door. Humid air, redolent with aromatic flowering vines, caressed her senses. She stepped forward into a round chamber and gasped in amazement. A hummingbird hovered for an instant before her, then zipped away to feed at a red flower erupting from a twisted vine with waxy green leaves. Somewhere in the expansive chamber, a fountain bubbled.

The late-day sun reflected off the moon of Baellen, beaming shafts of light through a rounded blue sphere overhead. A gust of sleet and snow swirled off the Great Crown and dashed against the barrier, only to slide away.

"By the Giver's hand," said Ksenia.

"It's really quite something, isn't it?" said a familiar aged voice.

Ksenia squealed in surprise, then recovered and turned to find Therek Lefledge sitting on a stone bench along a path in the garden. A middle-aged man sat beside him, dressed in fatigues that identified him as a member of the castle staff. The man held shears and a bucket with the clippings of flowers.

"Ms. Ksenia Balladuren, might I introduce Fagle Hoff? He is, among many things, our most talented royal gardener."

Fagle stood and tipped his head to Ksenia. "It's a pleasure to make your acquaintance, Ms. Balladuren. Your family's reputation precedes you." He nodded to the regent. "Your Grace, I appreciate your advice. I'll . . . consider what you have to say, and I hope my words offer you a measure of peace."

Ksenia tilted her head in polite respect. "I'm sorry to disturb you in your private garden, Your Grace. Bextle showed me in. Had I known you were here or entertaining . . . I would have waited."

The regent peered at her through his wispy eyebrows and flapped an arm in her direction. "Fagle and I go way back. Our wives were close friends, and the two of us like to sit and remember. You didn't interrupt anything that can't be rekindled easily enough. Besides, the Founder's Memorial is not more mine than anyone else's in Aarindorn. But I admit, I don't advertise its availability out of a selfish desire to have a few quiet places to retreat to now and again." He clasped his hands overhead and stretched, then yawned with uncharacteristic blasé. "The garden is open to all. I like to come here once a week. There's something good for the soul in seeing a bit of nature preserved as it is."

"It's incredible. How does the room stay so warm and still allow in the moon's light?" she asked.

"I can't say I entirely understand the mechanics of it all," said Therek. "What do you think, Fagle?"

The gardener pocketed his shears and cleared his throat. "Well, I'm no gifted, but to my understanding, the dome overhead is a selective barrier of zenith. It repels the elements but allows in other things of nature, light not the least among them. Living creatures can pass through it. I've seen birds come and go. When I was a boy, there was a flock of mourning doves we had to chase away. I mean, one or two make for a nice melody, but more than that, and things get messy."

Fagle reached forward and picked up a small stone, then tossed it high. The rock made a hissing sound as it passed through the translucent blue ceiling, then clattered and slid down the outside of the barrier. "At night, near the end of every week, the moon of Baellen hovers directly overhead. You can see it with such . . . clarity. Did you know there are pits on the surface of Baellen?"

Ksenia shook her head, indicating her ignorance of the topic.

Therek cleared his throat. "Lellen too. I think they might be lakes or valleys. In Callinora, they have a zeniscope that lets you see the moons like they were up close. A friend of mine thinks some of the pits are depressions on the moon's surface, and others are lakes of zenith. But, I apologize," said Therek. "If this is your first time, we should remain silent and let you experience the gardens for yourself."

They sat in companionable silence, staring up through the blue dome, for several moments before Ksenia spoke. "I don't mind. I did come here for a reason, though. Vin thought there was a monument here with words written in High Aarindorian. If that's true, I should like to see them. It might help my work."

"You're still at it then? Just like your mother, tenacious as a wolvryn," said the regent.

She felt her cheeks flush at the comparison. *Mother is more stubborn and persistent than most, to be sure. Moons . . . am I that bad?*

Fagle pointed down the path. "I think the fountain is what you want. There are words scrawled along its base. Just follow the path set before you."

"Thank you. I'll take a look. Nice to meet you, Fagle."

The gardener raised a finger to his brow and smiled. Ksenia followed the path of polished, fitted white stone that wound past flowering bushes, under broad-leafed plants, and ended with a fountain in the garden's center. A sculpture carved from the same white stone as the path stood in the center of the fountain. The sight made her wring her right hand around the symbols along her left wrist.

Ksenia sucked in her breath, thinking of the symbol of the Lacuna. Hewn from the same white stone, a circular torque, perhaps ten paces wide, defied gravity, leaning at an angle that suggested it should splash into the water of the fountain. At the bottom of the sculpture, the circular legs ended in rounded nubs, creating a gap that made her think of the symbol of the circle breakers.

Closer inspection showed an angular notch just to the right of the apex of the unique work of art. Blue veining on the inside of the torque created symbols that reminded her of the runes of the gifted. She walked in a slow perimeter around the fountain but discovered no other words.

It took only a moment for her to settle her mind, channel zenith, and empower her linguistics rune. She cast her gift across the runes of the sculpture for several minutes. The symbols tumbled before her awareness in a random cascade. She labored to bring them into some type of order that made sense, then stifled her connection in frustration.

The words are scrawled along its base. That's what the gardener said.

She squatted down to inspect the fountain. Water trickled over the edge of the rounded base to disappear beneath, and scrolling symbols appeared through the ripples. Stepping back allowed her to follow the script around the front edge of the fountain. She reached again for her gift, bringing it to bear on the archaic words of what appeared to be High Aarindorian.

Ellebrek darun un keska de' bolg, ut dervold un bitta ah.
Ellebrek wundarruh un eska de' Vron.

Ksenia paced back and forth in front of the fountain, pushing her gift to filter the symbols into any pattern. She continued walking in silent confusion until she reached the backside of the fountain. There, she discovered different characters.

"Wait a moment. I know these. That's Low Aarindorian," she muttered to herself, and her gift sifted antiquated symbols into familiar words.

Ksenia sucked in a breath. "By the Giver's shiny knockers . . . channel zenith to save the world, or nadir to destroy it. Channel confluence to become the Eidolon reborn."

"I don't speak High Aarindorian, and I don't doubt that the Giver's attributes are peerless. But . . . it sounds like you've discovered something useful?" asked Therek.

Ksenia barely registered that he had walked behind her, so intense was her concentration. In her mind, she overlapped the phrasing. An achy thrum of power resonated across the runes on her left arm for several seconds. She grasped her right hand around her left wrist, the pain dropping her to a knee.

Unbidden, the symbols and words she had wrestled with from the ancient tome collided into her like a deluge of spring melt cascading from the Great Crown to land on the valley below. The revelations enthralled her, keeping her cemented on her knees until, at last, she severed her connection to zenith.

With the regent's arm for support, Ksenia stood. Tingly exhilaration washed over her for the second time that day, but this time it blossomed from pure joy. She massaged the runes on her forearm in utter disbelief. Never had her gift bestowed such an onslaught of insight.

"Miss Balladuren, are you quite alright?" asked the regent. His brows drew together with an earnest look of concern.

"Alright? Yes . . . yes, much better than alright. I think I just unlocked the first steps to reading High Aarindorian."

Chapter Thirty-Seven: Scars from the Past

"This way, Mistress. Follow Eguma," said the small grotvonen.

As Volencia hurried to keep up, the sharp clack of her heels on the cavern floor triggered a memory. Years ago, she had paced a room, her boots clacking on the wooden floorboards of the cellar in her family's estate in Stone's Grasp. She had been turning a problem over and over in her mind, searching for any solution but the obvious answer. The voice of her master eroded the last of her resistance.

"The path to greatness requires more sacrifice than most are willing to pay. That's why you will meet only a few truly great people in your life," said Tarkannen. "The choice and that price, as always, are yours to pay. I cannot make it for you."

"Why does it have to be Veldrek? Why can't it be some gutter rat from the Sprawl? Someone nobody would miss?"

"That question is not one you are prepared to understand fully. But for now, if you want to acquire more strength, more power, you have to make a sacrifice. Only you can unlock that part of yourself and receive the ability to command more nadir. I can not do it for you."

Her breaths came rapid and short, unsustaining as she searched for clarity, hoping that a different answer would bubble up from the murky depths of her confusion and tell her what to do. She stood so long that the balls of her feet began to fall asleep.

Tarkannen stood after a time and turned to climb the stairs. "I can see that you are not ready. I'll offer the chance to another."

"No . . . I'll do it." She spoke the words with so little strength that her voice cracked. A numb coldness settled across her shoulders, and she cleared her throat. "I'll do it."

"You don't sound committed, Volencia. I'll not have you trifle with forces you are ill-prepared to command. If you proceed, be certain that it is because you fully understand what is at stake."

She allowed her eyes to roam across the sigil-ridden face of her master. Not once in all the time he spent with her did she ever feel fear or revulsion. Even when the wriggling lines of power rippled under his skin, all she felt was wonder . . . until now. When he turned and prepared to offer that power to someone else, she felt fear: fear of missing her opportunity to command more power and reshape the world, fear of sacrificing so much but gaining so little. That realization sealed the decision in her mind.

A tilt of her head was all she offered the abrogator. She turned on a heel and walked up the stairs, returning only a moment later with her brother a few steps behind.

Veldrek scratched errantly at the patch over his left eye. "Hello, Master Tarkannen. So, Vol, how can I help?"

Tarkannen stood at the far end of the room, refusing to instigate the deception. *Right then. It's all on you, Vol.*

"Yes, Vel. If you could stand over here in the center of the room, this shouldn't take but a moment." Volencia turned away from him and pulled hard on the currents of nadir. The thin sigils on her forearms pulsed with a tingly, eager quality. Without warning, she pivoted and lashed out with onyx cords. The leashes spiraled around her brother and constricted, bending to her will.

Veldrek gasped, and a puzzled question played across his face, but the constriction of her nadir prevented him from drawing breath. He mouthed at the air, red-faced, and writhed, trying to free himself from the suffocating bonds. Volencia held him fast.

Tarkannen's voice carried from the shadows at the back of the cellar. "Don't look away, Volencia. Look at your brother. Only if you see the shudder of his pain, his fear . . . only then will you unlock your potential."

Volencia blinked away the sting of tears that threatened to obscure her vision and forced herself to look directly at Veldrek. His face swelled and took on a ruddy hue that transitioned over the next minute to a dusky purple. His head tilted to the side, but instead of anger, his face held an expression of pity, and at that moment, she felt some part of herself split away. Like a spectator, she watched the scene before her in a mixture of horror and revulsion. Yet as Veldrek dropped to his knees in agony, she became fascinated by the magnification of her sigils.

The delicate black marks pulsed under her skin. Before she began the ritual, the sigils had an opaque appearance, as if drawn by a stick of coal. Now the onyx ribbons rippled with new dimension and depth. Complex swirls of ebony shadow played over their surface. She committed to the power, and the sigils flared, then entwined up her arms, sending shards of ice-cold pain lancing up to her armpits.

With a gasp of triumph, she turned her attention back to Veldrek. Something popped, and he fell to the floor. Volencia released her command of nadir and dropped to her knees beside him. His face appeared blue, and lifeless eyes stared past her into the dark corners of the room.

"What happened? I didn't mean for it to go so far. Master, he's not breathing. Veldrek's not breathing. I thought only to provoke his fear. You didn't tell me it would kill him. Oh . . . by the moons . . . Veldrek, wake up now, wake up! Master, help us. Do something! Veldrek, wake up!" She screamed and pulled at her brother's shirt, trying to coax him to sit up. His shoulders lifted off the floor, but his head flopped back at an odd angle. With frantic anticipation, she waited for his chest to move, willing him to draw a breath.

Volencia remained on her knees sobbing hysterically until firm hands reached under her arms and pulled her to her feet. She turned once again and looked past the dark sigils that shifted across her master's face to peer into his eyes. For just a moment, she thought she saw a flicker of something. Was it sadness or regret?

"There is no help for him, Volencia, but you did well. Your sacrifice unlocked more power than you can imagine," said Tarkannen.

Volencia shook her head in denial. "No . . . no, no, no! Take it back! Bring him back. Bring Veldrek back!"

Tarkannen considered her a long moment. "I am sorry for your loss but happy for your gain. This is the price you must pay to command more nadir. Restoring Veldrek is . . . beyond me."

She pushed away from her master and sprinted up the stairs, leaving the evidence of her betrayal in the cellar.

Volencia dismissed the memory, pushing it to the back of her mind. She jogged behind Eguma. The lithe grotvonen loped through caverns dimly lit by luminescent mosses. His calloused hands padded over cold stone in a rhythm that matched the primal drumming of the shamans. The slight creature paused and cast a luminous eye over his shoulder every now and again to be sure that Volencia followed. She waved a hand forward as if to say, "I'm coming. Lead on." And he did so.

Like endless rolling thunder, the shaman drums echoed through the Underdark. As she arrived at the summoning chamber, the chaotic storm organized into a recognizable cadence: two lone beats, a rolling trill, then another hard beat. Inside the large cavern, four shamans throttled hairy knuckles over hide drums while the rest of the chorus chanted in hoots and growls. In the center of the room, a large bowl rested on the floor. Its contents, a black liquid, vibrated and rippled from the clamor of the ritual.

She bent to speak in Eguma's hair-tufted ear. "Did the Consort distill liquid nadir?"

Eguma lifted both hands, palms up. "My dunno."

Volencia stepped farther into the chamber to stand beside Grasdok and a pair of umbral. The Brognaus chieftain nodded once, then fixed his beady eyes on the ceremony. One of the flat-heads tilted its bony head plate to her in what she assumed was a gesture of acknowledgment. Black symbols spiraled around the ridge of the plate, the charred remnants of a branding carried out long ago in the Drift.

I wonder if Mallic wanders about under the weight of a similar affliction. I wonder if I will too—a question for another day.

The drum cadence rose in intensity, and the chanting matched. A fat shaman rose to its hind feet and staggered to the center of the chamber. He appeared entranced, vacant eyes staring off into the distance, and he swayed to the cadence of the drums. In his arms, he cradled an infant grotvonen. The hairless creature with grey skin and oversized eyes wriggled and appeared to cry, but any wailing was drowned out by the percussive rhythms.

With trembling hands, the shaman lifted the infant overhead. Volencia understood what the shaman intended. The only way the shaman could manipulate the currents of nadir involved intimate sacrifice, an act that wounded the soul. *That must be your child, then.*

The shaman looked long moments on the face of his child, then something in the creature's bearing softened. He lowered the infant to his chest, cradling it. He appeared resolved to a different course of action and waddled to the perimeter of the circle before handing the grotvonen infant over to its mother.

The shaman strode back to the center of the circle and lifted the basin overhead. It cast one last look back at the mother of his child, closed its eyes in a slow blink, then drank the foul slick, draining the contents of the basin.

He staggered a few steps forward, then back, then fell like a sack of boneless flesh to the floor. The drumming and chanting reached a frantic pace until, at once, the room fell silent. Several long moments passed in which nothing changed. Then something writhed over the surface of the shaman's corpse. Rivulets of nadir snaked across the flesh of the dead grotvonen, appearing first as thin tendrils. The currents streamed over the corpse, growing in size and intensity until they became a writhing mass of onyx serpents. The tentacles folded the arms and legs of the grotvonen inward. Tendons snapped, and bones popped as the nadir consumed the shaman.

The others began to chant again, this time with low, sibilant whispers of encouragement. In response, the roiling nadir churned and condensed into a tight knot, then erupted with a shearing sound. The mass of what was once the shaman exploded. Instead of spattering the cavern with gore, the oily humors constrained into an oval on the floor. A ring of nadir streamed around the creation, and fresh air and light spilled from the portal.

Volencia stepped forward and looked through to the other side. A dimly lit corridor with walls of white stone appeared. A large painting with the twin moons over a modest dwelling hung on the wall. *The grinders did it. That's Callinora.*

She glanced once to the shamans, who continued their silent chanting. After pulling her veil tight across her face, she hopped into the portal. For an unsettling moment, she fell, then slid along icy currents of nadir that leached the heat from her body. Stinging pain seared across the exposed flesh of her hands and face. She lost all sense of balance as her body rolled through the conduit of nadir. The journey lasted less than a minute before she ejected through a similar portal and onto the floor of the corridor.

Gasping, she palmed her forehead and felt crystals of ice melt from her eyebrows. Everywhere nadir had contacted her exposed skin, she felt the lingering burn of pins and needles. Ignoring the pain, she inhaled. The air pulled in crisp and clean, laced with the faint fragrance of survivor's essence. Her head whirled, and she struggled to her feet, her hands finding purchase on smooth stone walls that, while cool to the touch, did not siphon the heat from her.

She stole into the shadows at the side of the wide hallway and waited for the swimming sensation in her head to settle. In the Underdark, she had lost all sense of day and night. A glance out a window showed the faint crescent of the red moon waning in the night sky. A small part of her desired to wait for the sun to rise, to soak in the vibrant colors as light spilled across the horizon. She dismissed the notion and turned her attention to discovering her surroundings.

The hallway stretched both forward and back. Several doors led to other rooms. Volencia ran to the end of the hall and discovered a wide set of stairs leading both up and down, each disappearing into darkness. Turning, she ran back to where she started and sidestepped the portal on the floor. Through the oval construct, she could just make out the grim faces of the chanting shamans.

She moved to a door at the far end of the hall, lifting its handle and feeling it crack open on silent hinges. Peering through, she finally got a sense of her location in the Sanitorium. Sconces and candles cast a yellow hue across the large foyer on the main floor of the building. She stepped back and latched the door closed, then investigated the side doors along the hallway.

The first door on the left opened to an empty room with a bed and nightstand. She walked to the next door and pushed it open. Inside, a shimmering blue husk covered something on a simple bed. Volencia stepped close to see a person cocooned in a web of delicate blue fibers. Soft currents of zenith flowed throughout the dozenth. Through the haze of filaments, she could just make out the body of a woman. One whole side of the patient's head appeared caved-in, and she was missing an arm.

Volencia channeled nadir and pushed a single probing tentacle through the fibers of zenith. She felt the extension of her will slide past several layers of the cocoon before meeting slight resistance. She pushed and felt a delicate pop. The dozenth shuddered, and an oily stain rippled across the life-sustaining cocoon. The lines of zenith retreated, and the entire construct sagged like a deflated wineskin. A loud, repeating gong rang out in the room.

Volencia hissed. *Of course, they monitor these with an alarm.*

She probed deeper, searching for any sign of her master. If this patient was tethered to Tarkannen, she would feel the abrasive shearing sensation as their nadir rasped together. Sensing no familiar connection, she withdrew and returned to the main hallway. Pushing into the next room, she found an old man snoring through the commotion of the dozenth alarm.

She walked to the last door, the closest to the stairwell, and sensed voices and shadows descending from above. She pushed the door open and closed it behind her. Inside lay another dozenth on a simple bed. The layers of the cocoon appeared reinforced compared to the first one. Volencia couldn't even tell if the patient inside was male or female. She drafted another probe and started to penetrate the fibers of zenith.

This time her efforts met significant resistance. Instead of allowing her probe to pass through, different layers of zenith redirected and diverted her along different planes. She withdrew and tried to bypass the obstruction several times. The sound of several voices coming from the adjacent room broke her concentration.

Volencia withdrew from the dozenth and gathered a ball of nadir in her fist. She stepped into the main hallway, where a man was kneeling beside the oval portal on the floor. He wore a hooded, tan robe commonplace among the acolytes and healers of the Sanitorium. The man held his hands over the portal as if sensing for any heat. A blue nimbus arose between his fingers, and the surface of the portal began to waver.

"That's enough of that," said Volencia.

She was preparing to throttle the healer with a condensed sphere of nadir when he looked up. The furrowed edge of a scar ran up the man's cheek and under a black eye patch. Volencia sucked in her breath in utter shock. "Veldrek? What are you . . . you're alive?"

"Hello little sister. Mother said you would return one day, but I hoped it might be under different circumstances."

Volencia's hand dropped, and her nadir globe dissipated. She walked forward and knelt to look her brother square in the face. A surge of confused emotions overwhelmed any apprehension she had about being discovered. "Veldrek . . . how are you? I thought you were dead. I . . ."

Veldrek gave her a half-smile, one that spoke more of sadness and loss than mirth. "You very nearly did kill me. But Venlith and the healers revived me and . . . we can speak of those dark days later. Vol, I need to close this, and I think a bit of zenith might do the trick."

Veldrek began to channel zenith into the edge of the portal once again, and the clarity of the images began to obscure. Volencia grabbed his wrist just as a female healer exited the room where she had triggered the dozenth alarm.

"What do you think you're doing here?" asked the woman.

The woman stepped forward and balled her hand in a fist. Her aggressive posture removed Volencia from any hesitation and indecision. She whipped a dense tentacle of nadir forward but pulled the full strength of her attack. The black extension of her malice caught her brother in the chest, and he flew backward several feet, landing with more force than she intended. She allowed the momentum of the swing to slam into the far wall, crushing the female healer just below the waist.

The woman cried out in pain and crumpled to the floor. Volencia watched to see her brother rise to his elbows. A burning cold sphere of nadir collected in her fist, primed for deadly release. But she was not prepared to kill her brother a second time. She dropped the orb to the stone floor, where it hissed and dissolved. The sigils of her arms rippled once, then stilled as she suffocated any desire to channel more nadir.

More healers arrived in the hall from the stairs and the door at the far end. Volencia dropped her head in exhausted defeat. She shared one look with her brother. A soft, compassionate expression played across his face, just like the last time she had seen him all those years ago in the family cellar.

The crowd surged forward, muttering with angry voices and demanding explanations. The clamor pushed her to action. *Grind it all to the grinding Drift.*

She hopped into the portal empty-handed and spilled back into the cavern. A hissing vacuum sucked the pressure from the cavern, and her ears popped as the portal slammed closed. Volencia staggered to her feet, holding her frost-nipped hands under her arms.

Without words or explanation, she retreated from the chamber. She had failed. Failed to find, let alone retrieve, the tethered host of her master, failed to subdue and apprehend the Baellentrell heirs, and now she failed to understand how her brother remained alive after all these years.

Chapter Thirty-Eight: The Vicissitudes of Voruden

Karragin walked a slow perimeter around their camp, which was set up on a hill in the Borderlands. Her Aarindin stood a few feet away and nickered once. In response, she awoke her gift and linked to the gelding. She had singled him out from the available mounts picketed back at the base camp.

Tacit had proved less talkative but more self-aware than her last several mounts. The gelding had been trained by the Balladuren daughter, Ksenia. Her touch on Tacit's mind made significant, noticeable differences. After the first day ranging, he already gripped when she mounted, a bond that often took weeks or longer.

"What is it, Tacit? I am listening."

A low voice, empty of strong emotion, resonated back to her. *"I smell your brother in the wind. He rides this way with one of my brothers."*

"Is there danger?"

A short pause flowed into their conversation, and Tacit nibbled errantly at the tall grasses. At last, he replied. *"I don't smell danger on my brother or yours."*

"Thanks, my friend," she communicated, then severed the link.

Karragin walked over to the small cookfire and probed at a large oval ball of clay with her sword tip. She rolled the compacted material in the hot coals. They had traveled by ghost protocol in the preceding week, but she'd agreed to lift the clandestine restrictions in the last day. Numerous groups of travelers had already established temporary camps with cookfires in the countryside north of Voruden.

The clay egg appeared solid and evenly baked, so she rolled it away from the coals, allowing it to cool. Fifteen minutes later, she cracked the outer shell with her blade. The clay casing split, and she pried apart the wedges to reveal a steaming game bird inside.

Savnah wandered over and frowned at her work. "I've never cooked a bird that wasn't plucked clean, stuffed, and spiced." The woman reached out and snapped off a steaming drumstick.

"Have a care not to burn yourself," said Karragin.

Savnah pinched her lips tight but held on to the piping hot drumstick. "Hunger makes monks of all of us. Ahh well, nothing a bit of my gift and some burn salve won't handle."

Karragin waited for the rest of the meat to cool and considered her friend. Savnah blew steam from the drumstick and eventually chanced a nibble, then a mouthful. She nodded in appreciation and raised her eyebrows. "It might be a bit overcooked, but grind me twice if that isn't the best thing I've tasted in the last week. Nice work, Karra."

Karragin parceled out generous servings to the others just as Nolan crested the hill on his Aarindin. "Why am I not a bit surprised that you arrived just in time for dinner, brother?" she asked.

Nolan smiled, threw a leg over, and slid off his mount. He hoisted a burlap sack over his shoulder. "Tell you what, I'll trade you a portion of that bird—the one I shot, by the way—for what's in my sack here."

Karragin handed him a serving wrapped in green leaf. Nolan tossed the sack to the ground, and a dense loaf of bread tumbled out. Tovnik placed the loaf near the hot coals and waved him over. "Seems you made contact. What do you make of Voruden?" asked the medic.

Nolan picked at the roasted fowl, and the rest of the group lingered close to hear his report. "I would guess Voruden holds at least ten thousand by its size. It's a monarchy state currently ruled by Queen Dressla Rudang. She seems to have the favor of the people I encountered.

"A robust palisade surrounds the city. The wall stretches all around, even to the north. There are three gates, but only the east gate is open, and it's closely guarded. They rotate guard shifts every three hours and have an active patrol. There are two towers for surveillance, one at the east gate and one on the backside where a river runs in from the Korjinth."

Karragin felt the skin between her eyebrows tense. "That's a strongly regimented security detail for an isolated city without any direct threats. Are they at war with a neighbor we have yet to discover?"

"I don't think so, but I thought the same thing about their security," said Nolan.

"What's it like inside?" asked Savnah.

"That's a very good question, and I would be happy to tell you, except I was turned away," he replied. "It seems you can't gain entrance unless you have something tangible they need or—"

"It's the only town for miles. What kind of monkery is involved with a decision to turn away travelers?" asked Savnah.

Karragin handed another portion of the roasted bird to Savnah. The prime bellyached on a good day, even more so if she was hungry. Nolan licked his fingers and winked at her in understanding.

"The palisade is new, commissioned to protect them from grondle incursions," he explained. "Apparently, grondle have ranged this far south. This past spring, fear of them drove too many settlers into town, and a flux broke out, killing hundreds. Now, nobody enters that doesn't have something of value to offer."

"How did you come by the bread?" asked Karragin.

"There is a mobile trading post outside the palisade that is fairly busy," said Nolan. "Most of the farmers bring their goods there, and locals come out to buy and sell."

"Is there anything that might get us inside?" asked Karragin.

"Just one," said her brother. "Grondle horns. Anyone who kills a grondle and returns with its horns is granted access and given a grace mark."

Tovnik leaned closer, a look of disgust on his face. "What's a grace mark? Do they brand people like cattle?"

"Nothing like that. It's what they call a writ," Nolan explained. "It's a hammered strip of metal imprinted with a person's name and identifying features. Somehow, the backside is stamped with a royal seal. The locals wear them on chains around their necks."

Savnah rubbed oily fingers on her pant legs. "Why don't we just sneak inside? A simple diversion outside the east gate would buy us enough time to enter by the river before they knew what happened."

"I had the same thought," said Nolan. "We could gain access easily enough, but renting rooms and doing business, let alone obtaining an audience with the queen, would be near impossible without the grace mark."

"Could we forge a grace mark, or possibly, I don't know . . . borrow someone else's?" asked Savnah.

"That's a gamble and undermines the legitimacy of our diplomatic interests," said Karragin.

"I agree. The grace seems difficult to counterfeit, and the punishment is chaining," said Nolan. "They wrap rusty chains around all the limbs and ribs, constrict them tight enough to crush bone, then hang the offender along the north wall as a warning to others."

"You learned a lot in just a few hours," said Karragin.

Nolan shrugged. "There's a whole row of portable taverns in the market. They specialize in a warm mead and something that could pass for weak resco. Anyway, it wasn't hard to find a farmer down on his luck. Two drinks in, and he told me all I needed to know."

"Dexxin, can you relay to your siblings that we reached Voruden? Only, hold off on the specifics of the grondle attacks this far south," said Karragin. "Let me know when you're finished."

Dexxin nodded and retreated into his gift. A distant expression played across his face. Moments later, his focus returned. "It is done."

"Good, can you not tell them this next part?" asked Karragin.

Dexxin cocked his head, considering her request, then unbuttoned the top of his Outrider uniform to reveal the dormant edges of his arca prime.

"Thanks," said Karragin. She turned to address the group. "It seems we have been given contradictory mandates: make contact in Voruden to initiate diplomatic discussions and avoid conflict with the grot or grondle.

"Since we can't have it both ways, I won't ask any of you to jeopardize your safety or your position in the Outriders. I appreciate that Nolan and I might be insulated from repercussions if things grind it to the Drift. We didn't come out here to hunt grondle, but that's exactly what I am proposing we do. There is no shame in returning to base camp. You all know the risks. Will any of you join me?"

Nolan licked the last of the drippings from his fingers. "You know I'm in."

"Do we have to travel by ghost protocol? Because a girl could get used to your cooking, Karra," said Savnah, a sly smile playing across her face.

"The way I see it, we blend in down here by setting up a visible camp," said Karragin.

She turned to the last two in the group. "Tov, Dex? I won't guilt you into coming, but it's a simple truth that our chances are much better if you join us."

Dexxin gave a curt nod, then lifted his chin to Savnah. "If she's in, then so am I."

"And I go where you go," said Tovnik.

She made eye contact with each of them, marking the moment and wondering if she was turning them down a path that would lead to their success for Aarindorn or their doom.

Chapter Thirty-Nine: Not Your Average River Chicken

Kaellor climbed the rolling foothills north of Voruden, backtracking his way to their camp nestled against a rocky overhang. His boots crunched over the icy sprigs of dried grasses that erupted from a thin blanket of snow. A gentle breeze, laden with moisture, carried across the plains.

An aroma of wet soil and damp leaves made him think briefly of Journey's Bend. For the first time since they set out, he released the memory of their home by the Shelwyn with little difficulty. Something about the feel of Northland soil under his boots just seemed right.

A heavy bag of goods jostled over his shoulder, but the weight caused him little discomfort after descending out of the thin mountain air of the Korjinth. He approached camp to find Lluthean sitting around a small fire, turning a makeshift skewer.

"I was only gone a few hours, and in that time, you managed to scrounge up food?" asked Kaellor.

"Neska caught the scent of a small group of herd animals. They resemble deer. It wasn't hard with her. I think she would have managed it without me. She was . . . very hungry."

"I'll bet," said Kaellor. "Hunger is a powerful motivator." He set the sack down and inspected the remains of the carcass. Lluthean had already quartered the lean animal. The brown and black striped hide lay discarded at the edge of camp with the head still attached. Its unusually long and wispy tail fluttered in the wind.

"You took a vestek," said Kaellor. "That's no easy task. They make the Southland deer seem like turtles."

"I used the Logrend bow. They're a lot like the gendek in the Valley of the Cloud Walkers. It actually wasn't much of a challenge. The plains are thick with herd animals, even close to Voruden. How was your visit there, anyway?" asked Lluthean.

Kaellor scratched at his beard. "The only gate open is on the east side, but the guards there turn away anyone without a writ. It's no matter. There is a thriving market outside the palisade. I was able to procure a few things: some blankets, a crude spyglass, and something that might pass for bread. The vendors also sell all types of leather goods. Weapons are costly; the price on a quiver of arrows was alarming." He knuckled the beard at his chin and sighed. "But outerwear is cheap, as spring is coming on early this year. I bought a large oiled tarp with the little coin I had left. Did Bryndor take Boru with Laryn?"

"Yes. They should be back soon." Lluthean tried to pick a piece of meat from the skewer but, finding it too hot, flapped his hand a few times then plunged his fingertips into the snow. "Taker's breath!"

His oath made Kaellor grunt a laugh. "You've been north of the mountains less than six days, and already you swear like an Aarindorian," said Kaellor.

"Thanks. I've been practicing. I figure the first time I slip and curse using the name of a Southland god, I might raise a few eyebrows." Lluthean sucked on his singed fingertips, then replaced them in the snow. "Gonna have to ask Laryn to help me with that."

"For a portion of roast vestek, I'm sure she'll be more than happy to help. Keep it in the snow until the initial sting subsides."

Lluthean relaxed his shoulders. "That already feels better." He withdrew his hand and inspected his fingers. "No . . . no, it does not . . . back in the snow."

Kaellor shook his head. *Some things you have to learn the hard way, I suppose.*

He unsheathed a knife and carved a small skewer from a tree branch, then jabbed the probe into the meat. A juicy, steaming hunk fell away. He walked back under the rocky ledge shielding their camp, waited for the meat to cool, then sampled Lluthean's cooking.

"Well, how is it?" asked Lluthean.

"It's missing Bryndor's touch, but I'm so hungry you'll not hear a complaint from me."

He finished his portion, then sat back and allowed his half-lidded gaze to wander across the plains. The thin trails of numerous cookfires from groups of settlers and merchants lifted into the sky. The afternoon sun warmed his legs, and he drifted to sleep. He awoke a short time later to Lluthean's soothing words.

"Easy, Neska, they'll be along soon enough." The wolvryn had been gnawing a thigh bone, working at the marrow. She dropped her trophy, sniffing at the air and searching the western horizon. Lluthean knelt beside her with the distant expression that indicated he was employing the wolvryn sight.

"What does she see?" asked Kaellor.

"Give it a bit. Laryn and Bryn will be along. It looks like they found horses."

A few minutes later, two figures rode around a hill leading four mounts. Ahead of them, Boru loped across the snow. Kaellor watched the late-day sun silhouette Laryn. She tossed her head back and laughed at something Bryndor said. *That sound . . . I could die happy if I could carry that with me to the Drift. Sometimes the Giver gives.*

He studied the horses as they trotted into camp. "You made out pretty well. I thought with the little coin we had left, you might get one or two, but not four." Kaellor let the statement hang in the air like a question.

"It was strange. I'm not sure I can explain it, but the rancher seemed eager to do business with us," said Laryn.

"I got the feeling we were the first customers he's had in a season," said Bryndor.

Kaellor worked to unsaddle one of the horses. "There's a strange tension in these parts. I couldn't gain access to Voruden. A sizable market thrives outside the city, but you need a writ to gain entrance. Was the palisade here when you passed through six years ago?"

"No," said Laryn. "I could tell people seemed . . . suspicious of outsiders, but the wall, the towers, all of that is new."

"Well, the sooner we leave it all behind, the better," said Kaellor. "How is it you managed to find mounts that aren't terrified by the wolvryn?"

"The rancher keeps several great hounds," said Laryn. "They aren't nearly the size of Neska or Boru, but they aren't well behaved, either. The horses were skittish at first, but once we sent Boru ahead of us, they settled down."

Kaellor turned his gaze back to the plains. "Assuming favorable weather, how long to cross the Borderlands and reach the Pillars of Eldrek?"

"I had an Outrider escort on the way here. Aarindin have more stamina than an average horse, but it still took us the better part of a month to reach Voruden from the pillars," said Laryn. "All of the lands north of here were open country. There were lots of small communities gathered around farmsteads that catered to travelers, and we were able to acquire cheap lodging."

"What's an Aarindin?" asked Lluthean.

"You'll see," Kaellor and Laryn answered together.

They settled in for the night, sharing good food and a secure shelter. Kaellor watched Laryn heal his nephew's minor burn and drew comfort from knowing that the dangers of the Korjinth were behind them.

We made it. Crossed the Korjinth and made it. We're coming home, brother. He thought wistfully of Japheth and sighed.

The following day, they broke camp and skirted the west side of Voruden, choosing to avoid the traffic of the market and any well-traveled dirt roads.

By midday, they journeyed far enough to the north that the plains and occasional forests overgrew any sign of foot traffic. They walked the horses along a game trail, skirting an abandoned farmstead.

Wood fencing, long ago neglected, lay more on the ground than upright, but the fence posts marked the perimeter of what had been a large estate like stark beacons. The blackened timbers of a barn and farmhouse jutted above the grasses. They stopped to survey the landscape.

"By the perimeter of the fencing, this was a massive operation," said Kaellor. "It carries on well over the next two hillsides. I wonder what happened?"

"I don't know, but that's the fourth abandoned farmstead we've seen in the last hour," said Bryndor.

"This entire region was thriving when I passed through," said Laryn.

Her words settled something cold between Kaellor's shoulders. The feeling niggled at him and made him think he was missing something. "Give me a moment. I'm going to try to reach out with my gift. I haven't done anything with it for a long time, but it can't hurt."

He retreated inside himself and channeled zenith, allowing the flow to infuse him but resisting the urge to empower his arca prime. With focused intensity, he imagined the journey before them, then sent the flows through his runes of judgement and perception. After several minutes, nothing rose to his awareness, and he opened his eyes. As the last remnants of his gift faded, he noticed a glowing blue nimbus around the wolvryn. *I didn't need to channel to know of their value.*

"Learn anything useful?" asked Bryndor.

"Not really. Did the wolvryn handler, Mahkeel, teach you . . . can you send them ahead of us to alert us to any danger?" he asked.

"Maybe," said Bryndor. "We can send them ahead tracking food or a particular person's scent. We didn't really have a reason to teach them to search for danger in the valley. They sort of *were* the most dangerous thing, if you know what I mean."

"What else can you direct them to do?" asked Kaellor.

"All the common stuff like stay, sit, heel. And then there's a whole set of stealth and attack commands," said Bryndor.

"Those, the stealth commands—can you direct them to scout ahead with those?" he pressed.

"Yes, but it mainly works if they know what we are sending them to look for," Bryndor sucked at his teeth. "What . . . are they looking for?"

"I don't—" Kaellor started in frustration. Laryn placed a hand on his forearm, and he gathered his thoughts. "I can't say. Just . . . send them ahead of us for now? They proved valuable in alerting us to dangers when we crossed the Korjinth, and before that with those hounds from the Drift. Humor me."

They continued across the grasslands, sending the wolvryn out in overlapping circuits. By evening they found another abandoned farmstead. The skeleton of a wood-slat single-story home stood empty; its roof had collapsed long ago, but the barn provided an escape from the elements. They made the best out of beds of moldy hay, then set off early the following day.

Travel along the edge of a stream brought them to a tract of timber. After a few hours, they emerged back onto grassy plains that rose and fell with rolling hills and valleys. On both the east and west horizons, massive herds of vestek and other plains grazing animals meandered. Once again, they deployed the wolvryn in circuits ahead of them, and Neska returned midday with a fat rodent in her jaws.

Lluthean dismounted and rewarded her with affection after receiving her gift. He grunted with the effort of lifting the prize. "What is this thing? It's all hind legs and buck teeth."

"That's a common river tuck. Neska must have come across a stream," said Laryn

"Is it edible?" asked Lluthean.

"Only one way to find out," said Bryndor.

After a long pause, Kaellor nodded his agreement. "We do need to rest the horses, so let's make this fast. A campfire will announce our presence for miles. I'll get the fire. Llu, dress the tuck. Bryn, send Boru on another circuit."

A short time later, they crouched near a small fire nibbling on roasted tuck. "Tastes like . . . river chicken," said Lluthean.

Kaellor had to admit "river chicken" did pretty much describe the delicate meat. They mounted up after finishing and began the ascent up a gentle rolling hill. Once at the top, they drew to a stop. Boru was racing toward them along the ridge, streaking through the grasses.

"Something's not right," said Bryndor. He hopped down and issued several hand signs. Boru sat, allowing Bryndor to inspect him, but remained oddly vigilant to something in the west.

"He's not hurt. Give me a moment," said Bryndor. He knelt and linked to the wolvryn's sight. After several seconds he startled to a standing position. "Kae, I can't explain what those are, but there's a group of something that looks like a cross between a man and a bull. They smell awful and—"

"How many?" Kaellor growled.

Bryndor blinked once but attended to his uncle's tone. He linked to Boru for a moment. "I count at least nine. Mogdure's breath, they carry spears. What are they?"

"They're not your average river chickens," growled Kaellor.

"Grondle. He's describing grondle," said Laryn. A look of astonishment played across her face.

"Nearly a full crush of them by the sounds of it," said Kaellor. He removed the crude spyglass he had purchased and scanned the west horizon. The faint, dark outline of something moving their direction was all he could make out, but he trusted Bryndor's description.

"Make sure your bows are strung, then saddle up, Bryn, and keep the wolvryn close," said Kaellor.

"What are grondle again?" asked Lluthean as he swiveled in his saddle to string his Logrend bow.

"Take a bull and cleave off the head, add the torso of a man, and plop the bull head back on. Mix in two parts rage and one part bloodlust, and you've got yourself a grondle," said Kaellor.

"I thought the Outriders hunted them to extinction after the Abrogator's War," said Laryn. "Where do you suppose they came from?"

"That's a puzzle for another day," said Kaellor. "But it does explain why Voruden erected a palisade and why the plains resemble one massive graveyard. Let's ride. We need to put as much distance between ourselves and the crush as we can. It's the Giver's blessing that we are downwind. Perhaps we can slip away unnoticed."

They pushed the horses hard over the next several hours, encouraging them to trot down the rolling hills and along flat ground. By late afternoon, Kaellor drew them to a stop along the top of a knoll. He scanned the west horizon until the sun brought tears to his eyes. Before pocketing the spyglass, he turned in the saddle, peering back to the south, and cursed.

"What is it?" asked Laryn.

"I think they follow us, and these mounts weren't bred for a marathon flight across the plains," said Kaellor. "Let's push as hard as we can."

The next hour elapsed in a grueling chase as they coerced the tired mounts to gallop down the rolling hills after allowing them to trot up. They passed stands of timber and tried to find egress through the plains by riding along game trails.

Kaellor had Lluthean lead them, picking winding paths intended to keep them from being spotted. He sensed, though, that his horse was struggling to keep up the pace. The animal lathered at the mouth and dropped its neck low.

"Hold a moment down here," Kaellor grunted as he drew to a stop at the bottom of a dry streambed.

He hopped down and ran to the top of a rise, crouching low, then raised the spyglass to scan the southern skyline. After a moment, he lowered it. "Taker's bitter breath." At the top of a rolling hill to the south, not more than five hundred paces away, the crush of grondle roared.

Chapter Forty: Dangerous Alone, Deadly Together

"Everyone, dismount! You have thirty seconds to center on me!" Kaellor shouted.

Kaellor never shouts. Without question, Lluthean hopped down, retrieving his Logrend bow. He signaled for Neska to attend him and gathered near his uncle with the others.

Lluthean tugged on the reins of his horse. He'd thought the mount was exhausted, but it whinnied with wide eyes and flared nostrils, straining to pull free.

"Leave him, Llu. I can't shield all of us and the horses. If we get through this, we might find them after," said Kaellor.

Lluthean released the reins only to watch his horse and the others scatter back down the hill to the north. He turned his attention to the south, where a gathering wave of thundering hooves announced the oncoming danger. The grondle galloped down the far side of a broad valley, churning up clods of mud and snow and trampling the grasslands in their wake.

The beasts would reach them within a minute. They roared with a cacophony of overlapping brays and howls. He felt Kaellor's firm hand on his shoulder and struggled to pull his eyes away from the stampeding herd.

"Eyes on me, Llu. I'm going to erect a barrier over us right before the grondle arrive. With Laryn's added strength, I think it will hold. Wait for them to collide, then try to shoot them. Aim low on the chest; they have long slits there, like fish gills. That's the only place your weapons will harm them. Your arrows should be able to penetrate my ward but wait for my signal. Keep the wolvryn close; turn them loose only when I say!"

Kaellor stepped in front of them and unsheathed the guardian sword. He looked once over his shoulder to Laryn. She stepped closer to him, placing a hand on his shoulder and nodding. His uncle then glanced to Bryndor, who nodded and nocked an arrow. Last, Kaellor turned a calm gaze to Lluthean.

Flickers of cerulean light seared across the depths of his uncle's eyes and played across the silver runes along his neck and jawline. "Wait for me, Llu, then aim for the lung slits."

They all turned their attention to the south as the grondle pounded up the rise to meet them. Several hurled crude spears at them. Kaellor held up a palm, flaring a crescent of zenith that dashed the missiles to the ground.

The crush surged forward in bloodlust, closing the last several feet. Lluthean shifted his feet and felt his legs turn to water. At the last moment, Kaellor drove the guardian sword into the ground and erected an opaque dome of azure light. More than half of the grondle collided with the barrier, hammering into the obstacle with all the grace of boulders rolling down a mountain. Consecutive, bone-crushing clacks that sounded like the splintering of massive timbers reverberated through the zenith dome. Kaellor pitched back under the onslaught, but together, he and Laryn held the barrier firm.

The enraged cries of the grondle pitched now as mewling bellows of pain. The tainted reek of blood, entrails, and something utterly rotting gusted out from the throng. Clods of muddy snow that had churned up onto the barrier obscured the grisly scene.

After several confusing moments, the slush slid from the barrier, showing five of the beasts incapacitated. Three of them lay before the dome, lifeless sacks of meat and broken bone. Two others writhed in agony with the glistening ends of exposed bones and joints protruding at unnatural angles. The other four grondle had careened off the barrier and were circling back to charge again.

"Now! Shoot now!" shouted Kaellor.

Lluthean drew back his bowstring, but relaxed it as Neska dashed away into the grasses. "No! Dammit to the Drift!"

Bryndor spared him a look before releasing an arrow. The missile passed through the dome but ricocheted off a grondle's shoulder. Boru stood next to him, attentive but waiting. "Didn't you command her to stay?" asked Bryndor over the din.

"No. I . . . grind it all . . . I didn't think." In anger, Lluthean pulled on the Logrend bow, thumb to jaw. He sighted one of the remaining grondle. The beast reared up, striking hooves and hammering fists on the guardian dome. Up this close, he had no trouble spotting the strange black and purple slits along its chest. He released, and the arrow sunk fletching-deep into one of the cavities.

The grondle lurched back with a grunt of surprise and staggered in a wobbly circle away from Kaellor's ward. It seemed to recover and turned around, glaring at Lluthean. A hind hoof churned up a clod of snow, and it prepared to charge.

Lluthean drew another arrow and waited. A blur of grey and black darted behind the beast, and it staggered again. A deep serrated gash opened up on one of its hind legs, and the grondle toppled back, bellowing in agony.

Bryndor must have released Boru because the big wolvryn charged through the dome in a bounding leap and caught another grondle unaware around the throat. The wolvryn's body weight wrenched the grondle around; the sickening popping of bone and sinew echoed from their collision. Neska flashed in again, opening up a rent in the beast's hind flank. In but a moment, Boru stood on the lifeless carcass, then bound into the grasses after his sibling.

Two grondle remained, pounding fists, scraping wicked curved horns, and screaming in rage against the ward. *These things don't learn fast.*

He trained an arrow on one and released, but it embedded into thick muscle and seemed only to anger the beast. Another arrow sprouted in its hairy upper torso, and Bryndor swore an oath.

Lluthean drew again, studied the rhythm of the creature, bounding up and down, throttling into the barrier, and finally released. This time, the arrow embedded deep into the lung slit. Dark ichor fountained out of the slit, and the grondle slid back on useless hind legs. A pitiful moan gurgled out once, then it flopped to the side, gasping in pain.

Without warning, Kaellor released the dome. The last grondle stumbled, and Kaellor swept the guardian sword forward. An arc of azure light trailed the path of his weapon as he took the creature out at the knee. He stepped back as the beast toppled to its side, then delivered a mighty overhead swing. The blade sheared deep through the muscled back and severed something vital. When Kaellor withdrew the weapon, the grondle crumpled to the ground.

A few of the wounded beasts moaned in the snow. Their stench made Lluthean bury his nose in his coat. Kaellor panted, hands on knees, and Laryn knelt on the ground. Both appeared exhausted, though the battle had only taken a few minutes.

Eventually, Kaellor stood. "I'll see to these last few." He picked his way around the carnage, thrusting his blade into the chest of any grondle still clinging to life.

Lluthean whistled, and the wolvryn both loped forward, panting and tails wagging. He made a quick assessment to be sure they had no injuries. While neither seemed hurt, they both gagged and pawed at their noses.

"I can imagine those things leave a nasty taste in your mouth. You did good, Neska," said Lluthean. He rubbed at her ears and ruffled her fur in affection.

The full measure of his awareness studied the scene as Kaellor attended to the grisly work of dispatching the remaining grondle. Even in death, the beasts gave him pause. Their smell revolted his senses, but their sheer size and muscular bulk provoked a sense of awe. *If there is a Giver, you have my thanks for all of it . . . Kaellor's abilities, Laryn's strength, and the wolvryn.*

"Have you ever seen them carry out that hamstring move?" asked Bryndor, interrupting his inner thoughts.

"Yes, but never up close. They're dangerous alone, but deadly together," said Lluthean.

He sensed Neska rumble a low growl, and she rose to all fours. "What is it?" Lluthean asked. He synchronized to her slow breathing, shifting his senses to hers. From the south, like stormclouds gathering, another crush of grondle stampeded their way, and by the resonance and vibrations, possibly a third wave was not far behind. Swelling over a distant hill, he counted a crush of eight galloping in their direction.

Lluthean severed his connection and patted Neska on the head. "Kae, do these things roam in big groups? Because I think two more are headed this way."

Kaellor flicked ichor from his blade, then wiped it clean against the flank of one of the grondle. He rubbed beads of sweat from his brow along his coat sleeve. "Two more grondle?"

"No," said Lluthean after a pause. "Crushes, herds, whatever. I can see the first wave maybe three minutes out, but I sense something else, maybe a smaller one behind even that. Can you manage that dome again?"

"I wager I'll have to." Kaellor shared a look with Laryn. "How much did you give me? How much do you have left?"

Laryn took a deep breath and lifted her chin high. "Enough; I have enough."

"Should we move away from these?" asked Lluthean, pointing at the grondle carcasses.

"Only far enough for them to make the same mistake of running headlong into the barrier. Once they rage, grondle lose the ability to think, but I like our odds if they have room to commit to a full charge," said Kaellor.

Kaellor led the way, trotting thirty paces to the east, keeping the high ground on the sweeping knoll. They huddled together, and the wolvryn nosed into their circle. Lluthean watched as the first wave of grondle surged over the far ridge and started their charge down the valley. Taking a cue from his brother, he made sure to issue the command for Neska to stay.

"How many arrows have you got?" asked Kaellor.

"Eight here," said Bryndor.

"Seven," said Lluthean.

Bryndor placed four of his arrows into Lluthean's quiver. "There's no time for false bravado, and I'm not very good at it anyway. Make them count," said Bryndor.

"Good," said Kaellor. He leaned his forehead against Laryn's and pulled Bryndor and Lluthean forward so that they all touched their heads together. "We didn't cross the Korjinth to be stopped here. Not by them. No matter what happens, we finish together. Are you ready?"

"Eyes to the horizon," said Laryn.

"Eyes to the horizon," the brothers echoed.

They turned as one to face the surging crush as it flowed over the grasslands and up the knoll. Once again, several grondle hurled spears. Kaellor kept his zenith in check as the weapons fell short or veered off the mark. Lluthean rattled his fingers on the bowstring, mindlessly tapping out a number game.

The ground vibrated, and the crush raged forward, baleful roars and screeching howls announcing their intent. At the last possible moment, Kaellor took a knee and erected the blue dome. The collision of the rushing grondle once again caused them all to flinch instinctively.

Instead of the horrific clamor of shattered bones of beasts crushed under their own weight, the zenith dome bent inward several feet. Its intense azure color faded to a pale blue, but as it repelled the grondle, only one of the beasts appeared incapacitated, crushed by the rush of two other grondle. All the others staggered back but remained on their feet.

Lluthean sighted an easy target, a grondle only steps away that seemed more disoriented than the others. He waited for it to turn and released a shot directly into its lung slit. The beast reeled in a circle on wobbly legs, slipped in the snow, then toppled.

Bryndor held his bow at the ready, waiting for a clear shot, but released Boru into the melee. Lluthean drew another arrow and released Neska to join him. The wolvryn tore off into the grasses. Somewhere to their right, the enraged howl of a grondle stifled into a painful squelch.

Lluthean sized up the five grondle trying to smash through Kaellor's barrier. He took a knee and waited, then fired up into the chest of one of the beasts. The arrow shaft wobbled as it sunk into place but failed to penetrate as deep as before until the grondle reared back and impaled the arrow deeper against the barrier. The beast grunted once in confusion and swayed to the side several steps.

Four grondle remained, thrashing against the barrier, and Lluthean looked for another target when Laryn groaned and flopped to the ground at his feet. Her face appeared pale, and her eyes fluttered.

"Oh, Giver," muttered Kaellor. He tossed his hand forward, releasing a blast of zenith. The four grondle staggered back and stumbled on wobbly legs for several moments, then wheeled around. The burst of zenith caused brief disorientation but failed to wound the beasts mortally.

Neska and Boru charged one of them, each striking a hind leg, and the beast toppled in a cry of rage. One of the wolvryn yelped in pain, but the other growled savagely. Lluthean struggled to set his concern for the wolvryn to the side.

He stared down an arrow shaft at three grondle. One of the massive beasts opened and closed fleshy dark purple tissue across its lung slits, and he realized for the first time that he was seeing them without the hazy blue nimbus of Kaellor's protective barrier.

The grondle kicked their hind hooves into the snow, settling in for a charge. They roared as one and erupted up the hillside.

Chapter Forty-One: Blood on the Borderlands

"I know your brother's a tracker, and that's a rare thing in the Outriders, but even I could follow that," said Savnah, pointing at a well-trodden path. "I'll shine the Taker's nob myself if that trail doesn't lead us to what we're after."

Karragin dipped her chin to glare back at her friend. Most of the time, Savnah's curses faded into the back of her mind like so much idle chatter. Every once in a while, though, she came up with a new one that made even Karragin wonder about the woman. "Savnah, did you learn to swear from your dad, or do you make them up as you go?"

"You have your gifts, and I have mine, Karra," said Savnah. "You can hide your thoughts behind that magnificent resting asshole gaze. Me? I have this rather fantastic gift of the Giver to share exactly what I'm thinking, and right now, I'm thinking that all this tussled-up mud and snow must be from a crush of grondle. What say you, tracker?"

Nolan shifted uneasily on his Aarindin, appearing reluctant to enter the contest of words between two primes. Eventually, Karragin turned her placid expression to consider her brother. Nolan shrugged his shoulders. "Those are grondle tracks, and I don't imagine you need me to know they are fresh."

Karragin blew warmth into her gloved fingers. They had spent the last six days following grondle tracks all across the plains. On two occasions, they'd arrived to find unwary travelers massacred by the beasts. The grondle consumed everything. Chicken, goats, and cattle were never safe when a crush of grondle attacked, but neither were dogs, horses, or humans.

Those last three bothered her enough to push on and exact some revenge, but as the days wore on, she wondered now and again if they should have gone with Savnah's plan to cause a diversion and sneak into Voruden.

"How fresh?" asked Karragin.

Nolan leaned forward on his Aarindin in concentration. His eyes seemed to focus on something unseen in the distance, then sharpened to normal again. "They passed less than two hours ago."

Karragin studied the muddy trail churned into the snow. *North. If this doesn't pan out, we'll end up closer to base camp than Voruden.*

She withdrew into her gift, connecting to her Aarindin. *"Can you smell the taint of the creatures that made this trail?"*

Nebulous images of death and gore transmitted back through their connection. Eventually, Tacit replied, *"Yes."*

"We are after the beasts that made this trail. They are close. Push the group until we find them. Nicker to me if you need a break."

She released her connection to the Aarindin and clicked her tongue on the back of her teeth. "Let's go." Tacit lurched forward, ranging across the grasses alternating between a canter and a gallop. The rest of the quint spread out and followed.

They ranged over the snow-capped grasslands with intense focus. Late in the afternoon, Tacit nickered, and she drew them to a stop by a stream to let the mounts rest.

Nolan disappeared over a knoll, taking Dexxin along. They performed their responsibilities without direction, falling into a seasoned routine. Nolan scouted the perimeter, assessing for threats or any deviation in the tracks; Dexxin served as his backup and another set of eyes.

Savnah had accompanied her brother on a few occasions, but her inability to filter any of her thoughts interfered with the fundamental secret nature of his mission. As a result, Karragin became the passive audience to most of Savnah's bawdy tales whenever they paused for a break.

"And that's why they called him Slippery Mic!" said Savnah. "Although it makes for a better story if you change his name to Dick, then that last line really jabs you in the ribs."

Tovnik squatted at the stream, refilling a waterskin, and chuckled as Savnah finished her story. The medic returned, offering them a fresh drink. "Savnah, tell me you did not share that with your niece. She was all of what, eight years old?"

"She was old enough to recite the tale at Harvestday dinner but young enough to claim ignorance. It was perfect, Tov," she giggled. "Don't judge! You've got to understand your audience, and believe me, at the Derrigand family table, that tale filled the quiver!"

"You absolutely have to invite me to dinner next season," said Tovnik.

Savnah tucked one thumb behind her belt and rested the palm of her other hand on one of her moonblade axes. She winked at them both. "Tell you what, we gain access to Voruden and make it back before the spring thaw, and you're all invited."

Nolan and Dexxin stumbled breathless back over the knoll. Karragin held forth a waterskin and waited. Nolan passed the drink to Dexxin, took a moment to catch his breath, then stood up, hands on hips.

"The trail we've been following, it's not just one crush, it's two. And they're only a few minutes ahead of us. We just saw some of them drop over the horizon to the north. If we ride hard, we can catch them."

"Slap my chapped ass with the Giver's blessing. Let's ride!" said Savnah.

"Wait," said Karragin. "If we have the tactical advantage of surprise, we can handle a few grondle, maybe a small crush, maybe. But two? Two full crush of grondle?"

"You're sucking at that scar on your lip, which means you're overthinking. After all this, we can't stop just because the odds might be stacked against us," said Savnah.

A sensation of fear and regret fluttered in her stomach and threatened to undermine her resolve. She thought briefly of Amniah, of all the close calls they had survived only by the Giver's blessing. After searching the grim faces of the others, her doubts withered.

Her mind settled into practiced, tactical determination. "No, but we need to be prepared to alter our strategy. All we need to do is kill one or two. If the numbers turn against us, keep riding north until we regroup. Hopefully, the grondle can't match pace with the Aarindin, and we have the advantage in timber. We kill one or two; then we can return and retrieve the horns when it's safe. Everyone, make sure you have ready access to your embertang eggs. Questions?"

She eyed them each, waiting. When none of them spoke, she nodded. "Let's bag a few grondle so we can finish this grind of a mission."

They mounted up and encouraged the Aarindin to push ahead. The elite mounts managed the effort without showing signs of fatigue. Within twenty minutes, Karragin could tell they must be close. The smell of freshly churned-up mud mixed with the familiar tainted funk of the grondle. She suppressed a shiver and stretched her neck against the inside of her Outrider collar but pressed on.

The cold wind numbed her face and brought fresh tears to her eyes as Tacit galloped to a rise on the plains. She drew the mount to a halt when something blue flashed on the northern horizon.

Savnah pulled up next to her. "What was that?" asked the prime.

"I don't know, but I'll personally buff your ass if that wasn't a release of zenith," said Karragin.

Savnah turned to her, fishmouthed. "Karra! Did anyone ever tell you that you sound like a Derrigand?"

Karragin cocked an eyebrow and felt her cheek tighten in a smile. "Those could be our people up there. Let's give them an assist, Outrider style."

She kicked Tacit into action. They raced down a valley, then back up the far side, following the well-marked path in the snow. As they galloped on, she opened herself like never before to the flows of zenith, feeling the runes across her forearms ripple with anticipation. Typically, she kept a tight rein on how much power she channeled through her gift, fearing the draft, but this time she allowed the currents to stream through her unbridled before gathering it all in her core in preparation to infuse her arca prime. The power strained to be released, pressing out at the confinement of her runes until, at last, she relaxed and gave over to the sensation.

The rising wave of zenith crested and crashed down upon her, pulsing throughout all of her runes. She felt lifted from the normal tempo of time. To her left, Savnah's Aarindin pulled its ears back, the muscles around its eyes tightening. The woman's lips drew back in a feral smile. The prime reached her hands down to grasp her moonblade axes and seemed completely at ease, gripped on the Aarindin's back.

To her right, Nolan galloped on. An earnest expression played across his face as he turned slowly and nodded once to her, then brought his attention back to the front. With one hand, he gripped the reins; the other clutched a pouch of embertang eggs.

Karragin's fingers strangled the hilt of her saber. Tacit's grip held her fast, and together they flowed ahead. The Aarindin's secure hold grounded her. With an effort, she relaxed her fingers and brought her focus to the carnage before them.

She watched as a full crush of grondle slammed headlong into a strange blue dome of zenith. One of the beasts impacted against the barrier and was then trampled by its own kind. A pair of massive wolves leaped out of the globe to subdue one of the grondle. An arrow erupted from the shimmering blue nimbus, felling another.

Fleetingly, thoughts interrupted her concentration. *These aren't Outriders. Elbiona would have told us through Dexxin if others were headed our way. And that has to be a guardian dome. Nobody has been able to erect that construct since the disappearance of the last Baellentrell. Giver help us, what are we riding into?*

She pushed all the questions out of her mind and drew her focus back to the grondle. Four of the beasts pawed at the ground, preparing to charge. With only moments to spare, her saber hissed from its scabbard. She ignited her sympath rune and linked to Tacit.

She directed the mount to release its grip and allow her to vault forward. The Aarindin performed as commanded, simultaneously releasing their connection, sliding to a stop in the snow, and dipping its head. Karragin used the forward momentum to surge into the melee.

Sliding on her knees, she swept under one of the middle grondle. The beast reared back to charge forward, oblivious to her approach. With a zenith-infused strike, she chopped her saber clean through the grondle's front leg, cleaving it below the knee.

She spun to face the creature, and for a few heartbeats, she remained obscured by the gouts of steam billowing from its lung slits. Up close, the hot, fetid breath took on a palpable gauzy quality and pressed in around her. It took all of her mental focus to resist the urge to turn her head and draw in a full breath.

The beast listed forward on the ruined leg in a grunt of surprise and turned to look down at her. Before it could react, she smashed an embertang egg into one of the breathing slits then rolled to the side.

The sharp scent of pine cut through the air. A glance showed her that Savnah had engaged the grondle to the left with similar tactics, her efforts assisted by Nolan's precision with an embertang egg. The grondle sputtered in surprise, and a whirling maelstrom of moonblade axes dropped the beast.

The massive wolves savaged one grondle that mewled in fright and pain. Together, the beasts tumbled into the grasses.

Karragin turned her attention to the last standing grondle. She sprang to its front, slashing at its legs, but it reared back, and her saber clanged off a hoof. A burning vibration thrummed up the inside of her forearm so intense that she might have dropped the hilt if not for her gift.

The beast reared back again to stomp down on her, and she gathered her strength for a focused attack. As the creature came down, she charged ahead and plunged her saber into the breastbone of the grondle, between the gill slits. The blade wedged in deep, and she twisted hard, bending the tang of the sword. The shudder of cracked bone traveled through the weapon. It staggered back dumbfounded, the hilt still protruding from its muscled chest.

Karragin backstepped and reached into her pocket for another embertang egg. From behind her, two arrows sped forth. One careened off the bony plate of the grondle's forehead, but the other disappeared into the purple fleshy tissue covering one of the lung slits.

The last grondle stood puzzled, grunting and panting. For a moment, Karragin thought she would have to find another weapon. The beast huffed with splinted breaths, but then its back legs slowly splayed out to the side. It collapsed, belly to the snow.

Karragin whirled to check for any other threats. Two young men who rivaled Nolan in age held bows at their hips: brothers, by the looks of them, same jawline, same grey eyes. An older man took a knee, holding a magnificent-looking long sword. Flickers of zenith danced behind his eyes and along the hilt of the weapon. In their midst, a woman lay unconscious.

One of the massive wolves sniffed at the still body of another of its make. The creature craned its neck, releasing a terrible, mournful sound. Its melancholy, moaning howl echoed across the plains. The young man with lighter-colored hair walked on tremulous legs and collapsed to his knees, sobbing beside the dead wolf.

Karragin studied the macabre scene with rapt attention. Where the grondle invoked fear by their savage nature, the massive wolf, with its silvery-black coat and rich blue eyes, instilled a sense of majesty by its powerful grace. She resisted the urge to reach out with her gift, as the timing felt wrong.

They all stood, studying one another while steaming panted breaths filled the air as the shock and intensity of the moment slowly subsided. Across the hillside, not more than fifty paces away lay the steaming corpses of at least eight other grondle. Karragin's mind struggled to make sense of it all.

Another crush? Who are these people?

Eventually, Savnah cleared her throat. "What say I check to make sure these are all dead while you . . . ?" She waved a hand toward the group of strangers.

Karragin turned to Nolan. "Assist Savnah, and mind not to let the grondle blood stain your skin." She turned to the man kneeling in the group. "You've got a woman down. Tovnik's a medic trained in Callinora. He can see to her injuries."

The man lifted his gaze, and something in his serious nature sparked a feeling of recognition, but she couldn't place it. His baritone voice pulled her from dwelling on the puzzle. "She's not injured. She just needs rest. She's a healer herself and would have your man save his reserve. She gave her strength to my guardian ward, but it's a kindness all the same."

"My name is Karragin Lefledge. That's my brother Nolan. Tovnik's our medic. Dexxin's our sender and Savnah's . . . Savnah, I suppose," said Karragin.

A grondle grunted as Savnah delivered a killing blow with her axe, the sound of butchered meat announcing her brutal but necessary actions. "I heard that. I'm right here, you know."

"Might I ask who you are and where you're from? I've not seen anyone craft zenith as you did," said Karragin.

The man sheathed his sword and knelt by the unconscious woman. He appeared exhausted and spent but moved with a tenderness that she would not have expected from anyone who had dispatched so many grondle. He gently turned the woman as if she were made of porcelain, laid her on her back, and propped her head up on a blanket. "We're from Aarindorn, trying to get home, you might say. And if you're a Lefledge, then I expect your father, Therek, will be anxious to see me. I'm Kaellor Baellentrell."

The realization stunned her in the moment. "You're him," she whispered, then cleared her throat. "You look just like the statue in the sanctum. You're the lost Baellentrell prince. And that's your wife, Laryn. Are these your nephews then?"

Kaellor smiled and nodded. "You have the right of thing—"

The man grunted in surprise and toppled forward. A thwack splintered the peace as one of Savnah's moonblade axes embedded between his shoulder blades. Karragin stood immobilized by utter confusion.

Savnah whirled and took one of the younger men with her other axe. He fell back as the prime wrenched the moonblade free, chopping a gash through his collarbone and deep into his chest. One, then two, then three arrows pincushioned the other young man. In an instant, the three Baellentrell men lay incapacitated, their lifeblood staining the snowy ground.

Karragin's paralysis lifted, and she screamed, then hurtled an embertang egg. The missile struck Savnah in the chest, splashing its contents into her face. "Savnah! By the Taker's shadow, what have you done?"

Savnah brushed fingers errantly at the embertang liquid. "It's a shame to waste an egg on me, Karra, my gift, you know . . . no pain."

The giant wolf snarled at Savnah, but the prime broke an embertang egg over its nose. The creature released a pitiful wine and turned upside down, wriggling its nose through the snow in agony. For good measure, she smashed another into its maw.

Savnah watched a moment to ensure that the wolf was out of the fight, then checked on the other two men. Finally, the brutal prime bent down to retrieve her other moonblade axe and wiped the blade clean on the prince's coat.

Karragin's feet remained rooted through it all; the depth of her friend's betrayal anchored her, preventing her from taking action.

"These three are dead, Dex, nice and tidy," said Savnah. "You see, Karra, your dad isn't the only one with the ability to glimpse something of the future. Turns out the Lacuna have a man like that too, and he saw that something like this day might be coming."

Karragin felt the heat of zenith surging and prepared to ignite her strength when Savnah tsk'd. "Don't go and do that. I can see your arca prime flaring. There's a place in the new order for you, Karra, and Nolan, even your father. Moons, we're working to make your father the elected leader of a free country."

Savnah shifted her gaze to the unconscious healer on the ground. "We'll leave the woman. You never know if the country might need the Lellendule bloodline when the moons turn, but the Baellentrells were never coming back. Never."

"Why?" Karragin growled the question and balled her fists so tight that the stitching of her gloves split.

"Why what? Why did I act to ensure Aarindorn becomes a free country? Why did I work with a group to lift the yoke of nobility that led us to the Abrogator's War in the first place? Why are we working to situate your father as the leader of our new country? Which question is it you want me to answer because I'll gladly oblige," said Savnah.

"Why didn't you tell me before all of this? Why did you . . . betray my trust?" asked Karrragin.

Savnah blinked and jerked her head back, as if struck by something more surprising than the foul taint of the grondle. Understanding played across her face. They stood there among the carnage, the iron tinge of blood and pungent resin of embertang steaming the air, their gazes locked together.

The vein along Savnah's neck swelled, and a ruddy hue flushed her cheeks. Eventually, the prime scowled. "Taker's spit, Karra. I'm doing everything for the greater good of our country—for all of our people. It's bigger than you and me. But . . . I can see I'm not getting through that resting asshole gaze of yours, am I?"

Savnah glanced to Dexxin. The sender sat on his Aarindin close to Tovnik. She gave him a curt nod, then looked back, keeping a wary eye on Karragin. "Scuttle it, Dex. She can't see it yet."

The twang of a bow sang, and Nolan grunted then folded over the fletching of an arrow protruding from his flank. Karragin turned in horror to see Dexxin lower his bow in one hand. Something silver streaked in the sender's fist, followed by the sick noise made when bone shatters and flesh splits. Tovnik fell from his mount, the hilt of a dagger protruding from his cheek.

Karragin raged.

She surged forward, clearing the three dead grondle, and prepared to obliterate Savnah Derrigand. Her fist hammered into the ground where she landed, snow and clods of mud spraying into the air from the force of her detonation. But Savnah had rolled away.

"Stop and think, Lefledge!" shouted Savnah. "Nolan isn't dead, and there's still an unconscious healer lying there. You can waste the next several minutes trying to kill me or attend to your brother."

Karragin crouched like a wild cat ready to pounce. Zenith surged through her arca prime, fueled by her need to exact revenge. Her gift thrummed through the tense chords of her muscles, causing her to quiver with murderous intent. She huddled there, trembling in indecision.

Nolan gasped to her side, his face already sweaty and ashen. At last, and with tremendous effort, she stifled her flow of zenith.

She turned a placid face to the traitors. "Ride to Aarindorn. It doesn't matter where you go. This isn't over. I'll find both of you, and your end will not be tidy."

A faint part of Karragin's awareness registered the twinge of fear that played momentarily across Savnah's face. "Come see me after your father assumes command of a free country, and we can settle the score if you still feel the need." She signaled and hopped onto her Aarindin, then led Dexxin off to the north.

Karragin shelved her wrath, tucking it away behind her wall to manage at a later time. She brushed away mud and snow from her Outrider fatigues, then walked over to Tovnik. The medic lay on his back, a dagger embedded in his cheek. A dark trickle of blood oozed from under an eye that bulged out unnaturally. More dribbled from the corner of his mouth, staining the snow.

She felt too numbed, too exhausted by Savnah's betrayal to mourn for her friend. Witnessing the treachery today and sensing its full accounting in the loss of royal blood left her bereft of strategic planning. Clumsy hands turned Tovnik's corpse to the side. She retrieved the medic's pack, then trudged over to Nolan to begin yet another field dressing.

Epilogue: Part One

Ksenia sat at her desk in the regent's receiving room, awaiting his arrival. She tapped her zeniscrawl against her teeth and stared out the window. A thin, late winter frost had collected overnight, glazing the forest of Stone's Grasp with white icing. As the afternoon sun climbed high into the sky, bits of color pushed through as the trees outside struggled to shrug off the icy insulation.

The private door to the chamber opened, and Chancle Lellendule entered, followed by the regent. The vice regent smiled and offered a greeting before checking on the petitioners in the reception room. Therek Lefledge swept in with his customary stork-like gait. Three long strides brought him before his raised chair. He pushed long fingers against rather unruly eyebrows, then turned to face her before dipping his head as if to speak to her in a conspiratorial manner.

"Good afternoon, Ms. Balladuren," he said. "I hope your fingers are nimble. I'm told by the vice regent that we have a full roster today. But if, say, your zeniscrawl ran dry, or the kingdom found itself short on paper such that we had to postpone some of the petitioners, I would understand."

Ksenia dropped her shoulders and offered him an apologetic smile, holding up a full stack of blank paper and three zeniscrawls. "Unfortunately, I have to report, I'm well supplied and ready when you are."

The regent sat back with a playful sigh. "I should only expect as much from one of our best."

Chancle returned from the front of the hall with an uncharacteristic look of concern. He looked at Ksenia, seemed reassured by what he saw, then cleared his throat. "There will be a slight change this afternoon. I'm afraid the petitioners will have to wait. Overwarden Kaldera has just arrived with the sender, Craxton."

Therek cocked his head to the side, considering the vice regent's news. After a moment, he humphed a sound of curiosity. "Bring them in. Let's see what news pulls Kaldera away from his post."

Ksenia gathered her papers and folio and stood to exit, but the regent's voice interrupted her departure. "You might as well stay, Ms. Balladuren. You've earned our trust, and we might have need of your skills."

Ksenia dipped her head and took her seat. Chancle disappeared back through the front doors. A murmur of disappointed voices echoed from the chamber when the door reopened. Overwarden Kaldera strode forward, looking every bit the soldier. He wore a tailored navy double-breasted top tucked under a broad belt adorned with silver filigree. More gold and silver stitching embellished the angles of his shoulders and left breast. A sheathed saber hung on his hip.

Straight black hair, grizzled at the temples and well-manicured, framed intense eyes that surveyed the room with a scowl that conveyed disappointment. When his gaze passed over Ksenia, she felt compelled to look away, and she sought out Craxton. The sender lifted a finger as a friendly wave but followed on the heels of the overwarden.

Kaldera approached and saluted. "Regent Lefledge, I apologize for the unannounced visit, but we bring news from the Borderlands that could not wait."

"You know that apologies are never required to attend to anything you might find meaningful, old friend. Tell me, what have you learned?" asked Therek.

The overwarden ushered Craxton forward. "Make a full report, son. The regent needs to hear all of it."

Craxton nodded and stepped forward. "Your Grace. As you are aware, my brother Dexxin rides in company with your daughter and son on the Borderlands. In this capacity, he has relayed that their mission to Voruden has been delayed. It seems that the people there have been suffering grondle attacks. A palisade was erected, and foreigners are prevented entry unless they have writ or submit evidence that they killed grondle by way of a set of horns."

"How long?" Therek interrupted.

"Your Grace?" asked Craxton.

"Did your brother mention how long the people of Voruden have been under attack?" he clarified.

"I will check, Your Grace," said the young man. A blank expression settled across his face, accompanied by flickers of cerulean light, which shimmered from the depths of his eyes. A moment later, his expression sharpened back to the room, and he lifted his head. "Your daughter estimates it has been nearly a year."

Therek settled his shoulders into the back of his chair, the news impacting him like a cold draft blowing through an errantly opened window. "Continue," he said.

"Their company, now numbering five with the extra reinforcement of Savnah Derrigand, pursues a crush of grondle as we speak," said Craxton.

"I see," said Therek. The regent turned his attention to the overwarden and seemed to consider the serious man a moment. "That is not the news you sought to bring me this day, is it?"

Craxton cleared his throat. "As you know, my sister was deployed to the forward staging area near the Pillars of Eldrek. She serves as the liaison to Warden Elbiona. Just this morning, they welcomed the return of one of our own. Warden Reddevek made it safely back to the forward staging area and is with Elbiona now."

At this news, the regent leaned forward, long-fingered hands gripping bony knees. "Was Reddevek alone? What news does the warden bring from his mission to the Southlands?"

"No, Your Grace," said Craxton. "He arrived with a young girl, an orphan from the port city of Callish. He claims her as his ward."

"No one else? Did Reddevek arrive with anyone else?" Therek pressed.

Craxton appeared puzzled by the regent's sudden intensity. "No, Your Grace, only the girl."

Therek deflated, appearing to wilt in his chair. The regent stood and paced a slow semi-circle behind this seat, appearing lost in thought. A strange silence fell across the room. The vice regent cleared his throat. "Is Mullayne in the company of Warden Reddevek now?"

Craxton accessed his gift once again, then returned to the room. "Yes, Your Grace."

"Ask Reddevek if he found that which he searched for in the Southlands. Did he recover the package?" asked Chancle.

Several minutes passed while Craxton managed the conversation. "Warden Reddevek found the package and sent it ahead months ago. He says it should have arrived intact but senses that something delayed its crossing of the Borderlands. He . . ." Craxton's eyes widened, and his cheeks flushed. "Your Grace, Reddevek stormed out of the building muttering something about . . . the Taker's anatomy."

The room fell into silence again as they waited. Therek continued to pace a slow circle, stopping near Ksenia's desk to gaze out the window. At last, Craxton spoke again. "Ahh, the warden, that is Reddevek, senses that he passed the package somewhere on the Borderlands and requests leave to retrieve it immediately."

"If Reddevek is able, convey that he should recover the package at all costs. Tell Elbiona to provide Reddevek with whatever resources he deems are necessary," said the regent.

"It is done," said Craxton.

"Good, tell Elbiona to keep me informed of Reddevek's progress," said Therek. The regent rubbed at his temples and returned to his chair.

He shifted his weight and turned to look at Ksenia. "Ms. Balladuren, I would like you to draft a communication for me—"

His words cut off as Craxton collapsed to his hands and knees, moaning in pain. The overwarden reached down and hoisted him up under the arm.

"What is it?" demanded Kaldera.

Fear hollowed out the young man's expression. "It's Dexxin, on the Borderlands. Something terrible has happened. His company engaged a crush of grondle. I can't . . . I can't sense Dexxin."

Epilogue: Part Two

Enthralled outside of the flow of time, Karragin tried to cry out, but her gift stifled her in place. She bore witness to their attack on the grondle. The images blurred as she and Savnah dispatched the beasts, then shifted. She stood outside herself, watching, listening. A conversation . . . introductions . . . *Why is Savnah creeping around like that?*

She gasped in anguish from the combined emotional and physical distress as Savnah committed one betrayal after another, culminating with the order to incapacitate Nolan and kill Tovnik.

The heat of the rune on her forearm subsided, and she sensed the flow of zenith diminish. Another conversation unfolded, and the images shifted. Then the vision faded like smoke as she watched herself recover the medic pack from Tovnik's dead body.

Her awareness returned to the present, and she listed on Tacit's back. The Aarindin grunted, and she sensed him firm up their connection, gripping her tightly. Her head reeled as she bumped up against the first stage of the draft.

Moments, Giver help me, I've only got moments to save them.

Tacit raced on, and she committed to action, sending zenith into her sympath rune. She took a chance and linked to the smaller wolf. A rapid stream of information poured out of her, and she hoped it was enough. It was all the time she had left.

Karragin redirected her link to Tacit, as she had in her premonition. Once again, she slid unerringly forward, activating her strength and taking the grondle out just below the knee. Crouched in the steaming, wretched breath before the beast, she leaned to the side and hurled an embertang egg, catching Dexxin directly on the forehead.

Giver, keep him down.

Karragin pulled another egg from her pouch and threw it into the grondle's lung slit just as the creature inhaled. As before, she rolled to the side, but this time the draft tilted the world, and she staggered a few steps, regaining her balance just as another grondle reared back, preparing to smash into her.

Flashes of silver crisscrossed behind the beast, the wolves assisting her. The grondle toppled backward, rolling to its side and groaning in agony. Dark fluids poured from fresh gashes on the backside of its hind legs. Arrows whistled past her. This time, one embedded in the fenestration over the grondle's lungs, and the other disappeared beyond the fleshy, purple curtain. The beast writhed and shuddered, sputtering dark, bubbly froth and choking on its fluids. It never rose again.

Karragin looked back. Dexxin's Aarindin sensed enough to understand that he wasn't engaging in the fight and had wandered off to the side. The sender screamed and cursed, then yelled for Tovnik to come to his aid.

Karragin opened herself up to Dexxin's mount. *Aarindin, you must release your grip on your rider and kick him off, now!*

She had never laced her messages with venom or heat, but she did so now, and the mount obeyed. Dexxin sailed through the air, landing on his shoulders. A sickening thump emitted when he crunched into the snow-covered ground. His cries silenced, and she hoped his wounds weren't mortal but gave it no more thought.

Finally, she turned, panting, and directed her attention to Savnah. The woman from Midrock had spun under the first grondle, as before in Karragin's vision. However, this time Savnah was battling two grondle. The giant wolf creatures had assisted Karragin with her kill, then returned to a defensive position by the royal family.

Giver's sweet breath . . . the royal family.

Kaellor staggered to a standing position. Blue light flickered from his runes and down the shaft of the blade he wielded. He took a step to aid Savnah.

"Hold, son of Kaellex, but keep your guard. There is more danger here than grondle. I'll help her," said Karragin.

Savnah parried and rolled, spun and twisted, her moonblade axes clanging off hoof and bone. When one of the grondle reared back in pain, she used the space to toss out an embertang egg, causing the beast to sputter and groan.

Somehow, the prime managed to keep the two grondle at bay, but that was all she managed, and she was tiring. Karragin timed her attack and leaped forward as one of the beasts tried to trample Savnah from the side. She chopped through a muscled arm, whirled, and plunged her saber into the grondle's chest, right between the lung slits.

The blade wedged deep into bone and twisted when she pulled on the hilt with both hands. The sword bent, but not before the shudder of cracked bone reverberated through the weapon. As before, the grondle seemed stunned by the sensation and paused.

"Move!" shouted Nolan. He dashed in, tossing an embertang egg at the wounded beast. The oily contents splashed into fenestrations along the creature's chest, causing immediate violent hacking and wheezing.

Karragin took a few wobbly steps back. Left to a lone grondle, Savnah harried the creature, feinting one way, then tumbling to the side. Nolan threw another embertang egg, startling the beast. Savnah used the distraction to dash back in and cleave through the grondle's leg. Part of Karragin appreciated Savnah's prowess and skill, but the memory of her treachery tainted any admiration.

Savnah whirled both blades through a wicked slice, toppling the last grondle, and then they all stood panting. Karragin sucked at the scar of her upper lip and struggled to separate what she'd seen in her vision and how this version of events had unfolded.

Nolan stands without injury, and Giver's mercy, Tovnik draws breath. Two wolves stand where before there was only one, wasn't that right? How do I even proceed? If I make introductions, will Savnah react as she did before? Taker's breath, she was so committed. Why couldn't we have more time?

Tovnik dismounted and looked to Karragin with an expression of uncertainty, then went to check on Dexxin, who lay motionless on the ground. *I can explain. All in due time, my friend.*

"Nolan, sweep the perimeter and check for any others. Savnah, would you check that the grondle are all dead? I'll see to our new friends," said Karragin.

She waited, holding her breath. Nolan nickered once, and his Aarindin lowered belly to the ground. He remounted and trotted off to the east.

Savnah eyed the small group, then shrugged. "Suits me. You were always the better ambassador." And she set to the gruesome task of killing the incapacitated grondle.

Karragin exhaled, then turned with her hands up, weaponless, and approached. Kaellor started to sheath his weapon and attend to the woman on the ground when Karragin interrupted him. She pitched her voice low. "Please don't do that. She will be fine; she spent too much zenith fueling your guardian ward, but she'll soon recover. For now, keep your blade in your hands until I see how this plays out."

Kaellor rested the blade on his shoulder, considering her words. "Alright, but in a moment, you're going to tell me who you are and how you know all of that."

"I'm Karragin Lefledge, daughter of Therek, and I inherited something of his gift for prophecy. I foresaw this moment, but it was different. I've only just learned that two in my company are in league with the Lacuna. They are something of a—"

The man twirled the blade of the longsword in his hands and brought it into a defensive position. Something in his bearing seemed suddenly feral, and the two younger men knocked arrows to their bowstrings. He said through gritted teeth, "We know what the Lacuna are. They've already murdered someone precious to us. Someone completely innocent."

Karragin nodded once. "I'm not surprised. Stay on your guard and give me a moment with her."

"If your friend counts herself among the Taker's minions, then stand aside," growled Kaellor.

Karragin held her hands higher. "Peace, please. If you held any love for my father, grant me this chance to talk to her. I owe her my life two times over. Give me one chance to . . . save my friend."

She waited for Kaellor to take his eyes from Savnah, who continued her butchery. When their gazes finally locked, she waited. A handful of heartbeats passed, and something in the man's angry fire soothed.

He nodded his head in disbelief. "Taker's spit, girl, you've got your mother's look about you. You have your chance, but I'll not be letting my guard down."

Karragin turned to regard her friend. Savnah hacked at the last intact grondle skull, removing another set of horns. Eventually, she rose and wiped a forearm across her brow. "Mind the grondle blood, Savnah. It's more toxic than you know."

Savnah smiled. "Thanks, but you could have reminded me before I got elbows deep into . . . the . . ." Something in Savnah's carefree manner shifted. She wiped her moonblades clean of any blood, then replaced them on her hips. A look of understanding rippled across her face.

"You tricky bitch," she smiled ruefully and hooked a thumb over her belt. "I don't know how, but you changed it, didn't you? You called him 'son of Kaellex,' and I missed it. I . . . missed it."

"What are you . . . ?" Karragin's voice trailed off in confusion.

Savnah withdrew her moonblade axes, flipping them both once as if testing their weight. Karragin heard bowstrings tighten, but Savnah tossed her weapons to Karragin's feet, then retrieved a waterskin from her Aarindin. She used the carcass of a dead grondle as a bench, plopping down unceremoniously, and pulled a long draw of water. "Did you take Dexxin out of the fight too?"

Karragin looked at her coolly but did not answer.

Savnah waved, releasing her from the obligation of an answer. "It doesn't matter. We're here, and I missed it, and that means you . . . you know, don't you? You know everything. Isn't that the Taker giving it to me in the backside and the Giver rewarding the golden child once again?" Savnah rambled now, appearing to talk more to herself.

Karragin wandered over to sit down beside her. She realized just how exhausted she felt as the draft rose up, threatening to make her vomit. She laid her palms on the grondle, attempting to ground herself and stave off the feeling of the world tilting. They sat in silence, and she struggled to think of what to say. "I had a vision of it all just before it happened."

The revelation made Savnah toss her head back. A throaty laugh escaped. "We go balls deep into grot territory, scrap it with grondle, and grind up in close calls too numerous count, and not once—not once!—does that . . . fragment of your gift awaken. Not until today. The Giver smiles on you, Lefledge."

"You can come back, Savnah. You can choose a different path," said Karragin.

Savnah sighed and handed her the waterskin. Karragin waved it off. Something about letting her guard down at that moment felt unwise.

"How accurate was your vision, Karra? What did I . . . how far did I take it?" asked Savnah.

"You went all the way. You butchered Kaellor and the princes, wounded one of those wolves, then ordered Dexxin to kill Tovnik and incapacitate Nolan with a gutshot. It was brutal and efficient. We spoke of the Lacuna, and then you left me here."

Savnah turned, and they stared at each other for long moments. "If you saw all of that, then you know I can't just . . ." She shook her head in disbelief. "I can't walk away from the Lacuna."

"What did you mean before, when you said I changed it?" asked Karragin.

"A seer told me this day would go down one of two ways." Savnah screwed up her face. "If direct an introduction is made, moonblades will rule the day. But if the title is one step removed, then the Giver will smile on another." She turned a defeated expression to Karragin. "I guess that means you."

"Did your seer tell us what to do next? Is there a path forward for all of us?" asked Karragin.

Savnah swiveled her head back and forth. Karragin wasn't sure if her friend was still in disbelief at how things had turned out or answering in the negative.

"Well, what would you have me do with you?" asked Karragin.

"It sounds like I was prepared to kill all of you. The way I see it, you should do the same," said the woman with a matter-of-fact expression.

"Hmm, maybe. But not today." Karragin stood and raised her voice. "Tovnik. How is Dexxin?"

The medic raised from a kneeling position. "He took a blow to the head, which is a mercy. I only just neutralized the embertang from his face. I knew these eggs were risky, but Giver, I never imagined anyone would douse themselves with it."

"How many doses of Veramanth's decoction do you carry?" she asked.

Tovnik scratched his head, appearing puzzled by the random nature of her question. "The customary pouch affords a three-week supply for several people if taken every other day. Dexxin is stable for now. Can I see to someone over there?"

"No, but I'll need two doses of the brew just the same," said Karragin.

Savnah sighed. "Have you ever tasted stiller's powder?"

"No, is it bad?" asked Karragin.

"I've broken more than my share of bones learning how to use my gift, so I've had plenty of experience with the stuff." She plucked errantly at the dried seed head of a thistle left from the prior season. "Suck on the ass-end of a dead mule for a bit, then come talk to me, and we can compare notes about being 'ranthed."

"I'm not going to kill you, Savnah, though by the moons I've every cause to, and by the sounds of it, so do the Baellentrells. You and I are going to walk back to Stone's Grasp. Dexxin too, though I've a mind to let one of them give him a gutshot so he knows what that's all about. You drink Veramanth's decoction every other day, and we'll go back to Stone's Grasp together. I'm not giving up on you. We can still sort all this out. What do you say?"

Savnah looked up at Kaellor, who stood assessing their conversation with a wary eye, hands on the pommel of his sword.

The woman from Midrock sighed and nodded her consent. "You're a stubborn grinder, Lefledge."

Epilogue: Part Three

Ksenia hoisted a small travel pack over her shoulder just as someone knocked on the door to her room. "Come in."

Vinnedesta stepped inside and eyed the pack. "All packed, I see. Off to make amends with your mother then?"

"Something like that, maybe. It will be good to have a break, even if it is only for a week. How about you? Any big plans with your time off?"

The scribe sighed. "Nothing as exciting as riding my own personal Aarindin in the countryside. My mother arranged a sitting appointment at a dressmaker in the Delve . . . for the spring assembly. I know it's still more than a month away, but mother says if you want to catch the eye of an eligible bachelor, you have to look the part, which means a new dress in the spring style."

Ksenia recalled seeing some of the displays when she last visited the elite market. The expense of the material alone would cost a month's wages. "I had completely forgotten about that. I wonder if there is a way to volunteer for some random scribe duty to get out of it all."

Vinnedesme backed a laugh. "Kess, you're absolutely a breath of fresh air. All of the royal offices close for the three days of the assembly. When you get back, I promise to help you get something presentable. You have to come; it's the event of the year."

She shifted her pack uneasily, staring past her friend to the hallway.

"Oh, say you'll come, Kess, please?" Vinnedesta pleaded. Then she wedged her feet inside the doorframe and crossed her arms. "Ksenia Balladuren, as your friend, I am not moving until you promise to come with me to spring assembly."

The two stared at each other a moment, and Vinnedesta lifted her chin and stared off into a corner of the room. Ksenia acquiesced. "Alright, I promise. Besides, my parents always return for the event, and I might need you to insulate me from my mother's meddling."

Vinnedesta hopped forward and embraced her, then stepped out of the way. "Safe travels then, and I'll see you when you get back."

"Can you do me one favor before I go?" asked Ksenia.

"Sure, anything."

"Are you familiar with the Golden Crust? It's a bakery in the Delve two blocks in," explained Ksenia. She retrieved a few coins and poured them into Vinnedesta's palm. "Buy a box of crownberry muffins and send them to the regent. You can say it's from the both of us. He's been distracted ever since that meeting with Craxton and the overwarden a week ago. It might be just the thing to make him smile again."

"Good plan, anything else?"

"Well, if you have time, this memo needs to be delivered to the royal offices on the second level. It's to be added to the formal invitations for the assembly. There aren't any state secrets, but it does hint at the urgency of attending this year."

Vinnedesta opened the memo and read through it. "His words hint at an important revelation to be shared and urges the attendance of all parties, even the minor noble houses. What do you suppose that's all about?"

Ksenia thought about the cryptic nature of the "package" which Reddevek sought on the Borderlands and how that might fit into the regent's plans. "I don't know," she sighed. "But I'm happy to leave it all behind for a bit."

"Well, get going then. I'll take care of this, and you have a good week," said Vinnedesta.

She said one last goodbye, then made her way toward the stables. Snowmelt left a palpable texture in the warm spring air. The early spring thaw meant muddy terrain for a good portion of the journey, but Winter wouldn't complain as long as she escaped the confines of the stables.

Ksenia pulled open the barn door and stepped inside. Munts walked down the wide row and dropped an armful of hay into a stall. "Hello, Ksenia. I've got Winter all sorted out for your ride back home."

"You didn't have to do that, Munts, but thanks all the same."

The stableman patted a meaty hand on the top of a gate post. "It's the least I can do after all that business with Annan. She made a complete recovery thanks to your advice."

"Glad to hear it. I'll see you when we get back in a week," she said and continued down the row to Winter's stall.

She turned the corner only to find a familiar Aarindin standing outside Winter's gate. More out of curiosity than alarm, she opened herself to her gift and linked them all in a conversation. "*Hello, Tacit. Are you here to escort Winter and me back home?*"

"*Yes, let's go home. Can we leave now?*" asked Winter. She nickered and rubbed the top of her nose on the rungs of her gate.

A mixture of words, phrases, smells, and images flooded through the link as Tacit tried to unload a complex message. "*I have a message from Karragin. She returns in private, in secret, she has a secret. What is a secret? Private, secret. Run, I must run. Not stop, secret run. Avoid the Lacuna.*"

Ksenia struggled to understand his meaning. She had spent time with Tacit on the ranch before her post in Stone's Grasp, but his command of language and ability to express himself was limited compared to Winter's.

She took a moment to inspect the Aarindin. He looked lean, with ribs protruding and fat pads atrophied around the hips. Road dust and mud stained his legs and belly, and burrs tangled his mane. She ran a hand along his neck and offered him a dried apple. The Aarindin took the treat eagerly, and she opened Winter's pen, ushering him inside to obtain water and hay.

"*Slow down, Tacit. You did well coming here. Try again. Tell me again.*"

The Aarindin drank long at the water trough, then nibbled at hay. He sent a confusing jumble of images laden with smells that conveyed emotion: fear, danger, urgency, and purpose all mingled together.

"*Winter, I can't make out what Tacit is trying to say. He seems exhausted or disorganized, I don't know. Can you understand why he is here? Where is Karragin?*"

"*If I say, you must promise me we will still go home.*"

"*I would love nothing more, but first help me understand,*" said Ksenia.

After a long pause, Winter dipped her head low, then lifted pink lashes to stare at Ksenia, who was brought to giggling by the human appearance of her expression of frustration.

"Karragin escorts a royal party. They return to Stone's Grasp but need to come in secret. The Lacuna tried to kill them, and she does not know who to trust. Craxton's brother is in the Lacuna, so Karragin sent Tacit to find you. You must tell this secret to someone . . . to Karragin's father. Can we go now?"

Ksenia leaned against an interior wall of Winter's stall. *A royal party . . . what does that even mean?*

The pieces of the last week all fell together . . . the package, Reddevek's mission, the regent's folly, the return of the royals. *That's why Therek wants so many people to attend spring assembly this year. He's going to announce the return of the royals.*

Winter's last words echoed in her mind. *You must tell this secret to someone.*

Suddenly, she felt as if the world shifted, and she had dropped into a crevice in the Great Crown. On one side, the Lacuna pressed in on her . . . Craxton, the Aspect, her brothers. And on the other side, the loyalists . . . Karragin, the regent, her parents. All these people held meaning to her.

"Moons . . . who am I supposed to tell?"

Glossary of names, places, and terms

Aarindorn (AIR-in-dorn)—a kingdom in the Northlands, surrounded by the Great Crown Mountains.

- Tacit—mount trained by Ksenia Balladuren with above average intelligence for the breed.
- Winter—Ksenia's personal friend, an albino.
- Zippy—Reddevek's loyal steed.

Abrogator (AB-roh-gate-or)—a term used to describe one who wields the reductive force of nadir.

Ahben (AH-ben)—a Cloud Walker herb gatherer.

Amniah (am-NIGH-yuh)—a young female Outrider gifted with the ability to gust (shape wind) who hails from Stellance. A member Karragin's quad.

Arca prime—the central rune of a zeniphile located on the center of the chest and determining the zeniphiles strongest affinity or ability.

Argul (AR-gull)—an Outrider with alchemic and munitions expertise. A member Savnah's quad.

Baellentrell (BAE-len-trell)—the last name of the current ruling family in Aarindorn.

- Bierden (BEER-den)—Kaellor's grandfather, capable of summoning rune fire.
- Bryndor (BRIN-dur)—oldest of two nephews to Kaellor. Older brother to Lluthean.
- Eldrek (EL-drek)—founder of the Baes line and first king of Aarindorn.

- Japheth (JAY-feth)—king of Aarindorn during the Abrogator's War. Father to Bryndor and Lluthean, brother to Kaellor.
- Kaellex (KAY-lex)—father to Kaellor and Japheth, grandfather to Bryndor and Lluthean.
- Kaellor (KAY-lore)—uncle to Bryndor and Lluthean.
- Lluthean (LOO-thee-in)—youngest of two nephews to Kaellor. Younger brother to Bryndor.
- Nebrine (neh-BREEN)—mother to Bryndor and Lluthean, wife to Japheth.
- Phethnem (FETH-nem)—mother to Kaellor and Japheth, wife to Kaellex.

Balladuren (bal-uh-DOO-ren)—family in Aarindorn famed for breeding Aarindin.

- Elbend (EL-bend)—father of the family, sits on the Aarindorian council.
- Madola (muh-DOLE-uh)—mother of the family, wife to Elbend.
- Kervin (KURV-in)—fourth brother, senior only to Ksenia. As a sympath, he can communicate with animals.
- Ksenia (keh-SEN-yuh)—youngest child of five and only daughter. Her runes enable her to channel zenith to empathically communicate with animals and decipher languages, among other talents.
- Rugen (ROO-gen)—oldest brother. Member of the city watch in Stone's Grasp.

Barl Fodensk—this zeniphile led his forces from the deep south by ship to fight against the abrogators in the Great War. His forces were gifted in controlling the forces of wind and water.

Burl Derrigand (Burl DARE-ih-gand)—a member of the inner circle of the Lacuna.

Bashing Ram—a tavern and inn at Journey's Bend.

Beclure (beh-KLURE)—a duchy in west Aarindorn.

Benyon Garr (BEN-yun)—a wizened trainer of the gifted in Aarindorn, member of the Aarindorian military, and adviser to the Outriders.

Berwek (BURR-wek)—a prime in the Outriders.

Besken (BES-kin)—a kingdom in the western Northlands of Karsk.

Bekson's Fine Restoratives—a tavern and eatery in the Delve in Stone's Grasp.

Bosulk (BO-sulk)—a.k.a. a greater driftian, a massive creature from the Drift.

Borsec (BORE-sek)—ruling monarch over the northwest region of the Southlands, including Riverton and Journey's Bend.

Braveska (bra-VES-kuh)—the royal family in Hammond and Malvress in the Southlands

- Leland (LEE-land)—duke in Malvress and youngest brother to Vendal.
- Lesand (leh-SAND)—niece to the king of Hammond and daughter to Duke Leland in Malvress.
- Shelland (SHELL-and)—queen in Hammond.
- Vendal (VEN-dull)—king in Hammond.

Boljer—a prime in the Outriders.

Callinora (cal-in-NORE-uh)—a city in northwest Aarindorn composed of erudites, scholars, and healers. The formal educational training of medics, healers, alchemists, and related fields takes place here. The city is a protectorate of Stone's Grasp with no specific familial loyalties but rather loyal to the welfare of Aarindorn. The kingdom's Sanitorium is located here.

Callish (CAL-ish)—port city along the northeast coast of the Southlands.

Cataclysm—the Great War in which the forces of abrogation caused a rent in the barrier between the world of the living and the Drift. The death toll was estimated at well over thirty thousand and led to the separation of

Karsk into the Northlands and the Southlands. The timing of this event is used as the source of the dating system on Karsk, with dates being either before cataclysm (bc) or post cataclysm (pc).

Cloud Walkers—a tribe native to the valley deep in the center of the Korjinth Mountains. Formally called the Damadibo (dahm-uh-DEE-boe), meaning "the people."

Consort—the Consort are the group of umbral pulled from the Drift and acting on Tarkannen's direction.

Crush—a herd of six to ten grondle.

Damadibo (dahm-uh-DEE-boe)—the Cloud Walkers, the term means "the people."

Dedicant—the Dedicant is the title given to the leader of the ungifted, or the runeless, in Aarindorn

Della—the proprietor at the Bashing Ram of Journey's Bend. She manages and owns the tavern with her brother Ingram.

Delve, the—a district in Stone's Grasp housing affluent merchant stores, shops, and wares.

Dressla Rudang (DRESS-luh roo-DANG)—the queen of Voruden.

Drexn (DREK-sen)—the name for the sun god in the Southlands.

Dulesque (doo-LESK)—a duchy in west Aarindorn.

Eguma (eh-GOO-muh)—a lithe and small grotvonen possessing more intelligence and the capacity for human speech.

Eidolon—prophesized in *The Book of Seven Prophets* as a person capable of wielding both zenith and nadir, and someone required to save the world.

Elcid—a bandit in Hammond.

Ellisina (el-eh-SEE-nuh)—a Cloud Walker child.

Elgruh—an adult female of the Cloud Walkers.

Endule (en-DUEL)—a family of nobles in Aarindorn related to and branching from the Lellendules. Currently ruling the duchies of Dulesque and Beclure in Aarindorn.

- Alvric (ALV-rick)—former Outrider recruited into the city watch in Stone's Grasp.
- Berling (BURR-ling)—a young man gifted in the healing arts

and a medic in the Outriders.

- Bextle (BEX-tul)—a member of the guard in Stone's Grasp, older brother to Craxton.
- Bexter (BEX-turr)—husband to Phelond, the matriarch of the family; he married into the family and assumed the Endule name.
- Chancle (CHANCE-ul)—the vice regent in Stone's Grasp in Aarindorn. He is the regent's close friend and confidante and runefather to the Lefledge children.
- Craxton (CRAX-ton)—younger brother to Bextle and representative speaker for several guilds in Stone's Grasp. A sender who is a triplet.
- Dexxin (DEX-in)—an Outrider, sender, and triplet to Craxton and Mullayne.
- Endera (en-DEER-uh)—the duchess of Beclure, mother to Velda.
- Mullayne (mull-AIN)—a member of the city watch in Aarindorn and sender triplet to Dexxin and Craxton.
- Phelond (feh-LOND)—the duchess of Dulesque, married to Bexter, mother to Berling.
- Velda (VEL-duh)—an Outrider skilled in archery. Daughter to Endera, from Beclure.

Exemplar Gre'Kanth (greh-KANTH)—the holy leader of the Immaculine, a sect founded in Caskayah in the deep south of the Southlands.

Fagle Hoff (FAY-gull)—the royal gardener in Stone's Grasp.

Festian Planes (FES-tee-un)—prairie and plains south of Callish in the Southlands.

Feth—a stableboy who works with his father, Steckle, at the Bashing Ram.

Firth—a name utilized by Lluthean while traveling anonymously.

fo'Vaeda and fo'Voshna—zeniphile sisters gifted in prophecy and prediction, both involved in a tangled relationship with Eldrek in the times of the Cataclysm.

Foden (FOE-den)—Southlander name for the god of the seas and wind.

Gavid Strictor (GAV-id STRIK-turr)—an official of the Immaculine.

Geddins (GEDD-ins)—a high family in Aarindorn.

- Ashrof (ASH-rof)—the oldest son gifted with the ability to survey and measure distances.
- Marsona (mar-SAW-nuh)—younger sister to Ashrof.

Grasdok (GRAZ-dock)—the chieftan of the Brognaus, a clan of grotvonen in the Torgrend Range.

Griggs—a guard at the southern gate to Aarindorn. He is a sifter.

Grotvonen (GROT-voh-nen)—The "grot" are humanoid creatures who live in clans underground. Their senses evolved to survive in that environment. They possess only vestigial lips and utilize a language of nasal snorts, clicks, and a guttural speech pattern.

Guster—a zeniphile who controls and manipulates winds or air.

Gwillion (GWILL-ee-un)—the former alchemy master in Aarindorn, disgraced by his addiction to vivith.

Hawklin—a family in Journey's Bend.

- Bruug (Broog)—the oldest brother.
- Heff—the middle brother.
- Rusn—the youngest brother.
- Gruus—the father of the Hawklin family.

Hillen—a deceased Cloud Walker. When he died, a pregnant wolvryn bonded to him (Vencha), became feral and slipped from the misted valley, later to become the mother to Boru and Neska.

Homnibus—the lead rector or abbot in service at the Abbey on the Mount in the Southlands.

Immaculine, the (im-MAC-u-you-leen)—a religious sect from Caskayah. They hunt and kill abrogators and zeniphiles alike.

Inasia (in-AY-shuh)—a member of the inner circle of the Lacuna, planted in Callinora.

Ingram—the proprietor and co-owner with sister Della of the Bashing Ram of Journey's Bend.

Journey's Bend—a rural Southland town not far from Riverton, childhood home to the "Scrivson boys," Bryndor and Lluthean.

Kal'maldra—a zeniphile who rose in power and assumed the title of the Eidolon in the time before the Cataclysm.

Kaldera (kal-DEER-uh)—Overwarden in the Outriders, he serves at the pleasure of the regent and sets strategy for the group.

Karsk—the continent of the Northlands and Southlands, used interchangeably by the people there to describe the world.

Kemp—an alias name used by Bryndor during anonymous travel.

Keska—chambermaid in Stone's Grasp.

Kindred—the term used to describe the common speech known by most humans on Karsk.

Korjinth Mountains (CORE-jinth)—the mountainous peaks of this range erupted, and the central valley was formed, after the Great War when Eldrek Baellentrell marshaled the zeniphiles to wield their collective zenith in tandem with Mogdurian's abrogators. The colossal release of force, poorly synthesized, resulted in the formation of this range on the Plains of Jintha, and divided all of Karsk. Currently, warring currents of zenith and nadir make crossing the summit nearly impossible.

Krestus (CREST-us)—a fallen knight from Malvress.

Kunzie (KOON-see)—a member of the inner circle of the Lacuna.

Lacuna (luh-COO-nuh)—a secret sect in Aarindorn seeking to replace the monarchy with a democracy. They seek to break the circle of recurrent or inherited familial leaders.

Lawn Whirik—constable in Journey's Bend.

Lefledge (leh-FLEJ)—a high family in Aarindorn

- Karragin (CARE-uh-gin)—an Outrider, sister to Nolan, daughter to Therek.
- Nolan (NO-lun)—an Outrider, son to Therek, brother to Karragin.
- Therek (THARE-ik)—the regent in Aarindorn.

Lellendule (lell-en-DOOL)—a noble family in Aarindorn

- Aldrik—oldest brother of Volencia.
- Chancle (CHANS-ul)—the vice regent in Aarindorn, brother to Hestian, cousin to Laryn. He is a trusted friend to the regent and has helped stabilize Aarindorn after the Abrogator's War.
- Charlest (char-LEST)—the last ruling Lellendule queen in Aarindorn and mother to Tarkannen.
- Elbare—Volencia's father, a disgraced drunkard.
- Hestian (HES-tee-en)—older brother to Chancle. He is a trusted friend to the regent.
- Kelledar (KELL-eh-dahr)—one of the first Lellendules, loyal friend to Eldrek Baellentrell.
- Laryn (LARE-in)—a healer trained in Callinora, she married Kaellor in a secret ceremony and returns to Aarindorn as his wife and a prominent member of the Lellendule family.
- Maelos (MAY-lohs)—the last king in the Lellendule line, father to Tarkannen.
- Phesteq (FEZ-tek)—a young man who attempted the Rite of Revealing only to perish in the trial.
- Shalla (SHAHL-uh)—mother to Volencia.
- Tarkannen (tar-CAN-en)—the Usurper who reintroduced the utilization of nadir over zenith and resurrected the abrogators. In real life, the author's daughters argue about the best pronunciation. Some prefer "TARK-anon," others "tar-CANN-on." The author is perfectly content to let the reader decide which pronunciation suits their worldview for Karsk.
- Veldrek—Volencia's middle brother.
- Volencia—born gifted with affinities in water manipulation, she never sat for the trial to unlock her arca prime and instead embraced the path of the abrogator.

Lemm Sogle—a drunkard from Journey's Bend

Lentrell (LEN-trell)—minor nobles in Aarindorn related by blood to the Baellentrells.

- Elbiona (el-bee-YOH-nuh)—an Outrider warden in Aarindorn. She is rumored to be exceptional with a bow.
- Venlith (VEN-lith)—a healer of the fourth circle (the highest rank) and referred to as docent. She is the leader overseeing the Sanitoruim in Callinora. A known master of the healing arts.
- Drevan and Bartoll—brothers who knew Volencia as a child.

Leveck—titled Commissioner Leveck, an officer of the court in Beclure in the employment of house Endule.

Lutn Egaine—an abrogator and famed mathmetician and tactitician who sought a neutral relationship between zeniphiles and abrogators. Because he was seen by some as playing both sides, he was later remembered as the trickster and in the Southlands incorporated into the pantheon.

Lutney (LUT-nee)—Southland god of luck, tricks, and the unseen.

Maedra (MAY-druh)—Southland god of nature and healing.

Maedraness—in the time of the cataclysm, this zeniphile, known as the Shaman Queen, joined Eldrek and the other zeniphiles. Their natural talents lay in the healing arts and communicating and controlling plants and animals.

Mahkeel (mah-KEEL)—the wolvryn handler of the Cloud Walker tribe.

Malldra (MAHL-druh)—Southland term for the mother of the pantheon of gods, thought to have died birthing the other gods.

Margrave Rolsh—the ruler in Riverton and by default the territories in Journey's Bend, loyal to King Borsec.

Miljin (MILL-jin)—an elder shaman among the Cloud Walkers.

Mogdure (mog-DURE)—the Southland god of death, darkness, and illness.

Mogdurian—in the time of the Great War, he led all the abrogators in his quest to bring order to Karsk.

Monk—affectionately, a Man of No Knowledge.

Moorlok (MORE-lock)—a vast and ancient tract of timber in the Southlands bordering Journey's Bend.

Munts—stableman in the royal stables at Stone's Grasp in Aarindorn.

Oren (ORE-en)—the captain of the city watch in Stone's Grasp.

Ozhen—a thug in the company of the Hawklin brothers in the Southlands.

Ranika (RAN-ih-kuh) —aka Nika, a waif following Reddevek from the city of Callish, one of the first innately gifted abrogators to walk Karsk since the cataclysm.

Reacher— a term used by the Immaculine to describe anyone who "reaches into the Drift" to summon power, whether it be zenith or nadir (they make no exception in using the terminology). Also called a thrall with the implication that anyone using the power is enthralled or enslaved by a lust for power.

Reddevek (RED-eh-vek)—a warden in the Outriders. One of the few gifted with tracking. He rarely uses his last name, Tain.

Riverton—a city adjacent to Journey's Bend in the Southlands.

Rolsh—the margrave in Riverton.

Rona (ROE-nuh) Scrivson—the aunt to Bryndor and Lluthean in the Southlands.

Runefather/mother—an adult zeniphile in Aarindorn who assumes a semi-formal relationship with a gifted child to uphold the cultural norms of society. This person is often involved in training and the rituals such as the Rite of Revealing.

Runeling—the gifted child who is the recipient of the mentoring relationship with a runefather/mother.

Runta—a mediocre healer among the Outriders in Savnah's quad.

Salveen (sal-VEEN)—the male leader of the Spicers, a gang running the vivith trade, gaming rackets, and brothels in the quarter known as the Sprawl in Aarindorn.

Sadeen Tunkle (suh-DEEN TUN-kull)—a townswoman in Journey's Bend.

Savnah Derrigand (SAWV-nuh DARE-ih-gand)—a prime in the Outriders, known for her battle prowess with twin moonblade axes and her rather colorful ways of expressing herself. From Midrock.

Senda—a Cloud Walker herb gatherer.

Sender—a zeniphile who can telepathically communicate with another sender. In the entire history of Aarindorn, senders have always been born as twins, triplets, etc. As such they are rare.

Shass—the former servant to the Volencia and Mallic at their estate in Callish.

Shaveen (shah-VEEN)—one of a set of five albino quintuplet zeniphile senders who lived in the time of the Cataclysm. Their arca prime gifts them with the ability to telepathically communicate with each other over any distance.

Shelwyn River (SHELL-win)—a river in the Southlands.

Sheshla (SHESH-luh)—a butterfly named in the Valley of the Cloud Walkers.

Sifter—a zeniphile who can recall people or events with an identic memory.

Skellig—a drug courier in the Sprawl.

Sprawl, the—the poor part of Aarindorn where houses are crammed into winding neighborhoods, overcrowded slums, and poorly maintained streets. The brothels, gaming houses, and taverns outnumber more reputable businesses.

Steckle (STEK-ul)—hired hand and handyman at the Bashing Ram in Journey's Bend.

Stone's Grasp—the castle and capital city of Aarindorn.

Suvi—an ungifted woman who manages several orphanages in the Sprawl.

Tellend (TELL-end)—a family of farmers in Journey's Bend.

- Emile (eh-MEEL)—wise matron of the family.
- Harland—son to Emile and Markum.
- Markum—Emile's husband.

Timson (TIM-son)—a stable boy at the Abbey on the Mount.

Tomlek (TOM-lek)—a rector in Journey's Bend.

Tovnik (TAHV-nik)—a medic among the Outriders.

Torgrend Range (TORE-gend)—a range of mountains in the far northwest finger of the Northlands.

Umbral—a.k.a. shadowmen, creatures wandering the Drift and wielders of nadir ruled by the forces there. Their origins are poorly understood, but they are likely abrogators who died while steeped in the frenze and are now enslaved by forces in the Drift.

Vaeda (VAY-duh)—Southland name for the goddess embodied as the red moon.

Valdesta (val-DEST-uh)—a member of the inner council of the Lacuna.

Vardell Becks—an assassin hired by the Lacuna from Aarindorn. He is gifted with gusting.

Vesta—servant to Mallic and Volencia in their estate in Callish.

Vinnedesta—a scribe in service to the regent in Aarindorn.

Voruden (voe-ROO-den)—a Queendom in the Northlands on the north face of the Korjinth Mountains, ruled by Queen Dressla Rudang.

Voshna (VOSH-nuh)—Southland name of the goddess embodied as the blue moon.

Weckles—the deceased former steward of the archives and master linguist in Aarindorn.

Winter—Ksenia Balladuren's albino Aarindin.

The Animals, Elements, and Plants of Karsk

Aarindin (AIR-in-din)—a prized stock of horses bred for their combination of stamina, speed, and intelligence and preserved for use by the Outriders, a branch of the Aarindorian military and elite classes. The breed standard are a jet black or ebony color. They can use zenith to grip a chosen or preferred rider and are most often ridden bareback for this reason.

Bandle root (BAND-ul)—a.k.a. stilben root in the Southlands or dreamsong among the Cloud Walkers. The herb can be steeped into tea or ingested raw. Low doses cause sedation, while concentrated dosing leads to dissociation or temporary paralysis and numbness. The herb smells and tastes like anise or black licorice.

Bear claw leaf—used to treat minor pain and fever.

Billow tree—a common tree along riverbanks in the Southlands. The tree produces seed pods with a woody outer husk of smooth, marbled brown. After a time, once exposed to water, the husk splits to release wispy seeds of white fluff, which billow into the air.

Blue trumpet—a vine that grows in the Borderlands and can be used to aid breathing/wheezing.

Broga's beard—a flowering plant that lives on its ability to absorb concentrated strands of zenith. Broga was a fabled mountain god from the Cloud Walkers, the native region of this plant.

Cave lark—a large cave-dwelling herbivore cat that uses its underbite to chisel away plants and lichen from rocks.

Darksun—a flowering plant that grows wild in the Borderlands and can treat the flux.

Eldrenol's solution—an oil that prevents abrogators from channeling nadir when ingested or inhaled.

Embertang—referred to as embertang in the Northlands and devil's tail in the Southlands, an antiseptic, hemostatic oil that, especially if undiluted, causes severe caustic pain even to casual skin contact. The less potent devil's tail is found as more of an oily resin.

Gellseed root—given with blackberry tincture to treat diarrhea.

Gendek—mountain relative to vestek, an elusive herd animal found only in the Valley of the Cloud Walkers.

Heh-gava—a powder used to treat a cough or wheezing.

Kaliphora—antiemetic.

Kevash—a juicy, tangy fruit that grows all year in the Valley of the Cloud Walkers.

Lammen—a bush that drops tart red berries in early winter, found in the Great Crown. The berries are restorative.

Maedra's pitchers—a plant that blooms south of the Korjinth Mountains and can be steeped into a tea that dulls pain and improves healing. Scholars suspect that the tea somehow enhances a body's ability to absorb zenith.

Nettle tea—a diuretic.

Resco—a distillate of wine akin to whiskey.

Spiritwort—a tea that lessens pain without causing drowsiness.

Veramanth's decoction (VARE-uh-manth)—a.k.a. stillers powder, mixed as a tea that prevents zeniphiles from channeling zenith for two to three days. When 'ranthed, a zeniphile cannot channel zenith.

Vestek—agile plains herd animal in the Northlands.

Vivith—an illegal stimulant. Brewed as a tea or smoked, it is highly addictive and often leads to paranoia. The smoke smells like pine resin.

Weeping bark—used to treat minor pain and fever.

Wolvryn—creatures related to wolves but much larger, far more intelligent, and gifted with unique abilities to see and smell through a spectrum of zenith.

- Boru (bo-ROO)—male companion to Bryndor.
- Ghetti—matriarch of the pack in the Valley of the Cloud Walkers.
- Neska (NES-kuh)—crafty female companion to Lluthean.
- Vencha—mother to Boru and Neska.

Don't miss out!

Visit the website below and you can sign up to receive emails whenever Lance VanGundy publishes a new book. There's no charge and no obligation.

https://books2read.com/r/B-A-LQHL-RYKTB

BOOKS 2 READ

Connecting independent readers to independent writers.

Also by Lance VanGundy

The Rune Fire Cycle
Awakened Runes
Runes of the Prime

Watch for more at https://www.lancevangundy.com/.

About the Author

Lance grew up in central Iowa, the product of public education and good parents. He attended Cornell College in Mount Vernon, Iowa where he obtained a Bachelor of Special Studies with anthropology and biology majors. Then he attended medical school at the University of Iowa. He has lived in central Iowa with his wife of more than thirty years where they raised three daughters. There he continues to practice emergency medicine and the whimsical art of escapism with all things Scifi and fantasy for as much as his wife can tolerate... that is significant... He is, after all, a very lucky man.

Read more at https://www.lancevangundy.com/.

Made in the USA
Monee, IL
14 December 2023

49207480R00239